Conflicts of Interest

Also by John Martel

Partners

Conflicts of Interest

John Martel

POCKET BOOKS

New York   London   Toronto   Sydney   Tokyo   Singapore

For Bonnie

The author is grateful to the mysterious and reclusive singer-songwriter Joe Silverhound for permission to use words from "Be Careful What You Pray For (You Might Just Get Her)" and "I Should Have Taken My Time (Now My Time's Been Taken From Me)." I belatedly thank Mr. Silverhound, whose lyrics tend to humble my prose, for use of a verse and chorus from "Survivor," with which I ended my previous novel, *Partners*.

This book is a work of fiction. Names, characters, places and incidents are products of the author's imagination or are used fictitiously. Any resemblance to actual events or locales or persons, living or dead, is entirely coincidental.

POCKET BOOKS, a division of Simon & Schuster Inc.
1230 Avenue of the Americas, New York, NY 10020

Library of Congress Cataloging-in-Publication Data

Martel, John.
    Conflicts of interest / John Martel.
       p.   cm.
    ISBN: 0-671-89094-8
    I. Title.
  PS3563.A72315C66 1995   94-45781
  813.'54—dc20   CIP

Design by Irva Mandelbaum

First Pocket Books hardcover printing August 1995

10 9 8 7 6 5 4 3 2 1

POCKET and colophon are registered trademarks of
Simon & Schuster Inc.

Printed in the U.S.A.

KENNEDY

Thanks to Fred, Bill, Dudley, Patsy, Kristina, Grant, Mark, Allen, Stu, Jim, all my tolerant law partners, and for their past wise counsel, Kathy and Linda.

It may happen that small differences in the initial conditions produce very great ones in the final phenomenon. A small error in the former produces enormous errors in the latter. Prediction becomes impossible.

—Henri Poincaré
Celestial Mechanics, 1882

Meteorologists are fond of saying that even the gentle movement of a butterfly's wings at point A can so impact upon Poincaré's "initial conditions" that "enormous errors" in predictability will result by the time a disastrous weather system is empirically registered at point B. Accordingly, students of Chaotic Dynamics call this phenomenon "The Butterfly Effect."

—Prof. Henry Daimler
Lecture, 1982

If you don't know where you're going, you'll probably end up someplace else.

—Will Rogers

Part 1

THE WORLD—TO BORROW FROM ABE LINCOLN—WOULD "LITTLE NOTE nor long remember" the trial about to start in an ancient courtroom in Modesto, California. But Seth Cameron knew his imminent battle with Sterritt Malm—one of California's top trial lawyers—could mean an escape from the quicksand of professional anonymity that had swallowed him up out of law school. Could mean one last chance at recognition and prosperity; a singular, potentially transforming event.

Little wonder his emotions oscillated between agitation and boredom as he forced the feverish Chevy up I-5—a seamless four-lane umbilical connecting the Mexican border to Canada—plummeting toward a confrontation that could change the lives of both people in the car he had just stolen.

The boredom came with the territory: I-5's hydralike capacity to seemingly generate two new miles ahead for every one mile left behind. Nothing in front or in back but asphalt and blowing dust. Frequent users like Seth knew that the biggest danger in driving the barren, unbending roadway was in falling asleep and running into a cow or a power pole.

The agitation part—with its compensating jolt of adrenaline—stabbed at Seth whenever he considered the significance of the case he was about to try. Not because of the money at stake—although it could go to six figures if things went badly—or monumental legal issues—it was just a bullshit product-liability case brought by his opponent's bullshit brother-in-law, who claimed to have swallowed part of a bug concealed in a can of garbanzo beans produced by Seth's client.

No, the case was significant because a victory against Sterritt Malm would earn Seth an interview with Miller and McGrath—one of San Francisco's top law firms—and a chance to put three hundred miles between himself and Bakersfield, California. A chance to prove that he was as good as any of those society hotshots on San Francisco's Montgomery Street.

Hotshots like Sterritt Malm, the man waiting for him in Modesto.

"You've got to beat Malm," his sometime friend and law school classmate Harrison Cooper had told him. Harry, like Seth, had labored in other fields before entering law school. Unlike Seth, however, Harry had finished second in their class, had been offered jobs by several of the top firms in the city. He had chosen Miller and McGrath over Stafford, Parrish and MacAlister—Harry's "short list"—and was now but two years away from the coveted election to partnership at M&M that would bring him tenured wealth and prestige.

Seth had also been a top student, at least until his third year, when an undergraduate named Trish Mayfair had ripped the heart out of his chest. His brain had hemorrhaged in sympathy, and he had spent his fifth semester in an angry, self-pitying haze, during which his thirst for knowledge was sated with shots of Cuervo Gold. As his grades spiraled into the tank, San Francisco big-firm recruiters who had been soliciting a commitment during his first two years suddenly developed communal lockjaw.

Upon graduation and with no offers in prospect, he drifted back to Bakersfield where he joined longtime friend Tom Huckins, who had graduated four years earlier, to form Huckins and Cameron. Tom handled the business clients—mostly contracts, wills, small partnerships—while Seth built a litigation practice of high-volume, low-fee insurance-defense work, and anything else that walked through the door. The fact that his father, a retired court clerk, was living alone in Bakersfield and crazy as a runover dog provided him a decent rationalization for his embarrassing return to the last place on earth he wanted to go.

You're taking a job in Bakersfield?

Yeah, my father's there. He's in bad shape.

"Beat Sterritt Malm," Harry had repeated, "and I'll be able to get you an interview, probably even an offer at M and M."

"That's it? Just beat one of the best trial lawyers in America?"

Harry had laughed. *"You're* the best trial lawyer in America, Seth. What's the problem?"

The problem was that Malm was indeed one of the best, a dominating trial lawyer and master of dirty tricks. Seth knew Malm would pull out all the stops for his sister's husband, even if the guy was a jerk and a deadbeat.

The problem was that Seth had no evidence to rebut the jerk's claim that he had in fact swallowed the damn insect, which had "caused Plaintiff, as a direct and proximate result of the ingestion thereof as alleged more fully hereinabove, to be rendered ill and to suffer, and to continue to suffer grievous physical and emotional pain and suffering."

The problem was that Sterritt Malm never lost.

"Schedule the interview, Harry," Seth had said as he hung up the phone.

A glance at his watch double-clutched Seth's stomach. His intense blue eyes—hungry eyes, deep-set beneath a brow too furrowed for a man in his midthirties—scanned the rearview mirror for black-and-whites. As if Malm and the high stakes weren't enough cause for anxiety, he was now running twenty minutes late for the 9:30 A.M. start of the most important trial of his life. Showing up late for court was unforgivable—like giving an opponent a two-hundred-mile head start in the Indy 500—and often produced an angry judge who could make it hard for the tardy lawyer's client to get a fair trial.

Which is how Seth had rationalized stealing the Chevy back in Avenal.

Stopping over there had definitely been a mistake, though Rosie's request had seemed reasonable enough at the time. Her aunt Claire—the oldest of three sisters of which Rosie's mother was the youngest—lived just off I-5, right on their way. At five-thirty the next morning, however, Seth had discovered that the El Camino had died in its sleep following a prolonged illness. Complications leading to a blown transmission leading to other complications.

Desperate, Seth had hot-wired the 1982 Chevrolet parked next door. Desperate circumstances, desperate measures. He felt a pang of remorse, but harbored no lingering regret, other than wishing he had stolen a faster car, maybe one with air-conditioning.

Rosie hated the idea, though Seth had explained that car rental agencies—like bowling alleys, Bob's Big Boy restaurants, and 7-Eleven stores—were among the facilities conspicuously missing from Avenal's storehouse of amenities. He had done what he had to do and hoped a check for $500 left in the owner's mailbox, along with a business card and a promise to return the car in four days, would discourage a call to 911. But precious time had been lost, including the extra ten minutes it had taken to coax Rosie into the car.

All clear in the rearview, so Seth kept the accelerator pinned to the floorboard and gulped the last of the coffee—still warm and bitter strong—straight from the plaid thermos. He was glad Rosie was asleep. She hated the way he drove, even in cars he hadn't stolen, which was also her excuse for refusing to ride behind him on motorcycles or horses. Didn't bother him. Nothing wrong with being alone once in a while.

The country-music radio station started playing "Be Careful What You Pray For, You Just Might Get Her," lifting a corner of his mouth into the sideways smile that had knocked Rosie's socks off when they met two years earlier. The song was his current favorite, though he couldn't imagine why someone would want something that wasn't good for them.

"Maybe I'm the guy to beat him," Seth had told his father the day before they left for Avenal. But Joe Cameron, caught between the crippling pincers of arthritis and Alzheimer's—complicated in recent years by a renewed and furtive fondness for wine of any color or variety—knew what his son was up to.

"Don't stay here on my account," Joe had said in a tightly wound voice that told Seth his father had descended into one of his dark moods. "Get the hell out of town for all I care."

Seth winced at the old man's words, just as he had as a kid, when his father had been abandoned by his wife, when he had discovered distilled spirits, when he had metamorphosed from a gentle soul into a bullying and emotionally abusive hothead in just one week's time—or so it had seemed to a frightened six-year-old boy. Four years later, Jimmy Maxwell, the superior court judge for whom Joe Cameron clerked—himself a member of Al-

coholics Anonymous—had personally put up the money to send
Joe off somewhere in Napa County to dry out, then made sure
he attended weekly AA meetings. After that, Joe had again become the loving father who had raised Seth single-handedly into
adulthood with hardly a complaint or harsh word.

But Joe was once again switching personas more often than
his underwear, howling and snarling at the full moon, only older
this time and even meaner. A stranger, a venom-spitting bag
of bones.

"Try to understand, Dad," Seth had said, opening a window
to allow the fresh air a beachhead against a room stinking with
age and neglect, then tossing off his leather jacket and sitting
next to his father. "It's now or never for me. It's my last shot at
being somebody." Joe Cameron's dull eyes stared straight ahead,
but Seth continued. "I'm suffocating in this place, Pop, and I
can't spend the rest of my life here, knowing that someday I'll
look in the mirror and see an old man looking back at me
through burnt-out eyes, an old man who never even tried to grab
the brass ring."

That didn't come out right, Seth realized, looking into the burnt-
out eyes of an old man who had never tried to grab the brass
ring: a career civil servant, a court clerk whose only ambition in
life had been to marry a decent woman someday, feed and clothe
his family, set a little aside. Instead, at the age of forty, he had
met Ruth.

Sure enough, his father's small head snapped around with the
suddenness of a bird taking flight. "You want to be somebody,"
he said in a mocking tone. "Sounds like a line from a hundred
bad movies. Your problem, kid, is trying to be somebody you
weren't meant to be." His peroration was interrupted by a
coughing seizure that left him wheezing and winded.

"Think just because nobody can beat you here in the bush
leagues you can make it in the majors," he continued, just as
Seth thought he had finished. Color rising in the old man's face
gave him a paradoxically healthy look as he paused once more
to catch his breath before adding, "Think you'll make a big
splash in the city and that'll bring her back. Am I right or am
I wrong?"

"Pop, let's not get into—"

"Well, I am right and you're *wrong,* damn it! Woman doesn't give a shit for either one of us. So forget all this Grand Achievement crapola. Besides—though it gives me no pleasure to say it—I've seen most of the great ones, *including* Sterritt Malm, during my twenty-five years in Department 3 and kid, you haven't got what it takes to beat him or any other world-class trial lawyer."

"I know you've seen a lot of great lawyers, Dad, but you've never seen me . . ."

"And what about your law firm right here in Bakersfield? What about Huckins and Cameron? You come crawling back to Big Tom, eh? Wanting to start all over? What's he going to say? He'll tell you it ain't no turnstile we're running here, playboy. Hell, you'll be replaced by the time you hit Fresno. Have you even *discussed* this with Big Tom?"

The reference to his partner angered and shamed Seth, who had always envied the easy relationship between his father and Tom Huckins. Big Tom. Big, handsome, red-necked, hard-drinking, womanizing, don't-give-a-shit Tom. Big Tom, his father's apparent idea of the perfect son, a real man: a man whose life ironically embodied the very traits Joe had raised his son to reject. Seth took a deep breath and moved to a chair directly in front of his father. He leaned forward, willing the old man to meet his gaze.

"Dad, can we stick with *my* life here? I called Harry Cooper because I'm dying here, shriveling up mentally, physically, professionally, financially, you name it. Has nothing to do with Tom Huckins."

"The hell it doesn't! You go off on this crazy frolic and I'm telling you Tom might not take you *back* after you flop!" Abruptly, Joe Cameron's expression turned to stone. He paused to catch his breath again, then gazed, trancelike, out the front window toward the street. He seemed to have forgotten Seth was there, but then startled his son by seizing his wrist with a powerful grip. "Don't you see it, Son? *She hated both of us!* Blamed you for wrecking her figure and me for wrecking her hopes and dreams—or so she said about a thousand times. Forget about her," he added in a sandpaper whisper, " 'cause I won't take *her* back either, no matter what she says."

The "she"—Seth's mother—had run off with a wealthy Los Angeles clothing wholesaler nearly thirty years before and was never heard from again—other than the annual birthday card to Seth with no return address.

Nearly thirty years.

Joe Cameron ran a veined claw of a hand across the thin white hair on either side of his creviced scalp. "So let's forget all this damn foolishness, kid."

Seth struggled for patience. "You got it all wrong, Dad," he said softly, searching his father's withered face, now a road map of fissures and inflamed capillaries. "I'm not trying to prove anything to Mom—hell, that's a lost cause. I guess I know how she must have . . . resented me. And I'm not running out on you or on Tom or anybody else. I'll be here whenever you need me. And with the extra money I'd be paid—over twice what I can make here—I'll be able to marry Rosie, get you full-time nursing care the doc says you need now or a place at Summercrest—"

"*Summercrest!*" Joe Cameron lifted himself to his feet, his face contorted as he limped off toward the kitchen. "Go wherever the hell you please," he growled without looking back. "But I'm staying right here. In *my* house where I belong. And when you see her, you tell her to just stay the hell *put*. I don't *want* her back. You hear? *Tell her to just stay the hell out of my life!*"

Rosie awoke on the outskirts of Modesto to the music of K. T. Oslin on AM radio and the bizarre sight of derelict skeletons of steel on both sides of a pockmarked roadway: wrecked automobiles, some twisted like cruller doughnuts, others crushed flat and stacked six deep on railroad cars or on flatbed trucks as long as aircraft carriers. The rusting junk was scattered across acres of bleached dust out of which had once sprouted lush peach, apricot, and walnut orchards, an endless, surrealistic car cemetery stretching as far as they could see down Crows Landing Road; endless and uninterrupted, except for Garcia's Fix-It, The Rodriguez Carnicería, and a Quonset-hut elementary school. All the used tires and hubcaps you could want.

Rosie yawned, saw that Seth was driving fast even for him, gave her thick dark hair a quick brush, and inspected her teeth in the mirror beneath the sun visor. Seth steeled himself for another discussion of orthodontia for her slight overbite, but she just leaned over to kiss him and ask cautiously if they were lost.

Seth was too busy hating himself to answer. Instead of staying

9

on I-5, taking McCracken Road up to 132, then straight east into Modesto, he had tried to make up time by cutting off at Crows Landing, then north up Crows Landing Road. He had immediately found himself in tight formation with a convoy of trailer houses, then a tractor-trailer behind a two-lane harvester. Finally, he had arrived somewhere on the outskirts of Modesto, completely disoriented.

"I think we're in South Modesto Acres," said Seth, twirling the car into a 180 turn in the middle of Yosemite Boulevard, his knuckles luminous on the steering wheel, "but nothing's like I remembered it."

South Modesto Acres had been a primary destination for hundreds of dust-bowl Okies over half a century earlier. Grandpa Tom Cameron—with a wife and two adolescents to feed—had been one of those migrating drought victims. He and Grandma had lived and worked in the fields here for whatever they could get, but made sure that Joe and his sister graduated from high school, no small task for rootless itinerant farmworkers. Joe Cameron had been proud of his heritage, but Ruth had reinvented the Cameron family history and told everyone Joe was old Boston Irish. It mattered little to Joe if it pleased Ruth, though neither Joe nor his father had ever been to Boston, and he couldn't think why Ruth went to such lengths. One of the last things he remembered before she left was hearing her tell someone on the phone that her father-in-law had lunched almost daily with Joe Kennedy in the old days.

The face of South Modesto Acres had changed since Seth had passed through years before, but the area still housed the poor and disenfranchised—now mainly Mexican transient laborers. Many were illegal aliens, fearful of strangers, existing in this steaming ghetto at the sufferance of the Immigration Service because of their willingness to pick insecticide-laden fruit nobody else would touch; to harvest the new grapes of wrath.

Seth glanced at the clock on the dash and muttered an epithet. It read 9:15 A.M.

"Look there, Seth!" said Rosie. "There's a boy might know the way to town!" Seth had also spotted the ponytailed Hispanic youth and jammed on his brakes. He leapt out of the car and shouted at the young man across spirals of withered air that rose from the Chevy's hood.

"Where the hell is Modesto?" he asked, noticing that the youth's left hand was encased in a filthy cast. "You know, the city center. *El centro?*"

The young man shielded his eyes with his good hand, then pointed the opposite way.

"*That* way? Not possible! *Es verdad?*" Seth ran both hands through his damp hair. "*El centro?* El Courthouse?"

These last words sent the boy scurrying into a nearby trailer house, bare feet moving across the white dust as soundlessly as a cat. His lair, like the hundreds of other four-wheel shanties, was separated from the next by little more than a few feet of space and looked about as sturdy as a Kleenex box. More wrecked cars were randomly scattered around the area like grazing sheep, but these at least appeared to be drivable.

"No green card," said Seth, his features pinched from smells as pungent as a Mexican border town mixed with the acid-metal stench of his boiling radiator and a tallow works a mile off the road. Seth remembered the Modesto rendering plant from years back. Wind blows the wrong way, watch out, especially on a day like this with the mercury already pushing the mideighties. Shirt soaked through. *Always look sharp in front of a jury, Son. Never call attention to yourself by being either sloppy or too fancy.* Fresh one in the suitcase if he had time.

"Kid's got no work visa," he mumbled to himself. "Afraid somebody will find out he's illegally conned his way into hell."

"It's sad," agreed Rosie, taking in the blight. No streetlights here, no gutters, no cable TV, no sidewalks, no McDonald's, no Burger King, no law, no stores. Just a scrawled sign in front of a shanty announcing Yard Sale, but the people on the porch had neither much of a yard nor much of anything for sale other than some colored bottles on a packing box, a handheld kitchen mixer, a bike with one wheel, some ragged clothes, a pair of shabby dolls.

Rosie leaned out the window and cautiously suggested they take the boy's advice, it being their only hope of making it on time, but Seth stood motionless outside the car, lost in his frustration.

He looked at his watch: 9:18 A.M.

Rosie jumped as Seth slammed his hand down on the hood of the car, muttering something about being fed up with working jerkwater towns like a fucking pencil salesman. Then he climbed back inside, jammed the gearbox into low, and spun the Chevy around toward where the youth had pointed and aimed it between a pair of circa 1916 full-size lions guarding the Seventh Street Bridge. Seth vanquished the Tuolumne River in seconds, then spotted a giant water tank off to his right with the word Modesto in letters the size of a man. A right on I Street and he suddenly found himself on familiar ground, crossing old Highway 99, then driving under the majestic steel archway that for nearly a hundred years had proudly proclaimed: "Water, Wealth, Contentment, Health!"

Seth wheeled left on Tenth Street—The Drag—immortalized by George Lucas (Modesto's only hometown celebrity) in *American Graffiti*. Now the barren street looked more like a set from another small-town classic, *The Last Picture Show*. Traffic lights were still working, however, and Seth's were all red. He shot through every one.

"Seth!" said Rosie. "This is a stolen car!"

Seth said nothing as he blasted through one more intersection, slammed on his brakes, and broke into a smile. "You're right, honey. So let's get the hell out of it." They were in front of the Stanislaus County Courthouse.

It was 9:27 A.M.

"Seth, darlin', this is a good omen. You run for it. I'll find a parking place and catch up with you in court."

"A good omen? Did you also happen to dream that I beat Malm?"

Rosie laughed at Seth's allusion to her dreaming, a subject that had once been no laughing matter in their relationship and one that could still generate tension. The major embarrassment in Rosie's life was her mother, Esther Wheeler, an L.A. psychic with a weekly column in a trash tabloid. Esther was the daughter of an Iroquois shaman named Amelia Moon. Her claim that she possessed the gift of precognitive dreams had been bolstered by sporadic incidents of apparent clairvoyance—she once helped the local police department locate a child who had fallen down an air shaft—leading to immediate tabloid veneration. Clawing her way up the highly competitive psychic-celebrity ladder from her outpost in South Dakota had not been easy, and Esther's early columns had indulged in the familiar excesses—"Mamie Eisenhower Drinks to Forget Her Virgin Birth," "How Sal Mineo Was Really Killed—Savaged by a Pack of Wild Dogs," and so on—

exposing young Rosie to the taunts of her schoolmates and seal-
ing her lips about her own dreams, which were sometimes fright-
eningly prescient.

Seth pulled his trial bags out of the backseat, then leaned across
to give Rosie a kiss. "Well," he said in a teasing tone, "did I win
or not?"

"Shoot, Seth," said Rosie, managing a smile as she eased the
manual shift into low gear, "I wouldn't *dream* of you losing. Not
with your record. See you inside."

Seth smiled back and put a cold hand over hers. His eyes—
intense even at rest—had become diamond edged and he seemed
to have grown an inch or so over his six foot height.

He was ready.

BUT THE NEXT FOUR DAYS OF TRIAL HAD BEEN A DISASTER, AND AS SETH
stared through the ancient courtroom's single south window into
the suffused glare of the San Joaquin Valley's midday sun—
barely listening to the Voice of Reason's closing argument as it
reverberated off the cracked yellow-oak walls—he wondered
where it had all gone wrong. Maybe the relentless heat in this
godforsaken coal-fired furnace Modestans called an All-American
City had finally fried a brain already weakened by thirty-five
years of life in the Valley—America's breadbasket—an area Harrison Cooper had described as "a great place for grapes and
peaches, but you wouldn't want to be a human there."

Seth's thoughts segued to Dante's *Inferno*. After all, losing is
hell to a trial lawyer, and Seth Cameron was about to lose a case
that could have been won. Not just any case either. *The* case. His
ticket to ride. The file hidden in his cake.

He forced his bloodless face back in the direction of the Voice
of Reason—that's what Sterritt Malm had already twice pro-

claimed himself to be—and saw to his dismay that the jury was still riveting all twenty-four of its approving eyes on Malm, and that its twelve sets of ears were vacuuming up every staccato word that issued from the stocky lawyer's electric mouth. Malm punctuated each point with a quick, forward thrust of his head, putting Seth in mind of a free-range chicken at suppertime. No, more like a banty rooster, pacing and preening in front of the jury, his closing argument crackling with righteousness as he railed against the foul misdeeds of Perfection Foods, Inc., a company so bereft of decency as to have "willfully and wantonly" permitted three of nature's ugliest creatures access to a can of its garbanzo beans, thereby allowing one of them further access into the very mouth of Malm's emotionally scarred client.

The Voice paused for a moment of reflective silence, then broke the ensuing tension with a swift backward tango that brought him alongside the defense counsel table. With an imperial sweep of his arm, as if intending to introduce Seth's client representative—an angular but decent-looking company vice president named Orville Baskins—Malm resumed his peroration.

"In whom," he intoned, his open palm extended to within inches of Baskins's flushed and penitent face, "do we repose greater public trust than in those who process our food, our very life *sustenance?*" (The personal-injury lawyer punctuated his last four words with a dramatic closed-fist blow to his own heart.) "And do not you and I—*and did not plaintiff Arnold Johnson*—have every right to assume that food processors like Perfection Foods would have taken such precautions as are necessary to ensure that when we purchase and consume their product"—quickly now, without even looking behind him at the clerk's table, Malm's manicured fingers closed around Plaintiff's Exhibit 1A, B, and C—"we don't also consume . . . *these?*"

Sterritt Malm continued to rail as he triumphantly crab-stepped across the front of the jury box, thrusting the moribund insects to within inches of each frozen-faced juror, causing them to recoil one by one like The Wave at a football game.

Seth, too, stared in disgust—not at the bugs but at his adversary—then turned his head away, back toward the window and its consoling rectangle of light, which now, however, had taken on the appearance of radioactive gelatin viewed through a dirty lens.

His mind drifted back to a similar feeling of solitary help-lessness he had experienced years before, staring out the window of his second-grade classroom the day after his mother had driven off into the night with Alfred Gamut.

Don't make life into a melodrama, kid. There's plenty of things to worry about already without inventing more of 'em.

Fatherly consolation.

Through the courtroom window, Seth now focused on a gaggle of cinnamon-colored leaves, emboldened by the absence of even a trace of air movement, clinging tenuously to the forked limb of a Modesto ash that looked as petrified as the three disgusting potato bugs now being displayed to the jury.

Seth shuddered and clamped his red-streaked eyes shut as Sterritt Malm finished his closing argument to the attentive jury with a "Thank you" as crisp as a hundred-dollar bill, then resumed his seat at counsel table, though not without first smiling at Seth—a sneer really—his chalk-colored bonded upper teeth sparkling beneath a thin upper lip curled inside out with contempt.

Malm had reason to gloat. The jurors' faces could have been read by a blind man. Malm would beat Cameron, and beat him badly. No one in the suffocating courtroom could rationally doubt the outcome now; not the dissipated pensioner who had wandered the courthouse for a decade, chewing on a lifeless corncob pipe and shifting his arthritic body from cheek to cheek on the unyielding oak seat; nor the enormous dowager who occupied the same second-row seats every day of the year, frantically fanning herself with a folded *Modesto Bee* as if bent on taking flight; nor even the beautiful but pale, dark-haired woman in the back of the courtroom. Not one among them could doubt that the flamboyant San Francisco plaintiff's attorney was about to hand the star trial lawyer from Bakersfield his first defeat in five years: a verdict that would surely exceed $100,000.

Seth Cameron managed to appear untroubled by any of this and took no apparent notice of Malm's arrogance. In fact, he nodded reassuringly to Orville Baskins and affected inspired scribblings on the yellow pad in front of him, his wiry frame draped over the defense end of counsel table, farthest from the jury as dictated by tradition. But his phlegmatic mien belied the internal combustion engine raging in his stomach, though it accurately depicted a brain gone stone dead, as moribund as the three tiny corpses that Malm had cleverly left sprawled across the evidence envelope at the far edge of counsel table in full, revolting sight of the jury.

Those jurors not preoccupied with the bugs stared impassively at Seth, waiting for the impression he would make on them, watching him rise from his place at counsel table and stride toward the court clerk's desk, ostensibly to peruse and organize the trial exhibits for his own argument, but really just to buy time. *Time? Time for what?* he thought, as he stared without seeing at the sheaf of documents being turned page by page by fingers he hardly recognized. Time was his enemy now: too early to be rescued by the lunch recess and too late to offer any real evidence in defense of Perfection Foods.

What it was time to do was take his medicine.

The judge, a political appointee obviously enamored of Department 4's illustrious visitor from San Francisco, scowled down at Seth, drumming zucchini fingers on a grapefruit cheek and conspicuously glancing up at the clock. Seth had seen from the outset that Judge Swinerton was not the sort to mask his feelings in front of the jury and that he possessed the judicial temperament of Jack the Ripper; the kind of sycophantic judge who, possessing few virtues of his own, sought to elevate his public image by aligning himself with those who had achieved a status that would forever elude him. Judge Swinerton was that breed of judge who could make the practice of law miserable under the best of circumstances, let alone with a dog of a case like Seth's that had been barking louder every day.

Seth willed himself to concentrate as he stared glumly at Plaintiff's Exhibit 2, a medical report describing how plaintiff Arnold Johnson, a two-hundred-pound union carpenter, had opened a can of Perfection Foods's garbanzo beans and spooned half of the contents into his mouth before discovering that he may have consumed some unwanted protein in the form of *Stenopelmatus fusci*, a small but exceptionally ugly insect, whose partial remains—a grotesque torso—were buried among the garbanzos together with two fellow uglies, equally dead, though in apparent possession of all their body parts.

Seth then picked up the complaint itself, which charged that the "shock to plaintiff's nervous system so exacerbated a preexisting pathological fear" of things that crawl, that Johnson had been rendered "unable to pursue his occupation for the past three years," i.e., forced to draw unemployment and become dependent upon his wife's earnings for his beer ration, an unquenchable regimen in which he engaged after every third race at Golden Gate Fields. Seth knew all this because he had hired Leviticus Heywood—a San Francisco 49er teammate for two months in 1978 and now a PI in the city—to tail the plaintiff for four days. But the jury would never hear about it because the one law-school graduate in a hundred who would consider such information to be "irrelevant and prejudicial" happened to be wearing a size extralarge black robe and sitting as the judge in this case.

Yes, Johnson was a phony—and undoubtedly a family embarrassment to Sterritt Malm—but Seth's observations of the jurors during Malm's argument confirmed his fear that they now saw the plaintiff through Malm's pleading eyes as an innocent victim of Perfection's imperfect canning process. "A broken man," the plaintiff's lawyer had called Johnson in a plea that skirted the edge of transparent melodrama. "A brittle insomniac," he had cried, "enduring unproductive days and endless nights crawling with fears that have haunted him now for three torturous years."

Seth replaced the exhibits with a minimal smile at Judge Swinerton, then returned to counsel table with the last words of Elston Winney—Perfection Foods's insurance claims supervisor— ringing in his ears: "You've got zip on this one, Cameron. Zilch, naught, zero. Offer this deadbeat a lousy fifteen grand. You'll be protecting your perfect record and my job."

You know who it is that exalts courage over judgment, kid? Dead men and other suckers. Courage is a vastly overrated commodity, probably because it's in such short supply.

"*Deadbeat* is the operative word here, sir," Seth had replied into the telephone. "You see it, I see it, I'll make the jury see it, too. The guy finds two or three dead bugs, vomits a few times, and expects twenty-five thousand bucks in settlement."

"Correction, Cameron," the claims supervisor had said, his metallic voice popping with sarcasm. "Mr. Johnson finds two dead bugs and *part* of a third. The jury will feel it was perfectly reasonable for him to infer that the missing portion of subject insect number three was at that very moment well on its way into his own small intestine. It makes me queasy just thinking about it, and I don't even believe the son of a bitch. Offer him the fifteen. He'll take it. The great Sterritt Winthrop Malm doesn't want to travel to Modesto fucking California to try this two-bit case."

"He may want to be a hero to his sister."

"All the more reason for him to put a quick fifteen big ones in her purse. Jesus, Cameron, I'm trying to save your ass here. We can't even rebut his assertion that the bugs got into the can at Perfection's plant. You inspected the place yourself and told me it reminded you of that scene from *The Naked Jungle* where the ants try to chew off Charlton Heston's ear or something."

Winney had him there. Seth had visited the plant outside Manteca on a steam-cabinet August day and would never forget his disgust as he undressed later at the motel and saw that two of the little nasties had made a break for freedom concealed in the cuff of his trousers.

"What *were* your reasons for not settling?" Rosie had asked the night before in their room at the Holiday Inn, not to rub it in surely, but in the hope of reestablishing some factual basis for positive thinking, something she had observed to be missing in action after three days of mauling at the combined hands of Sterritt Malm and Judge Swinerton. "Is it possible that this Winney person may have been right for once?"

"Left," said Seth.

"Pardon me?"

"More to the left."

Rosie said, "Oh," and rotated her massaging fingers over to the steel mesh that comprised Seth's left shoulder.

"I guess I just didn't figure on drawing a fawning airhead for a judge. Or on Arnie Johnson cleaning up so good. Or on Malm's high-budget graphics. Hell, that color blowup of the bugs was scarier than Jeff Goldblum's last scene in *The Fly*. Then he backdoored me with that whore psychiatrist from Stockton: 'traumatic neurosis' for Christ's sake!"

"I always figured the defense would buy its own psychiatrist to combat stuff like that."

"*Retain*, Rosie, not *buy*," said Seth, smiling and reaching back with both hands to caress her narrow hips. "Yes, honey, I usually do buy my own expert, but I didn't want to dignify his last-minute emotional-distress claim. It was a stupid gamble that left me with a defense case like watching *Lassie* without the dog."

Problem with some flies, Son, is they get complacent after a while. Figure they can get out of any trouble comes up. Spiders enjoy them best of all.

Meanwhile, Malm hadn't made a mistake for three days, and the jury had lapped up his case like starving dogs. Rosie considered asking Seth if he was scared, but knew better than to expect an answer. It was enough that he had stayed sober.

It was Seth's turn now, but he could already feel the icy hand of defeat at his throat. He realized he had stopped breathing—a bad sign for a trial lawyer about to deliver a closing defense argument in an indefensible case.

"Mr. Cameron!" Judge Swinerton's tenor voice flooded Seth's consciousness in surrealistic waves of sound that made his own name sound oddly unfamiliar. "Your closing argument. *Please!*"

The fat bastard is enjoying this, thought Seth, picturing the judge as a helium float in a Law Day parade and himself with an AK-47.

"Yes, Your Honor." The casual sound of his own voice encouraged Seth into a renewed resolve not to be deprived of his shot at joining a San Francisco firm by three dead bugs and a self-important stuffed shirt like Sterritt Malm. Seth drew a deep breath and tried to remember the other times he had felt devastated by an adversary's closing argument—words that seemed to erect a wall of logic his own rhetoric could not hope to breach— yet somehow, he had managed to win. "I'll be right there, Your Honor," he said, then added to himself, *as soon as I think of something to say.*

He listened to the familiar courtroom sounds: the clerk's muffled whisper into her telephone, a juror's self-conscious cough, the velvet key-taps of the court reporter's machine catching up on exhibit numbers, and a wheezing noise like a bicycle wheel in need of oil—his own breathing. At least he was breathing again, although it felt like something closer to hyperventilation. A shot of Tequila Gold splashed across his mind. Just one. Between pounding temples, his frontal lobes fought off an attack of vertigo and his pen had started writing nonsense, started writing nonsense, his pen had started . . .

His mouth was dry as asphalt. He wanted to lick his lips, but resisted the impulse, knowing the jury was watching him now as he twisted like an insect on the end of his adversary's pin, looking for the slightest indication of uncertainty, of fear.

He hated those jurors with their smothering eyes all over him, staring at his pock-scarred cheeks, expecting too much of him. He pictured himself rising to his feet, but instead of delivering his closing argument, simply wishing his client the best of luck and then walking out of the courtroom into the warmth of the late-morning sun.

An old trial lawyer's aphorism pushed the negative thought out of his mind: "If you don't have the law, try your case on the facts. If you don't have the facts, try your case on the law. If you don't have either the facts or the law, *try the lawyer on the other side.*" Fine, but try him for what? Having too much evidence? *Think, Cameron,* he urged himself, *this guy can't be perfect.*

Maybe, mused Seth, as thought jostled anxiety for space in his pounding head, *maybe I can make something of the fact that the son of a bitch really is perfect—or at least close to it—and like all "perfect" people, he reeks of self-importance and takes himself too damn seriously.*

"Mr. Cameron," repeated the judge, his voice flint-edged with impatience. "We are waiting for you. Are you or are you not going to favor us with a closing argument?"

"Yes, Your Honor, I'm sorry," said Seth, glancing toward the jury to include them within the reach of his apology. Then, with a supremely confident flourish the jury could not possibly miss, he twice underlined the sentence he had scribbled earlier on his yellow pad and began to will his anesthetized legs to stand and deliver.

What he had written was: *This is fucking hopeless.*

In the back of the courtroom, Rosie's delicate features were strained with anxiety, her eyes fixed on the immobilized back of her lover. Though worried, she was confident Seth would find his magic, pull a bunny out of his hat as he always did. But though she wanted to send him positive vibrations, Rosie was haunted by ambivalence concerning the desired outcome. She knew how much the San Francisco offer would mean to Seth, a knowledge that produced feelings of guilt—as if her thoughts might produce bad karma and influence the outcome. On the other hand, she had herself to think about. She was, after all, just a country girl, born and raised in the tiny town of Custer, South Dakota, nestled in the Black Hills, ill prepared to fit in with the cultured and well-dressed ladies of San Francisco. To Rosie, Bakersfield was plenty big enough, and she saw no reason to move far away from the only friends she had. And although from the looks of things, they wouldn't be going anywhere, she couldn't forget the dream she had had the night they were in Avenal.

Yet, despite her confusion and personal concerns, her heart ached with compassion as she stared at the man she loved. For now, at least, all she wanted was for Seth to get on his feet and somehow make the jury forget Malm's masterful polemic, an argument that even she had been unable to resist. Psychic powers were not needed to see that Seth was in deep trouble, but her hopes were fueled by the sight of him rising to his feet and the assured way he walked right up to the jury. Rosie held her breath.

"Your Honor. Ladies and gentlemen of the jury," Seth began, remembering other hopeless trial situations when he had forced himself to talk until he found a theme and gradually began to believe whatever it was he was saying—the first step in reversing the pendulum's swing. Then maybe one or two jurors would look as if they were also believing him, and that would feed his confidence until a tiny spark would fan into flame as more jurors seemed to be with him, and soon he might even get into The Zone and find himself sitting out there in the audience with the others, observing his own incredible performance with a father's pride as words rushed from his brilliant lawyer's mouth like little Phi Beta Kappa scholars, each one bearing its own unassailable logic, and then . . .

"I have listened to Mr. Sterritt Winthrop Maalllm," he began, "with great interest. In fact, this may surprise you, but I have no real argument with most of the things Mr. Sterritt Malm has come all the way from San Francisco to tell us.

"I can't, for example, prove that these little guys *weren't* there in my client's garbanzos at the time and place Mr. Johnson says he saw them. Shoot, he can say anything he wants; he was the only one around. I wasn't there and neither was Mr. Malm. Nor is there a single independent witness to counter Mr. Johnson's testimony that part of the thorax of Plaintiff's Exhibit C was missing when he first saw it, if in fact he saw it at all. Nor, for that matter, is there anybody who can say that he didn't get sick from *something* during those first two or three days. In fact, his work records—Exhibit 4—reflect that he has not done a single day's work since he met Plaintiff's Exhibit 1A, B, and C, who, by the way, since they are the silent but crucial witnesses in this case, deserve names. Let's call them ... Huey, Dewey, and Louie."

Seth noticed that juror number eight—a miniature peroxide blonde of indeterminate years—smiled openly at this, and that at least two other jurors stifled incipient grins. Seth also observed that Sterritt Malm tensed in his seat, started to object, but let the moment pass. Seth's strategy was forming in his head, bounding along like a foxhound just a few feet ahead of his tongue.

A strategy at last: *gentle ridicule.*

"Let me put it right out there, folks. What Mr. Sterritt Malm wants here is for you to give his client a whole lot of money because Mr. Johnson lost his zeal for hard labor after encountering Huey, Dewey and Louie—"

"*Part* of Louie!" interrupted Malm, exploding to his feet. "I mean part of Exhibit 1C," he corrected himself, provoking a chuckle from juror number three.

Seth continued, seeing that at least half the jurors were suppressing smiles now, "Mr. Malm's point is well taken, ladies and gentlemen: *part* of little Louie." Seth thrust his hands deep in his trouser pockets and walked closer to the jury. His tone remained relaxed, matter-of-fact, but now took on a serious edge. "But that, folks, is the *last* thing Mr. Malm and I agree on.

"In the first place, even if it happened, I just don't think it's right for people to exploit an honest error by a food company like Perfection, which, as you heard from its quality-control vice president—Mr. Baskins here—does everything humanly possible to provide food that is both appetizing and safe. And don't forget that Mr. Johnson doesn't even *claim* he was actually poisoned; he just says he was scared to death that he *might* have been poisoned and then, in a self-fulfilling prophecy, became ill. And what frightened this two-hundred-pound man right out of his honest job? A Bengal tiger? A werewolf at the full moon? Nope. It was Huey, Dewey, and ... part of Louie, that ended Mr. Johnson's career as a contributing member of society."

Yes, yes, thought Seth, feeling himself growing stronger, more confident. *They love it!* He stole a glance back at Sterritt Malm and wondered if the jury could see those aristocratic jaw muscles twitching.

"In summary, ladies and gentlemen, I submit that what *really* scared Mr. Johnson—and people like him who crowd our court-rooms every day looking to get rich off the misfortune of their neighbors—was the idea of having to work for a living."

Touchy ground. Easy does it, Boy Wonder.

"How else can you explain it? I realize that life is a matter of taste, but personally, I think if my stomach were tough enough to handle a half can of ... cold *garbanzo* beans, it could certainly tolerate the sight of a trio of God's own creatures without all this fuss."

This brought more smiles, and Seth knew he was making progress. *Rein it in, boy,* Seth again cautioned himself. He was certain now that Sterritt Malm *had* gone too far when he had thrust the bugs in front of each juror. Perhaps the shock and disdain on their faces had been directed not so much toward the insects as toward Malm for putting them through the experience. Seth knew that jurors, like good martinis, needed to be stirred, not shaken.

"Now, I am not going to bore you with a long dissertation on the law; it is pretty much as counsel has described it. But there is one important thing you should understand. Not even Mr. Malm is going to insult your intelligence by asking you to give him one hundred thousand dollars, or even five cents, because his client *saw* Huey, Dewey, and part of Louie in a can of gar-banzo beans. What he wants you to believe is that Mr. Johnson personally consumed half of Louie and thereafter became so sick that he developed the symptoms which Dr. Harris was so color-ful in describing and which nobody but God can prove or disprove.

"*So the thing to remember here*"—Seth moved another step forward, gently touching the jury-box railing with his fingertips and turning his voice volume up a notch—"*is that there is not one bit of proof by the plaintiff—who does have the burden of proof on this point as the court will soon instruct you—that Mr. Johnson did, in fact, eat half of Louie.*

"Now, you don't have to believe that Mr. Johnson is lying to you about this, because he doesn't even know whether he did or didn't, and cannot *say* that he did, and therefore has not *proven* that he did to a preponderance of the evidence, as required by law.

"I suggest, therefore, ladies and gentlemen," said Seth, extending his arms, palms up, then dropping them to his sides, "that this is a case of no harm, no foul."

Four jurors involuntarily nodded in affirmation, sending a rush of tiny electric needles up his spine. He had almost half of them now; the pendulum was swinging back. *God, what a great business to be in!*

There was, however, the One Last Thing, and the thought of it dampened his euphoria as he rushed headlong toward it.

"I'm not saying that I would not be pretty doggone mad myself if I paid seventy-nine cents for a can of garbanzo beans and halfway through it found these little guys—which Mr. Malm, you may have noticed, has conveniently left sitting right here on this white envelope in full view of all of you. By the way, folks, that's one of the oldest tricks of the trade. You see, that's supposed to put me in a terrible bind. Either you won't pay attention to my argument because you'll be distracted by these critters, or I'll have to be the one who puts them back in the evidence envelope, which would signify—as he would point out to you in his closing reply argument—that 'not even Mr. Cameron can stand the sight of these terrifying creatures!' "

Seth saw at least eight faces beaming back at him now in conspiratorial allegiance. The pendulum had swung back all right, but only the One Last Thing would keep it there after Malm had had the last word granted by law to all plaintiffs.

"Well, folks, Huey, Dewey, and Louie just aren't that terrifying. In some parts of Africa, these little fellas might be considered a delicacy." Seth turned to Plaintiff's Exhibit 1A, B, and C, picked up Huey, and cradling him in the palm of his hand, held him out at a comfortable distance from the jury. "If you can afford it, you can buy chocolate-covered ants in the gourmet section of your supermarket, and in some shops you can buy grasshopper delicacies much bigger than Huey here."

Seth paused, then ruefully shook his head and said, "No wonder the court system is clogged and companies are complaining about the skyrocketing cost of providing products to consumers."

At this, juror number four—a retired accountant whom Seth figured to be elected foreman—frowned and nodded in agreement.

Everybody's got a different button, Son, and you've got to be able to find a way to press 'em all—which is why it's a lot of bunk to say perspiration is more important than inspiration. If you don't have 110 percent of both, you better stick to drafting wills or partnership agreements and stay out of the courtroom.

"What's all the fuss about in this case? What's so bad about little Huey here?" Then, with a final look into the glazed eyes of *Stenopelmatus fusci* and an inward shudder, Seth wished himself *bon appétit* and popped Huey into his mouth. The twelve jurors inhaled as one, a vacuum gasp as palpable as a jet engine. Malm catapulted to his feet screaming, "Your Honor, Mr. Cameron is swallowing the evidence! Make him stop!"

"It may be too late for that, Counsel," said the judge, whose eyes had become golf balls in flight. "Have you, in fact, swallowed Plaintiff's Exhibit 1A, Mr. Cameron?"

Seth gathered himself. What was crucial now was not what he said, but how he said it. His mouth salivated formaldehyde, but it was that crunching sensation—like soft-shell crab—that would be lodged in his memory long after the last spiny segment had cleared his throat.

"I have, indeed, Your Honor, and would go for 1B and 1C as well, but I see that we are approaching the lunch hour."

More jurors were laughing now, relieving the tension.

"That's not funny, Mr. Cameron," said the judge, glaring at Seth and looking toward the bailiff as if for guidance.

"Mr. Cameron is in contempt, Your Honor!" cried Malm, dramatically snatching off his spectacles. "I cite him for misconduct and demand a mistrial. He has turned this case into a travesty of justice." Malm was whining, just as Seth had hoped and believed he would.

"With all respect, Your Honor," continued Seth, "I have only eliminated a redundant exhibit. Counsel has established through expert testimony that Exhibit 1A is identical to remaining Exhibits 1B and part of 1C. Thus, no prejudice has been done.

"As for turning this trial into a travesty, this case has been a travesty from the day Mr. Malm filed his frivolous complaint. I've only exposed it."

Feeling total control now, Seth turned his back on the judge and faced the jurors—all of whom had recovered from their surprise and were now regarding him with amused respect—and said, "In conclusion, ladies and gentlemen, I tell you two things: First, Plaintiff's Exhibit 1A could have used some mayo and perhaps a pinch of seasoning.

"Second, I have done my job. *Now go do yours.*"

"A PLAINTIFF'S VERDICT FOR SEVENTY-NINE CENTS? BE SERIOUS!"

"It's true, Harry," said Seth into the telephone just outside the courtroom. "Exactly the amount Johnson paid for his can of garbanzos. The jury saw right through him. Out less than an hour—and that's counting two interruptions by the bailiff to admonish them to hold down the laughter."

"*Laughter?* You're making this up, Cowboy."

"Hell, you could hear them all the way out in the corridor. Malm didn't even poll the jury after the verdict. Just lectured me, grabbed his trial bag, and lit out."

"Incredible!" exclaimed Harry. "His case sounded solid. How did you deal with his evidence?"

"Actually, Harry, I ate it. Part of it, at least."

"You what?"

"I ate little Huey, one of a proud but vanishing line of explorer bugs. Exhibit 1A to be precise."

"Jesus," said Harry, "what . . . what happened?"

"I threw up into my briefcase, but not until the jury—"

"I mean, what did the judge do?"

"The usual admonition to the jury to disregard, trying to unring the bell, with the usual result that it rang even louder."

"Jesus."

"Anyway, podner, as I told the twelve tried and true in closing argument, 'I've done my job, now go do yours.' "

"Fair enough, Cowboy. I'll take it up with an M and M hiring partner right away. How soon could you make it to the city for an interview?"

"I'm only four hours away. Just whistle."

"It shouldn't be a problem now. Not many trial lawyers have beaten Malm, plus we've just lost two trial associates. By the way, would you be able to bring any business clients with you if you got an offer?"

"From *Bakersfield?* You've got to be kidding. Huckins and Cameron has only one semimajor, continuing client. Mostly we do probate, divorce, small partnerships, leases. Pretty low-rent stuff by M and M standards."

"What does your semimajor client do?"

"Runs an independent telephone company that services about forty small towns in central California. I handle their disputes, Huck does their business work."

"Can you bring them with you to M and M?"

"I don't know. Is it important? I thought M and M just wanted my silver tongue."

Harry laughed, told him sure, that was what they wanted all right. "But these are tough times, Seth, and the partners are looking hard at a senior associate's ability to bring in business before electing him or her to partnership. We eat what we kill here in the big city."

Seth said he'd think about it, and Harry emphasized that it wasn't a condition: "It just might grease the skids a little. But tell me, what did Malm say to you after the verdict?"

"He said I danced too close to the edge. Told me next time he'd knock me off it. I told him that unless his balls were as big as his mouth, he'd better bring lots of help."

"Pretty harsh words, even from an ex-kamikaze defensive cornerback."

"He didn't much like it."

The telephone went silent for a moment.

"Harry?"

"Yeah, Seth," said Harry finally. "I was just thinking . . . and hope you won't resent a suggestion?"

"I'm all ears."

"Well," said Harry, now choosing his words carefully, "I know you've got to be yourself, but . . ."

"Don't worry, old son, I won't wear cowboy boots or come up in the elevator on my Harley. I'll be urbane and cultured, the best and the brightest, the cat's meow."

"That's reassuring from a guy who thinks pretzels and beer are two of the major food groups. But I had in mind the fact that everyone is going to ask you about your victory against Sterritt Malm, and it might be, well . . . prudent, not to mention the little matter of Exhibit 1A."

Another moment of silence passed between the friends.

"Guess I'm missing something here," said Seth. "I won, didn't I? Isn't that the bottom line these days, particularly with big-city partners? Don't they sometimes commit a little creativity there on Montgomery Street?"

"Well, sure, Seth, but it's not just that," said Harry, his voice strained with caution. "Some people here might think you bent the rules a little there; you know, maybe question the, uh, well . . . the ethics of it."

"*Ethics?*" said Seth, laughing again, but this time with a sardonic edge. "Where *you* work? Shit, Harry, I can understand them questioning my sanity, but my *ethics?* Are you saying those M and M three-piece suits who get paid four hundred bucks an hour to help takeover specialists swallow up weaker companies using borrowed funds so they can sell off the assets to repay the loans, trash the employees, then pocket the profits are going to get seriously righteous over a country lawyer who swallows one little insect?"

"Slow down, Cowboy. You can't blame them. Leveraged buyouts happen to be where the money is now."

"That's what Willie Sutton said when they asked him why he robbed banks."

"Don't get sanctimonious on me, Seth. They know they're not angels, and they don't expect you to be one either. It's more a matter of, well, style. I'm just suggesting you don't come on to them like some off-the-wall maverick. The personnel partner is already taking a chance, making an offer to someone while the senior partner's back at Yale on a teaching sabbatical."

"Who's that?" said Seth, his temper momentarily cooled by curiosity.

"Anthony Treadwell. He runs the place."

"I've heard him lecture. He's one of the great ones."

"If you come to M and M, you'll hear him lecture a lot. Up close and personal."

"I'm used to it."

"I'm sure you are. How is the old geezer?"

"You never know with Pop. The doc says it might be a tumor on the brain that turns him upside down every now and then. If I get on with M and M, I'm going to put him up at a good home."

"We need an experienced trial lawyer here, Seth. I think it's a slam dunk."

"Well, whatever happens, Harry, I thank you for your efforts."

Harry said nothing for a minute and Seth thought he might have lost the connection. When Harry spoke, Seth had to strain to hear.

"I'm still trying to square things, Seth."

Seth's features folded into a frown, and he drew in a quick breath. "That's history, pard. Forget about it. Give her my best."

Harry told Seth sure he'd do that and they said good-bye.

Seth stared at the receiver for a minute, then slammed it into the cradle and spun out of the phone booth, almost knocking Rosie down.

"What's wrong?" she asked. "Wasn't Harry excited about you winning?"

"Sure he was. Nothing's wrong. Everything's fine."

The peroxide juror approached Seth, congratulated him, enclosing his hand in both of hers. She then acknowledged Rosie with a tight-lipped smile and disappeared down the hall. Mr. Thorton, juror number five, came down the hallway, also smiling and wanting to visit.

"Beats anything I ever seen," he said, shaking hands with Seth. "Didn't know the law allowed it, but scarfin' little Huey like that sure did get our attention."

Seth forced a smile for the unemployed construction superintendent, a good-natured, rough-cut man. "As long as it's not a clear violation of the penal code," Seth said, reaching down for his trial bags, "Cameron's Law allows anything that works. So, if re-creating the event works, I'll do it every time."

The foreman scratched his head, then smiled again. "Well, I guess it's good this weren't no murder case."

"Even I have my limits," said Seth, trying to ease past the

burly juror. "Sorry I can't talk with you now, Mr. Thorton. Tight schedule."

The big man respectfully stepped back, then shuffled away as Seth started down the corridor in the other direction. "Let's get out of here," he said to Rosie, "before the local gourmet critic shows up wanting my recipe for Crepes Huey."

"He was just being nice."

"You're suggesting I wasn't?"

"Well, alls I know is that you just won the most important case of your life and you're acting like you lost it. What did Harry say to put you in such a black mood?"

"We'll discuss it later, okay? There's another elevator down at the end of the hall."

They passed the municipal court departments, weaving through a throng of dispirited people milling about, awaiting their fates: traffic violators, drug pushers, wife beaters, small-claims litigants. Several tried to catch Seth's eye, but he knew what they wanted and kept his gaze straight ahead. A lawyer in a courthouse, carrying his telltale briefcase, is a loaf of bread to a starving crowd. He has something the citizens want: familiarity with the arcane and mystical secrets of the intimidating world into which they have been unwillingly cast. He's a walking Rosetta Stone. Someone who can help.

"Señor, por favor! Please?" Seth turned to see a tiny woman who looked to be somewhere between the ages of thirty and sixty, smelling of fruit—peaches and apricots—with wiry hair stacked like an umbrella and skin as hard and dry-looking as a sidewalk. Seth figured her for a migrant cutting-shed worker. He picked up his pace in the direction of the elevator, but she scurried along beside him, then suddenly closed a callused hand around his wrist.

"Let go of me, ma'm," he said, still moving. Rosie paled and ran ahead to summon the elevator.

But the woman's fingers closed tighter. Hand like a chicken claw.

"Please, *señor abogado*," she said. "Only a minute." People were beginning to stare, some were following. "It's no for me," she continued breathlessly, "but to save a young life. Please. I beg of you, *señor*." She would have dropped to her knees, but a tall young man with a cast on one hand rushed up to restrain her.

"No, Mamá, no es necesario."

"Seth," whispered Rosie over her shoulder, "it's the boy from the car cemetery!"

The ponytailed youth smiled apologetically and, with his good hand, peeled his mother's fingers off Seth's wrist, one by one. "My boy is *muy loco* for what he did," she cried as the boy firmly led her away, "but we no have a lawyer and the judge he is going to deport him! Please, *señor, please!"*

Seth was at the elevator doors, staring at them, willing them to open. "The judge will appoint a lawyer for your son, ma'am," he said over his shoulder. When the doors finally opened, he pushed Rosie inside, pushed the ground-floor and door-close buttons until his finger was white and he felt the car's downward lurch.

"The judge will appoint someone," he repeated when the doors had finally closed, but Rosie stared up at lights inching sideways across the plastic numerals and said nothing.

"He'll plead political asylum," said Seth, inwardly cursing the lumbering elevator's seeming capacity to defy the laws of gravity. He exhaled, dropped his trial bags noisily on the floor. Rubbed his eyes but could still see the woman's dark, pleading eyes, aimed straight at him. "The process will tie up deportation proceedings for so many years they'll lose interest in him."

Silence.

"He'll be fine. Really."

Rosie sniffed, but offered a quick nod of her head, then the hint of an amnesty smile.

"Come on," he said as the doors finally parted into blazing sunlight, "it's time for Bonnie and Clyde to head back to Avenal and turn ourselves in."

A WEEK LATER, SETH CAMERON, BURIED IN VALLEY DUST AND CONVEN-
tion, mired alternately in the ennui of bullshit client meetings
and the fierce tension of the courtroom, awoke and prepared to
shave for the 210th time this year alone. His mind was an elevator, up and down, sometimes stuck between floors.

Rosie noisily hummed in the tiny kitchen as she served up his
210th bowl of oatmeal—she had long ago denied him his beloved
bacon and eggs—and topped the steaming mush with raw oat-
bran (you got to have your fiber, darlin'), rimmed with 2 percent
low-fat milk. Tupelo honey and raisins couldn't save it. Still
tasted like sawdust.

The week had passed at the speed of snail, and a dark, floating
anxiety had nested in his head. For one thing, as he put it to
Rosie, "the phone keeps on not ringing." For another, he felt
guilty about not being open with Tom Huckins about his conversations with Harry, about his intention to accept an offer if he
got one. Tom had his faults, but subterfuge was not among them.
On the other hand, Seth rationalized, why get Huck all upset
about something that might never happen.

Then it happened, and when the receptionist announced that
Harrison Cooper was on the line, Seth's emotions started dancing
like water drops on a griddle.

Harry skipped the preliminaries. "How about next Tuesday,
Cowboy?"

"Time?"

"You'll start at nine-thirty sharp. I'll introduce you to Vic Lydell—he's the personnel partner—and he'll start you on your
round of interviews. I shouldn't tell you this, but like I said, it's
practically a sure thing—barring, of course, the distinct possibility
that you make some sort of indecent proposal to Lydell's secre-

tary or urinate on his shoe. They're talking one hundred and fifty K to start as a lateral senior associate, then partnership in a year and a half after we sniff each other out."

"Sounds good. Have any idea how much a first-year partner makes there?"

Harry hesitated a minute. "I'm just guessing, but I assume we'd be bumped at least another hundred." Another pause, then a quiet chuckle. "I never realized that it was the almighty dollar that stimulated Seth Cameron's thalamus."

"That's because you always had enough of those almighty dollars."

Harry laughed. "There's never enough. Dostoyevsky called it 'coined liberty.' "

"The man had it right."

"So may I assume that's a yes?"

"My saddlebags are packed."

"That's what I thought you'd say," said Harry. "Plan on spending the night before with Trish and me. I'll tell you more of what to expect over some home-cooked San Francisco cuisine. Bring Rosie if she can get off."

Seth said he would be there, hung up, took a deep breath, and headed across the hallway to Tom Huckins's office.

"Seth, ol' pard! Meet Tammy. She's been telling me about her sexual harassment case against the manager of Big Burger."

"Tammy" quickly fastened the top buttons of her blouse— though Seth was sure not as quickly as his nimble-fingered part- ner had unfastened them—then asked directions to the ladies' room. Seth shook his head. "Started your research already, Huck?"

"You know I'm a hands-on kind of lawyer, Cowboy. Never too soon to begin dealing lusty blows for justice." Tom straight- ened his tie, brushed back his curly, dark hair, and glanced toward his scowling partner. "Okay, Seth, so she's a dog."

"That's not the point. I think she's trying to be a client. But since you mentioned it, she is in fact a real dog, which to my mind should make it easier for you to be a real lawyer."

"Come off it, pard. It doesn't interfere professionally and you know I never met a woman I didn't like."

"Nor a mirror either," said Seth dryly, thinking, *Just keep it up, Tom. Make this easier for me.*

Seth said it then, no preamble, just said it. Told him everything, including that if he got the offer, he'd accept it. Tom's salacious grin twisted into gaping disbelief, then tight-lipped anger as reality set in.

"You can't do this," said Tom, his handsome face suddenly strained, unbelieving. "We're just turning the corner here. Everybody knows you're nuts as a bunny, Cowboy, but I could have you shipped to the funny farm if you're crazy enough to walk away from what we've built here. Seth Cameron selling himself to a big-city firm? No way."

"Tom, nothing's for sure, but the fact is, I'm snakebit in this town. More to the point, Doc Farley says Pop needs round-the-clock nursing care now. Hell, Joe Cameron's so tight his ass squeaks even if he had any money, which he doesn't. I can't afford it either on what we take in here. So that's it. I told you because I thought you had a right to know. I'm not asking for your permission or your advice."

"Well, you're going to get my advice whether you want it or not," said Huckins, dropping into a seat behind his desk and staring thoughtfully at a pencil he picked up and held between his huge hands.

"Look, Seth, we both have friends at firms in the city and L.A., right? Are they as happy as we are? Hell no. They're always on guard. Right? Always under inspection: which club to join, which fucking fork to use, all that crap. That's not *you,* man. You belong right here with me and Rosie and the guys. Where you can be your shit-kicking self without some tightly wound asshole looking crosswise at you. Hell, Seth, your game's pool, not polo. There ain't a drop of blue blood running through that red neck of yours."

Seth just looked at him, knowing how Tom prided himself on his reverse snobbery. He was one of those self-absorbed people who assumed that all his buddies saw things the same as he did: that life amounted to no more—or less—than waterskiing on Saturday, watching big-screen professional football on Sunday, working hard all day, chasing hard-bodies all night, getting shit-faced Friday night at Jason's, then crawling out of bed Saturday noon and starting all over again.

Tom broke the silence. "Am I right? Or maybe the hottest trial lawyer in the Valley thinks he's a cut or two above the rest of us yokels."

Seth tried to generate a smile. "Jesus, Huck, let's not make this into some kind of major class struggle. Of course I don't think I'm better. What the hell's so damn evil about wanting to try big cases and getting paid top dollar for doing it?"

Tom pointed the pencil at Seth, heat flashing from his dark eyes. "Nothing, Seth. But you don't just want top dollar. You want top billing, top pussy, top everything. What's worse, you'll probably get it. But then you're gonna find you got nowhere to go. And I'll tell you this: You leave here, ol' buddy, you damn sure won't be welcome back."

"Tom, I can't believe you're saying—"

"*Well, believe it, asshole!*" said Huckins, spinning out of his chair and moving with surprising quickness to within inches of Seth. "I left a good job to join up with you! You *committed* to me, you son of a bitch!"

"Hell, Tom, you know I've never committed anything to anybody in my life," said Seth, holding his ground. "As for that 'good job,' you can go back to searching titles for the county at two grand a month anytime you want. They'll be glad to have you."

"And the white-shoe boys will be glad to have you, too, will they?"

"We'll see."

Tom began pacing like the trial lawyer he had always fancied himself to be. "And do they know just what they'd be buying?"

"Nobody's buyin' me, Tom."

Huckins snickered and bounced his pencil off the desktop, then deftly snatched it in midair. "Well, you just keep thinkin' that if it makes you feel better."

Seth turned toward the door, but lawyer Huckins was just warming up.

"Do they know, for example, about your brief but highly publicized career as a high school car thief?"

"They called it 'joyriding' and I wasn't the only kid—"

"Or how in your senior year you put Joe Hemphill in intensive care for three days for stealing your beat-up motorcycle?"

Seth bristled, but refused to be drawn in.

Huckins flexed his psychedelic suspenders, glanced sideways out the window, and made a clicking sound with his tongue. "Hey, ol' buddy, don't get me wrong," he said, flashing his most sincere smile—the one usually reserved for the girls at Jason's on a Friday night. "I understand completely. I'm only wonderin' if the blue-chip boys might construe crushing a man's jaw over a hunk of used metal to be a mild overreaction."

Seth drew in a breath. That 'hunk of used metal' was the only thing in my whole fucking life I'd ever been able to call my own."

"Okay, *okay*, I told you I *understand*. Might be they would, too. But how about your illustrious NFL career? Do those San Francisco cricket players know you were thrown out of football for high-sticking and other various and sundry dirty tricks?"

"That's bullshit, too. The 49ers just didn't renew me."

"How many games were you thrown out of before they didn't 'renew' you, Seth?"

"Look, Huck," said Seth, turning again for the door. "I know this is hard for you, so I've tried to hear you out. But this conversation isn't going anywhere."

"And neither are you, Seth," said Huckins. "At least if you know what's good for you. Just answer me one last question. Have they so much as seen your law school transcript? Your last year?"

Seth stood frozen in the empty doorway.

Huckins smiled. "I didn't think so."

Seth turned and stormed out of the building.

By the time he parked outside the Bakersfield Broadway Bowl and Bar, Seth had calmed down. He had not expected Tom to be happy for him. Too much fear at work. But Tom was popular around town and a good lawyer when his brain was on the north side of his belt line. He'd do fine, concluded Seth, once he got used to the idea.

Rosie would be another story. They had left Modesto for Avenal after the Perfection Foods verdict in the ecstatic mood of successful bank robbers, stopping first to celebrate with splits of champagne and dinner at Mallard's out on McHenry. Rosie had then slept most of the way—Rosie being one of those people who could sleep standing up—while Seth nursed a six-pack of Anchor

Steam and put the stolen car on cruise control. He didn't mind the quiet; it gave him the space to reenter planet Earth and the time to allow the narcissistic intensity of trial work to drain away.

But Rosie had awakened just south of the Los Banos turnoff to say that if Seth got the offer, she wasn't sure she should give up her job as hostess at the Bakersfield Broadway Bowl and Bar. She talked about having roots for the first time in her life, about not wanting to leave good friends and the Unitarian Church, which had been another source of tension between them.

"Hell, Rosie," he had said, opening another Anchor Steam. They've got all kinds of churches in Marin County. Must be a dozen of 'em."

"Unitarian?"

"Probably, Episcopalian anyway. Same difference."

Rosie groaned. "Would you go with me? To church, I mean. You know, if I went with you."

Bottle propped between his legs, rubbing his eyes, fatigue creeping in. "Rosie, you know I don't much cater to—"

"Anything you can't see, touch, or mix with tonic water."

"I just think you got to put your faith in yourself."

"I don't argue with that, Seth. Neither does any church worth the name. Nobody expects you to leave your common sense at the door, but it won't kill you to spend a few minutes a week considerin' the possibility of something bigger'n us."

Long swig, deep breath, rubs his neck.

"You know, some higher power?"

"You been dreamin' again, Rosie?"

Rosie gave him a sharp look. Knew what he was driving at.

"That's a whole 'nother thing, Seth," she said, the glow in her eyes now hooded into dark specks. It had been a mistake to tell him about her grandmother, and a worse mistake to tell him that the gift often skipped generations, making her the unwanted recipient of a capability she neither understood nor desired, like a tattoo on her brain that couldn't be wished away, that came unbidden in the night, dreams that could often be explained as coincidence, often turned out to be flat wrong, yet sometimes . . .

Seth had let it drop, then tried to persuade her not to get all worried about something that might not even happen, but Rosie would not be deterred.

"I bet Tom Huckins will tell you it's a mistake, Seth. He's

always sayin' about how the only real professional doctors and lawyers anymore are in smaller places like Bakersfield; that all they care about in big firms is how much you bill and their lowest line."

"Bottom line."

"That's it."

Seth was stung by Rosie's quoting Tom Huckins as an authority on his future. He had intended to sympathize with her concerns, but what came out instead was that Tom Huckins was full of self-serving bullshit and she was crazy to listen to him. Rosie responded to this demonstration of sensitivity by passing the next twenty-five miles in silence. Seth finally apologized, but insisted that she couldn't be serious about staying in Bakersfield. Rosie sat there holding firm, speaking in teary-eyed litanies about wanting to be with him but needing a life of her own. Her pain escaped in a torrent through lips that trembled with a heartrending sadness. By the time they reached Avenal, they agreed to cool it until he had heard something specific from Harry.

Now he had heard something specific from Harry, and as he watched Rosie roller-skating snake-hipped between the restaurant tables at the Bakersfield Broadway, flashing her smile at admiring customers, he knew he could never leave without her. The thought of losing her caused his lean face—a face more interesting in its expressiveness than handsome in repose—to tense and age beyond his years. He sipped his coffee and wondered how to persuade her that this could be her last chance as well as his.

But what if things didn't work out between them in San Francisco? He pondered their contrasting personalities, his poor track record in relationships, inwardly wrestled with his options as he watched Rosie snatch an empty carafe on the fly from between two people without even toe-braking her skates—swooping down like a gull, then soaring off. The people loved it.

Rosie plunked herself down at Seth's usual table—it was always quiet at the Broadway during the late afternoon—and began adjusting the laces on one of her skates with the purposeful concentration of a detonation expert defusing a pipe bomb. Seth could see she already knew.

"Tom called you, didn't he?"

Rosie busied herself tying a double bow on her second skate

with a vigorous flourish, almost as if she hadn't heard him. Then she poured fresh coffee for both of them and leaned back in her chair.

"I'm a little scared, Seth," she said in a mournful whisper with an emotional hitch in it that touched his heart.

"Hey, come on, babe," said Seth, watching her thick mane of dark hair as it cascaded off her lowered head like Niagara, flowing down around the steam off her coffee. "Hell, I might flunk the interview. If I don't, just remember how much you took to Mill Valley when we drove through it the day we had brunch at Sam's in Tiburon." Rosie wouldn't meet his eyes, so he reached over and touched her hand. "I was thinking we might find a spot right there at the base of Mount Tamalpais. You said something poetic that day about the rolling silence of the place, that it reminded you of the Black Hills."

Rosie continued to stare glumly into black coffee no darker than her eyes. "It's just all happening so darned fast. I feel like things are so good for us here, and all of a sudden we're just fixin' to throw it all away. Sometimes you can be pretty rash, Seth."

"Rosie, I hardly think of myself as a rash person."

"Oh? How about deciding to swallow Huey last week in Modesto or punching out Soapy Frederickson when he got fresh in here last New Year's Eve or—"

"Those were not rash acts, Rosie. Those were deliberate and premeditated acts of carefully considered insanity."

Rosie had smiled at that in spite of herself. Seth could usually jolly her out of a snit with a few words from *Blackstone's Law Dictionary*. "I do love it when you talk legal," she whispered.

But she wasn't finished with him. She hadn't dropped the big one yet. "What about your dad? We leave, he's all alone."

Seth looked away. The crashing of balls into pins and musty bowling-alley smell was beginning to give him a headache. "Thanks, Rosie, I really needed that little reminder. As a matter of fact, I'm on my way over there now to tell him what's happening."

"But what would he do? Seth, he's your *father*."

"I'm aware of that, Rosie, but I figure I'm about even with Joe Cameron and maybe I should start thinking about myself. If I don't grab this, I'll never get another chance. Not at my age and level of experience. It's too late for Pop, and if I blow this off, it'll be too late for me, too."

Now it was Seth's turn to gaze into his coffee cup. "Doc Farley says he's got to have twenty-four-hour nursing care or move out. Either way I can't afford it. If I get the job, I was thinking about putting him into Summercrest."

"A *home?* You'd put him in an *old folks' home?"* snapped Rosie in a voice loud enough to attract the sympathetic interest of a bowler over on alley number one. "Sorry, Seth," she added quickly, "I know it's been hard for you, and I love you for it."

"Well, *he* doesn't. Most of the time now, he doesn't even like me."

"That's just his head gone bad, honey." Rosie glanced up at a middle-aged couple coming through the front door, but they sat down at the counter. "Well, it's really none of my business anyway."

"It *is* your business, Rosie, but with the kind of money I'd be making, I could afford to buy his way into the one place I know he'd be happy."

"With the money *you'd* be making," said Rosie, her eyes suddenly sparking. Seth watched her get up, could see her mind shifting gears. "And just what the heck am *I* supposed to do in San Francisco or Mill Valley or wherever? I've hostessed here since 1988, Seth, and I'm finally up for evening manager. Either way, I'm making enough to live comfortable." She started to skate away, but turned and gave him a look that could bend a fork, adding, "You'll do just fine in the city. But have you given any thought to me? To *us?"*

Seth stared down at his hands. He could take on the world in the courtroom, but he hated conflict with Rosie. True, they were dissimilar people—he, the ambitious, quick-tempered, cerebral type; she, the warmhearted earth-woman who could see beauty in everything, even him. They had always managed to communicate, however, often without speaking. Even the decision to live together had been reached with absurd simplicity two years ago. Seth had spotted her skating around the Broadway and had begun to dine there regularly, attracted like a heat-seeking missile to her innocent, yet erotic aura. Rosie couldn't help noticing Seth's frequent appearances for dinner, the Bowl & Bar not being known for its fine cuisine. Soon they were small-talking, and Seth was able to get a good look into eyes that were both older and stronger than her youthful, fragile-looking body—eyes swimming with goodwill, yet reflecting the same passion for life he sometimes noticed in the mirror when he shaved.

Gradually they became friends. They talked about everything: her notorious mother, her Iroquois grandmother, her life growing up in the Black Hills, and her five-month marriage to a hard-boozing rock-and-roll guitar player who gave her four months in L.A. and a lesson in life she'd never forget. Seth told her about attending U.C. Berkeley on an athletic scholarship, laughed about his abortive professional football career after graduation, and his best friend, a three-legged canine named Fat Dog. They discussed his views on world affairs and politics, her insights into the spiritual nature of things. Touched on issues of freedom versus loneliness, power versus security. Shared favorite colors, songs, and wine. And laughter. Always laughter.

He solved a minor legal problem for her aunt Claire, and Rosie's gratitude made him feel as if he had won an appeal before the Supreme Court.

Though Seth's lust endured over these early weeks, he began to see Rosie Wheeler in a new light. He was in love with her.

They had never been on a date.

He could tell she knew about him. Bakersfield held few secrets. He wanted her to know he regarded her as something special, not another Seth Cameron one-nighter. Finally asked her to a movie.

They lucked into a parking place right in front of the theater, but neither one opened a door. They just sat there in his El Camino and stared straight ahead. After five minutes of this, Seth turned to her and told her he'd like her to move in with him. Rosie's quick, questioning glance went straight to his soul and stripped him of all pretense. His heart hammered in his chest, and he was relieved when she turned her gaze straight ahead again. Even now, two years later, he could still see the contours of her child-woman face that night, profiled in the back-lighting of the Strand Theater, as she pondered his proposal. "You know," he added, hardly breathing, "live together."

Seth would never forget that moment, that night, that warm, dry Valley night; the reckless joy of possibilities, of wanting something so much that fear and rationality never stood a chance.

"Okay," Rosie had replied at last, and they had driven straight to her apartment and tossed most of her things into the back of his pickup.

An added bonus was the way Rosie and Joe Cameron had taken to one another, maybe because Joe had never had a daughter and Rosie was on the lookout for a surrogate father. Her presence had become particularly helpful now that the seventy-nine-year-old man was having more and more trouble remembering things. Like eating. Like his own name.

Seth, on the other hand, had the gift of perfect memory, a blessing for a trial lawyer, but a curse for a boy who, at the age of six, had suffered an emotional wound that would never heal.

Joe had married Seth's mother—his first marriage, her second—in what he liked to call his "full maturity," which is to say he was forty years old and, Seth suspected, still a virgin. Ruth Hollander had been twenty-four, and virginity was to her but a distant memory. Beaten as a child by her father, then by her first husband, Ruth had apparently decided that marriage to a steady, middle-aged civil servant might represent a salutary change of pace. And so it was—at first anyway—as Ruth Cameron quietly endured nearly a decade of not being abused before she disappeared one night behind a sheet of rain and the cover of darkness in Alfred Gamut's mile-long Cadillac.

Seth, six years old, is awakened by a dream in which he is being kissed by his mother. Several minutes later he hears a car pull up in the alley and runs to his bedroom window in time to see a stranger roughly pinning her against the car door. The frantic child tries to open the window, but it's painted shut; stuck, just like his throat.

Now the man has jammed one hand up against his mother's chest while the other is trying to find something up inside her skirt. She spins around, but the stranger grabs her, bends her back across the front fender of the car, and starts to kiss her.

This seems too real to be a dream so he keeps pushing against the stubborn sill, his impotent mouth frosting the window as he sees that his mother has been able to get a good hold on the stranger's head with both hands and has wrapped a high-heeled foot around his back. But now it's getting weird because she's kissing him back and rubbing him between the legs with a spare hand that could have been used to sock him one. Then she kisses him on top of his head even though he's pulled up her sweater and buried his face in a bare chest glowing like white neon against her black sweater. Now she breaks free, but ... she's laughing and running, not toward the house, but around the front of that beautiful black car and now she's opening the passenger door and, oh, Mama, don't please, don't, Mama, don't leave! But the big, black car just swallows her up and drives away.

The boy returns to his bed in confused silence, touching the lipstick-marked cheek where his mother had kissed him in the dream, a red mark of betrayal that will still be there when he awakens in the morning.

Then he'll know it was no dream.

Alfred was a charmer from L.A. who had made his fortune in women's shoes. His genius had been in creating a system for getting crocodile skins out of Africa. A village of poverty-stricken Africans had been happy to club the child-killing reptiles for a bounty of two bits each, and Alfred had paid the chief another quarter to get the skins upstream to the town of Bukoa. From there they were shipped to Alicante, Spain, where he paid two bucks apiece to have them finished into boots and purses for which Imelda Marcos and her friends would later pay several hundred dollars in the shops of upper Madison Avenue. Alfred made a fortune until animal rights activists put a stop to it, and the crocs went back to eating village children, whom the parents were again having trouble feeding anyway now that the bounty was gone. Ecological balance.

In any event, Joe and young Seth Cameron suddenly found themselves alone. Gone forever was the smell of his mother's perfume when she kissed him good-night and the fresh bran muffins when she awoke him in the morning. No more ham and mushroom omelettes on weekends either, no more sounds of her monotone humming each morning as she laid out freshly ironed school clothes. No more freshly ironed school clothes.

These were some of Seth's thoughts as he approached the family home, hoping, but not expecting, to find his father in a lucid state.

Seth's car filled the empty driveway, unused by Joe since 1987 when he had permanently surrendered his driver's license for having entered a supermarket after hours. In his old Buick Roadmaster.

"You're friends with the DA, Seth," Joe had said, shamefully avoiding Seth's eyes. "Could you talk to him? I'm a prisoner in this house if I can't drive. Stir. The slammer. Up the river."

"This isn't just a parking ticket, Dad, though I doubt I could even fix one of those. I'll have a talk with him anyway."

Joe had winced at the word *fix* and nothing more was ever said on the subject. Seth did talk to the DA, however, and he did fix it—fixed it so his father would never drive again.

A by-product of Joe's incarceration had been the most beautiful garden on the street, a typical clean, wide Bakersfield street, with tall poplar sentinels on both sides and a five-foot strip of Bermuda grass running between the curb and sidewalk in front of each house on the block. Seth stopped for a minute to admire the new rows of impatiens on each side of the walkway that led to the front steps, then paused before the towering, espaliered bougainvillea Pop had planted when he went into recovery in 1967. Seth entered and found his father asleep on the couch. He smiled down at the old man.

Joe Cameron, a cruelly cuckolded philosopher king, trapped inside the body of a civil servant. Started out as a runner for the San Joaquin County Clerk's Office at the age of eighteen and was appointed court clerk of Department 3 by the time he was just twenty-three, serving under the illustrious Jimmy Maxwell, already known as the best trial judge in the county. Joe Cameron, who had been a good father to Seth after the four nightmarish years, which, for different reasons, neither remembered very much about and which, for similar reasons, they never discussed at all.

Dried out and sober, Joe had tried to make up for those lost years by teaching his son the one thing he knew well: trial tactics and courtroom survival rules. *I've seen the best of the best in my time, Son, and like Yogi Berra says, "You can observe a lot by watching."* Pop had also tried to instill the spiritual values he had picked up in his twelve-step recovery program, but these lessons made less sense to Seth—particularly the ones about doing unto others and the meek inheriting the earth, for while meek Joe Cameron had been busy doing unto others, Alfred Gamut had done him out of his wife.

Seth knew he should resent, even hate, his mother for what she'd done to them, but he had come to see his father's lack of ambition as a fatal, self-imposed weakness; and though he pitied the old man, he could understand, even identify with, Ruth's impatience with the life Joe offered her.

"I think I'm about to get the biggest break of my life, Pop," he whispered to his sleeping father, then brushed a wisp of white hair away from the old man's closed eyes. "I know you won't like the idea. You'll feel like you're being abandoned again. Oh, yes, I know all about that night, Dad. I couldn't tell you because at first I didn't understand it, and then when I did, well, I figured it would hurt you even more if you knew that I knew the truth. Well, I know all right, remember every goddamn detail. Still feel her lips on my cheek, hear her laughing; she hardly ever did that with us, you know. Laugh, I mean. Can still see that long black Cadillac driving off with your pride bein' dragged behind it like tin cans tied to a bumper."

Seth touched the old man lightly on the shoulder, but he didn't stir.

"You couldn't give her the luxury I guess she needed, Pop, but now you're going to have it for yourself—whether you want it or not. If things go well next Tuesday in the city, you'll be at Summercrest with the richest old farts in California, and you'll all be dressed the same. Old age and bad health, the great equalizers."

Joe Cameron's eyes slowly came unstuck, one at a time. "Hello, kid," he said, reaching down and arranging his legs into a sitting position.

"Brought your favorite, Dad," Seth said as he scanned his father's face and posture, gauging the lucidity of the moment, pleased to see the faded blue eyes unusually clear. "Raisin-apple pie from Rosie."

"Hell with the pie, Son," said Joe, taking in the smell of fresh cooked apples, "send me Rosie."

Seth laughed, then followed his father's slow passage through the small living room into a sunny kitchen shaped like a freight car. "I'm afraid she's a little upset with me right now, Dad."

"Well," said the old man with a laugh that crackled like green firewood, "I'm sure you're guilty of whatever you're charged with."

Encouraged, Seth decided there would never be a better time. "It's like this, Dad," he said casually, watching out of the corner of his eye for his father's reaction. "That opportunity I was hoping for in San Francisco may be coming through next week, and I want Rosie to come with me. She's not sure she wants to move."

Joe Cameron set the pie down on the cracked tile counter next to a dark-stained sink littered with cups and saucers. He gazed without blinking through a wood-framed window for a full minute, over the rear porch with its broken hammock, and across the overgrown backyard guarded by an ivy-choked chicken-wire fence he and Seth had built to contain a puppy Ruth had brought home. Had papers, she claimed, but neither the fence nor the papers had kept the pooch out of harm's way, and in the center of the enclosed area, over a hole Seth had tearfully dug as a child, refusing to let anybody help, a hunk of granite still rested.

Joe stood frozen there so long that Seth assumed he had slipped away from him again, but then he suddenly gave his head a jerk, said, "She's a good girl," and shuffled back into the living room.

"I can't force her to go with me, Dad. It wouldn't be right . . . even if I could." Seth's eyes fell on the picture of Ruth Cameron, amazingly still perched atop a dinette bookcase jammed with worn classics from Joyce to Faulkner, murder mysteries by Raymond Chandler and lesser students of the genre, a crumbling set of *Encyclopedia Britannica*, and a *Kern County Local Rules* manual. Seth realized he was now a year or two older than the sad-faced, hungry-eyed woman in the picture at the time it was taken.

Joe's eyes followed Seth's to the portrait.

"Don't lose her, Son," he said quietly.

"I'll try not to, Pop, but what I was wondering was, well, what with me and maybe Rosie leaving town, if you've given any more thought to moving out of here, maybe getting into a . . . more manageable situation?"

The old man's face was suddenly pinched and wary, but all he said was, "I'm fine right here at home."

"Dad, tell me what the doc thinks is wrong."

"He said it could be just old age hittin' me harder than some."

"Anything else?"

"He said it could be something called senile dementia, probably the same thing."

"Anything else?"

Pop gave his head a little jerk to the side. "Thinks it might be a tumor growin' on the brain."

Seth walked over and put his hands on Pop's gaunt shoulders. "What do you think it is?"

Joe Cameron gave his son a smile that pierced Seth's heart, then said in a hoarse voice, "I think it's bum luck."

Later, after dinner, exhausted father dozed on the sofa beside an ancient glass coffee table on which was spread a half-finished game of solitaire. Dutiful son, finishing up the dishes, heard Joe cry out, "Who's there?"

Seth snatched a dish towel and hurried into the living room, drying his hands. "It's me, Dad."

"What the hell are you doing here?" he asked, his face lined with suspicion. "Do I look like I need a caretaker? Go home to your wife."

"Dad, you know Rosie and I are not . . ."

Before Seth knew it, they were fighting again. Just like that. Seth said he was moving to San Francisco and that he was going to make arrangements at Summercrest for Joe. Joe said over my dead body, and Seth said that won't be long at all if you don't get the hell out of this house where somebody can take care of you, and Joe shouted something back and finally there was silence.

Seth slowly rose and went back to the kitchen. He poured two glasses of wine from the place where he knew his father had been hiding it for years and offered the glass to his father.

"Come on, Pop. Try to understand. It's a major opportunity with a top firm. I'd be able to make some big bucks there, eventually try some big cases against the best lawyers in the country."

Seth's father emptied the glass in three gulps, wiped his chin, and laughed sardonically. "And get eaten alive is what you'd do. I watched the great ones come and go from my courtroom for more than forty years—"

"And you can observe a lot by watching, right?"

"Huh?"

Seth found himself staring at a housefly, which, unnoticed by his father, had perched on the old man's right eyebrow, where it appeared to be grooming itself. "Never mind."

"There's only one thing standing in your way of being a top trial lawyer, kid."

"Yeah?" So easily sucked in. The head snaps up hopefully. "What's that, Pop?"

Pop eyed the empty glass and licked his lips. "Reality," he said, flashing Seth a bitter smile.

Seth said nothing.

"They'd throw your bones to the jury."

"Dad, don't start that again—"

"I'm just tellin' you flat out, kid: you don't have near what it takes to make it in the big leagues."

Seth fought back anger as he stared into a stranger's eyes, eyes cold with contempt.

"We'll see," Seth said softly, then soundlessly placed his untouched glass on the coffee table and walked out of the house— his father shouting after him that he'd soon come crawling home, that he'd be *begging* Big Tom to take him back.

Outside, Seth took a deep breath and gave his head a shake.

"We'll see," he repeated to the empty street.

Two weeks after his interviews at Miller and McGrath, and just as Seth had abandoned hope, Harry called with congratulations. They wanted him to "start yesterday." Seth told him he'd be there just as soon as he dealt with some "delicate personal matters," including sobering up from the celebration that was already forming in his mind.

First on his list of delicate personal matters was a final chat with Mrs. Delbert Spathe of Avenal, who, following a week of wrangling, had agreed to drop charges of grand theft auto filed with the regional prosecutor in return for "restitution" in the sum of an additional $3,000—substantially more than the full blue-book value of her 1982 Chevy. Seth knew the demand constituted extortion—particularly since her car was returned after just four days with a brand-new radiator—but Miller and McGrath wasn't hiring fugitives these days, and Mrs. Spathe was a woman who knew leverage when she saw it.

Seth figured that the ultimate fruit of his crime spree—a trial victory leading to M&M's offer—constituted a fair return and sent the check care of the prosecuting attorney, a pleasant-sounding country boy who mentioned that he happened to be Mrs. Spathe's son-in-law. Seth knew leverage when it had a bootheel on his throat.

Next was Tom Huckins. Seth checked his watch. Nearly six-thirty; Tom would be at Jason's.

Bakersfield still had fern bars. Jason's—the town's only hot singles saloon—looked like a botanical garden, with no less than eighteen of the plants hanging like shredded umbrellas from a fake cedar ceiling, plus twelve fake Tiffany lamps, four backgammon tables, and by five-thirty every afternoon, a roomful of small-talk junkies and sad-faced girls lonely enough to pay attention to them.

Seth entered and spotted his partner holding court at the end of the long oak bar, to the edge of which was attached a small brass plate inscribed THOMAS V. HUCKINS, ESQ.

"Holy shit, it's my partner, Seth Cameron!" shouted Huckins, his tie carelessly pulled open and obviously well into his weekend. "Back on the prowl again? Rosie out of town?" This brought macho chuckles from Tom's pals, Trigger and Lo-Ball, a pair of local Sheetrock contractors who listed Jason's phone number on what passed for their business cards. "Barkeep!" Tom shouted to Ken. "Bring Cowboy here one of these god-awful kamikazes you make. And bring me a couple more while you're at it."

"A beer will be fine, Ken," said Seth. "Tom, can I talk to you a minute?"

"Sure, but make it quick, old buddy," said Tom, emptying his glass. "See that little red-haired sweetie over by the juke? Definitely the next Mrs. Huckins."

"I got the offer from Miller and McGrath," Seth said quietly. "And I've accepted it."

Tom's hooded eyes slowly widened as the words registered. His head gave a little jerk and Seth could see his jaw twitching.

Huckins then levitated from his stool in a manner that caused Trigger and Lo-Ball to drift down toward the other end of the bar. There Tom stood, bent slightly forward at the waist, one foot well behind the other, shoulders hunched, eyes straight ahead, splayed palms on top of the bar supporting his muscular six-foot-three-inch frame.

"Just like that?" he said finally, still not looking at Seth.

"You said make it quick."

"That was quick, all right. Given any thought to how I'm supposed to service all our clients? Or are you taking them, too?"

"Just one, since you mention it. Central CalComm."

The last two words spun Huckins's head around. "Don't tell me, let me guess. You've already talked to Benson. Right? Told him how much better you'll be able to service all his needs with a big-city firm behind you."

"Something like that."

Huckins's eyes sparked hatred. "Another example of Seth Cameron's pragmatic philosophy in action: dog eat dog, every man for himself."

"It's always up to the client, Tom. You know that."

"*I'll* tell you what I know," said Huckins, his speech slurred. "It's un-fucking-ethical is what I know. I may be a lot of things, but I'm goddamn ethical."

Seth chuckled, took a quick swig of his beer. "Tom, you are to ethics what AstroTurf is to grass."

Ken paced behind the bar, listening to fragments of the conversation and watching Huckins's darkening expression. After Seth's remark, he scooped up the three dollars Seth threw down for his beer and headed for the other end of the bar where Trigger and Lo-Ball were watching the exchange from a safe distance.

"Central CalComm doesn't mean that much to me," Seth added, "if you feel so damn strong about it."

Huckins tossed off another kamikaze, then slowly turned to stare at Seth through narrowed eyes. "I always knew you were a cold and ambitious bastard," he said finally through clenched teeth, "but I put up with you because you were *my* cold and ambitious bastard."

"So you thought," said Seth.

"You son of a bitch!" No warning, just the huge fist bursting into Seth's face, sending him flying across the floor into a wall that stopped his backward motion and allowed him to keep his footing. The bar fell silent and everyone froze where they were: Lo-Ball with his hand in the cigarette machine, Ken drying a glass, the redhead coming out of the ladies'. Seth slowly wiped the back of his hand across his mouth and looked at the blood there.

"Jesus, Tom," he said with a wry smile, "maybe you should have been the litigator all along."

But Huckins wasn't smiling. Huckins was circling, closing in, that same club of a right fist cocked at the end of a wrist that looked like a two-by-four.

"Lighten up, Huck," said Seth, weaving from side to side against the wall. "Jason doesn't have a dance license."

Huckins's answer was a roundhouse right to the head, but this time Seth ducked down and to the right just as his partner's fist grazed his left ear, then passed through the Sheetrock wall, just missing a picture of Jason himself posed with a Hollywood starlet and local golf star Steve McClean. As Huckins struggled to extricate himself from Trigger and Lo-Ball's wallboard handiwork of eight years earlier, Seth slammed him with a quick left-right combination, then buried his left hand deep into the bigger man's solar plexus. Huckins groaned as blood spurted from his nose, then collapsed against Seth.

"Seth!" shouted Ken, as the smaller man, hunched over like a gravedigger, supported his dazed adversary by the shoulders and readied a deadly right-hand uppercut. *"Don't do it, man!"*

Seth, heart pounding so hard his vision was distorted, panting through slack mouth, eyes narrowed into burning slits, squinted in the direction of the voice. No one moved. Then finally, slowly and awkwardly, he steered Huckins into a nearby chair.

"You're right, Ken," gasped Seth, then slowly turned and dabbed at his cut lip with a cocktail napkin that read JASON'S: WHERE GOOD FRIENDS MEET. "Bring some coffee over here for Huck. Some ice, too."

"The hell with him, Seth," said Ken, hurling a towel into the sink behind the bar. "I saw what happened. Probably shoulda let you finish the fucker. Far as I'm concerned, he can go somewhere else for his goddamn coffee."

Seth leaned against the bar for a few seconds to catch his breath, then swayed toward the door. "Show some class, Ken," he said, turning and flashing the bartender a withering look. "Tom's drunk and you helped him get that way. Man couldn't scratch his own ass with a handful of fishhooks right now. Here's a twenty. Pour the coffee, then send my ex-partner home in a cab."

Seth reentered the Bakersfield Broadway Bowl and Bar just ahead of the dinner rush and fell into a chair at his usual table. Rosie ordered coffee for both of them, then sat down beside him and enclosed one of his hands in both of hers. "You don't look so good, darlin'. What happened to your face?"

"Tom had an attitude about my decision, so I smashed his fist with my mouth."

"I'll get you some ice, honey. It'll help the pain."

"Sounds good, assuming it comes with a double shot of Jack Daniel's."

Rosie said that could be arranged and took a metal key to her famous fuchsia-colored roller skates, which, as Seth had long ago observed, emphasized her trim ankles and gave her added height, the lack of which was the sole flaw in an otherwise perfect fashion model's figure. Seth put his head back to ease the pain in his neck and looked up past racks of hanging fluorescent lights at the ugliest cracked plaster ceiling he had ever seen—not that he had often confused the Broadway Bowl with the Sistine Chapel.

"Tom's just scared," she said.

"If that's scared, I'd hate to see him angry."

"Did you ...?"

"Yeah, but it could have been worse. He'll live."

Rosie gave him a worried look, but decided to change the subject. "How about your dad?"

"Tomorrow. I've had all the abuse I can handle for one day. He'll just tell me I'm not good enough. The usual."

"If his mood is right, he's just as likely to wish you well. Joe will go along when he's himself."

"I'm hoping you will, too."

"Go along or be myself?" she said, a ball-bearing hardness creeping into her voice as she tied the laces on her right skate with a flourish.

"Both."

"Well, both those things may not be possible, though I'm sure the notion of me havin' a 'self,' a life of my own, is somethin' that may not have crossed your mind lately."

Seth told her she'd been reading *Cosmopolitan* magazine again and Rosie said so what, then tried to cross her skate-elevated legs under the table, bumping her knee on the underside and spilling coffee from both mugs.

"I'm sorry, Seth."

"It's your table," Seth said, leaping to his feet and grabbing a napkin.

"I mean about jumpin' on you. You've got enough problems without worryin' about mine."

A dark silence consumed them as they sat back down. In fact, the entire Bowl went quiet for one of those awkward moments of coincident silence that seem orchestrated to embarrass. Then somebody picked up a number ten for a spare and the click-thud sound of the pin followed by the ball's hitting the canvas reverberated across the tense stillness. Seth figured that his Jack Daniel's was an idea whose time had passed, along with Rosie's good mood.

"Try to understand, Seth," said Rosie, gathering herself as the jukebox came alive and bowling balls resumed their rumbling attack on alleys two through six. "I'm just scared about quittin' my job. It may not seem like much of a job to you, but these people are my family now. Plus, leavin' my work at the church and all my friends. Aren't you worried about any of that? People respect you here, Seth."

"We'll make new friends."

"In San Francisco? Too many people there for findin' friends."

"Come again?"

"Too many people. It's like if we take a hike in the foothills on a weekday and we see somebody after an hour or so, we all smile and say hi to each other. But if we go out on a weekend and see people every five minutes on the very same path, we don't. Don't you know why that is?"

"I know I'm about to find out."

"It's because they aren't special anymore. In fact, they can become a darned nuisance. Same path, same nice people, but it's a whole 'nother thing. I read somewhere the same thing happens to hamsters when you put too many of them in the same space."

"Rats."

"I'm used to stronger language than that from you, but I'm glad you agree."

Seth smiled at her. "It won't happened to us, Rosie. Besides, we know Harry and Trish to start with."

"They're *your* friends, Seth. And anyways, it's not just that. It's the . . . whole *bigness* of the place. Even Bakersfield is gettin' too big far as I'm concerned, and now you're fixin' to move to an even bigger place? I don't know. I just don't know."

"I understand, baby," said Seth, lightly touching her hair. "I really do. But help me out here because I can't go without you."

Rosie's eyes misted up at this, but her resistance held. "Can't we wait till January at least? I'm due for a big Christmas bonus this year and was countin' on buyin' a decent car."

"Afraid not, Rosie. It's now or never for me. Big firms like M and M usually hire kids right out of law school so they can train them their own way, then exploit them for at least six or seven years before they have to cut them in on a piece of the action as partners. Hell, Rosie, I'm already over the edge in terms of years out of law school. I'd figured myself for dead. I happened to call Harry just as two senior associates defected to another firm. They're even going to bring me in at Harry's level, just as if I had joined them right out of school like he did. I'll never have another chance like this."

More silence.

"Come on, Rosie," Seth said, reaching over and caressing one of her shoulders. "What's happened to the old spirit of adventure?"

Rosie made a face. "Oh, it'd be an adventure all right, commuting to a new job I don't have in a dyin' Oldsmobile that burns gas like a 747. Comin' home to a place we also don't have and would have trouble rentin' because, as you may have forgotten, we do have a functionally impaired dog."

She should have been the trial lawyer, thought Seth. "I haven't forgotten, Rosie, but I've got to go to San Francisco. Like Yogi Berra says, 'When you get to a fork in the road, take it.' "

Rosie just played with her coffee mug, didn't help him with so much as a smile. "Don't you see, honey?" he added. "This is my fork in the road!"

Rosie looked up at him through liquid eyes, and Seth took

both of her hands in his. Getting her to go to the city with him was turning out to be his toughest case. No bugs to swallow this time; no tricks, no miracles. Nothing left but to resort to the truth, the whole truth, and nothing but . . .

"You've got to come with me, darlin'," he said, licking a bloody lip that was still swelling. "The thing is, if you don't, I'm afraid we'll lose each other." Seth then stood up, looked away for a moment, and let his arms drop helplessly to his sides. People in the restaurant area were watching them now, but neither Rosie nor Seth seemed to notice.

"I'm scared too, Rosie. Scared of the unknown, scared of blowing my last chance, but most of all, scared of losing you."

Rosie smiled, shook her head slowly, then rose to her eight-wheeled feet, put her arms around him, and buried her head in his chest. "Oh, Seth, you're just so doggone irresistible. I just hope they allow old Oldsmobiles and three-legged dogs in Marin County."

Seth tilted her head back and kissed her as if for the very first time. Ignoring the whistles and scattered applause, they stood looking at each other, and Seth could swear light was radiating from her pale face; light diffused by kaleidoscope tears into a shimmering aura that made him feel dizzy; light he knew he must be imagining, but light all the same.

Part 2

THE SMALL GARDEN COTTAGE WAS EVERYTHING ROSIE AND SETH HAD hoped for when they saw the ad in the *San Raphael Independent Journal*. They unpacked the last moving boxes by late afternoon and stayed warm their first night by burning them in the large fireplace. A grove of rhododendrons partially shielded their view of the landlord's house at the front of the large lot, and all that could be heard in the evenings was birdsong.

Beverly Jans-Becker, the rental agent, insisted that $1,400 a month was a bargain for a location at the very base of Mount Tamalpais in "picturesque Mill Valley," close to shopping, schools, and public transportation. Ms. Jans-Becker's rhapsodic sales pitch continued unabated—even after they had signed the lease and she was climbing back into the Marin County Realtor's standard vehicle, a Mercedes 190 sedan—still raving about the cottage's "convenient proximity to sunny Stinson Beach, mystical Inverness, and enchanting Bodega Bay." They smiled back at her and waved good-bye. Alone at last.

The owner of the cottage—an elderly widower—was so smitten by Rosie that he had approved the new tenants without a credit check. He was also a 49er fan, excited to meet his first real NFL player, even an *ex*-player he had never heard of, even an ex–*defensive* player who had played only one year for the 49ers and not very well at that. By the end of Seth's first full week at M&M, they were settled in.

"Put on your dancin' shoes, Rosie," Seth announced over the telephone, "it's party time."

"Tonight? You're actually takin' a night off? What's the occasion?"

"Since when do we need one on a Saturday night? But for starters, how about your job offer at Luchesso's, my completing a full week at M and M without grossly offending anyone, plus getting assigned to help on a seventy-million-dollar case today, *and*—last, but fastest—my hot new wheels."

Seth had just bought a '87 Porsche Targa from George Middleton, a seven-year associate who had been told he would not be making partnership at M&M. Harry had explained to Seth that nearly all metropolitan law firms still observed the harsh "up or out" policy for handling unwanted associate attorneys. Middleton was not going "up" to partnership, and this meant he had to go "out" on the street to find a new job.

He had not been fired, of course. Firing was a barbaric practice reserved for lesser enterprises, unworthy of a professional firm like Miller and McGrath. The time-honored solution at M&M was merely to inform the associate that he or she would not be making partner, coincident with the disappearance of any new assignments or salary increases. After a month or two of this embarrassing indifference, even the most persevering associate would tender notice of his or her "resignation," after which the relieved firm would close ranks behind its discarded employee with glowing letters of reference. Harry recounted an occasion when Anthony Treadwell had dismissed an associate named Evans Thompson on grounds of laziness, then later responded to one of Thompson's potential employers with a consummate example of devious and deliberate ambivalence. Treadwell's letter ended, "You will be very fortunate indeed to get Evans Thompson to work for you."

Later that night as they were driving to dinner in Seth's new car, Rosie expressed her concern over the three-way trade that had left Middleton with her antique Oldsmobile and herself in possession of Seth's relatively new El Camino.

"It was his own idea, Rosie. He's accepted an offer with a small firm up in Eureka and thinks your car will fit in fine up there. Besides, he needed the extra cash for the move. It worked out great for everybody."

Rosie was unconvinced. "It's not that I don't appreciate you givin' me the El Camino, honey, but I still don't see why he had to leave in the first place. You said he was a real brain."

"The guy was brilliant, but just being smart doesn't make it anymore. He wasn't producing enough billable hours, plus he didn't have a book."

"No book? How did he practice law?"

Seth laughed. "I mean no book of business. He wasn't a rainmaker and showed no signs of becoming one."

"Book? Rainmaker? Are we talking in code, Seth?"

"No, babe, it's law-firm economics. The concept has been changing, but it's still alive and well at M and M. To make partner, you've got to prove you can attract new clients in order to provide enough work to keep yourself and at least two younger associates busy."

"Why two associates?"

"To keep the ratio of associates to partners at around two to one. The idea is to get high billable hours from the young worker bees and to have two worker bees for every partner. Leverage—that's where the profit is."

"Leverage?"

"Well, yes." Seth's tone turned cautious as he felt himself being drawn in. "See, they get the associates doing monkey work behind the scenes—running up between 2,000 and 2,400 billable hours a year—for each partner doing the front work. The profit's in the associates."

"The monkeys."

"Right."

"Am I correct that you're the monkey in this situation?"

"It's a figure of speech." Seth spotted D'Angelo's and scanned the street in front for a parking place. He could use a drink. "Anyway, as M and M makes more partners, it has to grow to keep the two-to-one ratio, which means you need more new work coming in to keep the new associates busy."

"Which means you've got to have more partners to bring in that new work, right?"

"Exactly," said Seth, "which is where *I* come in."

"And this sounds like where *I* came in; talk about your chicken and egg!" Rosie leaned back in her bucket seat and looked out the window. Seth couldn't see her face, but didn't have to. She always got that expression—lips pooched out, dark eyes crinkled at the corners—when she was getting ready to say something weighty.

"You make a big-city law firm sound like some spreadin' forest fire in need of constant feedin'. Have you considered what happens if the fire runs out of fuel?"

"It doesn't," said Seth a little too quickly. "Okay, it would burn out. As a matter of fact, a few San Francisco firms have done that lately. Which is why associates have to show they can produce new business for the firm if they expect to be made partner. Middleton didn't produce."

"You don't sound very sorry about it."

"It's just the way it is, damn it! You produce or move on."

"But where will that put you when your turn comes? Won't you be held to the same standards?"

"Sure I will. Hell, Rosie, I didn't invent the idea of survival of the fittest, but I've got no problem with it. It's a bottom-line world out there. Besides, I've got a year and a half to make contacts and show them what I can do."

Seth spun the car around in the middle of the street and grabbed a parking spot close to the restaurant. "Enough economics, okay?" he said, giving her his best smile. "Let's party. Then I'm going to take you home and make up for a week of lonely nights."

ANTHONY TREADWELL'S IMPREGNABLE FEATURES TWISTED INTO A scowl—a look that had intimidated opposing counsel and witnesses for thirty-five years—as he stared at a three-month backlog of paperwork Miss Tarkenton had set out across his conference room table in neat stacks, each bearing its appropriate description: "Interoffice," "Rush," "Personnel," "Solicitations," "Correspondence," and so on.

"How was your last week at Yale, Mr. Treadwell?" asked the birdlike secretary, handing him a cup of his specially brewed Javanese coffee.

The question seemed to cheer the senior partner, who came as close to a spontaneous smile as the obsequious Miss Tarkenton could remember. He unwound his six-foot-four-inch frame from his chair and produced a small box from his briefcase. Miss Tarkenton's face lit up.

"It was most gratifying," he said. "My students expressed their appreciation with this lovely Waterman's pen set." Miss Tarkenton's eyes dulled with disappointment, but Treadwell didn't notice as he added, "The dean honored me with a farewell luncheon."

Just as quickly as it had appeared, the senior partner's relaxed countenance gave way to an expression more familiar to Miss Tarkenton, a pinched look in which deep lines across his forehead and around his mouth seemed to converge on his stiletto nose.

"The coffee."

"Yes, sir?"

"Is it the identical blend? Father's special Javanese?"

"Exactly, Mr. Treadwell."

"Ah, well, the palate must be atrophied from that paint remover they serve at the Faculty Club. Very well, Miss Tarkenton, I'll start through this mess now. Be so good as to call me the moment Mr. Addams arrives."

An hour later, Allston Addams, Treadwell's oldest and most trusted colleague among the sixty-five partners at M&M, entered the beautifully appointed office. The men exchanged a cordial handshake, and Addams seated himself in a genuine late-nineteenth-century Voltaire fauteuil, one of four that surrounded Treadwell's desk and four among only a few dozen known to exist in the entire world. He accepted a Davidoff cigar from the senior partner, and they proceeded to the business at hand.

At eleven-thirty, having provided details on the firm's activities during the senior partner's absence, Addams suggested they retire to the President's Club for cocktails and an early lunch, a setting he had concluded would be best suited for reporting a troublesome piece of news he knew would distress his friend. It might be more palatable once the senior partner was seated at his personal table with at least one single-malt Scotch under his belt.

"There is one rather distasteful item," began Addams, after Henri had delivered their second round of drinks and recommended the Norwegian salmon. "It involves a personnel matter, actually."

As he proceeded to report the hiring of Seth Cameron, Addams tried his best to minimize the significance of the matter. "Turns out I was probably wrong in opposing it, Tony. The young man bills time like an animal and appears to be quite bright as well."

Anthony Treadwell stroked his mustache, but said nothing, causing Addams to shift uncomfortably in his chair.

"I—we—realize," continued Addams with a vain attempt at making his voice sound more matter-of-fact, "that a litigator has never been hired without your prior approval, but with the department's workload and the unexpected departures of . . ."

Addams suddenly found the senior partner's laser eyes burning into him, shrinking him, silencing him.

"Don't try to placate me, Allston. If you didn't have the balls to stop it," Treadwell growled, "why didn't you just pick up the phone and call me?"

Inhaling the rest of his martini, Addams marshaled his defense. "The prospect—a young man named Cameron—was presented to us at a partners meeting without advance notice, Tony," he began (Addams was the only M&M partner privileged to use the diminutive), "and they insisted that a decision had to be made immediately to avoid losing him to another firm. Someone said that Rachel Cannon over at SP and M had heard about his victory over Malm and was about to approach him."

Treadwell needed no elaboration concerning "they" and "us." "They" were a cabal of young and midlevel partners—youngish men with hard eyes and slide-rule mentalities—who for three years had been pushing for a decentralization of power in a firm that had functioned autocratically since its founding in 1906, the year of the Great Quake. From Royston Miller to Samuel Peabody to Stanford Traeger to Anthony Treadwell: an unbroken line of dominant presiding partners, a papal-like hierocracy that had ruled efficiently—and most often peremptorily—for eighty-six years and had carried Miller and McGrath to its present prominence.

The "us" were the older or more conservative partners of the firm, many of whom were no longer the producers they had once been. They clung to a slim majority, however, and counted on Treadwell as their champion and protector, for Anthony

Treadwell was a man you could count on, a distinguished professional whose listing in *Who's Who in America* was engraved on a clock so strategically positioned on his desk that no client could miss it:

> TREADWELL, ANTHONY WINTHROP *lawyer; born Montpelier, Vt., Jan. 16, 1929; parents Winthrop Everett and Esther G. Treadwell; married, Charlotte Bateman Treadwell; children, Prudence and Winthrop Treadwell; B.S. Harvard, 1950, J.D. Yale Law School, 1957 (Order of the Coif); Lt. Commd'r U.S. Navy 1950–53; Presiding Partner, Miller and McGrath, 1983–present; Adjunct Professor, Yale Law School, 1975–Present; Author: numerous articles and legal treatises; Past President, California State Bar; Past Chair, American Bar Association Litigation Section; Member, A.B.A. Board of Governors; Diplomate, American Board of Trial Advocates.*

Treadwell, the proud issue of an aristocratic Vermont family, had succeeded newly appointed U.S. Senator Stanford Traeger as M&M's presiding partner in 1983 and had ingeniously guided the firm through one of the most difficult economic decades in the history of the legal profession, somehow managing to maintain average profits per partner at the high end of the *American Lawyer's* annual listings for California firms.

But cracks were appearing in the united front that had faithfully supported the autocratic senior partner. Profits were leveling off, and younger partners were growing restless. The profession had become a cutthroat business, complete with marketing departments and hordes of business consultants with their state-of-the-art computer and communication systems. Branch offices proliferated as large law firms swallowed up smaller ones, only to be swallowed up themselves by even bigger ones. Despite Treadwell's success, some of his key backers—loyal contemporaries who were old enough to have seen Neville Chamberlain returning with assurances from Hitler on the *Movietone News*—had begun to counsel that he make concessions to the rebellious young partners. They mouthed euphemistic clichés like "youth must be served," but Treadwell knew they meant "appeased." The crumbling old guard was fearful that defections by unhappy younger partners could threaten the funding of their own future retirements. Some, in fact, had taken early retirement, uncomfortable with the truculent antics now pervading what they had known as "the gentlemen's profession," including rapacious struggles between law firms for each other's clients and best lawyers.

"No one's questioning your leadership, Anthony," a moderate older partner had said to him at the beginning of the year. "You've made us all rich, for God's sake! The younger partners just want a voice in management. Nothing will really change." The senior partner had conceded that not even the Young Turks (or, as Treadwell called them, the Young Turkeys) were questioning his leadership genius; indeed, their proposal would guarantee him a three-year term as head of an expanded management committee—an offer that would have been taken as a vote of confidence by any other sixty-three-year-old law partner.

But not by Anthony Winthrop Treadwell. He was a survivor, a student of history who knew where appeasement could lead. Compromise was not in his vocabulary, and democracy was not his style. Instead of accepting the proposal or making even a modest concession, Treadwell had tightened his authority, leading to the recent defection of one prominent Young Turk, a star litigating partner. Two promising senior associates followed their mentor, which had made room for Seth. Treadwell, confident that he had squelched the "socialization movement," had accepted the prestigious Yale bid, only to find upon his return that a replacement litigator had been hired without so much as a telephone call to New Haven.

"Try to understand, Tony," pleaded Allston Addams, nervously finishing his appetizer of blackened ahi tuna, "we did what we could. It's all behind us now and we lucked into a seasoned trial lawyer who is not only brilliant, but billing at a clip of two hundred and twenty hours a month as well."

A glance at Treadwell told Addams he had failed.

"It may seem a small thing to you, Allston, but you are missing the point. Here, as in many things, the event itself is merely incidental to its true meaning. Hiring this yokel was a thinly disguised power play by the young partners." Treadwell paused to dab at the edges of his mustache with a napkin before adding, "The boy will have to go. Pass the bread, please."

* * *

The door to Seth's office swung open without a knock, indicating that either Harry Cooper or Anthony Treadwell was about to interrupt him; Harry didn't knock because he was a friend, Treadwell didn't knock for anyone.

"So what is Bakersfield's brightest up to today?" Harry asked, beaming with enthusiasm. "Developing new double-helix applications? Confirming the sixth quark? Rewriting the Constitution?"

"Not today." Seth barely looked up. "Preparing Charles Branch for his summary judgment motion in U.S. Minerals."

"Cocktail Charlie? You're aware, aren't you, that Branch is an all-day closet drinker. You'd better keep it simple, my friend, because you damn sure won't be able to keep him sober."

"Keeping senior partners sober is not in my job description, Harry. As for keeping this legal Rubik's Cube simple, nobody— not even you—could do that."

Harry acknowledged the compliment with a smile. "Well, it's not all bad. Charles Branch is a legend, you know, one of the best trial lawyers in town before the grape got him. And working for him beats being Treadwell's exclusive chattel."

"I'm the man's designated victim all right."

"I take it the two of you are not getting along well."

"You don't *get* along with Treadwell. You *go* along."

"You're learning fast. He can be an incredible bastard."

"Don't sugarcoat it, Harry. He's an arrogant prick, a slave-driving shithead, and a flaming asshole. Also vulgar."

"True," said Harry, laughing, "all true. You neglected to mention, however, that he's also a complete snob and feels that anybody without a lineal connection to the *Mayflower* is an aborigine who should be buried alive in an anthill."

"Then you guys must get along swell."

"Oh that score at least. Other than his record as presiding partner, he's probably most proud of his Brahmin lineage and spotless azure blood. His main liability right now is his refusal to let anybody else know jack shit about what's going on around here. As a result, he's isolated himself, and younger partners are finding ways to get around him. And you're right about the way he pushes people."

"Tell me about it. Our first meeting? Gave me a stack of files that required a U-Haul trailer just to get them into my office.

Then he takes off on a business trip; says I can handle it on my own."

"Ah, yes. The infamous True Valve case."

"You've heard. So, hell, it takes no more than an hour to see that the corporate officers are dead-bang guilty of the alleged fraudulent sales practices, so I go ahead and schedule a meeting with them to get to the truth."

"Of course. You erroneously assumed Treadwell meant it when he said, 'Handle it on your own.' Then mistake number two: attempting to ascertain the truth."

"So you've heard the rest. The miserable little shitheads come in and do the mating dance of the fly for about twenty minutes, then one of 'em pretty near admits everything but child molestation and tells me my job is to 'pull the right strings' to get 'em off."

"Is that when—?"

"Right. I threw them out of the office, and when Treadwell returned, he chewed my ass out for 'playing judge and jury' and blowing a major, big-fee client."

"Jesus, Seth, he's got a point. This is America, you know. Everybody's entitled to good representation."

"Not from me, ol' buddy. Anyway, I figure he's assigned me to the U.S. Minerals case because he knows it's a loser and he can blame me for it."

Seth dragged himself out of his chair, walked over to the window that signified his status as a senior associate, then stared into the adjacent brick wall that signified his status as a nonpartner. "The bottom line is I'm in trouble with the main man around here. Is he always this tough to please?"

"Don't feel bad. Treadwell offers up compliments as if they were his life savings."

"Hell, I never put much store in compliments; I'm just worried he's down on me for something and I don't know what it is."

"It's not you, Seth. It's what you symbolize. Try not to take it personally."

"Why would I do that?" said Seth, shrugging his shoulders and falling back into his chair. "It's only my life."

Harry seemed to be out of encouraging words. Seth swung a leg up onto his desk. "Look, Harry, I've been here three months now, and it seems like the only way I've disappointed Treadwell is by *not* missing an assignment or by *not* losing a motion. The bastard wants me to fail, Harry. Why?"

Harry slapped Seth on the foot and mustered another encouraging smile. "I meant it when I told you not to take it personally. Sure, part of it is the guy's upbringing and personality. Let's face it, Seth, you're not exactly the prototypical Pacific Heights socialite."

"No shit?" said Seth, feigning an injured look.

"But mainly, it's just politics. You happened to join the firm while Treadwell was off at Yale. First time so much as a janitor has been hired around here without his approval."

"So why does he take it out on me? I wasn't even aware of the firm's unwritten policy, much less consciously violating it."

"Irrelevant, Counselor. You're a symbol, remember? As you must know by now, there's a rebellion under way. Somewhere between fifteen and twenty junior and midrange partners are pushing for more say in the operation of the firm; specifically, they want more seats on an expanded management committee and less authority in the hands of King Treadwell."

"So how does a nice country boy from Bakersfield become a symbol in this high-level, internecine class struggle?"

Harry exhaled loudly, slapped his thighs, and stood up. "Hell, I'm partially responsible I guess. It was bad timing, and Treadwell took your hiring in his absence as a display of strength by the Young Turks."

"And what better way for the sovereign to show he's still in control than by ridding his kingdom of this leprous intruder."

"Exactamundo, my friend. Which is why he's finding fault with everything you do."

"Is there something I don't know about?"

Harry shifted in his chair. "Well, word has it he wasn't too keen on your recent appearance at the firm banquet in cowboy boots."

"Harry, those aren't just 'cowboy boots,' they're genuine anteaters."

"Whatever. He's also saying you aren't thorough enough to be an M and M litigator, that you take shortcuts which result in eliminating the need for lengthy depositions and interrogatories."

Seth rolled his eyes and sniffed.

"Well, you asked me, damn it, and it happens those are major

6 9

sources of revenue at M and M. He expects us to spend whatever amounts of our time and our clients' money is necessary to make life so miserable for our adversaries that they'll eventually settle just to get away from our sleazy, scorched-earth tactics."

Seth just stared at him, then said, "Any crimes and misdemeanors other than my footwear and saving clients' time and money?"

"That's about it," said Harry, looking at his hands.

"Which means there's more."

"Not really, though maybe Rosie could dress down a bit at the next firm social event."

"You mean dress *up* a bit, don't you, Harry? Jesus, she just got here; give her a break."

"Sorry, Seth. I'm out of line here. Believe me, I'm trying to help, and, well, Rosie's got an incredible figure and that skirt left no doubt about it."

Seth started looking at some documents on his desk.

"Okay, Seth, you asked me, remember? Besides, there is some good news. You are not without supporters. Let's face it, you've done great work in the time you've been here—a testament to my impeccable judgment in recruiting you—and you've tried more cases in your short but illustrious career than any associate and most of the partners. In other words, you are perceived as an asset."

"Assets can be liquidated," said Seth in a flat tone, "and these eighty-five-hour weeks are starting to catch up with me."

"Everyone knows he's loading you up. He's trying to ride you into the ground and out of the firm, just to show the Young Turks who's boss. So for what it's worth, it's not your work *or* you. It's the old fickle finger of fate."

Seth took a deep breath. "Okay, pard, thanks for leveling with me. I'll buy something nice for Rosie to wear next time."

"How's she getting along? It's tough adapting to life as an M and M widow."

"Not too well. Tell Trish I appreciate the support she's been giving her. I may be a pawn in a game I didn't create, but at least I know how to play. Rosie's a different story. She's missing her friends, her new job isn't going well, and she feels even more out of synch with the firm's social scene than I do."

"Trish didn't care much for it the first year or so, either. Then she decided she liked driving a 450SL and living in a four-bedroom house in Piedmont."

"Yeah, Trish would go for that."

An uneasy silence passed between them. "Look, Seth . . ."

"Forget it, Harry. I'm the one out of line this time. She was never right for me; I just didn't see it."

Harry fell back into his chair, ran a hand through his hair.

"I don't know what to say, Seth, except that I'm sorry it had to be you that got hurt."

"All's fair, Harry, and I can hardly blame you and Trish for the way I blew off my third year. I made my choices. Besides, thanks to you, here I am in the majors after all."

Harry brightened. "And by God, you're going to stay here. It'll just take some patience."

"Patience is right up there with black-tie dinners on the list of things I don't do well."

"Then keep on keepin' on the best you can."

"I'm okay. It's just going to take time for Treadwell and me to work out some kind of compromise."

Seth's secretary interrupted with a summons from Treadwell.

"Speak of the devil," said Seth.

"No such luck," warned Harry, walking toward the door. "With the devil, you can make a deal. There's no compromising with Anthony Treadwell."

"We'll see."

Harry turned in the doorway. "Let me know what happens and how I can help. Okay?"

"Don't worry about me, old son. I can take care of myself."

Harry shook his head. "Still the lone wolf, huh? Just like in law school. No help wanted. Trust nobody but yourself."

"I trust you, buddy."

"I doubt it."

"That's not very trusting, Harry."

"You're right. Okay, I believe you."

"I doubt it."

Seth's emotions went ballistic whenever he entered the senior partner's imposing corner office. Not just the anxiety of what-will-he-try-on-me-this-time, but something about the intimidating regal quarters themselves—the pristine opulence of the rosewood

desk, the Picasso originals, the huge conference wing that com-
fortably seated ten people, the private bar with its ebony surface and display of Waterford crystal, each piece etched with
Treadwell's initials. Then there was the unerring elegance of the
man himself—always immaculate in his tailored gray Brioni suits
that seemed to have been sprayed onto his slender body. The
richness of the senior partner's manner and possessions provoked
both revulsion and envy in Seth.

"I want you to prepare an analysis of the issues in the Sharpe
Steel case, Cameron."

No greeting, no false courtesy.

"I know you are rather busy at the moment," Treadwell added,
"so why don't you take, say, three days."

"This is Friday. Would that be due on Tuesday or Wednesday?"

"*Three* days. Monday by five will be fine," said Treadwell, who
still had not looked up from his desk.

"I've heard of the case," said Seth cautiously, "but isn't Ted
Arnold already working on a draft?"

For the first time, Treadwell's cavernous eyes came to rest on
Seth's. "I have his product. Now I want yours."

Pitting one associate against another was a big-firm technique
for building a case against both, since each would invariably
come up with something the other would miss. *Poor Arnold must
be in trouble, too,* thought Seth as he silently calculated the risks
involved in mentioning that he had already committed his weekend to another partner. *Fuck it, I'll get it done somehow.*

"The Sharpe Steel file boxes will be delivered to your office by
noon," said the senior partner, dismissing Seth by refocusing his
attention on the papers in his hand.

Seth stared at Treadwell, wanting to grab his skinny neck and
squeeze some color into that jaundiced face, break him in two
like a matchstick. But what he did was agree to have the memo
done by Monday, smile, turn, and walk the thirty feet of lush
Birvan carpet to the door.

"Oh, yes, Cameron," Treadwell said, still without looking up,
"I don't need to tell you how important it is to the firm—and to
you—that Charlie Branch wins that motion next month on the
U.S. Minerals case."

Seth stopped at the door and stared at the senior partner's down-turned head for nearly a minute, but Treadwell ignored him. "He'll win," Seth said, and walked through the door.

Outside, he encountered a ruckus between a surprisingly formidable Miss Tarkenton, her head thrust upward like a cobra, and an angular old man so tall and thin he appeared to be tottering on worn plaid stilts. His hollow eyes shone crazily, like naked lightbulbs, above an elongated aquiline nose, and his mottled skin was stretched taut over jutting cheekbones. Despite his appearance, however, the miserable wretch managed to wear his fragility more like a sword than a shield, and there was neither weakness nor apology in his lunatic whisper as he demanded access to Treadwell's office through a mouth contorted with rage.

Miss Tarkenton stood her ground. "Nobody sees Mr. Treadwell without an appointment, sir," she said, looking toward Seth for support.

Seth, however, stepped around them, catching the smell of stale tobacco and the cheap-perfume aroma of vodka as he passed. *Let Treadwell handle him,* he thought, but the old man reached out a bony, spotted hand and seized him by the lapel. Seth grabbed the dry talon, but could not dislodge it. Only then did he realize that the old man had but one arm. Their eyes met, and Seth was startled to see something weirdly familiar in the tubercular features.

"Do I know you?" he gasped, his heart pounding against the walls of his chest. "Who the hell *are* you?"

The old man released his hold, flashing a smile like broken piano keys as he smoothed out Seth's crunched lapel.

"Have a nice day, sonny," he said in a voice like a wire brush on cobblestone. He gave Seth's chest a firm slap, then disappeared through Treadwell's door even as Miss Tarkenton shouted at Seth to stop him.

"Sorry, Miss Tarkenton," Seth said. "I'm a symbol, not a security guard."

Inside the office, Anthony Treadwell was white with rage. "You *bastard!*" he exclaimed through clenched teeth. "I told you never to come here!"

"Well now, Mr. Society, is that any way to talk to your dear father?" said the old man, flashing his black-and-white teeth. "And as for the 'bastard' part, ain't that sorta like the pot calling the kettle black?"

Seth arrived home at 2:30 A.M. and was greeted at the door by Fat Dog. Seth gave him a quick rub and a special biscuit because he was too tired to give him time. He undressed in the living room, then crept into the bedroom, in part out of concern for Rosie, but mainly because he was too tired to deal with her mounting expressions of loneliness and discontent.

"Hi, Seth," she said into the darkness. "At least I hope it's you."

Seth put his arms around her and apologized for breaking their date for a late supper at Sam's.

"It was our anniversary. Our first date. Two years ago last night."

"Oh, Jesus. Is it September already? I'm sorry, babe."

She forgave him, conditioned upon a new commitment for Saturday night, but Seth explained what Treadwell had just done to him.

"How about we celebrate it a week from Sunday," he offered instead. "We'll pack a picnic lunch, take Fats, and spend the day at Stinson Beach if the weather's good. If it isn't, we'll stay here and make love all day."

"Umm. I'll brush up on my Indian rain dance," said Rosie. Seth stumbled off to the bathroom, relieved to see that she seemed to have fallen back asleep. Fat Dog padded after him.

Rosie waited in the dim light, however, watching Seth as he reentered the bedroom. He set the alarm for five o'clock—now less than three hours off—and fell into bed beside her without a word. He was asleep in her arms within seconds.

Rosie gazed down at his fatigued face, fissured by deep new lines, and touched his skin, cold as ice. Wished they had time to talk together. Might have risked confiding a recent dream. Scary. A little reassurance would be nice, even if cloaked in skepticism. He'd be upset because he wasn't in it. Rosie back in Bakersfield, surrounded by strangers and bags full of bills of various denominations. Bizarre.

As she warmed him with her body, her frustration faded first into pity, then love remembered. A sad smile crossed her face as she reconciled herself to the reality that there would be no day together at Stinson Beach or at home or anywhere else. His ambition had finally dug a hole deep enough to engulf him. Them.

She wondered how long she could endure it here—waiting for a future that hoped for little more than the joy of the past.

It made no sense to her.

Nor did it make sense that she had come all the way to the Bay Area to lose the only man she had ever loved—and not even to another woman.

THREE WEEKS LATER, STARING INTO THEIR COCKTAILS AT THE PRESIdent's Club, Anthony Treadwell and Allston Addams preached to each other's choir concerning the firm's culture and the need to prevent "further erosion of its great tradition."

"We can ride out this recession if we just stay calm, stick with what has served us well in the past," said Treadwell, snapping his fingers in the direction of Henri.

"Of course we can," agreed Addams, "but I, well . . ."

"Something's bothering you, Allston. Spit it out, for God's sake."

Addams tapped his lips with a pudgy forefinger, stared out the velvet-canopied window, then glanced sideways to measure his friend's mood. "I was just wondering whether it wouldn't be best to eliminate all this divisiveness by simple letting the young partners have their token expanded management committee. Hell, Tony, you would still be running the show . . ."

Treadwell exhaled loudly, something between a grunt of disdain and a forced laugh. "*Et tu*, Allston? Ready to give them an inch like the others?"

"It just seems . . ."

"It seems you have forgotten where appeasement leads. *No, sir.* Our dear ex-partner, Sen. Stanford Traeger—the manipulating bastard—kept me off the helm for five years, and now that I have it, I'll be damned if I'll surrender without a fight."

"I heard," said Addams, groping for a new subject, "that our former partner is now heading up the Senate subcommittee that monitors our infamous Stealth Program."

"Oh, yes. And wallowing in press coverage as usual."

"And his daughter—your godchild, as I recall—married now?"

"Sam something. A stealth test pilot of all things. Sam Barton. That's it."

"Like marrying the boss's daughter."

"Elena. Gorgeous child."

Addams was grateful to see the senior partner's features relax and even more grateful to see the waiter appear with another round of drinks. "Thank you, Henri," he said, but the old man merely raised an eyebrow in acknowledgment, more comfortable with the discreet silence that usually accompanied his approach to tables at the President's Club.

Treadwell took a sip of his Scotch, made a face. "Waiter," he said, refusing—as he had for nearly twenty years—to address "the help" by name, "is this my Linkwood Twelve?"

"Yes, sir, Mr. Treadwell, the 1959 from your private stock."

"Well, it tastes slightly off. Open a new bottle."

The waiter shuffled away, and Addams hastened to placate the senior partner. "About the Young Turkeys, you're quite right of course. I didn't mean to suggest—"

"Forget it," said Treadwell, tapping glasses with Addams, his annoyance spent. "I value your opinion. In fact, I'd be interested in your views on a related subject: the graceful elimination of this young maverick, Seth Cameron."

Addams, relieved and flattered to have the senior partner not only mollified, but seeking his counsel, was encouraged once again to risk speaking his mind.

"You're the general, Tony. Sack him if you want, but the kid's damn good, and we'll take some heat if you do."

Treadwell shook his head and pursed his thin lips into a fine line. "I *am* surprised the usual method has not worked with this hayseed."

The "usual method" for getting rid of an otherwise competent associate for personal reasons was to assign the prey more work than any lawyer could effectively handle. Treadwell had been confident that Seth, like other targeted victims before him, would either burn out in a few months and leave "voluntarily" or stay on and inevitably be late with an assignment or botch it altogether, thus giving the senior partner indisputable grounds for terminating him.

"So far," Treadwell added, "our Bakersfield cowboy has not fallen off his horse. But Charlie will be opposing the defendant's motion to dismiss in the U.S. Minerals case tomorrow based on Cameron's workup."

"And?"

"Charlie will lose, of course."

"What if he shows up sober?"

"Little danger of that, but even if he does, our position is fatally weak on the law. When we lose this motion, I suspect we'll lose the client as well, probably to Caldwell and Shaw as usual. My consolation is that I've laid the foundation for blaming Cameron's shoddy preparation, and Charlie Branch will be ill positioned to argue otherwise."

San Francisco's City Hall. One of the majestic grand dames of the city's architecture, once rivaled in her regal dignity only by Maybeck's Palace of Fine Arts and Timothy Pflueger's Four-Fifty Sutter Building. But somewhere along the way—like all beautiful women—she'd begun to show her age: the Grand Stairway now worn smooth, her soaring three-hundred-foot ornamental dome pockmarked and nearly opaque with sediment, her once flawless face filigreed by cracks from settling and small monthly quakes that don't even make the evening news.

Yet the old girl could still stop your heart, and as Seth exited the elevator at the fourth floor, he experienced the usual potpourri of trial-lawyer emotions: exhilaration, anticipation, hope, anxiety. In just ten minutes, presiding judge Lucille McCarthy would call the calendar and assign the U.S. Minerals case to a judge for argument on plaintiff's motion for summary judgment, the result of which could determine his fate at M&M.

Seth's work on the motion was finished: the analysis, the research, the drafting. Now it was all up to Charlie Branch, whom Seth tried to picture stalking these same hallways thirty years earlier, the walls then smooth with the smell of fresh paint, the venerable lawyer then young and eager, feeling these same mixed sensations.

At ten, Seth gave up waiting for Branch in the corridor and entered the PJ's courtroom. As she called the calendar, Judge McCarthy first elicited from each opposing set of lawyers estimates of time their arguments would require before assigning a courtroom and judge. When the clerk called out the U.S. Minerals case, Charlie Branch was still nowhere to be seen, so Seth stood and announced, "Forty minutes, Your Honor," then caught the look of surprise on the face of his opponent, Simon Stephens, of Caldwell and Shaw. Knowing that Stephens would now assume that M&M had sent a mere associate to argue a $40-million motion, Seth perversely reinforced the illusion by giving Stephens an assured smile across the room.

The key to this trial business, Son, is control—which means you always got to keep the other guy off balance. It's never too early to start playing games with his mind and never too late to crank up the confusion level even more. Never stop, and if you run out of ammunition, keep shooting anyway.

"I agree, Your Honor," said Stephens, barely concealing his relief, "twenty minutes each side."

"Judge Webster, Department 28," announced the PJ, and Seth, close to the front of the courtroom, affected as much confidence as possible as he strode through the rail and picked up the court file from the clerk for delivery to Judge Webster's clerk. Of all the feelings bombarding Seth, however, confidence was not one of them.

Where in the hell was Charlie Branch?

"I don't think we've met," said Simon Stephens, coming up behind him.

"How's it going?" said Seth, shaking Stephens's hand as they began to walk toward Judge Webster's courtroom. Seth was irritated that Stephens's hand was both warmer and drier than his own and that Stephens surely noticed it.

"Been at M and M long?" The game was beginning.

"I've been practicing for a few years in Bakersfield. Tried a bunch of cases around the Valley and came to M and M as a senior lateral associate."

"Bakersfield," said Stephens, as if trying to place it. "Drove through it once. Ever appear before Webster?"

"No."

"Minority appointment. Looks like he's right out of the bush." Seth said nothing.

"Your brief was interesting," said Stephens.

"Thanks. I'm hoping the judge has read it."

"Don't count on it," said Stephens, chuckling, "although I will say that Webster is more conscientious than most of the spades that affirmative action has shoved down our throats lately."

"Look, Stephens," said Seth, staring straight ahead as they approached Department 28, "I'm from Bakersfield all right, and there may be some hay sticking out of my collar. But if you look closely under that collar, you won't see a red neck anywhere. So spare me the racist bullshit."

Simon Stephens's eyebrows shot up in surprise, but he recovered as he opened the door to the courtroom. "Looks like the new kid in town is a bit touchy."

"See you in court," said Seth, and headed for the row of pay telephones down the hall.

"Mr. Branch must have gone directly to court from his home, Mr. Cameron," said Branch's secretary. "He hasn't been in yet this morning."

Seth delivered the court file to Judge Webster's clerk and noted with relief that another matter on the calendar would be argued first, giving Branch at least another fifteen or twenty minutes. He glanced at Si Stephens, who looked up from his files and flashed a confident smile. Seth wondered whether the Caldwell and Shaw star was right about Judge Webster, for it would take a smart and courageous jurist to comprehend and act on the theory that Seth had crafted for Branch to argue.

Ironic, thought Seth, that the fate of his partnership now rested in the hands of a judge he had never seen and a lawyer he couldn't find.

He glanced at his watch. Plenty of time to race to the main

entrance. Branch would be arriving by taxi, his driver's license having been suspended two years earlier for drunk driving. *Hurry and get up here, you brilliant old fart!* As Seth swept down the main entrance steps, he was relieved to see Charles Branch standing outside a taxi, engaged in animated conversation with the cabby.

"Mr. Branch!" Seth shouted. "Hurry, we're up next!"

But Branch did not seem to hear, and as Seth drew closer, he saw that the lawyer and the cabdriver were arguing.

Seth took Branch firmly by the arm and started to lead him toward the entrance. "We're up next, Mr. Branch. We've drawn Judge Webster, but you've got to hurry because the—"

"He ain't going anywhere," said the cabby, "unless you got twenty-eight bucks to cover the fare from Piedmont."

Branch was staring at Seth with dazed relief. "Thank heavens you're here, lad. I left my apartment without so much as a farthing. Be so good as to pay this parasite so that we may get on with the bishness of the day."

"Yeah," said the cabby, nodding to Seth. "He's drunk, all right. Got a bottle right there in his briefcase. I've been watching him in the rearview. You got the twenty-eight or do I call that cop over there?"

"Yes, of course I do," said Seth, watching Branch struggling to put on his topcoat, one arm now hopelessly entangled in a sleeve. "Are you all right, Mr. Branch?"

"I'm just fine, lad, thank you. But do I really need this coat?"

"No, Mr. Branch," said Seth, his heart sinking. "I don't think you'll be needing your briefcase either."

"You're right as rain, young man. I can pick a jury without this damn coat *or* a briefcase. Now pay the man and let's go over to Stars and have lunch."

Seth looked at his watch. His heart pounded as he reached into his wallet and fished out three twenties and a ten. "Take him back home, driver."

"Home?" muttered Branch, struggling against Seth's efforts to urge him back into the taxi. "The *hell* with home. I'm starting a trial today."

Seth saw that they were beginning to attract attention. He took a deep breath, removed Cocktail Charlie's homburg, put his hand on top of the old man's head to protect it, then gave him a shove that collapsed him into the backseat. "Go!" he commanded the driver as he slammed the rear door, and the driver went.

Minutes later he was apologizing to Judge Webster for the delay: "An office emergency, Your Honor." Lying to a traffic cop was one thing. Lying to a superior-court judge on the record was something else, but "an office emergency" was not only the truth in this instance, it was an understatement.

The problem was that *he* was now the emergency. He had assaulted an elderly partner, had not had time to report the situation to Anthony Treadwell, and had just been rejected in his request for a continuance of the hearing. Fate and Charlie Branch were conspiring to hand the senior partner the excuse Seth had so far managed to deny him.

"You've inconvenienced court and counsel long enough, Mr. Cameron. We're going forward, and we're going forward *now,* with or without your presence. For the record, this is a motion for summary judgment against plaintiff U.S. Minerals, which, I should say at the outset, Mr. Cameron, I am disposed to grant. I see no dispute in the facts, and the law appears to be with the moving party."

A bad start.

"State your appearances, Counsel."

"Simon Stephens of the firm of Caldwell and Shaw, Your Honor, representing the defendant and moving party."

"Seth Cameron, Your Honor. Miller and McGrath, representing plaintiff U.S. Minerals."

"Thank you, gentlemen. You may proceed, Mr. Stephens."

Stephens was elegant, articulate, and merciless, just as Harry had warned Seth he would be. "Standard equipment included on all Caldwell and Shaw models," Harry had said. "We're great here at Miller and McGrath, but C and S is the best. Average profit per partner according to the *American Lawyer*? Four hundred thousand a year! They're amoral, but they've got smarts, wealth, and plenty of power in the state capital. They've probably handpicked half the superior-court judges." *But not this one,* thought Seth.

"I've read your brief, Mr. Stephens," said Judge Webster, interrupting Stephens just five minutes into his argument, "and unless you have something new to add, I'd like to hear if opposing counsel can give me one good reason why I shouldn't grant your motion."

"In that case, I'll leave it right there, Your Honor," said Stephens. *C&S lawyers also know when it's smart to sit down and shut up*, thought Seth.

"Mr. Cameron?"

"Yes, Your Honor," Seth said, realizing he would have to take risks if he was going to turn the judge around. "As a matter of fact, there are *two* good reasons why this court should not grant the motion. The first is that you will be reversed if you do; though frankly, it seems as if the court has already made up its mind."

The judge scowled and leaned forward menacingly. "I'm listening, Counsel."

Step one, Son: you've got to get their attention—even if it means hittin' 'em upside the head.

"Mr. Stephens has correctly stated the law which should govern the trial of this case—"

"Then, sir, you are wasting the court's time. You and the defendant have already agreed on the basic facts, so if Mr. Stephens is right on the law, there won't *be* a trial of the case, because I'll be dismissing your complaint today."

"I hadn't finished, Your Honor," said Seth, his expression friendly, but his voice now hard-edged. "I said we may agree on the law governing the *trial* of the case. The problem for Mr. Stephens, and the second reason you should deny his motion to dismiss, is that *we just aren't there yet.* If you take a close look at *Harrison versus Excelsior Stores*, Your Honor, specifically footnote eight, you will see that the appellate court in that case required inquiry into *any* collateral evidence—even privileged information under certain circumstances—which might create a dispute in the facts during the *pretrial* phase of the case, evidence which your discovery commissioner has erroneously denied us."

"Let me understand you, Counsel," said the judge. "You're saying I should adopt your view on access to privileged and work-product information based on one footnote in just one case?"

"Not 'just one case,' Your Honor, but an extremely well-reasoned case out of our own appellate district which our Supreme Court has refused to review."

Judge Webster leaned forward, slowly shaking his head from side to side. "Mr. Cameron. What you're suggesting is that I permit you to engage in further discovery that you say could create a triable issue of fact you *admit* does not presently exist?"

"Exactly. Then let Mr. Stephens renew his motion—which, incidentally, he knows you will have to deny because by the time I finish taking depositions there *will* be a triable issue of fact. More important, justice will have been served by permitting my client its day in court on the merits."

Stephens started to rise, but the judge silenced him an imperious wave of his hand.

"And if I did buy your footnote eight argument, Mr. Cameron, just what would that fact issue be?"

Seth smiled broadly. "I haven't the slightest idea, Your Honor, but the law clearly allows us a chance to find out. My guess is that defendant's ex-employee—who won't speak to us without a court-ordered subpoena—has told Mr. Stephens a different story than the one being spun in these so-called 'uncontroverted' affidavits from the defendant's present officers. We're just asking for a chance to level the playing field here."

Stephens fought back, but the judge was intrigued. After another half hour of fierce debate, Seth left the courtroom with a favorable ruling.

"I'm pissed off," said Stephens in the elevator, "but also amazed. I'm a third-year partner at C and S, and they barely allowed *me* to argue this motion. They'd never let a rookie associate handle a matter of this magnitude. I was sure I'd be up against Charlie Branch; in fact, now I wish I had been."

"Mr. Branch," said Seth, looking straight ahead, "was forced to take a short trip."

"You *what?*" bellowed Treadwell through a telephone downstairs in the main lobby.

The conversation was not going well.

"Yes, I heard you," Treadwell continued, "but winning the motion in no way mitigates your flagrant abuse of office policy. We'll discuss this further when you report back here." He hung up.

"No, really, sir," said Seth into the dead phone, "I think a bonus that large would be excessive. I was just doing my job."

At ten the next morning, Charles Branch entered Seth's office and closed the door behind him. *Here it comes,* Seth thought.

"I don't know quite how to say this, young man," said Branch. "I'll start by saying I am both terribly embarrassed and eternally grateful. You saved me from a certain suspension, possibly even disbarment. I will be forever in your debt and hope you will accept my apology for my conduct and for putting you in such a position."

"Thanks, Mr. Branch. It's forgotten as far as I'm concerned."

"But I shall *not* forget it, Cameron," said the older man, smiling sheepishly as he added, "although my memory of the incident is a bit sketchy. You should also know that I straightened Anthony out concerning the true facts. All of them. It was most gallant of you, incidentally, to conceal my . . . condition from him."

"I just told him you were ill, and that was the truth."

Branch smiled sadly, saying, "You and I know that I've been incorrigibly 'ill' for years now, but thank you just the same. Whatever residuum of influence I have around here will be put in your service."

The old warhorse, head held high, left as quickly as he had come, and Seth grabbed his telephone.

"Rosie? The corpse has started breathing again."

SAM BARTON IS AWAKENED IN HIS ON-BASE STUDIO APARTMENT BY A grating sound he can't identify.

Is he dreaming?

Probably. Or maybe it's the lonely weeping willow in the backyard sidling up to the carport, nudged by winter winds rolling down from the mesa.

Probably. Or maybe just an attack of the malady Elena lovingly calls "stealth pilot's paranoia."

Whatever, his pillow is still broadcasting an accelerated heartbeat into his ear, so he considers getting up to check the patio door. Within a minute, however, fatigue and rational judgment prevail, and his heart returns to a test-pilot-perfect fifty-six beats per minute. He rolls over and begins to doze—a rare error in judgment as it turns out—for the sound he thought he had dreamed was made by a real knife blade slicing through a real screen door. And clutching the handle of the knife is a powerful gloved hand attached to a well-muscled arm, the other end of which is connected to a very tall, very real person.

The man is dressed entirely in black, and his face is covered with a ski mask, inside which his breathing is irregular. Behind him is a shorter man, also clad in a mask and black clothing, nervously peering into a room as dark as a shark's belly, trying to make out the location of the target's bed.

Despite the cold night, both men are perspiring as the tall man silently slides the patio door open and takes his first step inside. This is nowhere in my job description, he thinks as he begins to feel his way around an endless sofa.

In his bed, the stocky pilot is half-asleep again when he dreams another sound, the sound of footsteps. His eyes pop open and his heartbeat surges again, for it's clear now that he has company. A burglar? Should he reach for the bedside telephone? Fake having a gun? Just let him take what he wants?

Although adrenaline has now catapulted him into acute vigilance and his pounding heart is rocketing off his pillow into his temples, he's afraid to move anything but his eyes. Maybe if he doesn't move, the intruder won't even know he's there. But then he slowly raises his head and sees that the large rectangle of moonlight framed by the patio doors is now partially blocked by the moving silhouette of a man—oh, Jesus, two men!—and they are not stopping at his tape deck or his TV and are walking right past his new CD player.

What they must have come for is him.

He tries to clear his head, tries to remember that emergencies are his business. Analyze, then react. Analyze, react. He figures that although he can see them because of the moon's backlighting, they probably can't see him. Big advantage there. Means he can move and they won't know it.

He snakes his way over to the far edge of the bed. Good, they haven't seen him, but now what? He must either slide under the bed—where he could easily be trapped—or try to sneak to the front door, twenty feet away.

He decides to go for it and silently slides off the bed, crawling on his stomach toward the door and the safety of the public hallway. But they're close now and he hears one of them say, "Look! There he goes!" so he staggers to his feet like a flushed quail, running and stumbling toward the door. He hears grunts of pain from his pursuers and tables with lamps tipping over, but nothing seems to slow their progress as they try to cut him off before he can reach his one avenue of escape.

Reaching the door first, he jerks it open, but forgets the night chain. In panic, he jerks again and again—no time to unbolt the chain—but the damn thing holds and now a huge hand slashes over his shoulder and slams the door shut.

They have him.

He tries to scream out, but the hard heel of a hand is jamming his nose up into his skull. Despite the searing pain, he instinctively comes up with a knee, which produces a shriek from the taller man, but the shorter one counters with a paralyzing blow to his right kidney with something that feels like an iron bar. Though physically crippled by the attack, the pilot's head remains amazingly clear, adrenaline everywhere. This isn't just fight-or-flight energy: it's both, and he somehow finds the night chain and miraculously manipulates it out of the steel plate. Then he spins and pulls the front door open, slamming it into the shorter man's head as he hurls himself into the public hallway.

His prospects are buoyed by the bright lights and double row of doors, behind which any number of brave Samaritans surely await his call to arms, but when he tries to cry out for help, nothing issues from his throat but a gurgling cough, a ghost of his intention. He can barely even breathe, realizes he's choking on his own blood. And now an arm flies out of the doorway and snaps like a whip around his neck, dragging him back into the hellish darkness of the room as he struggles to resist, both hands clutching the doorjamb in a death grip. Slowly, one hand surrenders to the big man's superior strength, then the other.

He is back inside the room.

Desperate now, nothing to lose, he thrusts his head back into the face of the taller man. Now it is the assailant's nose that cracks, and the sandy-haired man, feeling renewed hope, spins out of the grasp of the tall man and races back the other way—across the room toward the wide-open patio door. He is wild with fear now, yet strangely exhilarated, panting like an animal. The smaller man tries to block his path, but the pilot is crazed, unmanageable, invincible, and the man gasps to his large companion, "Use the knife, for chrissake! I can't . . . hold the son of a bitch . . ."

The taller man stumbles back into the fray, still holding his nose in pain, but does not reach for his knife. "You know we can't," he grunts, spitting blood, "can't use a knife for this. Hold him . . . for . . . just another second." Then, while the two shorter figures continue to wrestle like bears against the moonlit screen, the tall man brings the steel pipe down hard toward his quarry's head. But the pilot has found the stocky assailant's eye with a thumb and twists free of his thick arms just as the steel bar brushes past his ear. Lucky, yet the bar smashes into his shoulder with such force that it partially paralyzes the right side of his body. Weakened now, he lurches to one side, hopping pitifully like a three-legged dog toward the patio, now just fifteen feet away.

But he makes only ten of them before he's again staring into the blood-soaked mask of the taller man. Instinct tells him to go for the vulnerable face again, and his gouging fingers seek out the broken nose. But all he gets this time is the mask, which he rips away, exposing the face underneath, shining with sweat and blood, yet unmistakably . . .

"My God!" gasps the sandy-haired man, his eyes round in amazement. "You?" But the pipe comes flying toward him again, and he knows there is no stopping it this time, no use even trying. Then he is strangely conscious of becoming unconscious, of a dull concussion, of scattered lights, thinking his last thoughts, of the wife he had loved, of the children he hadn't yet had, would never know . . .

The two men in black rest for a moment, hands on knees and gasping for air, looking down at the sandy-haired man and assessing their own injuries. Then they each grab an arm and drag the body roughly through the back patio door, down the cold, hard concrete steps, and into the driveway where their car waits idling under the gentle, swaying shadows of the moonstruck weeping willow.

In Mill Valley, Rosie bolted upright in her sleep, screaming words Seth could not understand, except for the last few: *"Stop! Stop! Please don't do this!"*

Now wide-awake, Seth tried to soothe her out of her nightmare, stroking her damp hair and reassuring her that it was a dream. But in the partial light of the moon, Seth could see Rosie's feverish eyes burning into him. She seemed to be hyperventilating, and Seth felt her pulse pounding in every part of her rigid body. It occurred to him that they had not yet found a doctor in Marin.

"Just a dream, babe," he whispered. "I'm right here."

Rosie fell against him, prespiring and sobbing, moaning into his chest. Finally, she found her voice and began repeating the same words over and over: "They killed him, Seth, they killed him."

"Come on, honey," Seth said, holding her close to him, "everything is okay. It's only four-thirty. Let's try to get back to sleep now. You've had a nightmare."

"No, Seth," she said, reaching for a Kleenex, calmer now. "It was real. They killed him."

"But a dream all the same."

Rosie blew her nose and sat up, herself again. "Maybe so, but it was like those other times, Seth, you know, when the things . . . when it turned out to be real."

"Even so, darlin'," said Seth, determined not to start something at this hour, "there's nothing we can do about it, and it's got nothing to do with us anyway."

Rosie turned toward him with a heartbreaking sadness in her dark, wet eyes. "That's just the problem, Seth. It's got everything to do with us. With *you!*"

"Oh, Jesus, Rosie. Let's not start that again. Okay?"

But Rosie just shook her head from side to side, then buried it against his shoulder. Soon, they fell back asleep, and when they awoke the next morning, nothing more was said about it.

TWO MONTHS LATER, A SUCCESSFUL FOURTEEN-HOUR WORKDAY BE-hind him, Seth popped two Dexedrine—just enough to get him home safely—and savored his victories.

Skimming across the fog-cloaked Golden Gate Bridge, the silver Porsche easily vanquished the sudden grade leading into the Waldo Tunnel. On the other side of the tube, the tarp of fog had lifted and the crisp December air was so clear that off to his right Seth could see all the way across the Bay, its dark waters as still as lead, and well beyond into the East Bay hills. With another ten-degree turn of his head, he was able to spot the brightly lighted Imperial Building itself, home of M&M. To his left, above the hills of the Marin Headlands, the full moon had painted a false dawn that glowed like northern lights. On an impulse, Seth turned off the headlights and drove at full speed, bathed in its glow. The advantage of commuting at three in the morning—you beat the crowd.

He considered popping the Targa to get that Harley feeling, but at eighty miles per hour and no hat or jacket the romance would turn cold. He settled for the thrill of high-speed invisibility, listening to Bob Seger belting out "You're Still the Same" on the custom sound system for which the departed Middleton, in his halcyon days, had shelled out six bills.

Jesus, what a day this has been, Seth thought. Sharpe Steel had been put to bed at last, with a smashing victory fueled by his research and analysis, an approach that had made poor Ted Arnold's memo look like *See Spot Run* by comparison. With a single, break-through idea, Seth had not only repelled another attempt by Treadwell to embarrass him, but had earned the gratitude and future allegiance of the partner who had argued the winning motion. In the process, he had also eliminated Ted Arnold—a member of Seth's own associate class—from the race for partnership. Making partner was like musical chairs: when the music stopped, not everybody would have a seat at the partnership table. Ted had been a bright enough guy, but he suffered the disability of a wife and three kids. Distractions could kill you in the jungle.

Like that unexpected appearance in his office by Trish Cooper today. She should have known better than to put him on the spot like that. He had wanted to ask her if she hadn't fucked up his life enough already, but decided it was enough to just say no.

Seth switched his headlights back on.

On the plus side, though nobody had noticed, today marked Seth's six-month anniversary with Miller and McGrath. He had planned to take Rosie to D'Angelo's for a celebration, but Treadwell had hit him with a rush job on an appellate brief—a reassignment from the late Ted Arnold.

As the twin cones of the Porsche's beams hit the carport, Seth began to give in to the fatigue that had been his nagging passenger from the moment he left his office. He was dismayed to see a light still burning in the bedroom. Though the sharp smell of pine and jasmine revived him a little on his way to the front door, he hoped neither Rosie nor Fat Dog entertained any expectations.

"Well," she said after the perfunctory kiss, "we're home from work early today."

"Very funny," said Seth, glancing at his watch and looping his tie over a peg in the closet. "It's been a killer."

"So what else is new."

Seth bent over to stroke Fat Dog. "We're a regular bundle of sardonic wit tonight, aren't we? How was your day?"

"Also the usual. Andre's thinks they can start me as soon as the weather warms up and people start going out to eat again." Rosie had quit her job at Luchesso's a month before when Luchesso made it clear she was on his menu. "And Lorraine called. Says your dad is getting to where he should have a full-time day nurse. She also said it would be cheaper and safer if you'd just go ahead and put him in Summercrest."

"Hell, Rosie, he won't go and I'm not going to make him. What did you tell her?"

"That you would say, 'Hell, Rosie, he won't go and I'm not going to make him.'"

"Would you call her tomorrow and ask her if she'll go ahead and get him a full-time nurse?"

"She said it would be expensive."

"I can afford it. We'll go to Bakersfield Sunday afternoon."

"Good. I'll bake him some Christmas cookies."

"Christ, it's almost Christmas?" Seth began to undress, fatigue suddenly overwhelming him. "Hear that, Fats?"

"That's right, and guess what else."

"I give up."

"Happy six months with the firm! You started exactly six months ago today—which means twelve more to go for partnership. I made you a strawberry pie."

"You remembered! Thanks, babe. That was real thoughtful. I'll take some to work tomorrow."

"Today."

"Right. Today."

"I put six candles on it."

Seth kicked off his shoes—wing tips he had purchased last

month—pulled off his tie, and slid out of his new Brooks Brothers trousers.

"Thanks, babe," he repeated, and fell into bed. But Rosie did not reach for the light on her side, signaling to Seth that she had conversation on her mind.

Seth pulled a blanket over his shoulders and turned away from Rosie and the light. "Can't this wait till morning? This day was a real bitch."

"It *is* morning, and no, it can't wait," she said in a tremulous voice. She paused for a minute, then seeing no reaction, continued, "I don't know if this situation is working out for us, Seth."

Seth groaned inwardly, dreading the conversation he knew she had been wanting to have, the pain she had been loading into words to be shot point-blank into his burnt-out brain. He tried to clear his head.

"*Every* day is a bitch for you, Seth. You're locked in some game with your Mr. Treadwell that's killing you, and there's nothing I can do to help. I never see you. We don't talk." Rosie folded her arms and waited, then added, "I don't hardly know you anymore."

Seth turned over and sat up. He told her he knew it had been hard on her and how much he appreciated her patience, but that all they had to do now was hang on—like she said—for just twelve more months, in return for which he'd have the coveted partnership in M&M. Was it too much to ask, he pleaded, to hold on just a bit more? Hadn't she admitted just last week that the Living in the Here and Now philosophy of the sixties and seventies was an anachronism? That the Deferred Gratification style of the eighties and nineties made more sense?

"That's exactly," said Rosie, slapping her hands hard into the bed, "what I expected you to say. Every time I try to discuss our relationship you start in spinnin' words I don't even understand until I feel like I'm the crazy one here. Words about makin' it, words about success and power and deferred whatever. I'm so tired of words. They're just darn poor excuses for themselves."

"But it's the truth, Rosie. I'm beating Treadwell and everybody knows it, even Treadwell himself. I've got heavy support now after winning the U.S. Minerals case. Every other partner I've worked for is behind me. All we have to do is hold on. I've become an asset."

"You used to be a person," said Rosie, her dark eyes flashing.

Seth wisely said nothing, but after a moment of silence, Rosie added, "Seth, darlin', don't you see? We're not gonna make it. *You* may make it, but *we* won't."

Seth ran rigid fingers through his hair. "Rosie, I'm not saying you're wrong, but I'm tired and it's late . . ."

"It *is* late, Seth, maybe *too* late. Don't you see? We've lost touch with each other. I spend more time talkin' with the lady at the dry cleaners or the guy at the butcher shop than I do with you."

"Are you still upset because I forgot our three-year anniversary?"

"Two. Two years."

"Two. Listen, babe, I'm so tired . . . I don't even know what I'm saying until I hear the words. My left brain and right brain aren't on speaking terms anymore. Let me get a little sleep, and I promise we'll talk it through on our next outing."

"*Next* outing? When was the *last* outing? We're livin' in the most beautiful area in the world, Seth Cameron, and we've taken exactly one weekend off together to see it."

Rosie paused to take a deep breath before dropping the bomb. "And we haven't made love in over a month."

Seth threw back the blanket and spun off the bed. "Oh, that's great. That's just great. With all the hassle I get at the office, I really appreciate coming home to this. Damn it, Rosie, *this isn't a good time!*"

Rosie stood up, too, facing him across the bed. "I'm sorry, Seth, but there's *never* a good time to talk to you anymore. Don't you see? That's part of the problem." Rosie seemed to be fighting back tears. She took in a choppy breath and folded her arms across her chest; then, in a more conciliatory tone, she added, "I know you're under pressure, it's just that I see them killin' you and you're too busy to notice."

"But I'm *winning*, damn it," said Seth, his face now pale as death, "and doing what it takes. I drove home this morning in a car that used to belong to a guy who *didn't* do what it takes. Then there's Ted Arnold, who spent nights and weekends with *his* wife and kids and now he's got to figure out how he's going to feed them because Treadwell sent him packing today. Even Harry might be headed for trouble."

"Harry *Cooper?*" exclaimed Rosie, momentarily derailed.

"Trish Cooper snuck into my office today to get me to help her with Harry's drug problem."

"Drug problem?"

"I knew Harry had been doing pharmaceuticals to keep up. Turns out he's also been doing cocaine. Big time."

"Oh my God. *Harry?"*

"And when he does take a few hours off, it's been for all-night trips to Tahoe or Reno. Trish says the money he doesn't lose gambling is going up his nose."

"What are you gonna do? What did you tell her?"

"I told her it's none of my business, that Harry would have to find his own way out of this. People have to save them*selves,* Rosie."

Rosie covered her face with her hands for a minute, then walked around the bed that had separated them. She stood in front of him, slim and steady as a fence post, planted her hands on her hips, and fixed her eyes on his as she began to speak.

"Seth, if people have to save themselves, that goes for us, too. If they can break Harry, they can break anybody, includin' you." She paused for another spasmodic deep breath, then added, "Look at you, darlin'. You're skin and bones from not gettin' enough sleep and decent food or from those little red pills I see you take when you get up in the mornin' and probably keep takin' all day. You're plain wore out, Seth. And I'll be darned if I'll stay here and watch Treadwell run you around the track like a juiced-up quarter horse until you drop!"

Seth's face went red, but for his lips, which were white and tightly drawn. *"Nobody* runs me around, Rosie. *Nobody!* I'm beating the son of a bitch and doing exactly what *I* want to do. This is the big leagues, damn it! This is what I came here for!"

"You came for *this?* Sleepless nights? All the time quarrelin' with me? Maybe an ulcer? Maybe worse? That's what you came for?"

"I came here to show them I *belong* here, Rosie. *Here,* where the action is. Where the *power* is. Arguing a motion with millions at stake against the best lawyers in town pumps you up like nothing you could imagine. I can't believe you'd want me to quit and crawl back to trying nickel-and-dime cases in that dead-end whistle-stop it took me thirty-five years to get out of."

"At least you used to *try* those 'nickel-and-dime cases,' Seth.

You dealt with *people* and *juries,* not just money and tons of paperwork and motions. Now all you talk about is big-buck cases
that eat you alive sixteen hours a day. Maybe Tom Huckins was
right after all. You've become less like a lawyer and more like a
plumber for a bunch of economic animals!"

Seth grabbed a towel and headed for the bathroom, but turned
at the door and said, "You call it what you want, but you should
be damn glad *somebody's* working around here!"

"And what's *that* supposed to mean?" shouted Rosie. "I've
carried my share here since I quit my job. Do you want me to
go on back there to be groped some more by Luchesso? Is *that*
what you want?"

Seth whirled in the hallway and stormed back into the bedroom. "You never told me he *touched* you. And you stayed there
four *months?* How could you let him do that?"

Rosie looked at him in disbelief. "Have you been on the moon,
Seth? You don't stop a two-hundred-pound man from grabbin'
you unless you carry a gun. And you don't up and walk out on
your job when your lover is the kind of person who might jump
all over you for not carryin' your share of the load!"

"What you really mean is when your lover *isn't* jumping all
over you and when being groped by a fat greaser is better than
no groping at all."

The cruel force of the words jerked Rosie's head back as if she
had been slapped. When she had stifled her tears of rage, she
spoke in a tone that sounded to Seth like someone else.

"You've always been selfish and quick-tempered, Seth Cameron," she said in that cold, alien voice, "full of anger and suspicious of everybody. Still and all, I've loved you with all my
heart." Her voice faltered on the last words, and her eyes seemed
to soften. "But Seth, I can't take this anymore." She was whispering now. "The city is going to kill you and . . . I'm not gonna
stay here for the funeral. I'm sorry, honey, but I think it's time
for me to—"

Seth spun around and threw up his hand as if trying to ward
off an onrushing projectile. He heard himself screaming,
"Don't—"

"—head on back home."

Rosie's last words—echoes from a nightmare past—continued
to rush toward him across the room, a building mass of bitter

hurt—$E=mc^2$—words that smashed into his heart at warp speed. He felt his knees start to buckle, his breath jammed somewhere in his resin throat. He took an unsteady step toward her, like a person who had been shot, then tried to gather himself.

"You don't mean that," he said, his eyes red and glassy. "Don't say things like that. You *can't* leave, Rosie. You just *can't*. Don't you see? I'm *making* it here!"

Rosie stared at him, shivered, but said nothing.

"You won't have to work at all once I make partner," he continued, his face flushed and contorted. "We'll take trips, go on vacations!" The words were splashing out of him now, like liquid from a broken vessel. "I'm going to be *rich*, honey. We'll travel. We'll buy a place, have kids, and ..."

Pitifully pale, shoulders and head sunk, he slumped onto the bed and put his arms around her hips, his head buried in her breasts. "Please. Oh, Jesus, don't ... leave, Rosie," he said, then looked up at her. "We can work this out."

Rosie saw the glint of tears forming in his eyes, heard the catch in his throat. She had been prepared for everything but this. She sat down on his lap, put her arms around his neck.

Overhead, the sound of a jet. A dog barked somewhere. Fat Dog answered.

Seth realized he was crying, his body convulsing, pulling Rosie closer to him, feeling her hands in his hair, mumbling nonsense like a crazy man.

Yeah, I'm going crazy. This is what it's like to go crazy. Nightmares while you know you're awake. Am I awake? Afraid so. Sleep. I've got to sleep.

"I promise," he heard himself say, "I promise you, I promise—"

He heard Rosie saying, "Shhh, shhh," and was aware that his body was trembling from the cold. Cold from what? *Of course, the window. From having his face against the damn window, the window that wouldn't open, painted shut, wouldn't open. Would never open.* "I promise, oh, God, I promise ..." *She's leaving and it's stuck shut. Everything's stuck.* "And I'm sorry about everything ... and forgetting everything ..." *If he could speak and hear his own words, he was okay. I speak, therefore I am.* "I'm sorry I said all those things about you and ... Luchesso. I didn't mean it."

A kiss on the cheek. Was it just a dream? No dream, shithead, she's leaving. She's good as gone, boy. "I'm sorry and I promise ..."

"Shhh," Rosie whispered, and kissed him lightly on the shoulder. Seth raised his head and tentatively kissed her cheek, then her lips. She touched his face, cold and white as marble, pressed her cheek to his, then kissed his eyes, his dry lips. Seth kissed her back, pulled her closer to him, then gently lowered her onto the bed.

SIX MONTHS BEFORE SETH'S UP-OR-OUT PARTNERSHIP VOTE, ANTHONY Treadwell sat with Allston Addams over cocktails at the President's Club, lamenting his decreasing support, the state of the profession generally, and miscellaneous other aggravations.

"It's not just us, it's rampant all across the country," Treadwell said, crossing his long legs with a pained expression. "Clients up to their ears in expanded in-house legal staffs bent on robbing us of our bread-and-butter work, destroying our ability to leverage our associates."

"And when they do deign to send us something, they complain about our rates," added Addams.

"Then we've got all these brash young female associates the Turkeys shoved down my throat, a bunch of no-talent Rachel Cannon wannabes."

"Most of whom will be married and producing babies by the time they're capable of producing good law work."

"And associates who would rather do *pro bono publico* work than tie into a good set of interrogatories," continued Treadwell. "Then you have the sharks like Caldwell and Shaw, stealing our top tax partner last month."

"With a guarantee of five hundred thousand dollars plus performance bonuses!" added Addams. "Let's face it, Tony, we'll lose more than a tax partner to C and S if we don't increase our own profit per partner."

Treadwell responded with a contemptuous grunt and snapped his fingers at Henri. Addams's eyes widened, for not once in more than twenty years had he seen Anthony Treadwell order a third drink before lunch.

"I see that Yale wanted you back this year," said Addams, trying to shift to a more pleasant subject. "You turned them down?"

"Of course I turned them down," said the senior partner, his words rushing out in a torrent of frustration. "Don't think I've forgotten that the last time I left San Francisco my dear young partners installed a computer system we can neither afford nor understand and hired a maverick lawyer—they call him *Cowboy* I understand!— with no discernible family background, whose baggage includes a bimbo girlfriend who I learned just last week worked in a *bowling* alley. Wearing *roller skates*, if you can believe it!"

"Though she did look lovely at the spring banquet last month," said Addams, feeling his second drink.

"Of course she looked lovely. That's what bimbos *do*, for God's sake. But can you picture her at a client's dinner? Entertaining a senator and his wife?"

Addams shook his head and seized a hunk of bread.

"I also learned last week that Cameron won the last case he tried before coming here by eating an *insect*, for God's sake, in front of the jury!"

"Incomprehensible," muttered Addams, shaking his head.

"*Reprehensible*," added Treadwell. "That's the kind of thing I would have investigated had I been here—family background, service organizations, and so on—before approving him."

"Of course you would have, Tony. And we *should* have."

"Well," said Treadwell, sipping his Linkwood Scotch, "thank heavens it's not too late to teach the Young Turkeys a lesson on that score, at least."

Addams stole a glance at the senior partner. "Tony, I, uh, had rather hoped you had given up on that particular project. You know I agree with you concerning the circumstances of the young man's hiring. But it's been a year now, and I doubt that anyone even remembers how he came to be here."

"*I* remember."

"All right. So do I. But my point is, we don't want to go to the mat with the Turkeys on a fight we can't win. Cameron's partnership might well be that fight. The kid's a hell of a lawyer, Tony. Relentless. Obsessive, in fact. Approaches a simple custodian-of-records deposition as if his very life depended on it." Addams sighed, then added, "And he's got Charlie Branch and several other partners lined up solidly behind him."

"Charlie Branch, that drunk!" exclaimed Treadwell, sucking down his third drink and slamming the empty glass down on the leather-topped table.

"Don't underestimate Charlie either, Tony," pleaded Addams. "Let's face it. He retains the mystique of his past accomplishments and the admiration of the younger partners."

"Branch and mystique be *damned!*" said Treadwell "I tell you the maverick bumpkin hasn't beaten me yet, and once I get him out of my hair I'll retire Branch. Then I'll get rid of Lydell for good measure."

"Vic Lydell? But . . ."

"For conveying the offer to Cameron!"

"Oh."

Henri approached, his spine in the deferential configuration of a question mark, and handed Treadwell a message. "From your secretary, sir," he muttered. "She said it might be urgent."

The message read:

> *Elena Barton is here, unscheduled, of course. I thought you should know. Marianne Tarkenton.*

"It is bad news?" asked Addams.

"Is there any other kind?" growled Treadwell, crumpling the note and rising to his feet. "Traeger's daughter, in my office."

"But . . . what about lunch?"

"Lunch?" said Treadwell, pushing his empty glass across the table. "I've just had it."

"Elena! What a pleasure!" said Treadwell, embracing his goddaughter in the reception area of the penthouse floor. "Why didn't you tell me you were back from your trip so we might have had lunch."

"I came back early on an impulse, Uncle Tony," said Elena.

"Well, my dear, the good news is that you're here. To what do we owe this good fortune?"

Treadwell knew very well why Sen. Stanford Traeger's daughter was in his office, and it wasn't good news at all. Her husband, Capt. Sam Barton, a U.S. Air Force top-gun test pilot, had been killed in the crash of an experimental X-215A stealth bomber about eight or nine months earlier. Traeger had warned Treadwell to be prepared for Elena's visit, that she might want him to bring a lawsuit against the government and InterContinental Aerospace—"ConSpace"—manufacturer of the doomed aircraft. She had told her father that she intended to vindicate her husband's good name by erasing the "pilot error" stigma from the Air Force's records, "no matter the consequences." Treadwell did not have to be told the "consequences": a suit by Traeger's own daughter attacking the X-215A—even if entirely groundless—could pose a major embarrassment to him as senior member of the U.S. Senate Armed Services Committee's subcommittee charged with oversight of the Stealth Program. Add the fact that the subcommittee Traeger chaired had endorsed ConSpace at the end of its fierce, four-year battle with chief competitor Winston-Ethridge Aeronautics for a $200 billion government contract, and the recipe for a personal political disaster was complete.

"My God," Treadwell had said, careful to keep the smile on his face from creeping into his voice, "that *would* be embarrassing!"

Traeger had then added that although Elena had unknowingly allowed the time for suits against the government to expire, she still had ample time to sue ConSpace.

"Talk her out of this latest foolish notion, Tony," Traeger had said, anticipating his ex-partner's reluctance. "Try to get her to understand she has no case. Remind her that test pilots knowingly live in death's shadow. Tell her," he added before slamming the phone into the cradle, "that's what the hell they get *paid* to do."

Traeger did not have to add that doing his bidding was what Treadwell and M&M got paid to do.

"But first just let me look at you, dear girl," said the senior partner, taking both of Elena Barton's hands in his. "Ah, yes, more beautiful than ever, even under the circumstances."

Elena smiled back and kissed him on the cheek. "It's good to see you, Uncle Tony, and I'm sorry I didn't call first, but it suddenly hit me: I need a lawyer. Can you give me some time?"

Not even Treadwell's dread of the dilemma confronting him could erase his pleasure at the sight of Elena Barton. He scanned her face, delicate features framed in long, softly curled blond hair, then gazed into eyes like pale jadestone set in eggshell. This young woman, thought Treadwell, is even more beautiful than her mother, who, before her death, had been the object of Treadwell's unrequited lust for twenty years. Even in mourning, Elena possessed a rare blend of seductive innocence, a virginal quality that tragedy and the passage of time had not yet stolen. *How many men have had this gorgeous child?* Treadwell wondered, then banished the thought as he realized how much he would like to have been one of them.

"I'm sorry you need a lawyer, my dear, but delighted to see you, if that's what it takes. I assume you'll be wanting to speak with Mr. Addams, the head of our trust and probate group."

"No, Uncle Tony . . ."

"Excuse me, dear, you remember Miss Tarkenton?"

The women exchanged pleasantries, Miss Tarkenton took beverage orders, and Treadwell seated Elena in a client's chair.

"Shall I ask Mr. Addams to join us, Elena?" Treadwell asked, then allowed Elena to explain the purpose of her visit.

"Elena, my dear," said the senior partner, his voice hypnotically soothing, "I would think you'd want to put this ugly matter behind you. And I must tell you that an attempt to reconstruct the crash of a top-secret aircraft—as we would have to do in order to establish a product failure—would be a fool's errand, doomed to failure. We wouldn't get to first base."

He studied Elena's flawless features, gauging the effect of his words, watched her as she began to dig through her purse. Was she going to cry? Not like her, he thought, remembering her stoic demeanor at Sam Barton's funeral. And Traeger had said that Elena was even more headstrong than usual concerning this particular quest.

Traeger, the bastard. Treadwell would never forgive his duplicity in 1978, but he had had to put it behind him. After all, the senator sent M&M even more business now than he had brought in as presiding partner. More importantly, the new clients were always referred directly—and therefore credited—to Treadwell, probably out of Traeger's understandable guilt. In any event, it was clear that Treadwell would have to do whatever Traeger wanted—and what Traeger wanted was assurance that this case would never see the inside of a courtroom.

Treadwell was pleased that at least he wouldn't have to lie to his godchild—it really *would* be next to impossible to bring a successful suit against a manufacturer in a case where normal pretrial discovery methods would be thwarted by high-level security protection.

Elena found what she was looking for in her purse, and it wasn't a tissue. "Look at these, Uncle Tony," she said, her eyes glowing. "I've been collecting handwritten statements from other test pilots—top guns—who fly the same aircraft. They all say Sam was *incapable* of pilot error, that he was the best of the lot. One of them, Jerry Murphy, will even say he has real concerns about the safety of the X-215A!"

Temporarily checkmated, Treadwell altered his tactics.

"My, you *have* been busy," he said, forcing an encouraging tone. "We just might have a job for you here, my dear."

They shared a laugh over this, and Treadwell promised to brainstorm the situation with some of the "experts" in his office and give her "a more knowledgeable evaluation" the following day. Elena thanked him, kissed him on the cheek, and left him alone to stare at the oil paintings of founders E. B. Miller and Gerald McGrath, framed in elaborately carved, gilded frames, hanging proudly in his conference area.

"And you fellows thought the Depression was rough," he said aloud to the silk-brocade-covered wall.

ATHERTON, CALIFORNIA, IS HOME TO MANY OF THE WEALTHIEST EXECUtives and socialites in northern California. Two million dollars nets the buyer a small lot and a demolition project. The horsey set prances just to the southwest in Woodside, on large parcels with private stables and training rings for Thoroughbreds, Morgans, and other equestrian objets d'art. Social wannabes who can't abide stuffy Atherton, Woodside, or nearby Hillsborough jet-set north across the Golden Gate to Ross or Kent Woodlands in hip Marin County, known for a more relaxed, peacock-feathered lifestyle. Old-money, A-list clubbies, who could afford Atherton but need to stay close to the opera and symphony for fear of losing their prestige seating on opening nights, reside in fragile, seventy-five-year-old Victorians that cost something considerably north of $4 million on high-security streets in the Pacific Heights district of San Francisco.

The rest of the world lives in Oakland.

Nestled in the heart of Atherton, in an enclave called Lindenwood—the first neighborhood in California to require that all electrical and telephone lines be buried underground and out of sight—is the ten-thousand-square foot, fourteen-room home of Charlotte and Anthony Treadwell—picked up cheap ten years earlier for only $3.8 million and change. A fixer-upper.

Inside the rambling mansion, seated in a dining room the size of a small restaurant, Charlotte and Anthony Treadwell discussed their respective days. Winthrop—named after his grandfather, an East Coast industrial baron—was out for the evening attending a fraternity meeting at nearby Stanford where he studied banking and finance. Prudence, twenty-eight, a member of the Boston Junior League and already well-married to an investment banker from a good family, had called the day before to announce that the miracle of amniocentesis had assured fulfillment of her most important function as a dutiful daughter: the imminent birth of a grandson to carry on the aristocratic Treadwell lineage.

But that was yesterday. Tonight, it was clear to Charlotte that something was wrong. Not that Anthony ever tried to conceal his moods from Charlotte. For one thing, he had learned many years before—as soon as his young bride decided to let him in on it—that she was even smarter than he. Also more ambitious.

"You seem particularly troubled tonight, Tony," she said, refilling his glass from a bottle of 1962 Château Margaux. "Want to talk about it?"

Treadwell tried to eat, but the chateaubriand tasted flat, indistinguishable from the eggplant. He shook his head, then pushed his plate away and stared into the bloodred liquid in his glass as if seeking a solution there.

"He's back," Treadwell said simply in a resigned, half-whispered tone.

"When?" she said, her glass stopping short of her lips. *"Where?"*

"He first showed up in my office seven or eight months ago. Caused a bit of a ruckus. Said he needed money. Wanted to go into business."

Charlotte grunted. "Doing what? Starting a fireworks stand?"

"I gave him ten thousand. I didn't tell you because I thought we were rid of him." Treadwell grabbed one of Charlotte's cigarettes—he only smoked hers, and never during the day—lit it, and inhaled deeply, feeling the deadly comfort of warm smoke invading his lungs.

"He called this morning. He says he 'wants to talk' before he leaves town for good."

Charlotte rose from her chair and hurled her linen napkin onto the table. "How much will your dear father extort this time, Tony?"

"I asked him that," said Treadwell after taking a long drink from his crystal wineglass. "He said he had enough to get by."

"He said *that?* Strange. What do you make of it?"

"I have no idea. He's *is* acting strangely, though—even for him. If I had to guess, I'd say he's now managed to blame me for everything."

"Bob blames *you?"* she exclaimed. "Doesn't *that* just make perfect sense: drunken mother confesses to drunken husband that he's not the real father of seven-year-old Tony. Drunken father runs out and shoots Romeo Bob's arm off with a twelve-gauge shotgun. How perfectly logical for Bob to blame the child nearly sixty years later!"

Charlotte, her anger spent, rested her hand on her husband's shoulder, then fell back into her chair, a flawless Louis XIV-style reproduction. "What are you going to do?"

Treadwell looked up at his wife and managed an unconvincing smile. "I've agreed to meet him next week."

"Isn't that risky?"

"I'm meeting him at Ranjits, in Santa Cruz. He's staying near there and nobody will recognize me."

"I don't like it," said Charlotte.

"Oh, yes," Treadwell added casually, staring down at his fingernails, "Elena dropped by today."

The mention of Elena's name caused Charlotte's eyes to narrow as if hit by a cold wind. When Treadwell had finished, she sat for a minute in fuming silence. "Well, dear, you *do* have a problem," she said finally. "The problem is that your precious Elena has always known exactly how to get around her worshiping uncle Tony, which means you'd better damn well figure how you are going to appease Stan when you fail to talk her out of her lawsuit." Abruptly, she rose to her feet again and swept up the china dinner plates. "I'll get the salads."

"Now don't be silly, Charlotte. Sit back down for a moment. I don't worship anyone. Except you, of course."

Bullshit, she thought, but let it pass.

"I'll find a way to talk her out of it," Treadwell continued. "Indeed, if she realized the difficulty of the position she's putting me in, she'd back off in a minute." Treadwell poured himself another glass of wine, then thoughtfully continued his peroration.

"Perhaps that's it. I'll combine the impossible odds against winning such a case with an appeal to her loyalty to her father and to me. I'll simply explain the difficulty of my position."

"Good luck, dear," said Charlotte, granting him a half-smile belied by the same cold, narrowed eyes. "Then you can tackle peace in the Middle East, AIDS, and race relations."

"Could you be a bit less sarcastic and a bit more specific? Or better yet, a bit helpful?"

"Elena is counting on the rivalry that existed between you and Stan before his election to the Senate. She knows how he tricked you into letting him become presiding partner ahead of you for 'just one year' to bolster his campaign résumé, then held you off for four more years while he nurtured his investments into a small fortune and bided his sweet time until the governor finally appointed him to fill an unexpired term."

Charlotte paused, folded her napkin into a perfect rectangle, then leaned forward. "She knows you'll always hate him for that. She also knows that a victory against his pet Stealth Program would give you an unexpected last chance to prove yourself a better man. Am I making sense?"

This was the old Charlotte, thought Treadwell, offering only a noncommittal shrug. Uncannily perceptive, unrelentingly blunt.

"Add to that," she continued, "the fact that Elena hates her father even more than you do for the shabby way he treated Beth before she died. Don't you see? Using you to humiliate him the way he humiliated Beth is part of her motivation in all this!"

Treadwell raised an eyebrow, but concealed his astonishment at Charlotte's insight. "You may have a point, my dear," he said. "It's quite true I wouldn't mind embarrassing the pompous little egomaniac, but I trust you realize I would never allow myself to be drawn into a father-daughter conflict for something as ephemeral as principle and vengeance."

"Translated," said Charlotte, her face relaxing again, "you won't risk the loss of that East Coast business he refers to you with the regularity that only guilt could motivate."

Treadwell decided to acknowledge the validity of her analysis with a bow of his head, and Charlotte, always gratified to think of herself as the power behind the throne, got up and kissed him on the cheek.

"Dealing with it, however, won't be easy," said Treadwell. "If I do fail to discourage her, the Young Turkeys will have an excuse for offering me up as a sacrifice to appease Traeger. I could be out."

But Charlotte was already a step ahead. "I've always believed, dear, that if there *must* be a sacrificial lamb"—here she paused to smile shrewdly and top off their glasses of Margaux—"it's good to make sure it's somebody else, not you."

Treadwell considered her words, then looked up from his plate and broke into the first genuine smile Charlotte had seen in weeks. "You've done it again, my dear. It should indeed be somebody else," he said, saluting her with his raised glass, "and I have just the man for the job."

"WELL," SAID ELENA THE FOLLOWING DAY IN THE SENIOR PARTNER'S office, "do I have a good case?"

"You have the next best thing," said Treadwell with a reassuring smile at his goddaughter, radiant in a pastel sheath dress and off-white Chanel jacket that complemented her eyes. "You have a good lawyer. I am happy to say that we recently associated an experienced personal-injury attorney; a young man, but with more actual jury trials under his belt than most of the senior partners here. *And,*" the senior partner added, having rationalized away any material distinction between canned garbanzos and supersonic aircraft, "he specializes in product-liability cases."

Elena frowned, but Treadwell continued before she could speak, "Naturally, dear, I'll be right here to keep an eye on things. But frankly, I've never tried a PI case, whereas Seth Cameron—that's his name—is a qualified expert in such matters."

"Well, if you really think he's the best choice . . ."

"There's not a doubt in my mind that he is suited in every way for this project," said Treadwell, imagining how Charlotte would appreciate the ironic touch.

"When can I meet Mr. Cameron?"

"Right now. Make yourself comfortable, dear, and I'll make certain he's available."

Treadwell excused himself and descended two floors to Seth's office. "Good morning, Cameron," he said in a friendly tone that signaled imminent danger to Seth.

"Good morning, sir."

"Cameron, I have a difficult assignment for you. A matter of the highest sensitivity, requiring the utmost delicacy and discretion."

Minutes later, after Treadwell had briefed Seth, including the potential problem with Senator Traeger, he left to fetch Elena. Seth slipped in a quick call to Rosie, eager to report his assignment to a matter of such political importance to the firm.

"I think I've won the old bastard over," he said.

Seth listened, scarcely breathing, to Elena's story.

His eyes wandered between her full lips and her eyes as she spoke, then—whenever she glanced away—to her shapely, white-stockinged legs. He occasionally managed a lawyerlike, even skeptical-sounding question or comment—*How would we be able to prove the aircraft was defective? How could we penetrate the wall of legitimate top-secret security that surrounds the X-215A? You realize, of course, that the time for filing against the government has expired?*—but was mainly content just to observe the intriguing woman across from him.

She told him everything, of her life with Capt. Sam Barton— whom Seth found himself envying even though the man was dead—of the difficulties of her transition from life as an Atherton debutante to the world of the military wife; of the vicious politics and backbiting among the wives, and the paradoxical bond of vicarious pride in their husbands' status and the imminency of tragic loss that bound them together.

She haltingly recalled the day it was her turn to be visited by the others: sad-faced women who really didn't like her, who spent their days gossiping about her. Women who lived in fear and loathing, who had sat waiting alone into the morning hours, worrying that their own late-returning husbands were lying somewhere in the twisted wreckage of a crashed aircraft, only to hear them creep into the house at dawn, reeking of vodka and cheap perfume. Women who then had to deal with the guilt of feeling their relief adulterated by malevolent disappointment.

This odd community of friends had consoled her at Sam's death and had promised (as she had done herself in the past) to stay in touch, only to disappear forever from her life. She understood. She was no longer one of them; the common fear that had bound them had been severed by its final, fiery incarnation. Besides, although it would never be hinted in her presence, Capt. Sam Barton had been charged posthumously with pilot error. He had blown it, screwed the pooch, fucked up. He—and thus she— no longer wore the mantle of the elite.

"Must have hurt," Seth said quietly, to which Elena replied with a shrug of her small shoulders that seemed to say, *Good riddance.*

Still she talked, displayed her meager proofs, tried to convince him. *Tops in his class of top guns ... not a single accident in six years of test-flying any airplane they could put on the tarmac ... told me this one scared him, scared him silly every time he flew it ... thought he knew what was wrong with it, but no one would listen ... got it down on the desert somehow that night, but he had to be identified by his dental work ...*

Against these images of splattered blood and shattered bone, white-gloved hands fumbled on a purse's catch, removed a handkerchief. A sweet, musk smell wafted across the laminated desktop, a smell that Seth thought fit her perfectly: innocent, yet fecund, ripe with possibilities.

"I'm sorry, Mr. Cameron," she said, her eyes glistening with tears. "I loved him so much. It's ..."

"I understand. Please. Call me Seth." He felt an impulse to leap the pine barrier that separated them and sweep her up in his arms, comfort her, assure her that her champion would dispatch the ConSpace dragon or die in the effort.

Instead, he stared down at his pen, saying, "Has Mr. Treadwell explained how difficult these cases are? That suing the U.S. government's major aircraft contractor is like taking on the U.S. government itself."

"Nothing good comes easy," she said, burning him with those pale green eyes, challenging eyes in which Seth, in his reckless, captivated state, saw the hint of a double entendre. "And besides," she added, "I haven't told you the best part. Crispie—Captain Jack Christopher—has heard that the X-215A has some kind of mechanical defect that is under investigation. This wasn't the first crash, you know."

She handed him a list, names and dates of other X-215A crashes, the pilot's name alongside each one. First Thomas Penrod, then Grant Wilburn. Now Barton.

"Your husband was the third pilot to die in the same type of plane?"

"And all on the same routine test mission. They fly some kind of triangular pattern; Penrod crashed not far from where Sam went down. Wilburn somewhere up in northern California. All top guns. All explained away as pilot error."

"Who's Christopher?"

"Sam's best friend and now the senior test pilot in the X-215A program. Another pilot—Gerald Murphy—told me he had heard Sam explain the problem with the X-215A to the base commander."

"What happened?"

"Nothing. The upper brass were trying to make Sam out to be a crackpot. After Wilburn crashed, Sam told me he'd take his theory public if anybody else bought the farm."

"But then Sam bought it himself."

She nodded. "Gerald Murphy could be helpful if he'd testify. Said he's heard other things and wants out of the program. Another stealth test pilot—David Ames—became so terrified after Sam's death he went AWOL and never came back."

"This fellow Murphy. You say he's heard other things?"

"About the aircraft."

"Like?"

Elean leafed through her handwritten notes. "Like—to use his words—'that InterContinental Aerospace threw the X-215A together with Scotch tape and baling wire to beat the government's bid deadline. Then to win the bid, they sacrificed many of the X-215A's safety features to gain speed and make it less detectable by radar.' "

"And these men would be willing to come forward and testify in court?" asked Seth, as if he didn't know better.

Now he had her.

"I know Crispie would come in and talk to you, Mr. Cameron," she said confidently.

"Afraid that's not enough, Elena. We need witnesses. In court."

Elena rose to her feet, walked over to Seth's window, and stared out at the building next door. His guilty 35-mm eyes framed her face, devoured her profile—the delicate nose, the loose curls tumbling over small breasts, which rose quickly now with each breath. He tried to clear his head, to remind himself that everything was at stake here, yet the voyeur lens panned relentlessly downward to take in a pair of hands, his own hands, enclosing the tiny waist, then sliding downward to that perfect platform of firm flesh jutting out from her low back, pulling her hips into his . . .

"I think Crispie would," she said, staring at him with liquid eyes. She turned, moved a step toward him, her hands clasped together in front of her.

"Sorry?" said Seth, flushed with guilt and desire. "Crispie would what?"

"Testify. Sam was his best friend, Mr. Cameron. At least talk to him. Something might develop."

Which was exactly what Seth was afraid might happen. The woman was determined, irrepressible. He began to feel like the proverbial goat staked at the edge of an African village to test the rumor that a lion was about. Thoughts poured in on him like a meteor shower. *She just might have a case after all, and she knows it. She's beautiful and knows that, too. I've got to get her out of here. How can I get her to stay?*

But one thought slashed through all the rest, penetrating his brain like an ice pick.

He's beaten me. The son of a bitch has beaten me.

HARRY COOPER WALKED IN AS ELENA LEFT, BEAMING WITH THE NEWS that he had "scored big time" at Tahoe over the weekend and that his "thoroughly appeased" wife was now driving a new Mercedes. His glasses began to steam up as he rambled on about how he had been working for years on a pass-bar system at the crap tables that had finally paid off.

"The system is slow, Seth. Excruciatingly slow, but it works! Seventy-six thousand in a little over ten hours. If they hadn't paid me the ultimate compliment of inviting me to leave, I'd have made more."

"Or lost it all back," said Seth, not looking up.

"No way. This system will beat any crap table in the world."

Seth told him he was Harry fucking Houdini all right, but he was swamped right now so buzz off. Harry just laughed a man's laugh and said, yeah, I noticed and just who the hell was she?

"A client. Sort of."

"You doing entertainment law now? She's got to be a movie actress. Come on, who *is* she?"

"She's trouble, that's who she is."

"If she's trouble, I'd like to get into it."

"Harry, I'm busy."

"Okay, sorry. But fact is, Seth, I'm already in trouble. Big trouble. I owe Treadwell an appellate brief tomorrow. I'd planned to do it this weekend and ... well, something came up. I guess I just snapped Friday night and had to get out of here. Next thing I knew I was at Harrah's Club."

"Next thing you knew."

"Seth. Give me a break. This could kill me with Treadwell."

"Let me guess. You want me to intercede and exercise my immense influence with Anthony Treadwell in your behalf."

Harry reached out and grabbed Seth's shoulder. "This is no laughing matter, Seth."

Seth looked up into Harry's feverish eyes. "I'm not laughing, Harry, but what do you want from me? In case you haven't noticed, I'm alone at the top of Treadwell's shit list."

"You could give me a hand tonight."

"Give you a hand."

"*Jesus*, Seth. I feel like I'm in a fucking echo chamber. Yes, damn it. A hand with the brief. Together we could kill it, you know, just like the old law-school study-group days."

"You mean where I'd do the work and you'd get the credit?"

"Seth, cut me a little slack here. It's got to be on Treadwell's desk tomorrow morning."

"In that case," said Seth, looking back down at his work, "you'd better get on it."

"Seth, don't do this. I've got only fifteen hours to salvage my whole damn career. My working tools to meet this challenge are a body desperately in need of sleep and a brain like burnt toast."

"And who's going to salvage *my* career, Harry?" said Seth, abruptly rising and kicking back his chair. "You of all people know what he's up to, what he's doing to me. I'm sleeping three, four hours a night, working my ass off while you're whoring around in Nevada stoned on Peruvian marching powder, elevating irresponsibility to an art form. Then you come stumbling in here and have the balls to—"

Spinning around, Harry pounded both fists onto Seth's desk. *"Seth,* it's not just my career, it's my fucking *life!"* He slowly straightened and dropped his arms to his side, trying to catch his breath. In a hoarse whisper he added, "I'm *begging* you, man!"

Seth stared at the piles of depositions and documents littering his desk, then shut his eyes and rubbed his temples for a full minute. Harry stood there, hardly breathing, watching Seth across the desk.

"Maybe I owe you one, Harry," said Seth, slamming his book shut, "but let's not make it a habit. *Never again.* Deal?"

A jagged smile cut across Harry's sallow face. "Deal," he said, and started to extend his hand until Seth's burning eyes stopped him. "I'll get the opening briefs," he added, reaching for the door instead. "And thanks, Seth."

It was all over by five the next morning. Actually, it was over for Harry by midnight, two hours after he snorted a final elephant-line of cocaine. Harry had offered Seth a "wee toot," then had become irrational when Seth refused. "Since when are you qualified to judge *me,"* he had said. "You with your bennies to stay wired at night, then shooters and red-birds to bring you down at bedtime!" Seth said, bullshit, that's different, and Harry said, yeah, a difference without a distinction, then accused Seth of being a hypocritical asshole, sending Seth to the door. Harry had then somehow managed a credible apology, and they returned to the books until Harry faded ten minutes later.

Seth's first draft went to word processing at around three-thirty, and he returned a final, marked-up draft to the sleepy-eyed night operator on his way out the door two hours later, leaving Harry passed out at a library table.

It was a good brief. Harry would be a fucking hero.

THE CAICOS ISLANDS LIE SCATTERED NORTH OF HAITI IN THE BRITISH West Indies, hidden like lost pearls from a broken string, lost but not forgotten. Two hours from Miami by Atwan Airways, Kew, the major city, boasts over a hundred banks in an area with a population smaller than many universities in the U.S. Once the haunt of corsairs and various picaroon vessels, the Caicos now offer the new pirates of commerce a special treasure: offshore banking facilities and a discreet tax haven. Although wealthy insiders go to the Caicos to scuba dive among the incomparable coral reefs and barnacled skeletons of unlucky sloops and schooners, most—including an enormous, perspiring American entrepreneur named Aubrey Olmstead—go there to make and protect their money.

Olmstead was perspiring on this particular occasion in a bar called the Noche Diablo—located halfway between Kew and the northeast tip of the central island in the chain—owned by a gay Baptist West Indian named Claude. Olmstead was perspiring partly because the Noche Diablo had no air-conditioning, partly because he was so overweight he once had to be lifted from the debris of a shattered platform rocker in a cargo net, and partly because the man across from him—to whom he referred only as "Father"—was either unable or unwilling to grasp the seriousness of the problem that had brought them together in this godforsaken place.

"You call it 'overreacting' if you want," said Olmstead, wiping his pumpkin of a head with an embroidered handkerchief, "but if the rumor is true, and ConSpace *does* replace our M-31 canopy system because another X-215A had to be scraped off the desert floor with a blotter, we'll have the tax division of the Justice

Department on our necks again, screaming we're nothing but a shell, a tax-evasion vehicle."

"Aww-brey, my *dear* fellow," said Father in his clipped pseudo-British accent, an effete Abbot to Olmstead's Costello, "even the government stumbles upon the truth occasionally."

"Damn it, man," said Olmstead, swatting in vain at a harassing fly, "this is no joke! If ConSpace hadn't installed our jury-rigged M-31 system on the X-215A, the feds would have seen our tax scam for what it is, and we'd be meeting on McNeil Island today instead of this one."

"It might be ever so much cooler," said Father, who, despite a humidity level bordering on rainfall, wore a Halston silk shantung jacket without evidencing a trace of perspiration.

"Fuck you, Father."

Father's eyes narrowed as he leaned toward his companion. "Easy now, my fat friend; perhaps it's time for a reality check. In the first place, your reference to '*our* tax scam' suggests you've got a very bad memory or a mouse in your pocket. The credit and blame for TDA's conception are entirely yours, Aubrey, and let us not forget it."

"As long as you don't forget that my 'conception' has rewarded you damn well, Father dearest, about five million American, tax-free, at last count!"

Father reached for his Mount Gay and soda. "A pittance compared with your own just rewards, my dear friend. At all events, just as it was *your* brilliant scam, it is well to note that it is *your* 'jury-rigged M-31,' not 'ours.' My sole involvement has been to funnel your ill-gotten money to ranking officers at ConSpace to ensure the exercise of good judgment in selecting *your* M-31 canopy system for the X-215A. In addition, I have willingly accepted the task of attempting damage control, necessitated by the bungling of *your* so-called genius, Ivor Tellman, God rest his tortured soul."

"Well, bra-*vo!*" grunted Olmstead, his froglike face beaming with sardonic appreciation. "Are you wearing a wire or something, Father? Should I deny I even know you?"

"Most people find that quite advisable. No, old boy, just keeping the record straight between us."

"And just how do you propose to 'control the damage' if yet another X-215A falls out of the sky like a rock?"

"We'll have to face that if it happens. Stop listening to rumors, Aubrey. After all, the Air Force has attributed blame to pilot error again—it can't afford to do otherwise—without so much as a whisper about your precious TDA and your rather dicey M-31. Not to worry, old sport."

TDA—Tellman Design Associates—was Aubrey Olmstead's masterpiece, the crowning achievement of a thirty-five-year career of scams ranging from street cons as a youth to complex pyramid schemes. It consisted of a limited partnership, purportedly formed to research and develop Prof. Ivor Tellman's concept of a high-performance, heat-resistant aircraft canopy system and associated electronics. One share in TDA required a minimum investment of $50,000, but only $20,000 in cash. The balance of $30,000 was satisfied by a non-interest-bearing loan available from Zenith Financial, a Caicos corporation also controlled by Olmstead. The carrot—for any wealthy investor looking for tax shelter—was that for every $20,000 he invested in cash, he got an immediate write-off of $50,000 passive income—a quick tax gain of $30,000! Likewise, a $500,000 "investment"—$200,000 in cash—would trigger a full $500,000 write-off, and so on. To make the deal even sweeter, the terms of the note required repayment to Zenith only out of future dividends, an unlikely occurrence, as TDA at the time had neither a real product nor a true intention to build one. Nevertheless, the investors freely took their giant deductions, and Olmstead kept their cash advances—over $100 million so far—less 5 percent to Father and generous salaries to a skeleton staff of "research scientists" headed by Tellman, a bona fide MIT genius who had dabbled for years in chaos physics and high-torque failure analysis. Everybody won, so nobody cared.

Except the tax division of the U.S. Justice Department.

A year earlier, a portly young assistant attorney general named William Torville had figured out enough of the scheme to seek an indictment, only to learn that TDA's spun-off manufacturing corporation—TDA, Inc.—had hastily come up with an authentic product and sold it to the U.S. Air Force and InterContinental Aerospace for use in its experimental stealth program.

"I hear you, Father," said Olmstead, swatting again at the pesky fly with one hand and spilling his lemonade on the other, "but that damn crash has safety engineers swarming all over the plans for every component of the X-215A. The antistealth wolves in Congress are howling, and the rumor is that the engineers have got to do something even if it's wrong; that at least twelve suppliers are going to be axed, and we're one of them."

Father ordered another Mount Gay, then leaned as close to Olmstead as the table and his companion's corpulence would permit. "Your paranoia is becoming quite insufferable, Aubrey."

"Paranoia? I've heard rumblings out of ConSpace that our canopy electronics might be directly implicated this time. So save your smart-ass remarks!"

Without warning, Father's right hand shot toward Olmstead, then opened in front of the fat man's bulging eyes to reveal a crushed fly. "You really worry too much, old boy," he added as he dropped the carcass onto the table. "Trust me to be quick enough to stay a step ahead of these fools."

Olmstead lapsed into a fuming silence, rattling the ice in his glass and glancing petulantly at the slow-moving bartender. Father appeared lost in thought, staring out toward the sea, which had borne the early white settlers of the Caicos: the turtlers, the buccaneers, the shipwrecked mariners.

"At least Tellman did the gentlemanly thing under the circumstances," said Olmstead. "If he hadn't put a bullet through his own head, I'd have done the job myself."

"Really? I rather thought you *had* shot him," said Father, but then paused and gave his head a quick shake. "No, that's not at all your style. Tell me, Aubrey, who *did* you engage to kill TDA's master of off-the-shelf electronics?"

"Don't be ridiculous. I was very fond of Ivor."

"So I've heard," said Father with a wry smile.

Before the red-faced Olmstead could respond, a waiter served their drinks and danced away.

"Now don't get huffy, Aubrey," added Father. "I'm not one to judge someone else's . . . personal preferences. You've made me so rich I wouldn't care if you were seen buggering an ape at high noon in Westminster Abbey. As for your desire that I keep the conscientious Mr. Torville off your generously endowed ass, I'm telling you that I'll see to it."

"Good. Because if you don't," said Aubrey Olmstead, calling

for the check, "you could be spending the balance of your miserable life rent free, all expenses paid, courtesy of the U.S. government. Let's not forget that either."

"Well, Aubrey," said Father, flickering a smile as he rose to leave, "the possibility of having you as a roommate provides strong motivation for me to succeed."

THE USUALLY SOMBER MAIN CONFERENCE ROOM AT MILLER AND McGrath was jammed to the walls with tired but wired associates noisily grabbing coffee and looking for a seat. Punctuality was prized at M&M, and the weekly litigation lawyers' staff meeting was an occasion where the lack of it was never more obvious. So obvious, in fact, that a lawyer not seated by eight sharp was well advised to stay away altogether and pray that his or her absence would not be noted—decent odds, as M&M's success of recent years had swelled the litigation side of the firm to twenty-seven partners and eighty-two associates.

The weekly meeting—called Show and Tell by the associates—provided the firm's trial lawyers an opportunity to hear what others were doing and to exchange ideas on how they might do it better. Treadwell ran the meeting, of course, keeping everyone alert with a brilliant blend of education, motivation, and castigation.

The first case under discussion was a sure loser about to be taken to trial by a young partner named Yancey, who described the bleak facts in a crisp, five-minute presentation. His case would be won—or more realistically, lost—on a single document that the defendant's comptroller, a Mr. Garner, steadfastly denied he had seen. A three-day deposition had failed to crack the stonewalling maneuver.

"Now, how might our Mr. Yancey hope to prevail in this apparently untenable situation?'' Treadwell always asked for solutions in a manner that implied he already knew the answer. And to prove his years as an adjunct professor at Yale had not been wasted, he scornfully shot down each suggestion, one by one.

"Brilliant, Mr. Butler. An answer worthy of a first-year night-school lawyer aspiring to a career searching title reports."

"This isn't Twenty Questions, Mr. Jackson. What we're seeking here are solutions, not recycled statements of the problem."

"No, Miss Farrell, and if you will read Hedgewood versus Atkinson *you'll see that the Supreme Court rejected that tactic two months ago."*

"Ah, good morning, Mathews. Thank you so much for joining us. If you had been here to hear all of Mr. Yancey's factual recitation, you would know that he already tried that approach."

And so on, until finally, *"Is that it?* No way out for our brother Yancey? No way for him to snatch victory from the jaws of defeat? How about you, Mr. Cameron? In view of the fact that you are now late with two assignments to me, perhaps you've been spending your time thinking about what Mr. Yancey might do to break this formidable opponent.''

Seth looked up, his eyes flashing, but he made no move to rise. The room went silent.

''Well, Mr. Cameron? Let's hear it. What should Yancey do in this untenable situation?''

As Seth slowly rose to his feet, he continued to meet Treadwell's eyes. Although the senior partner was grinning, their mutual hatred had never before been so publicly displayed.

''Yes, sir, I've been thinkin' hard on this one,'' Seth said at last, ''and I'd suggest that the best solution here would be for Yancey to challenge Mr. Garner to a duel.''

An outburst of laughter followed, and the smile disappeared from Treadwell's suddenly florid face. ''That's about what I would expect from you, Mr. Cameron. Please be so good as to stop by my office after the meeting, will you, sir?'' The laughter in the room dissipated into another sympathetic silence.

Forty-five minutes later, Treadwell closed the meeting by announcing that prospects for obtaining a reversal in the National Biometrics case had taken a promising turn, ''thanks to a creative new approach recently articulated in a fine appellate brief drafted by one of our senior associates. Stand and take a bow, Mr. Cooper."

Harry, his face flushed in what the audience took as a manifestation of humility, pulled himself into a standing position as the audience applauded, then quickly sat down. As the congratulatory din subsided, one person, behind and off to Harry's right, continued a slow rhythmic clapping for several seconds after everyone else had stopped.

Harry did not have to turn to see who it was.

As the meeting broke up, Harry spotted Seth in the hallway talking to Bill Yancey.

"—then I'd hit him with the March-sixth letter."

"That should do it, all right," said Yancey, "but what if he denies seeing it?"

"He won't," said Seth. "Not if you set him up like I told you. Remember, he'll be too afraid of looking even more negligent for *not* having seen it."

"Thanks, Seth," said Yancey, starting to walk away. "I'll give it my best shot."

As Harry approached Seth, Yancey stopped and turned back. "I'm curious, Seth. Why didn't you just say this when Treadwell—"

"Good luck, Bill," said Seth, signaling the end of the conversation.

"Right," said Yancey, and walked away, shaking his head.

Harry took Seth by the arm. "You won't say anything, will you, Seth? I read our brief after I rose from the dead the next day, and it's clearly your style, not mine. We both work for Treadwell. The man's a lot of things, but he's no fool. Did you hear the way he put it during the meeting? 'By *one* of our senior associates.' "

"I heard."

"So? What if he asks you?"

Seth gave Harry a droll smile. "I'll tell him the truth."

"*Shit!*" said Harry, turning away and slapping his forehead. "You *know* what that will do to my chances for partnership in January!"

"Don't worry, Harry," said Seth coldly. "The truth I'll tell him is that I've never expected any favors in life, and I don't grant any. Particularly here at M and M, where no good deed goes unpunished."

Harry exhaled and smiled. "Don't scare me like that, Seth, though God knows I deserve it. No shit, I'm really sorry about making you late on your own assignments. Maybe I can make it up to you."

"Forget it, Harry, it's my own damn fault. I should know better by now. Anyway, I owed you one. Now we're even."

Treadwell sat straight as a rifle behind his rosewood fortress.

"That was cute, Cameron. I hope you enjoyed your little joke at my expense."

"This place could use a few more chuckles."

"Is that so? You would do well, Cameron, to try to understand that this is a law firm, not a vacation destination, not a bird sanctuary, and certainly not a comedy house!"

Treadwell then delivered the anticipated lecture on the importance of submitting projects on schedule and concluded by saying, "You might also remember, Cameron, that he who chuckles last, chuckles best."

The senior partner then asked if he had heard from Elena Barton.

"It's been a week now," said Seth. "No calls. I suspect by now she's talked to a possible witness named Jack Christopher, a buddy of her husband's who heard some incriminating things from another pilot about the X-215A. The guy's undoubtedly scared to come forward. That should end it."

"Her silence is certainly a good sign," said Treadwell, smiling and nodding affirmatively for the first time in Seth's presence, "a good sign."

"Yes, sir, a good sign."

"By the way, Cameron, I'd like you to take a look at the brief I mentioned in the meeting today. Harry Cooper's. Imaginative work *and* on time. I know you two are close friends, and I think it might help you to see the kind of work we expect around here."

Seth held the brief in his hands, quickly leafed through the twenty pages, then glanced up at Treadwell's mocking smile. *He knows, all right. The son of a bitch knows.*

"I've already seen it," Seth said finally. "Harry's a smart lawyer."

"And creative."

"And punctual. Will that be all?"

"For now, but let me know if you hear anything else from Mrs. Barton."

"What if she calls and tells me she wants to proceed with her case?"

"Should she elect to file, we'll send her to off to a south-of-Market lawyer," said Treadwell, curling his lip disdainfully. "Who else would take a case this hopeless? But the more relevant question for you, Cameron, is whether you can succeed in obviating that bleak necessity. You are aware of the stakes."

"I think so. If I don't succeed, you'll be sending me off, too, won't you? That's what this conversation is really about, isn't it?"

Treadwell just smiled and said, "Let me know if you hear from her."

Two weeks later, Seth did hear from her. Unannounced, as usual, Elena Barton appeared in his office.

"Elena, I wasn't expecting you."

"I wasn't expecting me, either," she said, melting Seth's disappointment with a smile. "But my father asked me to meet him for lunch."

"Traeger? Senator Traeger is here?"

"A fund-raiser," she said, seating herself and crossing her perfect legs. "He wants to have lunch with me, which is strange, given the fact that we haven't spoken in years. I'm curious though and can't come up with a decent excuse not to meet him. You're a lawyer; maybe you can."

Sure, several, he thought. *How about you're being held captive in a hotel room by a sex-crazed lawyer.* "Don't tempt me," he said, not believing she had initiated this game or that he was playing it. *Get yourself together, man.*

"Wish I had known you were coming, Elena. The junior associate doing the investigation and research on your case is out today, and frankly I haven't talked to him lately." *You want excuses; you've come to the master.*

"My own fault, Seth," she said, finally calling him by his first name. "I didn't really expect you'd have ConSpace on its corporate knees in just two weeks."

"On the knees takes longer," Seth said lamely, trying to gather himself as she smiled. "Seriously, Elena, I hope you haven't forgotten what I said earlier about how tough this thing would be."

"Of course it will be difficult. That's why Tony assigned you to handle it."

You're closer to the truth than you know, Elena.

"Well," she said, rising and extending her hand, "it's show time with Senator Dad. You'll let me know when you come up with something?"

"Of course," said Seth, rising quickly. "Although," he added as casually as he could, "you must assume that no news is bad news."

He felt a tremor in her hand, and her smile vanished. "You don't think I have a case, do you." It was a statement, not a question.

"I'm afraid not," he said, walking her to the door.

"Sam's good name is all he left me. Please don't give up."

Seth could think of nothing to say.

Returning from lunch, Seth found a message from Marianne Tarkenton, summoning him to Treadwell's office for a brief meeting with Senator Traeger. Seth buffed his shoes with a paper towel and combed his hair. *Meeting daddy.*

Elena was gone. Traeger was even shorter and less attractive than he appeared on television. His small eyes were so close together a single silver dollar could have covered both of them, and his smile, which flashed on and off like a neon beer sign, revealed two dozen of the smallest teeth Seth had seen in a human mouth. When the mouth opened, words splattered the air in staccato bursts, holding even the formidable Treadwell at bay. This guy could not possibly be Elena's biological father, thought Seth, and little wonder the senior partner resents this ugly, dominating little man, remembering his conversation with Harry Cooper.

"Tony tells me you're just the man to straighten out my daughter on this latest fantasy of hers," spoke The Mouth, his pig eyes appraising Seth.

"I'm doing my best, sir," said Seth with a sideways glance at Treadwell.

"Excellent. Tell me about your meeting with her before lunch."

"I told her we weren't finished with our investigation and research—neither of which have actually even begun, of course—but that I was not at all encouraged by what we had found so far."

"What was her reaction? How was it left?"

"I tried to position her to assume the ball was in my court. Told her she'd hear from me if we found something positive, but not to be surprised if she didn't hear from me at all. My tactic has been to first win her trust, then encourage passivity on her part. My hope is that she'll eventually forget the whole thing."

"Excellent approach," said Traeger, flashing two rows of miniature teeth, "don't you agree, Tony?"

Treadwell swiveled a quarter turn in his chair, formed a steeple with his fingers, then directed his response to Seth.

"No, Stan, frankly I *don't* agree. Why, in God's name, Cameron, didn't you simply tell her that we *had* completed our investigation and that she had no case?"

"Two reasons. First, she's still too close to the loss of her husband, too angry. She'd just go out and get a second opinion."

"So?" said Treadwell.

"So the next lawyer she went to might . . . tell her the truth."

"The truth?" said Traeger. "What do you mean, 'the truth'?"

"That's the second reason. Even granting the difficulty of penetrating the government's security net and dealing with the causation issue, your daughter may actually have a case against ConSpace."

Seth saw Traeger's eyes flicker to Treadwell's glaring face, but Seth kept talking. "There are, admittedly, several major hurdles between filing a complaint and getting to a jury, but as you know from your own days here as a trial lawyer, Senator, if you can get your case to a jury, anything can happen. Barton was the third to die in little more than a year of testing the X-215A. A jury may think it strange that three of the best and the brightest were all guilty of pilot error. Plenty of hungry lawyers here in town would be willing to give it a try."

"That must be avoided at all costs, young man. Her psychiatrist has informed me that her emotional recovery from this damn mess could be delayed for *years* if it's not put behind her."

"I understand, sir. I'm just saying that although she's obviously an incredible woman, she's still looking for the catharsis that clearing her husband's—"

"*Catharsis?*" said Traeger with an outburst of laughter. "And to think I've spent all that money on a world-renowned grief counselor for Elena when I had an expert right here in my old firm."

Seth looked puzzled. "I had the impression you two weren't all that, well . . ."

"Close? Your impression is correct. She thinks it's part of the insurance, and you won't tell her otherwise. Now let's skip all this psychobabble bullshit and get rid of this problem."

"I only meant that all other things being equal—"

"Mr. Cameron," said Traeger, moving a step closer to Seth, "life has taught me that all other things are *never* equal. And apart from my fatherly concern about Elena, I want to be sure you understand that we are dealing here with a matter of grave national significance. Now, let's say some pettifogging ambulance chaser managed to prove to the world that the United States government couldn't make planes any better than Detroit can make automobiles. Can you imagine where that would put our national defense effort?"

The senator paused, then lowered his voice and smiled conspiratorially. "Between us, young man, Reagan's Star Wars project was always pure fantasy—just like the movie—and I'm a loyal *Republican*, for God's sake! But the X-215A is *reality* and only a few years away from mass production. It's got the B-2 whipped in every department, and we can bring it in for only a quarter billion per copy. The world out there already knows enough about it to be scared stiff of its capabilities, which means *we* own the ultimate weapon; the ultimate *deterrent*, Cameron!"

Seth wasn't sure how he had triggered all this or what he was supposed to say next. Traeger seemed satisfied, however, and

Treadwell interceded, assuring his ex-partner that Seth had "gotten the message" and would maintain control of the matter. On cue, Seth added his own assurances that he understood both his assignment and its importance, shook hands with the senator, and was excused.

"He'll be all right," said Treadwell. "What do you think?"

"I think," said Traeger, "that the boy wants to fuck my daughter."

Late that night, Seth visited Rosie at Andre's, where she had been taken on as hostess. He quickly downed a pair of Cuervo shooters. She took a break and he told her everything that had happened.

"It sounds like you think she has a case," said Rosie.

"If it were properly prepared and tried by someone with experience."

"By someone like you, right?" said Rosie, but Seth said nothing. "What's she like? Mrs. Barton?"

"She's okay," Seth said too quickly, then ordered another shooter and switched back to safer ground. "Sure, I'd like to be able to try a case like hers. Who wouldn't?"

"And instead, you're gonna make sure nobody else does?"

"Jesus, Rosie, a little understanding would be nice right now. My whole future—*our* whole future—is riding on the success of this . . . assignment."

"Well, pardon me if I don't start chirpin' like a cricket over a partnership you can only win by losing a case before it's even started." She shoved a stack of menus into a drawer with more force than necessary before adding, "This big-city law business is way more 'n I can figure. It surely don't fit you, Seth."

"We all have to play a role sometime."

"There's nothing wrong with playing a role, so long as you know you're playing one."

"Could you spare me the seventies mystics? You make this whole thing sound like some evil conspiracy."

Rosie's eyes confronted him with an unblinking accusation. "That isn't for me to say, but you seem to be leading someone who trusts you down a primrose path. You may be pigheaded and reckless, Seth Cameron, but you've always valued the truth."

Seth tossed down his shooter and slammed the shot glass down on the bar, saying, "So much for understanding."

"I think I'm understanding it exactly. That's the problem."

Seth said thanks for everything, threw a twenty on the bar, and drove back across the bay to Stars, where he drank four more shooters before Jeremiah Tower himself sent him home in a cab.

TENSION REIGNED BOTH AT HOME AND AT THE OFFICE FOR THE NEXT several weeks, but by late September, with less than three months before the vote on his partnership, still without a word from Elena, Seth began to breathe again. The breathing came in short gasps, however, because Treadwell, sensing that Seth might have disarmed the Barton bomb, had turned the pressure up yet another notch. Seth was now handling the caseload of three associates, supporting three partners, and supporting himself with increasing dependence on three substances, all ending with the same three letters and all providing various degrees of stimulation on demand: caffeine, Dexedrine, and Benzedrine. He was literally speeding through projects, yet somehow maintaining the quality of his work. He kept the pills well hidden, even from Rosie, but could not conceal an increasing discomfort in his stomach he feared might be an ulcer. His groans would awaken her sometimes at night, when the pain stabbing at him in his sleep felt like someone was trying to cauterize the hole in his gut with a soldering iron. She would kiss his cold, damp forehead and beg him to see a doctor. He would agree, then "feel much better" the next day. As the song goes, Seth was "running on empty"—coffee, Maalox, and bennies all day, then booze, red-birds, or yellow-jackets to bring it all down at bedtime.

To make matters worse, Joe Cameron's day nurse had quit in

utter frustration, and Seth had had to travel to Bakersfield to size up the situation. The day-care agency was refusing to send any more "victims," as they put it, and Seth's visit to his father merely confirmed the agency's concerns. Pop would have to be put in a home.

A half day of interviews and a $6,000 deposit settled it. A week later, however, Seth received a fax from Summercrest reporting that one of the attendants had suffered a mild concussion and a twelve-centimeter hematoma from an empty wine bottle hurled by his father. The director's carefully worded communication gave no hint as to how the reluctant exile had acquired the bottle of wine, but added that his "post-assault behavior left little doubt concerning the previous disposition of the contents of the aforementioned bottle." Seth took this to mean Pop was earnestly drunk.

The director had then suggested another nursing home "better equipped for exigencies of this nature" and promised return of Seth's deposit "under separate cover."

This meant another trip to Bakersfield to resettle Joe in a more heavily armed camp (as Joe described it) called Havenhill, and to engage in bilateral negotiations with the old man's dual personalities.

"Havenhill? Don't make me laugh," said Pop. "To start with, Son, there ain't a hill within twenty miles, and I guarantee the place ain't a haven."

Doc Farley went over the tests with Seth in private, explaining that Joe was suffering from an inoperable brain tumor that both explained his bouts of irrationality and rendered it impossible for him to be at home.

After his return to San Francisco, Seth began to slip behind at last, and Treadwell sensed that it was time to finish off his weakened prey.

"Well, Cameron," he said, entering Seth's office early one morning and speaking in his usual cold, military tone, "when can I expect the memorandum of points and authorities on the Jerome Frank case?" The assignment had been given only two days earlier, but Seth had spent all night in the office and had just delivered his first draft to the word-processing department. "By the way," added the senior partner, his face puckered disdainfully, "you look like the wrath of God. I hope you don't have any client meetings today."

"Nope," said Seth, thinking how much worse he'd look if Rosie hadn't brought a fresh shirt and his shaving kit into town after finishing her shift at Andre's. "As for your memorandum, I told you I'd have it by noon today and I will."

The passage of time had seen a further deterioration in the relationship between the two combatants, with all pretext of congeniality now abandoned.

"Heard anything from Elena Barton lately?" asked Treadwell.

"Sorry to disappoint you, Mr. Treadwell," said Seth without looking up as he continued to highlight a deposition transcript, "but not a word. She's apparently forgotten the idea." He could not resist adding, "As I expected she would."

Treadwell gave him a skewed smile. "You don't know her like I do, Cameron. Elena Barton forgets nothing she really wants, and she wants this lawsuit. She'll be back. She's not a quitter."

Seth rose to his feet and glared at the senior partner through unfocused, red-rimmed eyes. Something in the ragged intensity of the look caused Treadwell to take a step back toward the door.

"Then she's a lot like me, Treadwell."

Treadwell forced another smile as he turned to leave, saying, "You're a crude and offensive bumpkin, Cameron, but you are indeed persistent. I'll grant you that."

"Then grant me some *fairness*, for Christ's sake!" said Seth through clenched teeth as he charged around his desk and advanced on the senior partner, blocking his path to the door. Seth's pale face was so strained with fatigue he looked slightly deranged as he added in a hoarse whisper, *"I've done every fucking thing you've asked of me!"*

Their faces were but inches apart. "What are you going to do, Cameron," said Treadwell, calm again, "hit me?"

The two men glared at each other through narrowed eyes for several seconds before Seth turned his head away and gasped, "No, you bastard, that's one thing I won't do for you."

"A wise decision. Now get that temper under control, and you may yet be a good trial lawyer. Somewhere else, of course."

"Wrong on both counts, Treadwell," said Seth, surprising the senior partner with a broad, demented smile. "I'm *already* a good trial lawyer, and I'm not going 'somewhere else.' " Seth then reached up and patted the senior partner on both shoulders, adding, "I'm going to stay right here. I'm going to be your *partner*, old man!"

Treadwell recoiled from Seth's touch, then stared at the grinning associate with a mixture of repulsion and fascination.

"Not while I'm alive," he said finally, brushing past Seth and leaving the door open as he stormed out.

The senior partner was still fuming when Allston Addams entered his office fifteen minutes later. After hearing about the exchange, Addams tried again to convince his friend and benefactor that he had all but lost his case against Seth Cameron and those responsible for his hiring. "His support runs all through the partnership now, Tony, and you've got less than three months before the vote. The partners don't like what you're doing. They know he's taken your best shots—even apparently handled your problem with Traeger—and he's still on his feet ... though barely. Tony, please—just let it go."

"A lot can happen," said Treadwell, staring at his steepled fingertips, "in just three months."

The senior partner worked late that night, later than even the most diligent associate. He had spent the afternoon with computer director Barbara Erickson, who had been both surprised and flattered by his sudden interest in the various technical applications under her supervision. "Just part of my hands-on management style," he had told her as he took in every aspect of her department's activities, from the computerized litigation support system to the firm's fail-safe calendar procedures.

After a last-minute check around the office for stragglers, Treadwell took the night elevator down to the twentieth floor and unlocked the door where the master calendar-programming computer was housed. He sat at the console and soon managed to get on-line. After ten minutes of cautious false starts and recourse to the manual, he pulled up all calendar entries under the name of Seth Cameron. Next, he located an entry under Seth's file that read:

10/15/93 Barton vs. InterContinental Aerospace:
One-year statute of limitations expires today.

Treadwell carefully reviewed the checklist he had created after his meeting with Barbara Erickson and pushed the key marked BLOCK, then ran the cursor over the entire entry. Once the words were completely shaded, he took a deep breath and hit the delete button, then answered yes to the computer program's final fail-safe inquiry.

Treadwell found himself staring into a blank screen. The calendar entry had completely vanished—and soon, with or without the return of Elena Barton, Seth Cameron would disappear as well.

VENTANA, LOCATED TWENTY TWISTING, BREATHTAKING MILES SOUTH OF Carmel on Highway 1 near Big Sur, is one of California's best-kept secrets: a hideaway for those rare couples who have earned enough money to afford it while somehow preserving sufficient sensitivity to appreciate it. The rustic, yet elegant, resort can be either paradise or hell—the best of places, the worst of places— depending on the state of one's relationship, for there is absolutely nothing to do there ... except breathe the fresh ocean air, take in the most beautiful views ever created by nature, soak naked in one of the giant hot pools, partake of the restaurant's excellent cuisine, or just sit in front of a crackling fire and contemplate life. Those who become threatened by the silence and dreadful freedom of the place can be seen racing for their cars and rolling down the highway to Nepenthe, a bar and restaurant overlooking the Pacific that has served over the years as an off-beat hangout for celebrities as diverse as Henry Miller and Kim Novak.

Rosie had set up the trip well in advance, having secured Seth's blood-oath commitment that nothing would interfere this time.

She was typically up-front concerning her agenda: she was unhappy and again considering a return to Bakersfield. Although her job at Andre's involved less tension than Luchesso's, it paid considerably less money as well. She had little in common with the M&M wives and missed Seth's companionship, though the differences they brought with them to the city now seemed magnified. Even her dreams had abandoned her.

At first, Seth had waffled, wondering why they had to go so far, particularly to a place that wouldn't take Fat Dog. He came around in the end, however, pledging to let nothing stand in the way of the trip, and promising to "sit her down and give her a good listening-to." Still, Rosie could hardly believe it when Friday afternoon arrived and they were actually packed and on their way across the Golden Gate, then winding south down Highway 1.

They had stopped in Carmel at Clint Eastwood's Hogsbreath Cafe for a supper of cheeseburgers and beer, warmed their feet on the hearth of the outdoor fireplace, laughed together for the first time in weeks. By the time they reached Ventana, they were both too tired to do anything but fall asleep in each other's arms.

The uncommon silence and a soft light spreading across the spacious room awakened them the next morning, and Seth built a fire while Rosie made coffee. They decided to try the coed hot pool before breakfast and were delighted to find themselves alone. Playful games soon turned to deferred passion, and they took full advantage of their privacy by making love at the edge of the healing waters. After an icy shower, they returned to their room and started over again on the rug in front of the fireplace.

This time, however, they were not alone, for visions of Elena Barton invaded Seth's mind, then raged unchecked down his spine, culminating in a convulsive release that left him physically drained but filled with guilt.

"What's she like, Seth?" Rosie had asked that night at Andre's. *"Mrs. Barton."*

"She's okay," he had said.

They got dressed and joined a half dozen other couples for a continental breakfast in the main room, where two massive fireplaces warmed the spacious area with a sweet oak smell. They exchanged friendly glances with other couples, but few words were spoken. Ventana was not a place for making new friends or setting up a golf date.

After breakfast, they headed out on one of the mountain paths to have their talk. Rosie started by telling Seth the ways in which the city had changed him, noting, for example, how his cowboy boots had gathered dust in the closet. "You used to be a pretty crazy person, Seth. You did what you wanted. Now you're more crazed than crazy, all the time worryin' about what *they* want."

"Sometimes you have to do what other people want in order to get what *you* want. It's called compromise, Rosie. It's called adapting to a new environment. It's the way people survive. You should try it."

"What's that supposed to mean?"

Bad start.

"Never mind. It's just that I had asked you to dress a little more . . . appropriately for the M and M wives' tea last month. Trish told Harry you showed up in a miniskirt."

"It was *not* a miniskirt."

"Well, it was described as looking like it had been spray-painted on you."

"It wasn't a hoopskirt, if that's what your old girlfriend Trish meant."

"And you had to wear that sweater I hate."

"It's colorful. Makes me feel good."

"It looks like something that came with batteries."

Rosie started to snap back, then paused to calm herself. "It never bothered you before. Back home you used to say, 'If you got it, flaunt it'; you used to be proud of me, not ashamed."

Seth had no answer.

"See what I mean?" she continued. "I feel lately like you're all the time either ignorin' me or judgin' me. Somethin' in between would be nice once in a while."

"I'm sorry."

Rosie let it go and switched to concerns about his health. "That Treadwell person is killin' you, Seth. Last week, I found another bottle of pills you're takin' and I don't even know what's wrong with you. Is it speed? Is that how this 'adapting' works? You go on drugs?"

"It's just Benzedrine. Coffee's not always handy."

Rosie gave him a look.

"And the caffeine was hurting my gut."

"Amphetamines will hurt it worse."

"Well, thank you, Doctor Edell. While we're on the subject of just saying no, how 'bout that pot you've been smoking? Have I ever bugged you about that? I suppose you'll say it's a peace pipe, integral to your religion?"

Rosie, miraculously inoculated at birth against temper tirades, reddened at Seth's demeaning reference to her Native American heritage. "You bastard," she said, clenching her fists. "I don't even know you anymore."

"See? It's not fun bein' judged, is it?" Seth ran fingers through his hair. "So how about a little live-and-let-live around here?"

The anger in their words stained the air and they withdrew into an edgy silence, fiddling with the grass at their feet, confused and troubled.

Ten minutes later, Rosie made the first move, suggesting they start over. Seth took her hand and they headed up a new trail, this one carpeted with pine needles with a creek running far below. Rosie was calm again, measured and reasonable, as she moved into the main item on her agenda: reassurance concerning their future. She held nothing back, spoke of her hopes for a house and a child of their own someday, and wondered aloud about Seth's view of their future, now that he had apparently won his battle with Treadwell and would soon be elected to the partnership.

They stopped to rest on a huge rock, worn smooth by time, where Seth listened to Rosie and stared through the tall pines at the shimmering Pacific and the cloudless sky overhead. He tried to stay focused on her words, but he had been living a day at a time for so long it was almost inconceivable for him to think in terms of five, ten, or twenty years ahead. He felt flat and exhausted, without sufficient resources to deal with Rosie's candor, yet unable to deny her right to honest answers. His face felt cold, and he put a hand to his stomach.

Rosie was looking at him, waiting. He stood up, squatted down to pick up a rock, carelessly tossed it into the trees, sat down again. "I don't know what to say, Rosie. My ideal dream home has always had wheels on it. I need some time to digest all this."

"That's why we're here, Seth. This may all seem sudden to

you, but I've been wonderin' these things for almost three years, and now I need to know where you stand. Where *we* stand."

Seth rose, hands thrust deep in pockets. "I hear you, honey. Give me another hour or two to think about what you've said. You're asking me to decide our entire future in just one weekend."

"More than that," said Rosie, taking his hand and turning him around to face her, "I'm askin' Seth Cameron to make the first emotional commitment of his entire life."

They separated, and Seth headed off on a trail winding northward, high above Highway 1, rarely out of view of the vast Pacific. Ten minutes into his walk, he was excited by the sight of two rare California condors soaring high overhead in and out of a film of stratocumulus clouds that had moved in from the west. Less majestic crows and magpies exchanged insults in the dense forest on either side of his path.

He picked up his pace, seeking a place where the lush pine and oak would not impede his view of the Pacific. Panting for air, he finally broke into an opening atop a large knoll and found a natural seat on the trunk of a fallen madrona. The burning in his stomach had eased, but Rosie was right: he was in terrible shape. She was right about other things as well, but her comment about emotional commitment had seemed pretty harsh. Sure, he was careful. You had to be.

As for his inattention to their relationship, he had no answer for that one. Did she really blame the work, or had she sensed his confused but tenacious longing for Elena? *Elena,* a disquieting song that he couldn't get out of his head, like a catchy commercial for a product you know is bad for you. Bad? Not really. A woman like Elena would be a tremendous asset to a partner in a white-shoe firm like M&M. *What am I thinking?* Was the clairvoyant Rosie reading these thoughts? She had not mentioned a psychic dream in almost a year—thank God—since the nightmare about the man being murdered. *Am I killing her dreams as well as her hopes?*

He leaned back into the tree's natural saddle and again scanned the horizon beyond the vast sea, but saw no answers there. All he saw was that the two "California condors" had circled much lower now, and that they were actually a pair of common turkey vultures.

*   *   *

On Monday, Seth was back in the office, facing a new day and, with luck, his last month as an associate at Miller and McGrath.

The weekend at Ventana had ended without resolution, but with a compromise that Rosie had accepted, influenced in no small part by the tranquil surroundings and Seth's renewed amorous attentions. On Sunday afternoon, she had granted him a four-month, pressure-free reprieve, to permit him to settle into his new and hopefully more relaxed life as an M&M partner, before demanding a decision about their future.

Rosie had resisted using "the M-word" all weekend, but marriage was a mutually understood objective, as was a dramatic change in Seth's lifestyle and focus. Otherwise, it was also understood that Rosie would return to Bakersfield.

Seth had gratefully accepted the arrangement and had even extracted conditions of his own. Rosie had agreed to make more of an effort to fit into the firm's social fabric, and to help Seth meet a partner's responsibility to attract new clients and entertain old ones. After a conversation that ranged from awkward to acrimonious, they negotiated a new "dress code" for partnership events, and Rosie volunteered that she would like to begin studies at Marin Community College in January.

Seth conceded that the pills had played no small part in the way his life was careening out of control, but they both realized he could do little to change things before the partnership vote. As a symbol of his new resolve, however, he had slept in until six that morning, and his first act upon arriving at the office had been to remove Elena Barton's telephone number from his Rolodex. She was, it now seemed, no longer a factor in his professional life, and now she must be excised from his personal fantasies as well.

But Seth was wrong on both counts, for late that very afternoon, following months of silence, Elena Barton appeared at his office and casually asked about the status of the case.

Summoning his poise, Seth told her that he had assumed she had lost interest and, therefore, had done nothing more. Elena seemed upset and assured him that she was as determined as ever to clear Sam's name. She had reluctantly avoided the "legal aspects" of her life on the advice of her grief counselor.

"The other reason I'm checking in," she said, relaxing into a smile, "is that my one-year period of mourning ended yesterday, and I've come to buy my lawyer a drink."

Seth's first reactions—surprise and disappointment, mingled with the unwanted pleasure of seeing her face—gave way to shock and anxiety as her words sunk in. *One year!* A seismic shudder of anxiety sent Seth's heart pounding against his rib cage. *"One year period of mourning . . . ended yesterday!"* Shaken, he took a deep breath and managed some casual conversation as he moved to a cabinet, removed her file, and checked the date of Barton's death recorded on his first memorandum. She was right. The date of accident was October 15, 1992. A glance down at his calendar confirmed his worst fears: the one-year statute of limitations for filing Elena's suit had run the day before!

He lunged back toward his desk, vaguely aware that Elena was saying something. Eyes darting back and forth across his desk, he rummaged through the mass of papers on his desk until he found the printout of his master calendar memo for the previous week.

There was no entry for *Barton vs. InterContinental Aerospace!*

He grabbed the case file again—Elena's presence now forgotten—the date of death still read October 15, 1992. He collapsed into his chair as his mind raced frantically. *Why didn't the expiration date show up on my master calendar memo? Did I forget to enter the date of death when Elena first came in? Did my secretary forget? Could I have written down the date incorrectly when I first met her, then carried the error over onto the calendar? But shit, it's not just in the wrong place, it's not* anywhere! *No mention of the case!*

"Seth?" Her voice drifted in as if from a great distance. "Is something wrong?"

He started to reply, but his mouth was already dry as resin and his overloaded brain was too busy trying to reason away the apparent reality. *Maybe you don't count both the first and last dates in computing when the statue-of-limitations period expires. If that's the case, screw the master calendar, I could still file a complaint today!*

"No," said Seth, forcing a smile and glancing at his watch. "I'm sorry. It's just that I remembered something I'm supposed to be doing right now. I wasn't expecting you, remember? Can you maybe kill an hour shopping and return at five?"

"Killing an hour shopping is easy. Stopping after the hour is up is the problem. If I'm not back by five, call 911 and give them my description."

Seth couldn't think of a witty rejoinder as he escorted her out the door to the elevator. He started to ask his secretary to go get him a plaintiff's personal-injury form, but thought better of it. *Can't trust anyone with this for now.* Instead, he called an independent court-filing service, ordered a rush pickup for an immediate filing, then pounded down two flights of stairs to the law library, snatched a wrongful-death complaint form from the files, and hurriedly filled it out. In the space for "Plaintiff's Counsel," he inserted his own name—an interim device to avoid embarrassment to the firm if the complaint later had to be dismissed—then sealed the document in an envelope together with the filing fee, handed it to the receptionist, and ran back to the library.

Deep in the stacks, he grabbed a copy of the annotated *California Code of Civil Procedure* and pawed through the index. Half-blinded by anxiety, he stared at a page that he had inadvertently ripped right out of the book.

Words. Confusing, obfuscating, legalese bullshit words. *Why can't they just fucking say what they mean?* After five frustrating minutes in the *Code of Civil Procedure* and the *Government Code*, he found his answer, an answer as clear and definitive as death itself. The statute of limitations had run on the fifteenth, yesterday. Elena's case had irrevocably expired, as had his dream of partnership in Miller and McGrath.

Or anywhere else in the free world.

"Are you *certain?*" She smiled, as if she thought he might be testing her. "It just sounds like a technicality, Seth. You lawyers are supposed to be able to leap technicalities with a single bound."

"Elena, I'm sorry, but this is no joke. The statute has run."

"There *must* be some mistake! The law can't possibly be so unforgiving!"

Seth could not meet her eyes.

"Law is by definition 'unforgiving,' Elena, and my disregard of it is both irreversible and inexcusable. Your only recourse now is to the firm's malpractice insurance. You should consult an independent lawyer about that. A *real* lawyer," he added bitterly, then swept an arm across his desk, sending pens, papers, paperweights, and a desk clock flying. He kicked his chair out of the way, sending it smashing into the adjacent wall, then turned his back and stared out the window.

A grim silence followed Seth's outburst of self-flagellation, broken finally by the soft, childlike sound of Elena's giving way to tears. Seth wanted to turn, take her in his arms, beg her forgiveness. Put his life in her hands.

But he couldn't bear to face her. Nolo contendere.

"I'll call in the morning," she said at last, and silently left his office.

I've seen 'em all, kid. I've seen the wise ones, the cool ones, and the smart-ass punks who'll fight like a tiger, then turn around and beat themselves.

BUT IT WAS TREADWELL, NOT ELENA, WHO CALLED THE NEXT DAY TO request Seth's immediate presence. Elena was there, wearing a dark midcalf dress, a gray scarf and hat, and a mood as somber as the first day he met her. Allston Addams was there, too. A witness to the execution.

"Elena—Mrs. Barton—has informed me of your dereliction, Cameron, and of her justified intention to sue this firm for malpractice. It appears to her to be the only remaining means by which she might achieve her objective. In the circumstances, I can hardly dissuade her. Do you have anything to say for yourself?"

Seth glanced at Elena, but she stared resolutely at the floor.

"Nothing," Seth said.

"All right, then," Treadwell said crisply, turning to Elena. "Would you excuse us now, dear. I'll call you at home later."

Elena left and Treadwell started in. "You've caused nothing but trouble since the day you arrived, Cameron. Despite this, I've given you every opportunity to show us you belong here, but—"

"Spare me the lecture, Treadwell," Seth said, rising to his feet. "I'm out of here."

"Cameron, Cameron," said the senior partner to Seth's back, "you are so predictable."

As Seth passed through the reception area on the way to clear out his desk, he saw Elena waiting at the elevator.

"Elena," he said, "I'm real sorry about all this. I'd like to talk to you. Later, of course."

An elevator door opened. "There's nothing you can say or do now," she said, then brushed past him and entered the car. He took her by the arm, but she spun away.

He held the door to keep it from closing. "Elena. *Please.* I know I screwed up, but I'd like to explain how it all happened."

Elena said nothing.

"Christ, woman, give me a break. I've lost *everything!*"

Fire suddenly swept through Elena's lifeless eyes. "You dare speak to me of loss? A year ago a friend reported the death of my husband. Yesterday, you reported the death of his honor. Now release the elevator."

Seth was out of words, and the doors closed between them.

Typical of M&M efficiency, a young man from administrative services was waiting in Seth's office with Bekins boxes. "I've been asked to help you with your things," he said with the detachment of a priest offering to administer the last rites. *He's done this before,* thought Seth.

It was finished in under twenty minutes, and now it was Seth heading for the elevator. He heard footsteps behind him and turned to see Harry Cooper puffing down the hallway.

"Jesus, Seth, I just heard. What the hell?"

"Yeah, Harry, what the hell."

"I'll call you tonight. Is there anything I can do to help?"

Seth shook his head. "We all have to help ourselves, Harry." Seth took his friend's extended hand and added, "Good luck on your partnership vote next month," as the elevator doors closed on Harry's forlorn face.

Part 3

THE HIGH-PITCHED RINGING SOUND ROCKETED OUT OF NOWHERE AND ricocheted around his brain, pushing against the back of his eye sockets like pressure trying to release itself. He could neither stop the sound nor identify its origin, so he knew he must be dreaming.

But now an explosion, closer to the surface of his consciousness. A door slamming? Footsteps? *Where was he?*

"Seth! Wake up."

The ringing stopped but the pressure was still there. He was being shaken. He was waking up.

Rosie's voice cut through the fog. "Didn't you hear the phone, Seth? It's Leviticus Heywood. He says he worked for you as an investigator on the Huey case and at M and M."

Seth muttered a pessimistic appraisal of his ability to form a complete sentence and added that he didn't want to speak with anyone, save perhaps a doctor.

"He says it's important," she insisted.

Seth was aware of his legs being roughly grabbed, then swung around so that his bare feet were now on the cold hardwood floor. He hurt everywhere, so at least he must be alive. Another comforting thought because, despite everything, he wanted to be alive. It was the business of living he wanted nothing to do with. Like talking on telephones. Dealing with people, calendars, regulations, computers. Failure.

"Yeah," he managed into the telephone Rosie had jammed into his hand.

"You sick, Cowboy? You sound awful."

"Just a mild stroke, Lev. What's up?"

"I've got this client in San Fran. Good lawyer. I do all her family-law and personal-injury investigation work. She's interviewing, looking to hire an associate. You interested?"

Seth rubbed his temples, took the coffee cup Rosie handed him. Tried to remember where he had been last night, how he had gotten home. His jaw ached and he noticed that his knuckles where skinned and bruised.

"Can I call you back in a few minutes, Lev?"

Rising unsteadily to his feet, he hung up the telephone and told Rosie it was Leviticus Heywood, a guy he had worked with, and Rosie reminded him she had just told him that. Her ubiquitous smile was nowhere in sight. Nor in prospect.

"I smell coffee," he said hopefully.

"It's in your hand," she said, and there it was. "I thought you'd given up interviewin' here. You said you were a piranha in San Francisco; that fourteen rejections in five weeks was enough."

"A pariah."

"Whatever. A dead duck once they checked your references."

"All roads lead to Treadwell."

Seth drank from the cup, but the process of awakening only intensified the pain in his head and jaw. "Has it really been five weeks?"

"And three days," she said, beginning to make up the bed with him still half in it, "though you've slept and drank your way through most of them. When you weren't watching daytime TV."

He went to the kitchen and splashed cold water on his face.

"You look terrible," she said. "I think you lost."

"What?"

"The fight you must have been in to end up lookin' so poorly."

He didn't remember a fight, but couldn't deny it.

"So what will you tell this Leviticus person?"

Seth looked at his reflection in the kitchen window, raked his wet hair back, collapsed in a dinette chair.

"I know what you're thinking, Rosie, but I can't go back to the Valley. Not yet."

Rosie stared at him for a minute, then opened the back door that led out into the garden. "Your cereal's in the pot," she said, and left him sitting there, his head in both hands.

* * *

"Let's not waste time bullshitting each other, kid," Allyn Friedlander told Seth the next day, only moments after they had been introduced. "Leviticus here has filled me in on your misadventures with the blue-blood barons of Montgomery Street."

Seth could think of nothing to say, so he nodded into the ensuing silence.

"He also says you're a tough guy; bounced around the NFL for four years."

"Three seasons, actually."

"Says you were tough, but too small."

Lev shook his head. "I said he was too slow. The kid had white-man's disease."

"You're both right," said Seth. "I was small, but slow."

Allyn let out a cackle. "Then you must have been a fighter to survive three seasons."

"He made Jack Tatum look like St. Francis," said Lev, "but you know what they say about livin' by the sword? The man took so many chugs to the head, couldn't keep the defensive signals straight anymore. Nothin' left but to quit and become a lawyer."

Seth had to smile, seeing Lev selling him so hard. Courage and grit must be near the top of this particular job description.

"At least," Seth rejoined, winking at Allyn, "I left the league on two feet."

"Okay, boys," said Allyn, "let's cut the macho bullshit and talk some business." Rings dazzling on ropelike fingers, hands like baseball gloves, an incongruous turquoise squash-blossom necklace adorning the multilayered throat. A piece of work. Swinging her cigar like a baton between them every time she made a point, Allyn Friedlander's gruff directness and formidable size—Seth figured her for just under six feet and 180 pounds—was neutralized by eyes that outdazzled the rings and a broad smile that, like a prison riot, broke out at unlikely times and seemed even to surprise herself.

Seth liked the rough-cut woman immediately, but the weeks of Cuervo meditation following his departure from M&M had rendered his stomach particularly vulnerable to the ominous cloud of gray-blue smoke that engulfed him every time she waved the cigar. Nonetheless, he fought off the impulse to wave back, for his ego had been savaged to the point where even the act of boarding a bus in the morning—the Porsche was back in the body shop—was seen as a test of competence and courage. He also refrained from telling Allyn Friedlander that Lev had filled him in on her as well.

"I got to know her when I was a cop before I went private and started doing her investigation work," Leviticus Heywood had said. "She chain-smokes industrial-strength cigars, chews nails for breakfast, and washes them down with high-test caffeine."

"She sounds lovely," Seth had said.

"She's always looking to bag the big-time case, the Big Score, but her practice has been the typical Mission Street stuff: divorce work, defending junkies, DWIs, anything that can make it up two flights to her office. No elevator," Lev added unnecessarily with a shrug of his shoulders.

"Sounds lovely," Seth repeated. "Any other glowing reasons I should want to work for her?"

"Three that come to mind. First, she's as smart as they come. Savvy. New York transplant. Might even teach a hotshot honkie cowboy a thing or two if he keeps his eyes and ears open. Second, she was a lady trial lawyer long before the women's movement made it commonplace; balls as big as her heart. I figure she wouldn't be afraid to . . ."

"Take a chance on a screwup who nobody else in town will give the time of day to?"

Lev had shrugged again before adding, "You need a job?"

"Hell, Lev, you know I do."

"That's the third reason."

"Look, kid," said Allyn Friedlander after Lev had run off to pick up his wife, "we all make mistakes. Problem is we trial lawyers can't hide our fuck-ups like builders can or bury 'em six feet under like doctors do." She paused to knock a two-inch ash off her cigar. "So a mistake—even a big one—doesn't bother me so long as it doesn't bother you. Know what I mean? So forget about it, okay? It's old business. You've obviously got a brain, and Lev says you're a hell of a trial lawyer. My only question is whether you can contribute to the moral and monetary welfare of the law offices of Allyn Friedlander; namely me." This said, accompanied by another vigorous brandishing of her cigar, she leaned back in her swivel chair and slung a long leg up onto her desk before adding, "*If* I hired you."

"What would I be doing for you?" asked Seth as Friedlander paused for a moment, winded from her peroration. "If you hired me."

"All the things I don't want to do myself. That straight enough?"

Seth said it was.

"It's lunchtime," she said, abruptly slamming a wooden gavel down on her desk so hard Seth nearly jumped to his feet. "No intercom," said Allyn as her secretary floated into her office.

"You called, madam?"

"Meet Mr. Cameron, Ramon. You hungry?"

"You bet, Boss Woman," said Ramon, eyeing Seth as he spoke.

"I was referring to our honored guest, Ramon."

"So was I, Great Mother."

Allyn rolled her eyes. "Don't mind Ramon. He fantasizes a life in stand-up comedy. He's using me as a temporary stepping-stone."

"I live only to serve thee, mighty Queen of Jurisprudence."

"Oh, Jesus," she said, replacing the gavel. "So, Seth, how's about a kosher submarine?"

"Sounds good."

Scribbling their orders on a piece of paper, she stuck it on a large paper clip tied to a string and, without looking, pitched it out the window down into the alley below. She noticed Seth's look and explained that a boy named Miguel walked by just before noon every day and would deliver their order by twelve-fifteen. "I also hate telephones," she added. "Now, if you're through asking questions, shall we get to work?"

Seth rose to his feet and stared out the window, down the alley into the dusty din of traffic and predominantly Latin humanity milling on Mission Street. A carpet company across the street announced it was Going Out of Business! in letters so large people might believe it this time. Every shop within his vision had a 40%-60% SALE sign. A Hispanic street sweeper, probably a misdemeanor probationer working off soft time, speared discarded advertising handouts from the sidewalks and gutters nearly as fast as the woman across the street could distribute them. Seth's mind drifted back to his encounter with the boy from El Salvador the day he and Rosie were lost in the outskirts of Modesto, heading for his confrontation with Sterritt Malm.

So full of hope. A hundred years ago.

"Hello? Earth to Cameron!" Allyn Friedlander's gravel voice jerked him back to the here and now. He stared out the window for another few seconds anyway, his gaze drifting northward toward Montgomery Street, where the Pacific Towers loomed above its older neighbors. If Allyn Friedlander could have seen Seth's face at that moment, she would have observed lips suddenly tightened into a straight line and his hand pushing against his stomach. She would have seen those bloodless lips move slightly as he silently vowed that somehow, someday, he would find his way back onto Montgomery Street.

And once there, he would deal with Anthony Treadwell.

"That was an offer, kid," she added.

"I know," he said. "Let's get to work."

Odd that it would be the money that set Rosie off. Odd, because money was usually the last thing on her mind. Even now, as they stood glaring at each other in their Mill Valley kitchen, it was not the paltry amount of Seth's new salary that had shattered her determination to fake an enthusiastic response to his "good news," but the fact that not only was he staying on in the city, but for even less money than he had been making in Bakersfield. That cooked it for Rosie. Less money for the privilege of working for a divorce lawyer on Mission Street!

"It's a living."

"It's surviving, not living."

"Well, Jesus Christ! What happened to my barefoot girl from the Black Hills? Does the granddaughter of the Sioux need more wampum all of a sudden?"

"That's crude, Seth, even for you. Besides, they were Iroquois."

"Well, I got nothing against Indians—Sioux or Iroquois—but I read somewhere that ninety tribes own casino licenses now, which in my book doesn't do a hell of a lot for their spiritual image."

Rosie's dark eyes flashed. "Perfect, Seth. Here we are in a country that makes three hundred guns every hour of the day and you want to jump on Native Americans for playin' bingo."

Seth glowered back. "My point is simply that we'll still have more money than most Americans, certainly most Native Americans."

"And my point is that it doesn't matter how much we've got if you hate what you're doing. What is it you really *want*, Seth Cameron?" she added, throwing her hands in the air, then slapping them to her hips. "Do you have a *clue?*"

"Sure, I know what I want, and so do you."

"No, I *don't* know. Alls I know is we're miserable here, you're drunk most of the time, and now you're commencin' to take a job doin' work you'll hate, for less money than you could make back home where we have friends and could live for half what it costs us here!"

"Since when did you worry so much about money?"

"I'm worried about you. And *us.*"

"A second chance," Seth whispered.

"*What?*"

"You asked me what I want. That's what I want. A second chance."

Rosie stopped what she was doing and turned toward Seth, her eyes searching his face as if for the first time. The sadness in those beautiful eyes as she studied him broke his heart. He felt his own eyes tearing as she reached up and, like a blind person, gently traced the lines etched in his face. Her fingers were warm on his skin and he turned his head so that he could brush his lips against the palm of her hand.

But Rosie gave a quick shake of her head and slowly withdrew her hand. "You'll never leave this place, will you, Seth?" she said in a voice like muffled gunfire. "No matter how I feel or what they do to you and no matter how little they pay you or what you have to do for it. You'll never quit until you find whatever it is you came here for."

Seth rubbed his face with open palms, but said nothing. Rosie straightened, brushed imaginary lint from the front of her skirt, and took a deep breath.

"Seth, darlin'," Rosie said, a tremor invading her voice, "I talked to Aunt Claire a while ago. She's decided to move directly. Back to Bakersfield."

Seth took a step toward her, but Rosie turned sideways and moved back as she continued speaking. "I was thinkin' I might pay her a visit next month, seein' you're settled in a new job now. Maybe see . . . you know, what's available there."

Seth started to speak, but Rosie stopped him with the slightest motion of her hand. "I've been in the slow readin' group, Seth, but now that it's plain where *your* heart is, I think it's time for me to stop listenin' to mine."

"Rosie, I—"

"And maybe start listenin' to my head."

She turned and was down the hall before Seth could begin to breathe again.

SETH'S NEW OFFICE WAS A CONVERTED SUPPLY ROOM BARELY LARGE enough to accommodate his worktable—Allyn had said a month earlier that a desk was on its way—and two cast-off client chairs. The only similarity with his old office was that his view through the west window featured the east brick wall of the adjacent building. He shared Ramon with Allyn, an arrangement that would never have worked out but for Ramon's incredible job skills and his obvious infatuation with Seth.

Files were spread everywhere in the cramped quarters, mostly divorce matters and collection cases, plus a smattering of insurance subrogation claims, a plethora of *pro bono* landlord-tenant disputes, and three fender-bender personal-injury suits that Seth prayed would get to trial without settling.

Allyn kept the infrequent trials for herself, the sole bone of contention between them during their first nine weeks together. Thus Seth's days were spent appearing at show-cause matters before the family-law magistrate, taking quicky depositions (for which he had no time to prepare), writing dunning letters to debtors, and fighting eviction notices for deadbeat tenants. He told Lev he had no idea how she had kept it all going before taking him on.

"What's keeping *you* going, my man?" Lev replied. "Not that I feel responsible, you understand, but you're working in a shit-hole doing shit work and it escapes me how this ever gets you back on Montgomery Street. Not that I feel responsible."

"I'm still in San Francisco, Lev, which means I'm still in the game. For now, I'm just surviving, one day at a time."

"That's what prisoners I interviewed out at San Quentin used to tell me, Cowboy. Then one day they'd die."

"Don't worry about me, Lev. I'm going to save dying for last."

Lev opened his notebook to copy names and addresses from the file Seth had asked him to work on. "Uh-huh," he muttered, and began scribbling. As he wrote, Seth studied his friend and concluded the years had not been kind. The ex-49er halfback had gained weight in all the wrong places, and his massive brow sprouted beads of sweat now with the slightest exertion. His features forged a contrast in force and kindness—carbon-black skin tightly drawn over a montage of flat surfaces that surrounded eyes too large and gentle for the rest of his face. His short-cropped hair was nearly white.

The two men had met during the 1978 season, but Seth had been surprised Lev remembered him. Seth had been a rookie cornerback on the taxi squad and Leviticus Heywood was a star. Their relationship that year was purely physical: Lev's foot planted briefly in Seth's chest as he ran over him during practice.

As for Lev's current skepticism concerning Seth's professional future, Seth could have thrown the futility issue right back in the face of a Vietnam vet who had been a hot running back for the 49ers—a first-round draft pick, then runner-up rookie of the year, headed for the Hall of Fame—until a torn anterior cruciate ligament in his knee early in his second season ended his football career and his hopes for fame and fortune. After a hitch in the S.F. Police Department's burglary detail, he went private in 1986 and, like Allyn, had survived since that time mostly on divorce tails and intersection crashes. From Heisman Trophy runner-up at Southern Cal and NFL stardom to peekaboo work and a one-bedroom box of a house in South San Francisco, all accomplished in eight short years. Seth had managed to get his friend two lucrative assignments at Miller and McGrath—making Lev the only black man Seth had ever seen at M&M during daylight hours—but with Seth's demise, Lev was back to the ragbag business.

Seth wondered if Lev knew he was really talking about himself when he had characterized Allyn Friedlander as someone looking for that One Big Score that would be her ticket out of the purgatory of mediocrity to which she had been consigned.

Or if Lev knew he was also talking about Seth Cameron.

THE DAY SHE CAME WAS LIKE ANY OTHER. SETH WAS BURIED IN FRENzied efforts to get Ramon's attention to complete a filing on schedule while at the same time frantically looking for some lost documents so he could prepare for the deposition of a father in a bitter child custody case, plus screaming at a landlord who had just filed a three-day notice against his client on one line, while screaming at his client for not paying his rent on the other.

A day like any other. The day she came.

Elena Barton was the last person on earth he expected, yet when he heard a voice say his name, he didn't have to look up to see who it was. He turned slowly in fact, concealing his eagerness and savoring the moment of first sight, momentarily forgetting his embarrassment at his surroundings. At what he had become.

"Hello, Elena," he said, sounding as cool as she had. Hard to imagine, but the woman was even more beautiful than he remembered. He rose to his feet and worked his way around the table to turn a chair for her to sit down. The chair got caught in the leg of the table, and when he gave it a jerk, the leg of the chair broke off. She tried not to laugh and he said, we're redecorating, can you tell? and they laughed together, the tension relieved.

"There's a coffee shop downstairs that makes a tolerable *caffé latte*," he said, and soon they were sitting in a booth, facing each other, taking each other in. Elena's pale green eyes were just as he had remembered them, though softer now, forgiving. He found it hard to keep his head clear. Glancing around, Seth saw that all eyes in the restaurant—men and women alike—were on her, wondering who she was, this woman with a face that drew attention to itself without effort. *What was she doing here?*

Then, finally, she told him.

She told him that no capable lawyer would take her case against Miller and McGrath. She told him of her anger and frustration, of her feelings of isolation and helplessness. Then she told him that another X-215A had just crashed and killed Lt. Lee Andrews—"labeled pilot error again, of course"—and that had given her a new idea.

"Four crashes in less than two years can't all be pilot error, Seth. Sam was right—there's something terribly wrong with that airplane. I've talked to the senior test pilot. Remember Crispie— Major Christopher—Sam's best friend? I told you about him . . . before. Anyway, my thought is that if we could just get some kind of evidence against ConSpace now that they've had this new failure, we could force them to admit Sam's crash wasn't his fault. What do you think?"

The waitress brought their coffee, giving Seth a minute to think. "You understand," he said, the words nearly choking him, "that we have no recourse to the courts whatsoever."

"But we have access to the *public*, Seth," she said, leaning toward him. "Our lawsuit may be dead, but we can still threaten a public relations battle they won't dare fight right now. Look at how quickly the media goes into a feeding frenzy these days."

"That's usually murder cases."

"I'm sure my father will seriously consider doing me in." Seth couldn't miss the spark in her usually soft eyes, the firming of her chin, when she mentioned her father.

"It's impossible, Elena. With no lawsuit, we'd have no subpoena power. Besides, the stuff that would help us is probably all classified top secret and beyond the reach of a subpoena anyway."

She nodded to show she knew that, but didn't he at least owe her a shot at it? An effort at coming up with something creative? She was fighting back tears. Didn't he know an investigator who could go undercover or something?

Seth looked down at his coffee cup because he couldn't bear to meet her gaze. Someone behind him spilled a glass of water and shouted for a towel.

"Please, Seth. Just say you'll try. Sam's good name is all I have left of him."

He stirred the nutmeg into the whipped cream into the coffee, then carefully laid the straw beside the cup.

"There may be one way in. The recent widow—Mrs. Andrews—would she bring a suit?"

Elena shot him a pained look. "Not a chance. Shirley Andrews is the daughter of an Air Force general. Whole family's gung ho and she's moved back in with her parents now. She stopped speaking to me when I make the mistake of telling her I was trying to hire Miller and McGrath after Sam's death. Wouldn't even take my calls last week."

Seth hesitated, seemed to go inside himself for a minute. Elena sipped her *latte*, her eyes locked onto his.

"I do owe you, Elena," he said at last, "and I'll look into it. Give me Major Christopher's telephone number and I'll talk with him. But first, I'll have to clear it with Allyn Friedlander."

"The boss?"

"She could be held responsible if anything goes wrong, plus she keeps me busy ten hours a day."

"But you will talk to her?" Elena said, putting her small hand over his.

It was the touch of a supplicant, not a seductress, but it sent an electric current up his spine and into his temples, stinging his face. He could hardly bear the intensity in her eyes, which—was it the light?—seemed to have turned a deeper shade of green. He felt a dampness across his back. Her voice was pleading, as gentle as Vivaldi, yet sounding an alarm somewhere deep in Seth's intuitive nature, a crazy sense of irresistible danger.

He drained his coffee cup with his free hand, then tapped on the tabletop with the straw.

"All right, let's go up and talk to her."

ALLYN WENT ALONG, BUT NOT BEFORE TELLING SETH HE SHOULD SEE A shrink; anybody in his right mind could see that Elena Barton was a disaster looking for a place to happen.

"Hold your horses, Cowboy," she told him. "First, nobody, I mean *nobody*, is *that* gorgeous. Even Ramon's salivating. Second, she's got the desperate but determined look of E.T. trying to get home. Third, you're messing with the military industrial complex, and fourth, you're too damn busy. You're up to your chin in swamp water and she's handing you an anvil." But Seth stood his ground and promised to do whatever he did for Elena on his own time. In the end, Allyn agreed, but insisted on complete deniability. "If the shit hits the fan, Cowboy, I don't even know you."

Rosie was tougher. "I can't believe you're doin' this, Seth. Not even a dumb ol' cat jumps up on a hot stove twice."

"I owe her, Rosie," he had said, sitting down to the dinner table. But Rosie just said "umm-hmm" and reminded him that she had seen Elena Barton's picture in the newspaper. Seth's efforts to convince her that this was a chance to salvage a measure of self-respect fell on deaf ears. A meal taken in silence.

Lev had been the easiest. "Give me a chance to screw the U.S. government and I normally do it for free." Then he smiled his big harmonica smile and added, "In your case, however, I'll need expenses and two hundred and fifty dollars a day."

Within a week, Elena returned with Maj. Jack Christopher in tow. He had flown out military transport on short notice; figured he owed Sam that much, he said, and would do whatever he could to help. The problem was he was unable to add much to what Seth's search of reported news events had already revealed.

Yes, Sam was one of the best, probably incapable of pilot error. No, Sam never told him what he thought was wrong with the X-215A, just that he was fairly sure what it was. Yes, Gerald Murphy—another test pilot in the unit—claimed to have talked with Barton about a specific problem with the aircraft, but Murphy was now refusing to say anything for fear of compromising his request for transfer to the Nellis Gunnery School at Las Vegas. No, Murphy wouldn't meet with Seth. No way. Yes, Christopher would keep his eyes and ears open. No, he could not compromise his top-secret clearance by providing any documentation on the aircraft. Yes, he realized that if Sam were right, he could be the next to die, but that was his job. And so on.

When pushed concerning possible problems with the X-215A, Christopher just shrugged and said, "The bird is tricky, but that's why we have test pilots."

"But Elena here tells me that Sam was sure something was wrong," said Seth, "that he was pushing the brass to ground the X-215A until the true cause of the failures was corrected. She thinks he was nearly certain what was wrong. Didn't he even give you a hint?"

Christopher crossed his long legs, glanced uneasily at Elena, and exhaled. "Sam wasn't always . . . rational."

"What do you mean?" asked Seth, dreading the answer.

"Sam *was* a great pilot, but he was also an obsessive worrier," said Christopher, lighting a cigarette and glancing at Elena again. "Hell, Lanie, you know that better than anyone. He had the talent of a top gun, but not the temperament. After Grant Wilburn crashed—Grant was the second one to go down, Penrod was first—Sam became obsessed with finding out why. He was driving everybody on the base batshit."

Seth looked at Elena for a reaction, but she was staring out the window.

Seth tried a small fender bender the next day in municipal court, but went back to work on Elena's case as soon as he could. Got nowhere. Managed to pry the name of ConSpace's senior technical representative out of Crispie, but when he finally got through to Harold Bostwick, he received the standard reply: "We are not free to discuss any aspect of top-secret classified information."

Three weeks later, still nothing and nowhere to go. He dreaded making the call to Elena, becoming the agent of yet another wounding disappointment. He stared at a sheaf of newspapers Ramon had collected for him from October 15 to mid-November 1992: the *Times*, the *Post*, and the two local dailies, the *Chronicle* and the afternoon *Examiner*. He read and reread the various news accounts about the crash—small articles on back pages. When Ramon interrupted to get his signature on several dictated letters, Seth signed without even reading them or looking up.

"Well, aren't we Mr. Warmth today," said Ramon in a hurt tone. "Here's the subpoena in the Dickson custody case."

Seth grunted a thanks.

The third time through the clippings, however, a short article in the business section of the *Chronicle* caught Seth's attention. One of ConSpace's suppliers and its chief executive officer had been under attack by the Justice Department for securities violations and income tax evasion. Nothing had come of either the SEC or the Tax Division investigation. Ramon came back in with fresh coffee and a cookie "to soothe the savage beastie," which Seth accepted with a nod.

"Oh, wonderful!" said the secretary in a sardonic tone. "It's *coffee* and my very favorite raisin-oatbran cookie! How can I ever thank you enough, Ramon dearest."

Seth looked up. "Sorry, Ramon. Did you say something?"

"I said you'd better review that subpoena, you heartless slave driver."

Seth raised his head. "Subpoena?"

"Yes, you asked for a subpoena."

"*Subpoena!*"

"Are you all right?"

"That's it! Of course! A *subpoena!* That's how we do it!" He grabbed the article and headed for Allyn's office. "Ramon, you *are* wonderful."

"Dinner tonight, then?" said Ramon to the empty doorway. "Shall we say, eight?"

"I have an idea," Seth began as Allyn lit a fresh cigar. He laid out a plan to file a stockholders' suit against TDA, Inc., the incriminated manufacturing company, seeking damages from its billionaire chief executive officer for subjecting his company to charges of illegal activities.

"It works for both of us, Allyn! You could hit big time if even half of the stories about this con man are true, and I'd get the subpoena power against a major supplier that might lead me to something on ConSpace."

Allyn thumbed through the clippings, humming occasionally and ignoring the ash that extended precariously from her cigar. Seth watched her, wishing for the first time in years that he had a cigarette.

"Where's your business plan?" she said at last, staring at him over her thick glasses.

"Business plan?'

"Is there an echo in here? Yes, a *business plan*, as in how much is this going to cost me versus how much I stand to make if we hit? You know, risk-benefit analysis? I'm running a business here, Cowboy."

They argued the matter for another twenty minutes as Seth became increasingly impatient. Abruptly then, he placed both hands on her desk, leaned as close to her as the stench of the ubiquitous cigar would permit, and unleashed a white-water torrent of words: "Jesus, Allyn. You want a fucking risk-benefit analysis, here it is. You fund the costs of litigation up to fifty thousand dollars. That's your risk.

"Anything over that I fund on an IOU against future salary. I do all the work on my own time except for what you want to do yourself. This guy has cost his company nearly ten million dollars in legal fees alone, plus another one hundred million dollars or so the SEC claims he ripped off his stockholders. Your fee if we settle or win a verdict could run into tens of millions— and you keep every cent. *That's your goddam benefit, okay?"*

Allyn slammed her gavel down hard, but Seth didn't blink. "Some coffee, Ramon!" she said. "Make it high-test."

She began shuffling through the clippings again as a siren screamed out on the street below. Seth's eyes burned from the cigar smoke, but he kept them locked on hers, looking for a sign. The large clock behind her desk struck three o'clock.

"Oh, all right, Seth," she said finally, leaning so far back in her huge leather chair Seth was sure it would collapse, "let's sue the fucker. I'll draft a simple but unconscionable agreement between the two of us, and you go ahead and draft a complaint against . . . what's his name?"

"Olmstead," said Seth, leaping to his feet. "Operates out of the Caicos Islands. Aubrey Olmstead."

For the first time since he had arrived in San Francisco, Seth left his office at four in the afternoon. And for the first time since his firing, he felt the spine-tingling hope of redemption. His strategy seemed laid out as clearly as stones on a desert floor. The derivative suit would be filed in three days. Subpoenas would follow. If Elena was right, he would find fire under the smoke of four deadly X-215A crashes. A private threat to go public, and ConSpace would cave in to his simple demands that they pressure the U.S. Air Force to correct the record on Sam Barton's file—the hell with the others—and hand over a modest hundred thousand or so to buy Elena's eternal silence.

Then he would put himself back on the market. *Well, yes,* he would say, *there was a problem at M&M, but it was strictly a personality thing with a key partner. I'm sure that the most senior trial lawyer there—Charles Branch—would be happy to provide you with the firm's perspective. In confidence, of course. The statute problem? A tempest in a teapot. The client is completely satisfied; got just what she wanted without the anguish of reliving the experience in a public courtroom. Here is a copy of her letter of appreciation, and I'm sure she would also be happy to talk with you.*

His mind raced with the possibilities. But first things first: a surprise celebration dinner for Rosie she would never forget. They'd start with a bottle of decent champagne at home, then special reservations at Star's at six. He would assure Rosie he was himself again—off the tequila—and lay out his plan for getting back on the fast track, but this time starting without two strikes against him. That would be the hardest sell—out would come the bottle of champagne at this point—convincing her it would be different next time around. Change her mind about leaving. She would be a part of the new firm from the start, and no more all-nighters at the office either. She'd be skeptical, but she would listen.

He stopped at the little flower stall on Lombard to pick up two dozen Sterling roses, her favorite.

* * *

He could tell she was gone long before he saw the note—tell it the minute he walked in the door—but he ran from room to room anyway, shouting her name. Checked all the rooms, every empty dresser drawer, every barren closet shelf. Ran to the kitchen and saw there the note with his name on the outside. Stared at it for a minute, eyes blurred by his pounding heart. He knew what was written inside, and from inside himself came a gravelly roar, a convulsive animal protest against the reality of what he also knew: he was alone again.

The flowers fell from his hand as he picked up the note. He turned it over and over, then pressed it against his cheek and let the tears come.

He awoke the next morning at nine. Allyn would be pissed, though she ought to be impressed that he still had a pulse after the amount of tequila his liver had been processing the past fifteen hours.

He climbed the two flights of stairs, panting at the top like Sir Edmund Hillary astride Everest. He headed straight for the coffee, then locked himself in his office to reread Rosie's note for the fortieth time.

> Dearest Seth:
>
> You knew I would have to go sometime and now your settled and everthing in your new job so it just seems to me times good as any. Or as bad as most. Anyways, I love you Seth and always will, but I can't watch any more. It hurts to much.
>
> I know now you cant stop what your doing so please don't call me it will just hurt us both. Cause I cant change any more either.
>
> Love always,
> Rosie Wheeler

The brief letter he scribbled to Aunt Claire, enclosing a check that cleaned out his savings, asked her to anonymously parcel out the money to Rosie whenever she needed it to get resettled.

Seth turned to the mail. A square envelope from Miller and McGrath announced Harry Cooper's election to partnership. Despite everything—including a sudden stab of pain in his stomach as the words sunk home—he was glad for Harry and vowed to write him a note.

Grabbing another cup of coffee, he began to draft a shareholder derivative complaint against a man he had never met, in behalf of a class-action client he had yet to find.

A MONTH LATER, SETH FOUND HIMSELF MIRED DOWN IN ALLYN'S "RAG-bag" of trivial disputes and lost causes, still getting nowhere with his investigation of ConSpace or Aubrey Olmstead's TDA, depressed over Rosie's departure, and generally miserable. Desperate to ward off a growing sense of déjà vu failure on Elena's problem, he persuaded Allyn to fund a trip to New Orleans, where he had arranged a meeting with the deputy U.S. Attorney in the tax division of the Justice Department who had tried to indict Aubrey Olmstead. To his amazement, Allyn had decided at the last minute to go along.

"I won't get in your way, kid," she told him the day before his departure. "I just want to see Bourbon Street and try some of that crawfish gumbo and étouffée I've heard so much about."

"You didn't like my famous Étouffée Cameron?" Seth had been a short-order cook as part of his athletic scholarship program at Cal, and with Rosie gone, he had taken up cooking as a practical avocation.

"Just want to check out your imitators."

Allyn turned out to be more useful than either of them expected, first serving as a referee between Seth and William Torville, a condescending and priggish graduate of Harvard Law whose IQ obviously exceeded his not inconsiderable weight. It was enmity at first sight as Seth listened to the young deputy pontificate on the quality of the evidence he had compiled during his campaign to obtain an indictment against Olmstead. He showed them documents, employee records, and witness statements demonstrating "beyond peradventure of doubt" that the TDA limited partnership was a tax-evasion shell with no conceivable commercial purpose. But just two weeks before his presentation to a federal grand jury, TDA's manufacturing company, TDA, Inc., had miraculously come up with the M–31 canopy system, which, when accepted by ConSpace for installation in their X-215A, provided the company and parent partnership with instant legitimacy, and his case with a swift and simple burial.

"The contract lent substance to an otherwise blatant tax scam?" said the corpulent deputy, oozing self-importance and indulging in one of Seth's least favorite mannerisms: ending each declarative sentence with a rising intonation. "A week later," Torville continued, "I was told that someone very 'high up' had scuttled my investigation? To avoid 'further embarrassment to the Department'?"

"You mean," said Seth, "that with all this evidence, you just quit without knowing who was ordering you to do it? With this slam dunk of a case, you just walked away and—"

Allyn jumped in. "I don't think you should assume that Mr. Torville has quite the same authority as the U.S. Attorney General, Seth. No offense intended, Mr. Torville."

"None taken," said the deputy, his round face burning. "By *your* remarks at least?" he added with a withering glance at Seth and ending with an inflection that soared upward like a flying buttress.

Torville went on to explain that three months after TDA's amazing deliverance, ConSpace shocked the industry by winning the biggest government contract in U.S. military history. "ConSpace's bid and prototype X-215A design simply decimated the XB-3 submitted by Winston-Ethridge, the world's leading supersonic-aircraft manufacturer."

Seth bolted out of his chair. "Jesus, Torville, isn't it *obvious* what happened? Olmstead got ConSpace to take on his M-31 system in return for Olmstead using some kind of juice to help ConSpace beat out Winston-Ethridge!"

"It's, uh, not entirely beyond the range of reasonable possibilities?" said Torville, the concession choking in his throat. "Olmstead is an extremely wealthy and unsavory character, indeed dangerous? Nothing he would do would surprise me?"

"Is that why you backed off?" said Seth. "Were you afraid of him?"

"Ms. Friedlander," said Torville, rising to his feet. "I consented to this meeting because I speculated that there might exist the possibility of synergism—that's common ground, Cameron—wherein both our objectives might be furthered? After meeting King Kong here, I doubt that we could ever have *anything* in common."

"I couldn't agree with you more," said Seth, grabbing his coat, "and I can't tell you how much I'm comforted by the knowledge. By the way, you talk like some goddamn Valley girl."

Outside, Allyn shook her head and glared at Seth.

"What," he said, but she ignored him and started writing. Seth saw that she was reproducing with amazing accuracy the government's entire witness list including many addresses and telephone numbers. When she had finished, she turned and headed for the parking lot. They walked in silence, Allyn a step ahead all the way, not looking at Seth. Only when they were inside their rented car did she turn to face him.

"Seth Cameron, you may be a hotshot trial lawyer inside a courtroom where everybody's fully expecting a buttoned-down alley fight and knows what the rules are, but you don't know shit about how to get what you want out here in the real world."

Seth started to reply, but Allyn wasn't finished.

"Despite your best efforts to fuck it up, however, that tightly wound asshole told us how to get inside this conspiracy. Did you pick up on it?"

Seth thought for a minute, then said, "The Caicos Islands."

"Bingo!"

"Then I can leave tomorrow?"

"Absolutely. You can leave tomorrow for San Francisco, California. Somebody's got to hold down the fort. *I'm* going to the Caicos."

"But—"

"*But* nothing, 'King Kong,' " she said, smiling for the first time since leaving Torville's office. "This is going to require a modicum of finesse and tact you have yet to demonstrate."

Allyn tossed her notebook into her briefcase, slammed it shut, and added, "In other words, this is woman's work."

TWO NIGHTS LATER SETH WAS AWAKENED BY A JUBILANT ALLYN FRIED-
lander, calling from Kew.

"We've got him, Cowboy," she shouted, "we've got the
bastard."

"That's great," mumbled Seth, trying to focus on the bedside
clock that read 2 A.M., "but which bastard, how did we get him,
and who the fuck is this?"

"Olmstead," she said in a slurred voice that told Seth she was
drunk. *"That* bastard. Okay, here it is."

Allyn laid out Olmstead's involvement in the tax scam in a
raucous voice that Seth could have heard from his kitchen.

"Two questions," said Seth, still trying to clear his head. "First:
How could an investor get the whole deduction past the IRS
without proving a valid note for the balance due? Second: How
in the hell did you find out all this stuff?"

An uncharacteristic giggle issued from Allyn. "Olmstead set
up a dummy Caicos lending institution called Zenith Financial,
which issued the note and a check drawn on First Southern Bank
of Kew, a chartered bank in the Caicos Islands. This gave the
note authenticity."

"Doesn't that make Southern Bank another deep-pocket
defendant?"

"Give that kid a ci-gar!" More giggling. "The bank had to
know what was going on. The investor signed the note to Zenith
and handed over Zenith's check for, let's say, six hundred thousand dollars to TDA. It's all just paper, of course, because the
investor only agrees to pay back the note out of dividends from
TDA, which would never happen because TDA had neither a
product nor an intention to build one. And since everything was
controlled by Olmstead, the money from the 'check' just went in

a circle—back into Zenith's account with First Southern Bank to be 'lent' to the next greedy schmuck."

"And Olmstead keeps the four-hundred-thousand dollar cash down payment himself."

"Multiplied over and over again. Hundreds of millions of dollars, and his only real overhead was Dr. Ivor Tellman, an authentic but alcoholic MIT professor who, incidentally, later killed himself. Tellman had a few technicians and ran a small research lab that photographed well for offering circulars."

"But TDA *did* build a product, the M-31 system."

"Which came about only because—you ready for this?—Olmstead learned from his *very* silent partner in TDA—a phantom power-broker—that your best pal Torville was about to get an indictment against them. You were probably right on target when you speculated that there had to be some kind of deal between ConSpace and TDA."

"And don't forget the United States government," said Seth. "The insider who rigged the deal must be one powerful mother."

"Father."

"What?"

"The power guy. He's known only as Father. It's a code name. Nobody but Olmstead knows who he really is."

"Which brings me back to my second question," said Seth. "How and where did you get all this stuff?"

"Straight from an ex-bookkeeper for Olmstead's companies named Cecil Kimbrough. He was on Torville's list."

Seth swung his feet over the edge of the bed as he considered the source. "I would think anyone as powerful as Olmstead would control ex-employees very carefully, either by reward or intimidation."

"Correctamundo, my skeptical friend," said Allyn with another high-pitched giggle. "But I outpromised Olmstead, then I outthreatened him."

"You're drunk, Allyn."

"An unavoidable consequence of the promise phrase of my short-lived relationship with dear Cecil," she said, a wistful tone in her voice.

"You *slept* with the guy?"

Allyn's insane cackle pierced Seth's ear. "You know what they say, Seth: 'Promise them anything, but give them a summons and complaint."

"A *summons?* You threatened to sue the poor schmuck? What did you do? Write out a summons on a cocktail napkin?"

Allyn explained that she had matched Kimbrough drink for drink until she could get no more information out of him, then ordered black coffee and hit the hapless Don Juan with a copy of Seth's draft complaint and a summons.

"Unorthodox," said Seth, "even for you."

"But effective," said Allyn, laughing again. "And as soon as I sober up and get back home, we'll be able to put together a real stockholders' complaint against Olmstead."

"That's very nice, Allyn, but it might be a more effective class action if we had a representative client."

"Thought you'd never ask. Dear Cecil supplied me with a copy of the list of stockholders of the spun-off manufacturing company. At least a dozen are from the Bay Area."

"Okay, but what about *my* case? Did you learn anything about ConSpace? Problems with the X-215A? You know, the reason we started this stockholders' suit in the first place?"

Seconds of silence hummed through the long-distance wire.

"I'm sorry I'm not more enthusiastic, Allyn. It just seems to me the tail's beginning to wag the dog here."

"I understand, kid," she said lightly, "but what you've got to understand is that your case *is* a dog."

Seth said nothing.

"Okay, Seth. I'm sorry. But I don't expect this guy would have known anything about the M-31 system anyway."

Even if you had thought to ask, thought Seth.

"Safe trip home," he said, and hung up.

He was angry, yet knew he couldn't blame her. He had violated his code and fallen into a trap foreign to him—counting on another person. If something was going to happen with Elena's case, he was going to have to make it happen himself.

He picked up the phone again and dialed Lev's number.

"Lev, this is Seth. Call me at the office when and if you wake up and get this. I've got an idea."

THE REQUEST WAS NEITHER UNEXPECTED NOR RUDELY DELIVERED, YET it set Seth's heart ricocheting around his chest cavity like a squash ball. It wasn't the question itself, so much as the mongoose eyes of the questioner—an Air Police sergeant guarding the gate at New Mexico's Symington Air Force Base—compounded probably by the three cups of black coffee with the viscosity of a winter racetrack that he had inhaled at Bertha's, just outside the gate.

The request was: "Your identification please, gentlemen."

He and Leviticus had spent an hour at Bertha's, staring at black velvet art and absorbing caffeine, refining their plan to penetrate a top-secret air base, secure an interview with the ConSpace technical representative most responsible for the maintenance and safety of America's most protected weapon, then get him to commit a federal felony by revealing enough top-secret information about the X-215A to enable them to extort ConSpace into settling a case on which everybody knew the statute of limitations had already run.

"That's it?" Lev asked the week before. "That's all we need to do?"

"The ConSpace tech rep won't come to us," said Seth, "we've got to go to him."

Lev was unpersuaded. "Whoa, Cowboy. Even if it could be done—which I seriously doubt—espionage against my own government is way outside my strike zone. I have no idea how to get us inside Symington Air Force Base."

So Seth was all the more surprised when Lev had spread out three cards on the table at Bertha's: a fake press card, identifying Seth as Jason Arnold, a reporter from *Scientific Aeronautics*; a New York driver's license with the same name; and a phony American

Express credit card. Lev had another set for himself—the handiwork of a friend who owed him one.

"We swallowed the whale," Lev had said, "let's not be chokin' on the tail."

"Why did you decide to do this?" Seth had asked him as they paid Bertha's bill and put on their coats. "I don't even know why *I'm* doing it."

"Yes, you do," Lev had said. "It's your last shot."

"Okay, but why are you doing it?"

Lev stood for a moment as still as a boulder of scarred granite. He seemed to be wrestling with his thoughts—half-angry, half-embarrassed.

"I guess it's partly for you, asshole," he said finally. "Old times' sake and all that shit. Gettin' me in the door at M and M."

"Too bad Treadwell got me out the door before I could do more."

"Fuck that place. You were the only guy there who didn't walk around like he had a broomstick rammed up his ass. Also the only one who treated me with real respect. You get to know the phony stuff by the time you're seven years old.

"As for what's in it for me? Hell, man, this beats trackin' some husband with his dick out. Call it fourth and ten on the thirty with twenty seconds on the clock and you're three points behind. I ain't interested in no tie game. I don't think you are either."

So here they were, only sixty seconds into the caper, being hauled into the gate office by an air policeman—trained to distrust his own mother—who was now looking doubtfully at the fake cards.

"Yes, Sergeant," he heard Lev say to the lanky AP, "we're reporters for *Scientific Aeronautics*. This gentleman with me is Jason Arnold."

Jason? Why not Benedict? thought Seth.

"I'll have to check with Mr. Bostwick, gentlemen, so just have a seat there," said the red-haired guard in a tone that signified an order, not an invitation. "Is he expecting you?"

"Not exactly," said Seth, feeling his stomach flinch under the sergeant's gaze, but pleased and surprised at the confident tone his own voice had managed. "We travel a lot and got a break in our schedule on the way back east."

"Thought we'd drop by and try to give the Stealth Program a

boost," added Lev, but Seth could see that the sergeant was spring-loaded to the negative position and that what he was hearing over the telephone from Bostwick wasn't helping.

"Not only is he *not* expecting you," said the air cop, an even harder edge in his voice now, "he's never even *heard* of you."

"May I speak with him?" asked Seth in an indignant tone, extending his hand toward the phone. "He's damn sure heard of our magazine." As he leaned forward, he felt an uncomfortable coldness across his back as a light breeze from the security shack's open door touched his soaked shirt. *This is crazy*, he thought, and wished he were sitting back in his cottage in Mill Valley with Fat Dog, watching the fog slip in over the Marin Headlands, turning the valley below him into a goose-down lake.

But Seth picked up on Lev's theme and managed to persuade the tech rep not only that their magazine's editorial point of view was Stealth-positive, but also that a favorable article might help to balance the current attacks being leveled at the program by Congress and the press.

Seth handed the phone back to the AP, who directed the relieved impostors toward Hangar G.

"This is going to be delicate," Seth said, nervously glancing from side to side, "so let me take the lead, okay?"

Lev stared straight ahead over the steering wheel as the words hung in the air. "For a guy who played defense," he said at last, "you can sure be offensive."

They rode in silence past rows of olive-colored Quonset huts and scraggly trees that seemed to have lost their struggle for survival against the cruel New Mexico winter.

Lev was still smarting. "Would you like to drive, too, Mistah Seth, sah?" he added, looking straight ahead.

"Come on, Lev, I just meant . . ."

"Forget it, Cowboy," said Lev, spinning the car neatly into a parking place and slamming on the brakes harder than necessary. "It's your gig. I'll try not to screw it up."

ConSpace's on-site facility looked like a typical construction shack—walls covered with flow charts, blueprints everywhere, drafting tables, computer printouts, and Kmart furniture. Both uniformed and civilian personnel sat in close quarters, milling through a snowstorm of paperwork, shouting into telephones and at each other. A bespectacled airman second class directed them to a huge desk at one end of the temporary building, behind which sat an intense, round-faced man caressing his telephone.

A glistening bronze plate identified Harold Bostwick, who glanced up and motioned them into chairs while he continued his conversation, giving Seth an opportunity to scrutinize him, probe for openings, clues, and cues: a cheap but ostentatious watch, a fraternity ring, a Countess Mara tie adorning an inexpensive, monogrammed dress shirt, coffee in a cup and saucer—affectations suggesting to Seth's practiced eye a man of frustrated vanity who had not achieved his expectations and was probably angry about that and a lot of other things—his job, his thick lenses, the image in his mirror every morning. A nose besieged by spidery tributaries spread out across a puffy face, betraying an affection for the grape. It all fit.

Such a man must be flattered, Seth knew, for he would consider himself to be swimming—or treading water—in an undeserved sea of mediocrity. Such a man usually held deep resentments toward his superiors and might be vulnerable if handled just right. And such a man might possess little tolerance for an interloper should he be able to expose and apprehend one.

"Well now, gentlemen of the press," said Bostwick, dropping the receiver onto the cradle with two fingers, "what can I do for you?" As he addressed them, he rubbed his hands together as if intending to make a fire and offered up his version of a smile, in which an upper lip like a sausage curled northward under a nose the size of a minivan.

Seth eased his way in by offering further assurances concerning their magazine's favorable bias, and Harold Bostwick, sensing an opportunity for recognition, began to take the hook, interrupted only by a sporadic sprinkling of sanctimonious reminders such as, *you understand, gentlemen, that I can only discuss information already in the public domain,* to which Seth would respond *we understand completely, sir,* and Lev would nod sympathetically, and Bostwick would keep on talking. The only problem was, he really *was* confining himself to public and self-serving technical data vouching for the X-215A's superiority and safety. So, after twenty minutes of Bostwick-ese, Seth decided to take the matter head-on.

"There has been speculation, sir, that these X-215A crashes—

four of them now, and all within less than twenty months—were actually the result of some kind of technical defect, not pilot error. Would you like to take this opportunity to put that rumor to rest?"

Tactfully done, thought Seth. But the tech rep commenced a liftoff from his chair that caused heads to turn all over the shack, and Seth realized it had not been tactful enough. As Bostwick lurched forward, a renegade ray of sunlight invaded the shack through a waffle-sized window and glinted off his thick lenses, behind which now lay bulging goldfish eyes as suspicious as an IRS agent's.

"Are you guys researching a scientific project or doing an exposé?" demanded Bostwick through teeth that looked like the grill of an Oldsmobile. "This interview has just ended."

Seth stared at the red-faced man and realized Allyn had been right in her stern lecture after his confrontation with Deputy U.S. Attorney William Torville.

Cases aren't really won in the courtroom, Seth; they're won in the streets. Out in the field, where you have to learn the patience and skill to scrape together support for your client's view of reality; where the witnesses you have to have can still be had—if you're clever enough and patient enough.

You want good testimony? Don't expect it to come knocking on your office door. Out there in the streets—years before you get into the courtroom—that's where your fate as a trial lawyer is being decided.

Although Seth could see she was right, it didn't make this part of the process any easier. He just wasn't cut out for it. He preferred the straightforward encounter within the walls of the courtroom, where both sides know they are in a bare-knuckle fight, the roles clear-cut and understood:

In this corner—a lying or exaggerating witness who can say damn near anything he or she wants to say without fear of a lightning bolt striking the courthouse. In the other corner—possessing the home-field advantage and the sworn duty to do anything he can legitimately get away with to expose the witness's deception—the trial lawyer. Everything up-front, the battle lines drawn, the rules clear. Shake hands and come out fighting.

Field investigation was just the opposite. Now it was the lawyer engaging in deception and the witness who had the home-field advantage.

And the home team had just ended this game with a shutout.

"You've got us all wrong, Mr. Bostwick." Seth loved this part, too—the begging. "We're on *your* side. But I'll just make a note here that you preferred not to respond to the allegation."

That did it. The tech rep was positioned squarely on the fence—with suspicion on one side and the possibility of good press and even some personal recognition on the other—a tension that seemed to drain his vitality. It was like watching water run out of a bathtub. The huge head settled into the gap between his shoulders, which in turn slumped down and forward around his chest. Then the upper lip slowly curled upward again and the whalelike body sank back in its chair. "Now, boys," he said, "I think you got me wrong, too. Let me put it this way. It's not that I don't *want* to comment, it's just that we're not allowed to discuss cases where litigation is a possibility. You know how those fucking lawyers are."

"Assholes," ventured Leviticus, "every damn one of them."

"Well, good news on that front you might not have heard," said Seth. "The statute of limitations has run on the first three crashes, including Sam Barton's, and the widow from the most recent one is the daughter of a career Air Force general."

Bostwick had heard, and Seth could tell by the way he slowly nodded his head that resistance was diminishing.

Extra innings.

"Okay, boys, I see no harm in being quoted as saying that the X-215A was state-of-the-art perfect just before the Barton and Andrews accidents."

"I don't doubt that for a minute," said Seth, "but how do we convince our readers? Take Barton, for instance. People say he was the hottest top gun on the base."

Bostwick's mouth worked its way into a wry smile as he said, "Then people don't know shit about Sam Barton."

"What do you mean?"

The smile disappeared. "Forget about that. All your readers need to know is that I was there that day before Captain Barton took off. I personally supervised the master preflight check on the X-215A that he crashed. It's required by our contract."

The harsh ring of Bostwick's phone set Seth's heart pounding again. Too much coffee. Too much deception. Hook him up to a polygraph, ask him his own name, and he'd blow up the fucking machine.

As Bostwick spoke to the caller, Seth affected a casual review of his notes, while Lev affected an equally casual study of Bostwick's diplomas and extravagantly framed Defense Department efficiency awards.

"Yes, sir," said Bostwick, "yes, sir, I'll be right out there."

Seth's heart stopped pounding and began to sink. *Just as we were getting somewhere.* Bostwick shook his head apologetically as he hung up the phone. "Sorry, boys, but we've got a snafu in the hangar and I gotta run. Another time, maybe."

"I'm sorry, too, Mr. Bostwick," said Seth, desperately reaching for words as the tech rep reached for the door, "because . . . well, frankly, sir, we're, uh, returning east today, and we'll have no choice now but to go with the rumor." Bostwick stopped, his hand on the doorknob. Seth tried to take the desperation out of his voice. "I know this will disappoint our editor, since he sent us here to try to put all that antistealth crap to rest."

Lev played along by folding his notepad and giving Bostwick a consoling look as he extended his hand in farewell.

The tech rep turned, his close-set eyes batting with indecision. "Oh, shit, you can come along, I guess. The hottest thing out there today is an F-15, and the old Soviet Union had a full set of plans and specs to that bird by the time it was tested." Bostwick lurched back to his desk and pulled a drawer open. "Here. Put these badges on next to the ones you got there."

The three men quickly covered the twenty feet from the shack to a steel door, where another robotic AP—whose hard eyes belied his tender years—checked badges and waved them through. Once in the hangar, Bostwick told Seth and Leviticus to wait just inside the door while he solved his problem. Lev let out a low whistle as they looked down into a blindingly lighted, cement-lined bunker, carved deep into the earth. Only three aircraft, all different, were scattered around the vast floor—bigger than a football field—each attended by a half dozen or so guards and workers. Seth was surprised as Lev identified each plane, together with details as to airspeed, thrust, and armament.

"So what do you think, Cowboy? Worth the trip?"

"Not yet, but he knows something about Barton we'd best find out," said Seth as they watched Bostwick leave an office at ground level and waddle back toward them along a steel catwalk.

"Is it okay for us to go down below as we talk?" Seth asked the tech rep.

"No harm in it," said Bostwick, "but stay close to me."

The men descended four stories to the floor of the hangar.

"What are those structures that look like railroad tracks spanning the opening?" asked Leviticus.

Bostwick smiled his baboon smile. "They're railroad tracks," he said dryly, then explained how a steel-reinforced concrete mat could be activated to seal off and protect everything below ground level in an emergency.

"I assume," said Seth, "that the X-215A is out on a training mission or something?"

"Or something," said Bostwick. "Let me put it this way: you can assume that if the X-215A were here, you guys wouldn't be. Now where were we? Oh, yes, the night of the Barton crash."

The tech rep then explained that it was ConSpace's standard practice and contractual obligation to check all systems before each test mission and that he did so personally just before the fatal flight. Seth asked him if he would show them "either on or off the record" the maintenance records for October 15, "just to prove the point."

A ripple of laughter exploded from deep within the tech rep. "Hell, boys, why don't I just give you a complete set of plans for the X-215A and be done with it."

"I know you can't do that," said Seth, forcing an accommodating smile, "but we aren't asking for secrets, only some corroboration of our editor's theory that the bird is as perfect as you say. Let's face it, sir. This Sam Barton was a top gun, the best the Air Force had, and the liberal dissidents on the Armed Services Committee have got the muckrakers calling for ConSpace's head."

"We can handle it," said Bostwick in a tone so lacking in conviction that Seth decided to take off the gloves. He looked at his watch, shrugged his shoulders, and snapped his notebook closed.

"I understand your position, Mr. Bostwick, and I hope you understand ours. We'll have to inform our readership that you were unwilling or unable to document ConSpace's claim that the X-215A was flight ready before takeoff on the night of the crash."

The tech rep's eyes narrowed into razor slits for a second, but then The Lip curled into another contrived fake smile as he said, "Boys, how about a cup of coffee."

Seth said sure, and within five minutes they had struck a deal. In recognition of the need for national security, *Scientific Aeronautics* would accept Bostwick's undocumented word, in return for which he would provide them with an off-the-record statement that would erase any doubt in their minds concerning the X-215A's airworthiness on the night of the Barton crash. If they deemed it insufficient for their purposes, of course, they would be free to go their separate ways.

"Okay, boys, here it is. I'll tell you just what I told the inspector general. I give you my word as a gentleman that the maintenance records and my personal daily reports could back it up." Bostwick paused for dramatic effect, then took a swig of coffee and continued, "We started the final preflight at five-thirty the afternoon of the fifteenth. Before that—at four—I checked with all systems chiefs, as usual. Each one of them is required to check every element of the aircraft they're responsible for and sign off with me. There are eighteen systems chiefs, and every damn one of them is the best in the business. After they finish, I do it all over again. Now, here's what you're looking for, boys: everything was one hundred percent *perfect,* and you can quote me on that. If it isn't perfect, it doesn't fly until it is. Just like the space shuttle. You have my word on it."

"What time was Barton's takeoff?"

"I wasn't on the flight line. My security clearance stops right here at the hangar. Can't say."

"Who can?"

"Nobody will. Flight-line information is *the* highest level of confidentiality in the U.S. Besides, there's been a complete rotation of the flight-line personnel since then."

"Have you heard of anything unusual?"

"Hell, man, this is the military. You can't pay attention to rumors."

"What are the rumors?"

Lev put his pad away and added, "Off the record, of course."

"Well, I hear the takeoff was delayed."

"What's normal takeoff time?" asked Seth.

"I understand that pattern goes out around twenty-two hundred."

"Ten o'clock?"

"Right."

"How long was the delay?"

"Don't know. An hour, maybe two. It happens."

"So what started a rumor?"

"Well, let me put it this way, Mr. Arnold," said Bostwick, cautiously framing his words. "Captain Barton maybe needed a little more preflight himself."

"I don't follow," said Seth. "Was he sick?"

"In a manner of speaking."

"Could you be more specific? Off the record, of course."

Bostwick's eyes flickered between the two reporters. "Let's just say he needed a coffee break, okay?"

Seth and Leviticus gave him a blank look that irritated the tech rep even more. "*Jesus*, you guys are dense. Nixon would still be president—thank God—if you guys had been working for the *Washington Post*. Okay, here it is, but strictly off the record. Deal?"

"I swear to you as a gentleman," said Seth, "that what you tell me will never appear in any magazine."

"All right, here it is. I've heard rumors about Barton's blood alcohol that suggest he was flying high long before he took off."

Seth shot Lev a worried look that said the tech rep seemed to be reporting the truth, at least as he knew it.

"Barton was *drunk?*"

"That was off the record, Mr. Arnold, and I'll say no more about it. The Air Force suppressed it out of deference to the widow."

Lev looked at Seth and shrugged his shoulders. Seth felt beaten, exhausted. His pancreas was reacting to the new dose of caffeine by secreting fresh insulin, and he could feel the rapid drop in his blood sugar all the way down to his ankles. He needed to sit down and was relieved when Lev leapt into the brief vacuum of silence; Lev, playing bad cop.

"Still, sir," said the investigator, removing his empty pipe from his coat pocket and thoughtfully chewing on the stem, "they are saying that all this 'pilot error' explanation is just a cover-up, that your bird is trying to do too much with too small a budget compared with Northrup's B-2 program or Winston-Ethridge's XB-004. They say the X-215A is so burdened with antiradar coatings and other devices that it's forgotten how to fly. They say what you're doing is blaming the dead pilots who can't speak for themselves."

Bostwick was glaring at Leviticus now, but the investigator seemed not to notice as he added, "Even the folks in Congress who still think the U.S. needs a deterrent force are beginning to doubt the X-215A can get the job done."

"That's ridiculous," said the tech rep, apparently relieved to be on safe ground again. "Let's say the Russkies get frisky again after they get around to dumping Yeltsin. Our detection satellites give us a thirty-minute warning of their incoming ICBMs, which is all we need to take out Moscow within minutes after they hit Washington, D.C. The X-215A's SRAMs—short range nuclear attack missiles—will score a hell of a lot more accuracy than any long-range robotic rocket system can deliver."

Leviticus shook his head, saying, "What about the Asat system like the one based at Tyuratam?"

Seth glanced at Leviticus with new interest.

"It's true," Bostwick conceded, "that the old Soviet Union's air defense early-warning system was one of the best in the world—"

"No, sir," said Leviticus interrupting, "not one of the best. *The* best. And not *was. Still is.* In addition to satellite bases, they've got their high-frequency OTH radar—that's 'over the horizon,' Jason—plus eleven tracking radars at six sites around Russia, and six more phased-array radar sites from the Kola Peninsula in the northwest to the Caucasus in the southwest, with approximately seven thousand air-surveillance radars."

Now it was Bostwick, not just Seth, trying to conceal his amazement as Lev continued his rapid-fire litany. "Then you got to throw in their twelve hundred and fifty interceptors and God knows how many thousands of surface-to-air missiles with ranges up to one hundred eighty-six miles—"

"Hold on there," interrupted the technician, involuntarily drawn into an attempt to regain the initiative. "You may be right about Russia's defense capability—I'm not saying you are, understand—but that's exactly the defensive array our performance specifications were designed to *beat*, for God's sake!" The red-faced technician then continued to reveal technical information about the X-215A's capabilities that, to Seth's continuing amazement, Leviticus seemed to comprehend.

"But you can't deny," responded Leviticus, like a fisherman in familiar seas but angling for something in deep water he can't see, "that when you gave up afterburners to beat the enemy's infrared sensors, you sacrificed half your engine thrust."

Bostwick bit, freely discussing the X-215A's capability to fly nearly twice the speed of sound because of its "twin high-thrust turbofans and its blended airframe designed to provide a low profile with minimum drag and high speed with low kinetic heating."

Seth was totally lost, but Leviticus maintained his self-assured, yet casual probing. Seth realized he was watching the ace investigator in *his* courtroom. He also realized that Lev was trying to bait the tech rep into betraying a flaw, some weakness in the perfect killing machine.

But over Bostwick's shoulder, Seth saw a person approaching, a familiar person, the last person in the world Seth wanted to see right now: Maj. Jack Christopher. *And the pilot was walking straight toward them!* To be recognized now that Lev was finally getting somewhere . . .

Desperate, Seth took advantage of Lev's girth, casually strolling around the investigator, using him to partially eclipse Christopher's view as the major passed within twenty feet of them, headed toward the steel stairway. Just as it seemed to have worked, Christopher's head turned in their direction. Now he was staring straight at them! Seth whipped out his handkerchief and covered his lower face as Christopher addressed Harold Bostwick.

"Hey, Hal. How's the wife getting along?"

Seth feigned a sneeze attack into his contrived mask. "Oh, hello, Major Christopher," said Bostwick. "She's fine now, thanks for asking."

Leviticus, hearing the officer's name and realizing the reason for Seth's charade said, "Geshundheit," and made himself even larger than usual. Seth prayed that the major would keep moving toward the exit stairway, but to his dismay, Bostwick beckoned him over.

"Oh, Major," he said, "I'd like you to meet a couple of—" But

Bostwick was interrupted by a maintenance specialist shouting at Christopher. "Major!" came the voice of divine intervention. "We need to see you right away. We've got a hot one over here on this F-15 you're taking up this afternoon." Crispie shrugged an apology as he turned and hurried toward the aircraft, and Seth began to resume normal breathing.

"Sorry," he said to Bostwick. "Hay fever." *Another bullet dodged,* he thought, but wondered if Lev would be able to get Bostwick's mouth moving at Mach 2 again.

Without hesitation, Lev resumed his probing. "Lockheed is way ahead of you with its F-19. Then you have Northrup's B-2 with four F-118, GE-100 nonafterburning engines with nineteen thousand pounds of thrust. You got ramjets? Slush hydrogen?"

Bostwick took the hook again. "Don't need it, Mr. Smith. The F-19—which, by the way, the Air Force denies even exists—has only two sixteen-thousand pound-thrust engines. We've got *four* of them, each developing thirty thousand pounds of thrust and with no higher fuselage profile than Lockheed's. Let me put it this way: our X-215A is as thin as a razor blade up front where it really counts. It's even flatter than Grumman's stealth design, plus it's lighter and twice as fast as Northrup's B-2, not to mention more controllable in terms of vertical stabilization."

At this, Leviticus began chewing on his unlit pipe again. Seth saw that though he had Bostwick in verbal overdrive again, something was bothering the investigator.

"Take the highly publicized B-1B bomber," the suddenly garrulous rep continued, *"please!"* Lev and Seth accommodated the tech rep's attempt at humor with a courtesy smile. "It's junk! Antiquated junk. Sure, it has a reduced radar cross-section—the frontal silhouette or radar signature we call RGS—so that a formation of one hundred of them looks about the same as one B-52. But *our* bird has an even smaller RGS than the B-1B, with a hell of lot more power. Every part of her body—inside and out—flows into everything else so there is only minimal radar reflection back. Plus she flies as cool as a Popsicle—hydrogen, you know—so a Sidewinder-type missile has nothing to grab on to."

Leviticus raised his eyebrows to show he was impressed, then casually tapped his pipe and added, "But what about your bubble-canopy design? The slightest glint from that shiny Plexiglas surface could be a real grabber for radar."

Bostwick looked as if he had been hit between the legs. His eyes narrowed and flickered between them, his chin jutted out, and he shot Lev a hostile look. He then composed himself and looked at his watch. "Sorry, gentlemen," he muttered, just as Seth spotted Christopher coming toward them again—"but I'm really running late."

"Would that be the M-31 canopy system designed by TDA?" said Seth.

"Really, gentlemen, I've got to get back to the office."

Lev spotted Crispie, too, and quickly extended his hand to the tech rep. Seth knew they had to escape, but something in Bostwick's last stonewalling remark—"running late"—nagged at him, even more than the obvious nerve they had struck on the canopy.

"Running . . . *late*." Hadn't the tech rep said something earlier about the unscheduled flight leaving 'late that night'? Seth's heart was pounding through his chest as he saw Christopher turning toward them, but his mind raced with new possibilities and hope. Suppose the flight *did* take off an hour or two late as Bostwick had heard, rather than the ten o'clock time reported by the Air Force? What if the flight took off so late that Sam Barton died *after* midnight—on the sixteenth—so that the statute of limitations had not run on Elena's case after all? *Jesus!*

"Just one more thing," Seth said as casually as possible. "If the rumor about Barton is true, the X-215A gets a clean bill all the way around. When did you hear he took off? Closer to an hour or to two hours late?"

Bostwick seemed relieved at the change of subject and appeared to be racking his memory, but Crispie was now swiftly closing the gap between them. Seth saw perspiration break on Lev's brow for the first time today.

"Oh, yes, I remember now," said Bostwick. "I heard the flight left at twenty-three thirty hours, an eleven-thirty takeoff."

Seth could hardly believe what he was hearing and could not stop probing, even though Crispie was closer now and seemed to be eyeing Seth curiously.

"And how long," Seth asked quickly, his throat tightening as the test pilot was now only twenty yards away, "was the flight?"

The tech rep replied that although the flight was unscheduled, it was undoubtedly the standard sortie, probably "an hour, maybe an hour fifteen." Seth knew they should run for it, that

Christopher could have them arrested, that both of them could end up in federal prison. But his brain was on afterburner, and new hope for a rekindled professional career had incinerated his judgment. He took Bostwick by the arm and started marching him toward the stairway with Christopher now only ten yards behind them and closing. "And how long," he asked the tech rep, "would it take to get from takeoff at Symington Air Force Base in New Mexico to the crash site in Arizona . . . under normal circumstances."

"Depends on how he got there," replied the tech rep. "We aren't told the exact test-flight routes, but there's a standard triangular flight pattern. If he had gone straight to the crash site, he would have been there in ten to fifteen minutes."

"But what," asked Seth, praying that the hangar floor would open up and swallow Christopher, "if he was on the *last* leg of a triangular flight path when the crash occurred?"

With Christopher now only several steps behind them, the trio started up the stairs. After a seemingly endless amount of head-scratching, earlobe pulling, and panting, Bostwick answered the question. "Well, it would have taken roughly forty-five minutes or so, say to . . . oh, about twelve-fifteen the next morning."

Bostwick turned back to see Christopher coming up behind him, as the "reporters" began taking steps two at a time. "Oh, hello again, Major. I'd like you to meet these gentlemen from the . . . That's funny, sir; there they go, late for their plane I guess."

Neither Seth nor Leviticus spoke until they had returned their visitors' passes and traveled a full mile from the base. Only then did their eyes meet, followed by a high five and raucous sounds of unrestrained joy.

"Are you sure," asked Leviticus, "that you filed a complaint on the sixteenth?"

"It was the first thing I did, still hoping I was on time. Turns out I *was* on time—if we can prove what Bostwick just told us."

Another high five.

"Okay," said Seth after they had traveled a few miles in silence, "let's hear it. *How?*"

"How to you, too, Chief."

"Come on, Lev. *How the hell did you do it?* How do you know all that stuff?"

Leviticus went silent for a moment, his big fists tightening around the steering wheel. Seth waited, knowing it would not come out until Lev was ready, and when it did come out, it would be understated, the square root of the total equation.

"I wanted to be a pilot during Nam," Lev said several minutes later. "I had two years of junior college—as did a few of my more fortunate friends—but they got into the aviation cadet program and I didn't."

Lev swung the rented Ford out and around two slower cars, and Seth wondered if the act of passing on the two-lane roadway was temporarily preoccupying the investigator or if that was the end of the subject.

"By 'more fortunate' you mean 'less black,' don't you?" Seth said finally.

"Bingo."

"So what did you do?"

"I did what I could," said Lev, expertly passing another car with only a few feet to spare, "to get close to jets. Became an Air Force jet mechanic."

"Hell, Lev, that must have been tough to get into, too."

"Oh, yeah," said Leviticus, the words propelled with ironic laughter, "rigid entry requirements—like half of us had to be a different height than the other half."

Seth laughed. "But you weren't talking golden oldies from the midseventies back there to our friend Bostwick, Lev. You seem to be up to speed on everything that flies."

"I never lost interest in jet aircraft. Never will. I devour everything I can find. I live for the next volume of *Jane's* out of the U.K. I guess a shrink would say it's become more of an obsession than a hobby."

"But why didn't you tell me, for God's sake? Before, when I was ... asking you to stay in the background."

Leviticus stared straight ahead as he said, "Would it have made any difference?" A trace of coldness had returned to his voice.

Seth's mouth was already forming a facile response, but he thought better of it and said nothing.

Back in San Francisco the next day, Seth and Leviticus reported the good news to Allyn. She responded by producing a bottle of

Jack Daniel's from her lower right-hand desk drawer, but then turned serious.

"One word of caution," she said, waving the ubiquitous cigar. "Be careful what you ask for—"

"You just might get it," said Seth, finishing the aphorism. "So what's your point?"

"My point is that this is not your everyday lawsuit you are launching here. These are not nice people. Remember what Torville said? And Cecil Kimbrough? Consider the power this guy Olmstead and his pal 'Father' must have to be able to rig the biggest governmental contract in history. And are we sure that Dr. Ivor Tellman really committed suicide? And then there's the U.S. Air Force, which will not take kindly to your public criticism of their most cherished secret weapon."

There followed a moment of tense silence while Allyn and Lev studied Seth's face.

"So what's your point?" Seth said.

The three friends burst out laughing, and Allyn poured them another drink. Seth removed a copy of the summons and complaint from his coat pocket and slapped it into Leviticus's hand.

"Serve the bastards," he said, and returned to his office.

Weeks later, Ramon's melodious voice announced that a Mrs. Johannson was calling "about your father." Pop had made a break for it, and although he had quickly been captured, subdued, and resettled, he was unhappier than ever and demanding to see his son.

"Dr. Farley suggests we move him into the full-care ward, Mr. Cameron. He doesn't think your father has much more time."

Seth said he would come right away, and Allyn agreed to cover his schedule.

His first destination upon reaching Bakersfield late that afternoon was not Havenhill, but Poplar Street, where he found the large For Sale sign tilting at a thirty-degree angle and looking as neglected as the house to which it had failed to attract interest. Not a nibble since the property was listed a month after Pop was transferred to Havenhill. "Flat market," was the broker's reply whenever Seth inquired. "Sure money's cheap, but nobody's buying."

The front yard had become an uneven mattress of leaves and branches from a fall windstorm earlier in the day. He picked up some dead sticks from the walkway and threw them over the picket fence at the side of the house. Leaves had also blanketed the small front porch, and he used the side of his foot to sweep most of them down into a border of geraniums that were already surrendering to autumn and neglect.

He realized he didn't even have a key, but he had seen enough. *"Fuck 'em all,"* he said out loud, then jerked the real estate sign, post and all, out of the ground and threw it over the fence, too.

"I'm sure you realize, Mr. Cameron, that the cost of full-time nursing back at Mr. Cameron's home will be twice what you've been paying here at Havenhill."

"I'm sure, ma'am."

"I realize you think your father should be able to live wherever he wants to—"

"I'm more interested in seein' he gets to die where he wants to. I'll take him with me now, if you don't mind."

After a fitful night in his old bed on Poplar Street, Seth was relieved to see Mrs. Alice Jenkins at the door at seven the next morning. She had been the best of Pop's previous day-care nurses and had just become available. Seth had forgotten that Mrs. Jenkins was herself a cripple, one foot covered in a boot attached to a primitive six-inch metal prosthesis.

"You're a courageous woman, Mrs. Jenkins."

"Oh, he's not so bad. We're both a little afraid of the other so it works out just fine. Most of the time."

They went together into Joe's bedroom. Seth was again shocked at how much his father had failed. The old man had shrunk to no more than a hundred pounds, and extending his hand to Seth seemed to require great effort. Seth looked into his father's surprisingly clear blue eyes and felt a cold shudder rippling down his spine as he saw something he had never seen there.

Pop had decided to die.

"I'm glad you're here, Son," said Pop, trying to pull himself more upright on the double bed. "Maybe you could persuade the warden here to mark the occasion of my return with a child's portion of Chianti."

"I think a modification of the house rules would be in order," said Seth, wrapping his left arm around his father's bony neck and shoulders.

"How about it, Nurse Ratched?" said Joe. "Hell, I know you'll water it down anyway." Pop seemed either to have forgotten he had been away or to be thinking that Alice Jenkins had been there all the time he was gone.

"To mark the occasion," said Mrs. Jenkins, flashing a good-natured smile as she left them alone.

"How's it going, Pop?"

"Can't complain. Well, I could complain, but that would only fuel your plans to dump me back in some other old folks' home."

Seth smiled and shook his head. This seemed to be the Good Pop Cameron. The one he would remember.

"You can stay here as long as you want to, Pop."

The withered face relaxed a bit. "I know the warden is expensive, but you can refinance the house. It's yours now anyway." Seth saw no point in reminding him that the house was already mortgaged to the hilt.

Joe used his elbows to shift into a more comfortable position. "My goals are simple, kid, two to be exact. The first is to die here in my own home with whatever dignity I can muster."

Mrs. Jenkins entered and handed each of them a glass of wine. Pop took his in both hands and eagerly lifted it to his lips, despite a tremor that threatened to spill the contents.

"What's the second?"

"To do it as soon as possible," said Pop, wiping the back of one hand across his mouth. "I've lived too long."

"Don't talk like that, Pop."

"It's true. You'll find out someday. The nurses have to clean up after my messes, then force-feed me so I'll do it all over again.

185

All that's left of me is a receptacle for pain and a vessel for the conversion of food into shit.''

He then told Seth that Rosie had visited him "in that other place," but he couldn't remember how many times. "Has she been here today? I don't think my head is working so good.''

"Not yet," Seth said.

"She's working in a bank," said Mrs. Jenkins.

Seth's eyes flickered surprise. Aunt Claire had refused to tell him what Rosie was doing or where. "Where?''

"Valley National. My bank. I see her all the time, standing there pretty as a picture, surrounded by money. Main branch.''

Joe Cameron—momentarily forgotten—began to cough, pausing only long enough to accept the cough medicine offered by the nurse and to demand more.

"I remember now," said Alice Jenkins, smiling broadly, "he's heard that cough syrup has alcohol in it.''

"Seth, tell this old bat to bring me another glass of wine or I'll write you out of my will. Come on, Lady Ratched, hit the kitchen. I hope you're not paying much to this one, Seth.''

Seth laughed uneasily as Joe's mood seemed to be changing. "Maybe just a half a glass?''

Mrs. Jenkins sighed and shook her head. Seth knew she would water it down and take her sweet time doing it.

"What the hell, Seth, I'll be a prisoner in my own house. Sometimes I get spells when I can't even walk to the toilet by myself. Can't even *walk* for Christ's sake!" Joe was starting to wheeze, gulping for air. "How can I blame you for not coming around here? Hell, I don't even want you to.''

"Easy, Pop.''

"Fuck easy! You had it easy right here, but you had to go off and try to be a big-time L.A. lawyer.''

"I'm in San Francisco.''

"That's what I said!" Seth saw that his father's eyes were darting around the room as if trying to focus on things that weren't there. "*She* went to L.A.," he shouted, the eyes narrowed, his head slowly nodding. "What the hell difference does it make who went where anyway?" The old man was seized by another convulsive coughing spell that racked his entire body. Seth glanced uneasily toward the kitchen where Mrs. Jenkins stood like a guard at attention in the doorway, looking on sadly. He removed his handkerchief and wiped spittle from the old man's contorted face.

"Point is," Joe continued after he had begun to breathe normally again, "you all disappeared and the only reason *you've* come back is to put me away in some goddamn home."

"That's not true, Pop. I just got you out of one."

"So why *are* you here? Did they kick you out of that fancy firm you went to? Are you here to beg Big Tom for your old job back?"

Seth felt helpless, as if he were watching his father oozing deeper into quicksand and had no rope to throw to him. "I'll get you a glass of wine."

"Couldn't make it in the major leagues, could you!" Joe shouted to Seth's retreating back. "Didn't I tell you, damn it, I told you! But no. You had to go be a big shot, didn't you! You and that alley-cat mother of yours!"

"I'm sorry, Mr. Cameron," said Mrs. Jenkins, viewing Seth with concern as he entered the kitchen, pale as chalk, holding his stomach as if he'd been shot. "He gets like this all of a sudden. It's the tumor. I know he doesn't mean all those things."

Seth shrugged. "Most of them are true."

"He'll be asleep in a minute or two. The cough syrup I gave him was from before. It's laced with lithium and phenobarbital. Doctor says it's the only way to deal with him when he gets like this."

"Maybe I should try some," said Seth, and slumped into a kitchen chair beside her.

As soon as Pop dozed off, Seth headed for Valley National Bank. There, looking like a bird in a cage, he found Rosie.

Rosie Wheeler! A bank teller!

Looking far too beautiful for the role but seemingly relaxed, she had a smile for everyone, just as when she had been at the Broadway Bowl. A hundred years ago. Rosie was so absorbed in her duties she didn't see him until his turn in line came up and suddenly there they were. Face-to-face.

"Hi," he said.

She said, "Hi," back, but the smile disappeared. She said sorry she couldn't talk to him while she was working, and no, she couldn't see him after work either because she was busy and it wouldn't be a good idea anyway.

"Please don't make a scene, Seth," she added when Seth persisted, much to the chagrin of the restless man waiting behind him. "We are not allowed to socialize. There are people in line behind you, and my supervisor is behind me. *Please.*"

Seth smiled his best "thank you, ma'am" smile and nodded his head vigorously in case the supervisor was watching them, then took out his pen and grabbed a deposit receipt from the dispenser. He scribbled a note on the receipt and shoved it in front of her. The note said:

I've got to see you. Please, Rosie. PLEASE!

Rosie slid the receipt back and pointed to it with her pencil, as if indicating a problem with the way he had filled it out. "Seth," she whispered between locked teeth, "please don't do this to me. I worked hard to get this job and I know how you can be. Please, just walk away."

The man in back of Seth cleared his throat. Again.

Seth turned to see a glowering giant in jeans and a T-shirt. Seth smiled at him and at Rosie, but the intensity of his voice matched hers. "I loved you, Rosie. I still do."

Rosie exhaled, glanced toward the ceiling, raised and lowered her shoulders. "And I loved you, Seth, but . . ."

"But not enough to stay with me."

"I'm calling my supervisor," said Rosie, and started to turn.

"Rosie, *the statute never ran on Barton.* I've served ConSpace."

"What? It didn't run?"

"None of this had to happen. All I need is for you to come back. I'll be back on Montgomery Street in two years. Maybe sooner."

Rosie gave Seth a look that mirrored failure. "I'm happy for you, Seth, but the statute of limitations was not the problem for us, and a change in the status of the case is not the solution."

Seth saw tears forming in her large dark eyes. She said, "Goodbye, Seth," then turned away from him and addressed a mousy little man with a saberlike nose looming over a mustache as thin as a straw. "Mr. Turner? I'm having a problem over here."

The nose turned and pointed in their direction, and the man

who had been clearing his throat behind Seth said, "It's about time, lady. This guy belongs in the cooler."

"Stay out of this, pardner," said Seth over his shoulder as he picked up his pen and the failed note. "Okay, babe," he said to Rosie. "I'll go."

"No way, buster," said the man. "You've fucked up my afternoon, now that there supervisor's gonna fuck up yours. You ain't goin' nowhere!"

Everything happened quickly after that. Seth remembered feeling something like a forklift coming up under his arms, then wrapping around his chest, then his own right elbow finding its target deep in the man's solar plexus while his foot crushed the guy's left instep. But he would never be sure who connected with the first real punch, or when it was that the security guard intervened with a stunning blow to the back of his head. Or who all it was dragging him toward the entrance like a common drunk.

Or how life could fall apart so fast on a person.

Within hours, Seth found himself on Highway 99 heading toward San Francisco, thanks to a deputy district attorney who had been a friend and law school classmate. His last words, delivered without a hint of a smile, were, "Straight out of Dodge, Seth. Okay?" Seth needed no urging.

Once behind the wheel, however, the silence of the road forced him to deal with the demons of remorse in a head crowded with visions of his father's unrelenting condemnation, the looks of disgust on the faces of the security guards as they had shoved him into the police van, the blood of a total stranger on his sleeve, Rosie's vain and plaintive cry.

The pitiless miles of highway stretched beyond his headlights—infinite, inexhaustible. Time seemed to have stopped to take pleasure in his pain.

He remembered lines from an old Joe Silverhound tune:

> When he's the one, havin' all the fun,
> The devil takes his time.

Mostly, he thought of Rosie. If ever she had needed confirmation of her wisdom in leaving him, God knows she had it now.

He stopped by the office to check his mail. At the top of the pile was a document called "Answer to Complaint" in the case of *Barton versus InterContinental Aerospace*. And at the top of the pleading was the name of the lawyer who would be defending the case.

Anthony Treadwell.

Part 4

"I CAN'T AFFORD TO PACK A ONE-TRICK PONY AROUND HERE," ALLYN said as she pushed through Seth's door two weeks later and tossed another thick file onto the stack covering his desk.

"Never considered myself one," said Seth, engrossed in something, not looking up. "By my count I've got about forty-five active files working."

Allyn leaned against the paint-chipped doorframe and lit a cigar. "Now you've got forty-six; which is maybe how many it takes to divert your attention from the Queen of Lost Causes." She took a deep puff. "And Outflowing Capital."

"Pardon me, Allyn," he said, putting down the deposition he was reading. "Is there a criticism in there somewhere?"

"Forget about it, Cowboy. I'm having a mood. My hair looks like it got caught in the ceiling fan, and my allergies have my nose feeling like a saxophone. Plus Ramon and I are trying to balance the checkbook today. Anyway, take a look at this file."

Seth took a look.

"I thought it might interest you."

"Only if it requires no care and feeding within the next week or two."

"You might want to take a closer look then," she said, "since the trial starts day after tomorrow."

"A trial?" said Seth, snatching up the file again. "You're giving me a jury trial? Must be a loser."

"Wasn't it you who said a world-class trial lawyer can win any case against an inferior trial lawyer—no matter how bad the facts?"

"Sounds vaguely familiar. So who's the world-class trial lawyer in this case?"

Allyn made a face. "Modesty jokes don't suit you, Seth. You'll be up against an old friend of yours. Didn't you win a big motion against Si Stephens of Caldwell and Shaw? Well, I thought I'd give Mr. Stephens a chance to get even. Besides, I've got that Johnson child-custody hearing in Oakland starting Thursday."

Seth's new client was the widow of a doctor who had ingested large volumes of alcohol and Librium, a potentially lethal combination. Her death-benefits claim for the policy limits of $500,000 had been rejected by the insurance carrier on the grounds of the suicide exclusion: the decedent was in poor health and, as a physician, must have known the blend was deadly; ergo, suicide. "I filed for the policy limits," Allyn concluded, "plus punitive damages for their bad-faith refusal to pay."

"Did he leave a suicide note?" asked Seth, flipping through the file.

"Fortunately, no. But Pacific Sigma Insurance investigators have dug up a parade of witnesses who will say the doc was gambling and severely depressed."

"And Stephens will argue that the widow Brownstein destroyed any note he might have left."

"Exactly, because Stephens knows no one can prove a negative."

"I'm beginning to see why you gave me this one."

"You said 'give me a trial.' "

Seth nodded soberly. "Well, I beat him once, I can do it again."

"You beat him once, but don't underestimate him. He's a self-centered stuffed shirt like all of them at C and S, but he's damn good with a jury and as treacherous as they come. Pacific Sigma is a big client even for C and S, so they'll pull out all the stops."

"Any other encouraging words?"

"No use sugarcoating it, Cowboy, your case has problems. Stephens will blow every one of them up the size of a Buick and shove 'em up your cute little ass in full view of the jury."

"I won't turn my back. Besides—"

"Just listen to me for once, kid. Caldwell and Shaw got the label 'Hall of Shame' the old-fashioned way—they earned it. They build their cases with unlimited budgets. They've got money—partners average over a half million a year—and plenty of power to go with it. It's common knowledge that Eldridge Shaw runs the mayor's office."

"So? He won't be picking my jury."

"That's right, Cowboy, but he's probably already picked your judge. So try to bluff Stephens into a settlement on the courthouse steps."

"How much you looking for?"

"Any goddamn thing you can get."

Seth was halfway through the file when Ramon announced that a Mr. Tucker was waiting to see him. Seth had noticed the poor soul dragging himself up the stairs and had assumed he was just another street guy bumming a handout. Knew that Ramon had standing orders from Allyn to give anyone who could make it to the second landing a cup of coffee and a card to the Episcopal Homeless Sanctuary over on Eighth and Howard.

"He says it's about the Barton case. He's read about it."

Within fifteen minutes, Seth had impatiently culled the pertinent facts from Ben Tucker, a man who claimed to be fifty-seven but looked at least twenty years older. A persistent smile failed to conceal a certain sullenness around his eyes, like a needy but mistreated dog. His was a scar-spangled face, eyes like bombs bursting in air, a nose that preceded him into the room like a flagpole. Even the smile had a bemused, ironic quality, the corners of his mouth turned down and blocked by deep grooves in his skin, engraved concentric half-circles that spread from his mouth like ripples on a disturbed pond.

In November of 1989, Ben Tucker had inherited a six-unit motel near Trinidad, California, from a distant aunt. To hear him tell it, his aunt's death by drowning was the first break he had ever had in his life. He had been out of work and nearly penniless when contacted by the probate lawyer, but had hitchhiked to Eureka to claim his prize, then borrowed against the run-down property in order to feed and clothe himself. Used the rest of the money to patch up the place. By the summer of 1990, he was beginning to turn a small profit, when a "hunk of metal the size of a horse" came out of nowhere and set his legacy ablaze.

"I reckon I shoulda expected it, sir," said Tucker from behind his mask of pain. "Never had nothin' and guess I never will. But then I read about your case and figured you might take me on."

"Why me?"

" 'Cause the Eureka newspaper back in early '92 said it was a secret jet airplane that crashed on a beach called College Cove near where my spot is and scattered parts of itself over the whole area. Hell, by next mornin', the army was all over Trinidad and Arcata, commencin' to rope off places and all hush-hush about it. They said the part what hit my motel was a piece of the damn motor."

Tucker produced the clipping from the *Eureka Times-Standard*, which speculated that the craft was a an experimental stealth jet. Seth's interest rose slightly when he read that the pilot was identified as Capt. Grant Wilburn, a name Seth recognized as the second X-215A fatality.

"How much do you estimate your damages to be, Mr. Tucker?"

"Lost one unit and damaged another, which put me into the red. Got no insurance and behind on loan payments. I'll lose the whole thing if I don't get some help, but nobody will take me on 'cause to them it's just mousemeat damages and goin' up against some big defense contractor with big bucks."

"I was asking how much you've lost, sir?"

"I'm not rightly sure, but probably about twenty-five thousand dollars to fix 'em up, plus I lost some rentals."

Seth paused, trying to conceal his irritation at the interruption. "I'm afraid I can't help you either, Mr. Tucker. You obviously can't pay an hourly rate, and there's not enough involved to justify taking your case on a contingency."

"But you got one filed already, ain't you? Cain't I just sorta piggyback?"

"The Barton case involves the identical plane, but the similarity ends there. We're going for over a million dollars in damages in that case. Yours is small change by comparison, plus a different crash at a different time with a different pilot. I'm sorry, sir, but we can't take your case. There's just no profit in it."

"No profit. Story of my life."

"Look, I'm sorry, but I've got a trial starting tomorrow, Mr. Tucker, and have to get back to it."

"A trial," he said to the floor, "one's got some profit to it, I reckon."

Seth looked at his watch. Tucker got the point. "I guess I'll be goin'."

"I can't help you, Mr. Tucker. Good luck and good-bye."

Tucker sat staring at callused hands. "I ain't had a run a good luck in my life, Mr. Cameron, 'ceptin', of course, the inheritance, and it turned sour, too. So save that wish for somebody else. Much obliged for your time anyhow." He rose slowly, steadying himself on Seth's desk, then made his way out the office.

Seth sat back down and picked up the Brownstein file, trying to find his place. The pages were now a jumble in his distracted mind. *Damn!*

"Ramon?"

"Don't worry, he's not even down to the entrance yet," said Ramon, smiling through the door. "Well, your door *was* open!"

"Well, close it and give me some privacy, okay? And when he gets back up, sign him to the standard one-third contingency and tell him I'll call him as soon as I finish the Brownstein trial."

Two days later, as Seth and the portly Mrs. Brownstein were hailing a cab to court, Harry Cooper—his expression as flat as as a sheet of foil—appeared on the sidewalk in front of Seth's office. Ignoring Mrs. Brownstein, he ushered Seth aside to tell him that Trish had left him and was threatening to file for dissolution of their marriage.

"You're coming to *me* for advice on relationships?"

"I've got to talk to someone, Seth." Harry's breath was spiced with the sweet, telltale perfume of raw vodka. "If they find out at the firm that—"

"Look, pard, I'm starting my first meaningful trial in more than a year and I'm up against C and S. You of all people know what this could mean to me. So I can't talk to you right now, understand?" A taxi pulled up. "Call me later if you want," he said, watching as Mrs. Brownstein laboriously urged herself through the cab's rear passenger door, "but if you're still into the blow and playing bingo in Reno, save your dime."

Harry began to examine his shoes and to move his lips without saying anything. Seth gave his head a quick shake, then followed Mrs. Brownstein into the cab. As they sped off, Seth refused to look back at what he knew would be Harry's most forlorn pose.

The first day of trial had its typical peaks and valleys, but as Seth began working on his closing argument late that night, he permitted himself some guarded optimism. If Mrs. Brownstein could just hold up on cross-examination the next morning, he could hit big.

The phone rang. It was Elena, her voice crackling with excitement. "I tried you at home. I *have* to talk with you. You're still working?"

"I'm in trial."

"Seth, I've got something, maybe the break we've needed!"

"Calm down, woman. You sound like one of those singing squirrels."

Elena took a deep breath, then told of having dinner that night with Gerald Murphy's wife. Murphy, according to his wife, had explored every avenue in an effort to escape the X-215A test program after Sam's death. He didn't want to go "over the hill" as Lt. David Ames had done the day after Sam's crash. Elena paused, then digressed to explain to Seth that the U.S. Air Force public information office had issued a terse statement claiming that Lieutenant Ames had been "suffering marital problems," presumably to discourage the press from branding one of their top guns as a cowardly deserter. Murphy didn't want his own marriage sullied, nor did he savor spending the rest of his life looking over his shoulder in some South American village—but he did want to spend the rest of his life.

"As a last resort," Elena continued, "he had applied to be an instructor at the Nellis Air Force Base gunnery school—just like Crispie told us. Only now, with the help of a good friend in Headquarters Records, he has his orders and they've just moved to Vegas!"

"Is there a point in there somewhere, Elena?"

"Murphy and Sam were close. I just reached him by telephone at Nellis. *He'll talk to you!*"

Seth almost came out of his chair. He grabbed another legal pad and started writing.

"I'll fly to Vegas the minute this trial is over."

"I just told Crispie, and he's as excited as we are. He said that with Murphy out of the stealth program now, he might open up to you."

"What else did Murphy tell you? If he can help us pin down Bostwick's rumor that Sam took off as late as eleven-thirty P.M. and that the standard flight pattern would put the crash area more than thirty minutes away from Symington Air Force Base, we'll have wiped out Treadwell's statute-of-limitations defense."

"He did say something about the route starting out toward

someplace in Washington near the Canadian border, then down over an Air Force base at some little town in California. Sounded like a fortress or a castle."

"Could he have said Castle Air Force Base? That's not too far south of Modesto."

"Yes, that was it."

"Perfect! that puts Sam in the Arizona desert after midnight. I'll take Murphy's statement the minute my trial is over. By the way," he added casually, hoping to blow it by her, "I hope you don't mind sharing top billing, but I've taken on a codefendant named Ben Tucker. He lost a unit in his motel to an earlier X-215A crash."

The silence told him she minded.

"Is that wise?" she said at last. "Doesn't that demean the seriousness of *my* case? A *unit* in a *motel*, Seth? Are you serious about this?"

Seth felt heat rising in his face, anger at himself that he had picked this particular moment to bring up something he knew would be touchy. He took a deep breath and spent the next ten minutes rationalizing his moment of weakness in taking on the poor bastard, explaining how it would benefit her case to have an identically designed and manufactured X-215A crashing on the identical flight pattern.

"Captain Wilburn didn't even make it to Arizona, Elena. Crashed near Eureka on his way south from the Seattle marker. Anyway, Tucker is old and broke and will engender a different kind of sympathy from a different kind of juror. Trust me, Elena, this makes for terrific synergism."

Her voice grew sleepy and softer, the level of skepticism receding with her energy.

"Well, I guess if you think it's best . . ."

"Combined with Murphy, we're on a roll here."

"All right. Anyway, it's after midnight, Seth. You'd better get some sleep."

Seth copied Murphy's telephone number onto his calendar and took a bottle of pills out of the desk drawer.

"Sleep? I'm in trial," he said, added a goodnight, and hung up.

Three days later, the jury retired to begin deliberations in the case of *Brownstein versus Pacific Sigma*. Allyn had come out for

the closing arguments and now approached Seth with an uneasy deference.

"Your argument was surgery, kid. You had Stephens and the
Pacific Sigma folks sweating bullets." Allyn started to say something else, but stopped herself and began to scan the ceiling of
the courtroom instead.

"You lose something up there, Allyn? Finish what you have
to say."

"Well, it seemed to me you danced close to the edge of the
proof a few times, at least as I recall the evidence."

"Yeah? Well, so did Stephens."

"If I remember correctly, Stephens isn't my associate, working
in a firm with my name on it."

Seth jammed the last of his files into a trial bag. "Is that all
you've got to say?"

"No. What I've got to say is thanks for turning a sow's ear
into a silk purse. You're good, Cowboy. *Really good.*"

"As good as Treadwell?" asked Seth, snapping both trial bags
shut and looking at her with eyes that still sparkled from the
intensity of his closing argument. "Well? Am I? You've seen us
both."

Allyn's thick eyebrows knitted together as she realized he was
serious. "You're already as good as Treadwell, Seth," she said,
then added gravely, "In five more years, you could be even
worse."

"What the hell's that supposed to mean?"

Allyn abruptly shook her mop of tight ringlets, jumped to her
feet, and slapped her enormous thighs. "Oh, shit, forget it, Cowboy, it was a joke. You were terrific! Tell me how you found out
that Doc Brownstein sent a desperation beeper signal to his office
just before he died."

"I went through his medical group's records covering the night
of his death. Wasn't it you who told me cases are won in the
field?"

"So I did. Let's go grab a drink while these jurors decide to
give you policy limits plus a million in punitive damages."

"I'll be with you in a minute."

In the corridor outside the courtroom, Seth joined a small
group—an attractive Japanese woman, a black man, and four
others—whom Allyn had seen sitting in the back of the court-

room. After fifteen minutes, she became tired of waiting and waved him over.

"You about ready? I've got work to do back at the office."

"Sorry, Allyn, I can't have that drink. I've got to find Si."

"What the hell's going on here?"

"I'll explain later. Come along if you want to."

They found Stephens at the cafeteria. After an exchange of perfunctory reciprocal praise, Seth got down to business.

"You know it and I know it, Si. You're going to get hit with three to five million in punitives."

"You been smoking that Mission Street loco weed, Seth?"

Seth just smiled. "All right, Si. But don't forget to tell Pacific Sigma you had a chance."

"A chance?"

"To buy out now—before the jury comes in—for policy limits plus two million five."

"You'd make a bad comedian, Seth. Keep your day job as a lawyer."

"I plan to," said Seth, then turned and began walking toward the door. *One, two, three ... come on, Simon ... four, five, blink, you bastard ... six, seven ...*

"Hold on, Seth." Seth held on, turned just slightly.

"Yeah?"

"Maybe I can get you the policy and another five hundred thousand dollars."

Seth smiled and shook his head. "I'll have to report your offer to Mrs. Brownstein, but I won't recommend it and she won't take it."

"Oh, really? Well, then, tell her that the offer expires in exactly fifteen minutes or when the jury comes back—whichever's first."

Seth started walking again. "I bet you're a good card player, Simon, but keep your day job."

Allyn followed Seth out the door. "You *will* take the million if you have to?" she asked, barely containing her excitement.

"Sure," said Seth disappearing into the men's room, "but I don't reckon I'll have to."

Seth emerged three minutes later and took Allyn by the arm. "Let's go break the bad news to Mr. Stephens."

"Bad news? You haven't even talked to Mrs. Brownstein yet."

"Don't like to pester my clients with details."

"Seth!" Allyn shouted as she pursued Seth back into the cafeteria, panting and careening around corners on her midsize heels. "A million-buck offer is hardly a detail."

"Trust me on this one, Allyn."

"I *can't* 'trust' you, Cowboy," said Allyn, stopping Seth in his tracks with one arm, then turning him around to face her. "Brownstein could sue *me* for the million if your bluff backfires. Stephens is right. You've gone loco."

"Nobody's going to sue you. Si will take my deal, Mrs. Brownstein will be rich, and so will you."

"Bullshit! Si Stephens is a savvy trial lawyer, not some easy roadkill like you used to run over when you were working the Valley courts."

"Give it a rest, Allyn," said Seth, setting off again for the cafeteria. "I'm working here."

With surprising speed, Allyn moved in front of him. "You'd do well to remember that you're working for *me!* It's *my* case, *my* malpractice policy, and it's my *law firm!*"

"Your law firm? You call this thing we do a *'law firm'?*"

Allyn shuddered as if he had struck her. Her broad shoulders sagged and her face paled. Seth tried to reach out to her, but she backed away from him.

"It may or may not be what a hotshot like you calls a law firm," she said through trembling lips, "but it's my *life,* God damn it!"

Seth had never seen Allyn Friedlander like this, never thought her capable of tears. He reached out, and this time she stood her ground. He took her gently by the shoulders.

"Allyn, listen to me. I'm sorry I hurt you. You may be the best friend I've got. So tell me the truth: Do you really *want* this 'life' you talk about? Two-bit cases? Staying one step ahead of your overhead? Trying to balance the checkbook every month with red ink? Offering cut-rate legal plumbing in a rat-infested, walk-up-and-save building?"

Silence.

"Then hang in with me. If it goes bad, I'll spend the rest of my life paying you back. You've got my word on it. Plus there's always the jury." Seth bent his head down under her eyes so she could see him smile as he added, "You know I hardly ever lose."

Allyn just gave her head a small shake, but still said nothing as Seth moved on to his rendezvous with Simon Stephens.

"Your offer is rejected, Si. Mrs. Brownstein will, however, be willing to accept the policy limits of five hundred thousand dollars plus one point eight million dollars."

Now it was Stephens who smiled and shook his head. Seth kept talking.

"Face it, Si. Your alleged expert had a whole lot of trouble explaining why a man bent on killing himself would try to call someone to help him stay alive."

"I think the jury will believe Brownstein just chickened out. Happens all the time."

"You know what else happens all the time, Si? Insurance carriers get hit for millions of dollars in punitive damages because the common folks on the street hate them. And guess who's sitting in the jury box, Si? Twelve common folks from the street."

Si smiled again and kept shaking his head. "The company won't buy it, Seth, but I'm duty-bound to report it to them. I'll be right back."

But Seth seized Stephens by the arm and spoke into his surprised face with an intensity that caused the smaller man to pull a step away. "I'm not horse-trading for a higher number, Si. We won't even *entertain* a counteroffer, understand? Our negotiations end with a simple yes or no to a total demand of two million three. If it's a no, then it's in the jury's hands, and that's just fine with me."

Something passed across Stephens's eyes, something his laughter arrived too late to disguise.

"I'll tell them," he said through a frozen smile.

"Oh, Si," shouted Seth to the retreating figure, "the offer expires in exactly fifteen minutes, or when the jury comes in— whichever's first."

Stephens paused for a moment without turning, then moved on out the door.

Seth exhaled and winked at Allyn, who had followed him into the cafeteria and had caught most of it. He went over to order coffee for both of them.

"Thanks for coming back," he said.

She managed a smile. "In for a dime, in for a dollar."

"Have some coffee."

"All I can say is that you must have a lot of confidence that you'll do better than a million when the jury comes in."

"Well, now," said Seth, staring grimly into his coffee as if seeking refuge there. "About the jury. I'm afraid we can't count too much on them."

"*What?*" Allyn Friedlander was on her feet again.

"Those people you saw me talking to in the hallway? The Japanese woman is Dr. Senko Mitsui, a jury consultant, the best in the business. She owed me a favor from my Miller and McGrath days. The others you saw with her are a perfect demographic match for the real jury. They sat through the whole three days of evidence, then came up with their own verdict."

"A shadow jury? *You used a shadow fucking jury?*"

"A downsized economy version, but effective. They came to a verdict of policy limits with *no* punitive damages."

"No punies?"

"Zilch."

"Zero? The *shoe?*"

"Planted right on Mrs. Brownstein's generously endowed ass. They didn't like her, so they bought Stephens's note-burning scenario. To top it off, the jury consultant says the obvious choice for foreman on the real jury is a blatant anti-Semite."

Allyn stared at Seth in silence, then planted her fists on the table and leaned in close to his face. "You could have told me that a few minutes ago in the hallway."

"Yes, that's true," said Seth, putting a hand on hers.

"Don't touch me, you bullshit artist!" she said, but didn't remove her hand. "Jesus, Seth, why do I sit here putting up with this?"

"Because I'm probably the best friend you've got, too. Plus, deep down, you know I've got a shot at pulling this off."

The big woman stared out the window. Her lips trembled, and Seth thought she was going to cry again, but she was struggling to hold back an ironic smile.

"A shadow jury was ingenious, Cowboy. But if the real jury is going to shut the door on you, would you mind telling me what the hell kind of game you're playing with Stephens?"

"Poker. Didn't you see his eyes when I told him I wouldn't accept a counteroffer?"

Allyn just shook her head slowly, too drained by the roller coaster of emotions to argue. "Big balls are part of your charm, Seth, but—"

"Hold the flattery for later. Here he comes."

A pale Simon Stephens entered the cafeteria and extended his hand to Seth. "Okay, Counselor, you can tell your client she's got her two point three million ... and a damn good lawyer."

"I'm sure she'll value your opinion on that Si," said Seth with a wry smile. "We'd better tell the judge to release the jury."

"I'll go tell him," said Stephens, smiling back. "But for the record, you bastard, I told them I thought you were bluffing about not being willing to listen to a counteroffer. Were you?"

"If I said no, would I be bluffing you now? You know better than to ask to see my hole card before the money's in the bank."

"Touché," said Stephens, grabbing his coat and heading for the door. "But I'll get you next time. I guarantee it."

"Always a possibility."

The woman and the younger man sat in silence for a few minutes, sipping their coffee. "Congratulations, champ," said Allyn.

"I'm sorry about hurting your feelings."

"Don't be. Everything you said is true, and we can damn sure use the money."

"For 'lost causes.' "

Allyn smiled, but ignored the remark, too happy with the sudden inflow of a fee that would exceed a half million dollars. "I still can't believe it. Hell, and to think I would have grabbed less than the policy limits in settlement if I had had the chance."

"Scary, isn't it," said Seth, shooting her his crooked smile.

Allyn smiled and shook her head. "Stephens was right about the bastard part."

"And you're a stingy old miser who probably won't even bonus me for achieving this minor miracle."

"Hey, I'm lavishly funding your Normandy-like assault on the forces of airborne evil, aren't I?"

"You are now," said Seth, smiling. "I'm going expert shopping."

30

STARS, THE GLITTERING JEWEL OF SAN FRANCISCO RESTAURANTS, SITS in relative obscurity in an alley a block from City Hall and even closer to the Federal Building. Thus situated, it provides the perfect informal venue for what passes for decision-making in San Francisco's local politics. The mayor of Stars is internationally acclaimed chef Jeremiah Tower, who efficiently greets guests while keeping a close eye on the open kitchen to ensure that the cuisine never disappoints. The "mayor's" board of supervisors consists of an equally competent cadre of maître d's whose job is to seat visiting celebrities and local power brokers according to their status and need for relative privacy.

The inconspicuous location—the front door is in an obscure alley—is Stars' only understated element, for this is where Assembly Speaker Willie Brown brushes velvet-clad elbows with Pacific Heights socialites before opening night at the opera, where Baryshnikov dines when in the city (causing a near-riot one night when spotted by Russian tourists), where judges huddle around their drinks, and where beautiful young singles huddle around each other.

Seth managed a table in the Club area, where the churning, fecund maneuvering could be observed from an elevated platform of relative tranquillity and where conversation could be undertaken without shouting. Not a typical setting for a client meeting, but Elena Barton was not a typical client. Besides, it was time for a celebration.

"It sounds as if things are going beautifully, Seth," she said, extending her glass of Veuve Clicquot—the house bubbly—in a toast. "Here's to your great victory."

"And to continuing good luck."

"I'd say good instincts."

"Credit Dr. Mitsui for my good instincts. By the way, our interview of the real jury foreman confirmed they were going to give her only the five-hundred-thousand-dollar policy. Just as our shadow jury had predicted."

"Was your opponent crushed when he heard that?"

"You don't crush Caldwell and Shaw lawyers, maybe just ding 'em a little."

"They're still the best, are they? I'm a little out of touch."

"They're tops all right. The ultimate firm."

"Sounds like the place *you* should be," she said, then caught herself. "I'm sorry."

Seth gave his glass a swirl, reading her mind reading his. "They don't hire rejects. Only beautiful women do that."

She laughed excessively at this, then gave further substance to her wish that she had not gone off on this awkward subject by changing it.

"Isn't that Luciano Pavarotti over there?"

"Looks like him."

"Pavarotti and Placido Domingo are my favorites!"

"They're okay, I guess, but I'd give the edge to Hank Williams and George Jones."

She nodded, but wasn't really listening.

"What's on your mind, Elena?"

She looked up, slightly flushed.

"I guess I just need to say that I feel responsible for your ... problem at M and M. If I hadn't gone to Uncle Tony in the first place—"

"Hey. That's all history now. Besides, Treadwell had decided I didn't belong on Montgomery Street long before you entered the picture."

"You'll make it back there."

"Hope so. Also hope I fit in better next time."

"You will. Just play the game."

"Afraid I never learned the rules."

For the next few minutes Seth sat dumbfounded while Elena recited "the rules" as if she were reading a grocery list. Get on joint partner-associate committees, even if they don't do anything, particularly the practice development committee or anything related to finance. Get a mentor and make sure he's got a book of business so you know he'll have the client clout to get you admitted to partnership when the vote comes. Make sure you get credit for victories, even small ones, using the firm newsletter or getting out a memo about something you "learned." Get your name out there and keep it out there.

Seth stared at her in amazement. "How do you know all this stuff?"

"Have you forgotten that I was an M and M kid? Grew up there. Learned the politics of success from the master himself."

"Daddy."

"And Uncle Tony, too, of course. I'd sit there and listen to them by the hour. Something had to stick."

"Any other tips for the master of the politics of failure?"

"Sure. Be sure to ask dumb questions of other senior associates, never a partner. Speak up at firm-wide meetings, but never dominate or try too much humor. Con the new, junior associates into helping you with projects when you get behind. Whenever you finish an assignment, even a small one, leave a note to the partner in the file suggesting the next steps. The partner will love you for it." She paused, sipped her champagne. "I guess no one tells associates these things."

Seth saluted her with his glass, imagining what it would mean to have a woman like this at his side.

The appetizers arrived, crab toasts with lobster sauce for Elena, and cornmeal pancakes with salmon for Seth. He wondered briefly what Allyn and Ramon would think about this $200 "client meeting."

"More champagne?" asked the waiter.

"Bring us another glass, Lee, then open a bottle of Mondavi reserve cabernet to go with the lady's duck confit. I'll have the lavender-honey roasted lamb loin. Hold the fava beans."

Their glasses touched again, and Seth felt himself drawn into her gray-green eyes. It killed him the way her lips were always parted a little, as if she were about to speak, full lips surrounding a row of perfect, chalk-white teeth. *Is this another woman come to wreck me?* The piano soared through the theme from *Dr. Zhivago*.

Then she did speak.

"You seem to have more than a passing knowledge of gourmet dining. I thought you said you were from Bakersfield."

"I'm a decent cook," Seth said, smiling. "Comes from years of being on my own. I'll give you a private demonstration some evening if you'd like."

Elena gave him a look that sent a tremor through his groin. "Your place or mine?" she said, and burst out laughing.

"Pretty subtle, huh?" said Seth, forcing a smile.

"Somewhere between a boiler explosion and a train wreck."

"Well, I *am* from Bakersfield."

Elena turned serious. "I've heard that it's a bad idea to mix business and pleasure, particularly between lawyer and client. Are you afraid to get it out in the open, Counselor?"

Seth put his glass down. "You want it out in the open? Okay. I've been living alone for nearly six months now and I'm horny as a hoot owl. On top of that, you're the most beautiful woman I've ever seen, on or off a movie screen. So I'd like to go to bed with you as soon as possible. That open enough?"

Elena stared into her own glass for a moment as the corners of her mouth gave way to an incipient smile. "I suspect that you're obsessed with urges less primitive than sex."

"None come to mind at the moment."

"How about power for starters?" she said playfully, then turned serious. "I'm curious, Seth. What *is* important to you?"

Seth straightened in his chair, thought for a moment, then nodded his head.

"Getting," he said.

"Getting? Getting what?"

"Lots of things. Getting a second chance at Montgomery Street. Getting even with the son of a bitch who booted me off it." Seth paused and smiled again. "I think I may already have mentioned getting you in bed."

I'm talking too much, he thought. *Running off at the mouth like a damn goose with diarrhea.*

Elena's face gave away nothing, and Seth resolved to knock off the Joe Romeo crap. This one would have to come to him, when and if she wanted to.

"So tell me," she said, her eyes now steadily fixed on his despite the distractions around them, "about the case."

Seth resisted trying to speculate concerning this typically sharp turn in Elena's thought processes and was almost relieved that she had broken the tension. Back on solid ground, he gave her a detailed update. He told her that he had set up a meeting with

Gerald Murphy at Nellis Air Force Base. He reviewed his trips to New Orleans and Symington, then concluded by explaining that with the fee from the Pacific Sigma case in hand, Allyn had approved the retention of Dr. Henry Daimler, one of the country's foremost avionics experts, now teaching part-time at the University of California.

"Avionics?"

"The field of aviation electronics," said Seth. "Dr. Daimler speculates that Sam—and the others—died from some kind of electronic systems failure."

"How far do we get in court with speculation?"

"Fair question. The answer is not very, but I'm meeting with him tomorrow and hope to persuade him to come up with a specific theory on how the X-215A's electronics failed."

"How do you 'persuade' an expert to do that?"

"Pay him three hundred and fifty dollars an hour for starters. The rest is an acquired skill, called gentle persuasion by some, shameless manipulation by others."

"What do *you* call it?"

"The successful seduction of your own well-paid whore—if you'll excuse the language."

"You're excused. Here's to a successful seduction," she said, then added with a coy smile, "of Professor Daimler."

Seth acknowledged her repartee with a smile of his own, and they toasted, eyes locked over the rims of their brandy snifters. Seth asked Elena what she would like for dessert.

"How about one of those private demonstrations you mentioned?"

He couldn't resist. "Your place or mine?"

Her eyes never wavered from his as she completed the exchange. "Mine."

While Seth slumbered in the silk-sheet luxury of Elena Barton's four-poster in San Francisco's Pacific Heights, Aubrey Olmstead glowered at his silent telephone and paced the floor nearly four thousand miles away in the Caicos Islands. At 4:30 A.M., he heard the sound he had been waiting for, and his huge fist snatched the phone out of its cradle in midring.

"*Yes?*"

"Good morning, Aubrey," came Father's soothing baritone.

"*Bullshit* good! You send me one of your cryptic goddamn messages, then you fucking disappear on me. What the hell does 'One of the sheep has strayed' mean and what have you done about it?"

"Aubrey, Aubrey. I sent that elliptical message only to alert you to exercise particular caution as regards our . . . sales activities during the next few days, not to launch you into one of your paranoid orbits. If I had wanted you to know precisely what is at hand, I would have told you. Rest assured that our little problem will be taken care of—indeed *is* being taken care of in Las Vegas even as we speak."

"Well, then, Mr. Fixit, here's another 'little problem' that's popped up today. That Mission Street punk's suit against Con-Space has provoked a new government investigation!"

For a moment, all Olmstead could hear in the telephone was his own labored breathing.

"Torville?"

"Who else? The fat little prick issued a subpoena today to my ex-bookkeeper."

"Will he talk?"

"Not now."

"Oh, Jesus, Aubrey, you didn't . . ."

"No, of course not. We just scared the shit out of him and sent him to Uruguay to work under the close supervision of one of my associates."

"Ah. The 'Aubrey Olmstead Witness Protection Program.' "

"Something like that. But now there's Torville and this fucking Cameron, who's scheduled to start trial soon against ConSpace. A public fistfight like that could get very sticky."

"Not to worry, deah boy. Mr. Cameron will be on the canvas before the first round even starts."

"What if he won't stay there?"

"Then he'll be put *under* the canvas. Disposal is my job, Aubrey. Your job is to keep the money coming and to *relax* for heaven's sake!"

"Christ, Father, we can't just go around killing people . . ."

Aubrey Olmstead stood alone in the middle of the room, aware that his perspiring hand was clutched around a plastic dial tone.

Sᴀᴛʜᴇʀ Gᴀᴛᴇ, ʟᴏᴄᴀᴛᴇᴅ ᴀᴛ ᴛʜᴇ ɴᴏʀᴛʜ ᴇɴᴅ ᴏꜰ Tᴇʟᴇɢʀᴀᴘʜ Aᴠᴇɴᴜᴇ, is not really a gate at all, but an ornate wrought-iron arch that majestically marks the entrance to the University of California at Berkeley. Walking beneath it the next morning was for Seth like passing under a waterfall of nostalgia: girls he had dated or tried to date, drug vendors, pangs of anxiety en route to final exams, People's Park, clashes with police, bongo drums, runaways begging for spare change, atheists and Jesus freaks screaming at each other and at other demonstrators loudly exhorting the memory of Mario Savio. He wouldn't have missed it for anything, nor could he imagine anything that could make him do it over again.

Seth was surprised at the modesty of Prof. Henry P. Daimler's office when he finally found it buried in the east wing of the Barrington Memorial Science Building. The professor's cubicle was even smaller than Seth's own and every bit as poorly furnished. Two leather chairs, finely corrugated with age, took up the only space not jammed with bookcases overflowing with technical treatises. Sandwiched between the bookcases was a small student's desk that seemed incapable of accommodating the professor's long legs. The austere milieu was capped by an odor like rotten eggs drifting in a tiny window from one of the labs below.

"Come in, Mr. Cameron," Daimler said in a surprisingly youthful voice for a man in his seventies. He was six feet four inches tall, and his manner suggested an apology for taking up so much space. A mangled tweed suit hung from his lanky frame like moss from an ancient oak, and a trumpet of a nose protruded from a friendly face that was largely concealed by a full red beard, slowly surrendering to gray. His hair, though also in retreat, was flaming red, which, when combined with his height and pale, elongated forehead, created the image of a volcano in full eruption.

"Have a plum? Some grapes? This," he added with a diffident smile, "is my version of lunch."

"No thank you, sir. Just ate."

"I have a more comfortable office in Los Angeles," the professor continued with the comfortable air of a man disseminating information, not boasting. "I teach only one day a week here, so this is what I get. Have a seat and tell me more about this case of yours."

But Seth was not to be rushed. This was a time for investigation and appraisal. His father, who had seen many fine expert witnesses come and go in his courtroom, used to say there is no one—not even a trial lawyer—who can turn a losing case into a winner, or a winner into a loser, faster than an expert witness.

He's got to be smart, of course, and have all the right credentials, Joe had said, *but down-to-earth, too; not always talking down to folks.*

"In a minute, sir," Seth said, his critical eye taking in everything: a UC honorary Ph.D. certificate, photos of a forty-something couple with teenage kids—presumably grandchildren—propped on his desk, the unpolished shoes, the tie of many colors, the gray, unkempt beard, the incongruously bright red hair—*does the professor wear a rug? Probably not, but jurors might think so, which is just as bad.* "Tell me about your work."

Fifteen years at MIT, another twenty at Cal Tech, a Ph.D. in physics, and an endless list of publications—articles and books on molecular physics, materials failure, nonlinear dynamics, and avionics—comprised a curriculum vitae that would qualify the professor to testify in any court in the land. Seth had already studied Daimler's paper on stealth avionics, a definitive work on aircraft electronics known to have influenced President Carter in his decision to kill the Rockwell International B-1 bomber. Professor Daimler was also an authority on chaos dynamics and its application to materials-failure analysis.

Seth was fully satisfied with Daimler's academic pedigree, and the soft-spoken way in which he described it. His trial lawyer instincts also sensed that under the expert witness's mild manner lay a formidable strength and will. The game now was not only to make sure Professor Daimler was the right man for the job, but to manipulate him into becoming an advocate for the case.

Seth knew from his father's early stories that the best expert witness in the world cannot be of help unless he will come into court, raise his right hand in the air, face the jury square in its collective eye, and persuasively sponsor the trial lawyer's theory of the case. *Make 'em want to help you, Seth. Spin your sad tale of widows and orphans, evil corporate empires and wrongs to be righted. Help your expert get up on that white stallion, kid, then hand him a sword.*

The Investigator was finished; time for the Manipulator to jump in with a quick peroration on the nobility of Elena Barton's purpose in bringing the suit—no money-grubbing litigant in our corner, no sir. (Seth didn't burden the monologue with his own motivations.) Time to speak of undetected government dereliction, the agony of other stealth widows, and the countless lives that could be saved by forcing an open review of the X-215A's deficiencies.

The professor nodded sympathetically at each point. Progress was being made.

As Seth then steered the expert into a general discussion of stealth technology, he was relieved to see the professor scratch his head with a vigor no toupee could have survived. *Good,* concluded the Investigator, *no rug.*

Prof. Henry Daimler steepled his fingers, then gave Seth a where-do-you-want-me-to-begin look over his Ben Franklin spectacles. Seth told him wherever he wanted to start would be fine.

"The ultimate stealth aircraft will look either like a carrot or a pancake," he began, speaking in a voice ripe with experience, and conveying the authority of a pioneer. He explained how Con-Space, like Northrup with the controversial B-2 bomber, had opted for the pancake-design configuration, which meant that the forward fuselage "ended up looking like it has been run over by a steamroller."

In his most recent paper, Daimler had researched the accessible public data on stealth designs by Northrup, Grumman, Con-Space, and others and had correlated various designs with currently available accident data.

"Sort of an epidemiological approach," he said with the weary smile of an academician delivering a bad scientific joke. "The bottom line is that stealth aircraft are, by definition and necessity, inherently unsafe. Sure you don't want an apricot?"

The Investigator was ready to conclude that the professor was a trial lawyer's dream—imposing but likable, articulate but not overly cerebral, and though a high-profile critic of stealth technology, ostensibly objective. Seth took in a deep breath and decided to go for the jugular. No use wasting time with a man he was paying $350 per hour.

"So unsafe," Seth said, picking up a yellow legal pad, "as to rule out the probability of pilot error as the cause of a crash?"

The professor tapped the side of an index finger on pursed lips and let out a melancholy sigh. Seth made a note to eliminate these revealing mannerisms before his deposition.

"Not without an opportunity to examine the craft, I'm afraid."

Seth had feared this response. "You know they won't let us do that and the court probably won't make them. How far can you go without it?"

Daimler gazed at his liver-spotted hands for a full minute before answering. "Well, Counselor, my recent paper to the Institute of Advanced Aviation Research in Boston takes the position that pancake designs simply cannot safely accommodate the ten to sixteen miles of electrical wiring a stealth aircraft requires."

"Good. Why is that?"

"Too many elements. You've got fly-by-wire electronics, systems to reduce the aircraft's RCS, ECM equipment, infrared and other detection gear to beat ground-based bistatic and OTH backscatter radar—"

"Hold on, sir, you just lost me and most of the jury. You've got to speak English in a courtroom or you're no good to me. Why don't you pretend you're explaining the things you've just told me to your grandson in the picture there."

"All right," said Daimler, and tapped a pipe with an empty bowl on the heel of his hand. He then jammed it into his mouth, and deep furrows fanned out in all directions from his eyes as he drew imaginary smoke. Seth could feel the energy of his concentration. Then Professor Daimler lifted his plate of fruit and thrust it in front of Seth.

"I'd tell him it's like trying to cram six pounds of these grapes into a five-pound bag. Some are bound to get broken."

"That's better," said Seth, relieved to see that Daimler did not suffer from the need to protect himself from contradiction by speaking in an unfathomable interlingua. Seth had found that this narcissistic patois turned off nine jurors for every three it impressed.

Daimler shrugged, seemingly disappointed at Seth's bland reaction to his idiomatic pearl. "We get a little isolated here in academia. Become conversationally handicapped."

Seth smiled. "Verbally challenged?"

Daimler smiled back. "Linguistically dysfunctional."

Good. He's got a wit and can laugh at himself.

"I'll catch on," he added. A grape vanished into the dense beard.

"We'll work on it," said Seth, knowing better at this early stage than to pamper or patronize an expert. *Make them want to please you.*

"Based on what I sent you, Professor, can you provide an opinion as to what happened to Sam Barton out in that Arizona desert?"

"That just sounds like a different approach to the same problematical question, and I'm sorry to tell you I can't really say what happened out there. My guess—which I suppose carries little weight in a court of law—is that the root cause for the X-215A's problems has to do with taking reckless shortcuts in its efforts to surpass Northrup and its B-2 bomber. In the process, ConSpace built an unsafe aircraft."

Back to generalizations, thought Seth, trying to remain patient.

"Then can't we draw a fair inference, Professor, that this very lack of safety probably caused the crash?"

"I'm afraid not."

Seth glared at the old man and tapped his pen on the yellow pad.

"Peach?" said Daimler into the silence. "They're from South America, I believe. Wonderful."

"Look, Professor," said Seth, color rising in his fatigued face, "I need some help here. I've got a widow whose husband's career and reputation have been disparaged by a not-give-a-shit U.S. Air Force. I've got four deadly crashes in less than two years with the best fliers in the world at the wheel. I've got six pounds of grapes crammed into a five-pound bag, and now I've got an expert who won't attribute the crashes to what he's described *himself* as a fucking 'unsafe aircraft!' "

Professor Daimler looked sympathetically at Seth and responded in a voice so serene and supportive that it made Seth feel like a patient in therapy. "I don't believe," he said, grinning, "that my description made any reference to fucking."

Seth fell back in his chair and exhaled. "I get carried away sometimes."

"Its all right," said Daimler in his soothing, almost hypnotic voice.

"Rub people the wrong way."

"We all do at one time or another."

"Sorry."

"No apology necessary."

"Let's start over."

The good trial lawyers know when to quit, Son. The **great** *trial lawyers don't even know how.*

"Tell me how the B-2 is different from the X-215A."

"Of course. For one thing, the X-215A flies nearly twice as fast as the notorious B-2 stealth bomber. The trade-off is a radar signature several times larger. ConSpace bet its money that the development of impulse radar by foreign military powers would soon render speed more important than stealth."

"Impulse radar?"

"It will be able to profile a sparrow and render the half-billion-per-copy B-2 obsolete before it's fully operational. This inspired the Armed Forces Subcommittee on Aviation Technology to move into a further design evolution of manned delivery systems, resulting in the X-215A."

"So," said Seth, "it was their earlier mistakes on the B-1 and B-2 that spooked the committee, then Congress, into funding the X-215A."

"Exactly, and now the X-215A might be a clunker, too."

"On the phone, you mentioned electronics as a possible cause of ConSpace's problems."

"Just a guess, but I think their problem is improper interfacing of numerous electrical wiring systems, compounded by the extremely limited storage space imposed by the flattened-out fuselage and crowded canopy-cockpit area."

"Too many grapes for the size of the bag."

"Exactly."

"How did the grapes break on Sam Barton's flight?"

The professor smiled and reached for his pipe again. "How

many different ways of asking the same question do they teach you fellows in law school?"

Seth reached over and grabbed a grape off the plate. "As many ways as necessary to get the answer we need."

The professor sighed and picked up his pipe again. "I'm not trying to be difficult, but . . . okay. A grape is fine until its skin breaks. I suspect it starts with a failure to the harness that encloses and shields the wiring from contact with other wiring or other objects."

"What could cause failure of a harness?"

"It could be some kind of maintenance mishap, though that seems unlikely to have happened on four separate occasions, unless of course it was sabotage—which wouldn't help your case much. Failure could also result from friction caused by rubbing or chafing."

"Then?"

"Once the harness deteriorates, sparking can occur between wires, or between a wire and some protruding object like a bolt or screw, resulting in systems failure or even a fire. But whether that happened and how it happened, I must repeat, is pure speculation on my part."

I'm sitting with the expert of all fucking experts, thought Seth, staring glumly at his nearly empty yellow pad, *and he can't do a goddamn thing for me.* Another wave of sulfuric acid drifted into the room. Seth tasted a bitterness in his mouth. He was beginning to feel sick.

"As you know, Professor, the court won't let you speculate, so I'm afraid we've got problems." Seth closed his briefcase and thanked Dr. Daimler for his time. "I'll be talking to one of the X-215A test pilots tomorrow, and I'll tell you what I learn at our predeposition meeting on Thursday."

"Who will be taking my deposition?"

"A lawyer named Anthony Treadwell."

"Sounds familiar. Is he good?"

Seth turned at the door. "He's good."

As he passed under Sather Gate again, Seth experienced a déjà vu feeling from fifteen years before; a sense of having just flunked a final exam.

SETH'S WELCOME AT THE ENTRANCE TO NELLIS AIR FORCE BASE THE next day was in pleasant contrast to his earlier experience with Lev in New Mexico. Captain Murphy had put his name on the visitors' list, and Seth was given a full salute and VIP treatment from the moment of his arrival.

"This is Corporal Hawkinson, sir," said the guard. "He'll be your driver. Please park your vehicle right over there, sir."

Five minutes later, Seth was escorted into a large office in the headquarters complex. The walls were covered with squadron emblems, plus a family portrait of a seated but erect uniformed officer, beset by two gleaming, erect, towheaded boys and one gleaming, erect, bleached-blond wife whose mushrooming bouffant hairstyle threatened the otherwise perfect composition of the scene. There were crossed regimental swords, an Air University diploma, photos of diverse high-ranking officers and gray-haired civilians chatting amiably in front of airplanes of various vintages. An airman first class indicated a chair and offered Seth a cup of coffee, which he gratefully accepted.

"Do all pilots have offices like this?" asked Seth.

"Only if they also happen to be a base commander," said the airman, who vanished before Seth could ask the obvious question.

He didn't have to wait long.

A tall, distinguished-looking man extended his hand. "I'm Gen. Clement Farnsworth." Seth noted the steel gray hair, chiseled features, and one white eyebrow as the general continued. "I'm the base commander of Symington Air Force Base. I'm here at Nellis as part of an accident-investigation team. I'm afraid you won't be meeting with Captain Murphy today."

"He had an accident?"

"A fatal one it seems."

"He's *dead?*"

"I'm sorry to report to you that Capt. Gerald X. Murphy crashed on takeoff this morning at oh seven hundred hours," said Farnsworth with the cold precision of an information officer reading an accident report. "It was a routine mission in a time-proven F-16. The captain was just putting in his minimum flight time." His report completed, the general seated himself behind the desk, and his tone shifted to that of a chaplain breaking bad news to a family member. Warm and soothing. "May I ask your purpose in coming here to see Captain Murphy?"

A knock on the door interrupted Seth's dazed thoughts.

"In!" shouted the general in a different voice, so different that Seth thought for a moment someone else was in the room. It was the coffee, hot enough to burn Seth's mouth, although he hardly noticed.

"But I just spoke with him. Last night."

"He crashed this morning," repeated the general, resuming a soothing tone that overlooked the irrelevance of Seth's remark. "I know it must be a shock. Were you friends?"

"No. I had only spoken to him on the phone."

"May I ask why you came here to see him?"

"Just wanted to chat."

"About?"

"I'm a lawyer, sir. I'm on a case."

"Was Captain Murphy involved," asked the general, swiveling casually behind the desk, "in your case?"

It dawned on Seth that he was being interrogated. He thanked the general, picked up his briefcase, and got to his feet. General Farnsworth rose as well and moved swiftly toward the door.

But he didn't open it. He blocked it.

"I asked you," he repeated, but in a voice now hard-edged, "whether Captain Murphy was involved in your case."

"And I told you," said Seth, mustering a steely tone of his own, "that I'm a lawyer on a case. That means I can't discuss privileged information. Now, General, I'll be leaving."

The two men exchanged a challenging look, neither blinking. Finally, the general stepped aside, saying, "All right, Mr. Cameron, you're free to go, of course. But you are *not*, I say again, *not* free to return—either to Nellis *or* to Symington. Particularly Symington."

Seth didn't move. "Why do you mention Symington?"

"Because I know you and your spade friend were nosing around there," said Farnsworth, his voice menacing and razor raw. "Show up there again and I'll shoot you myself as a spy." He flashed Seth a sinister smile as he swung the door open, adding, "Military law."

Seth's momentary anxiety was swept aside by anger. He slammed the door shut with the heel of his hand and stood nose to nose with Farnsworth. "What the fuck is going on here, General? What are you afraid of? You say you're here investigating Murphy's accident. What caused it? *Who* caused it?"

Farnsworth's unblinking eyes were like clear ice crystals within a face that had become a frozen mask. Abruptly, he brushed past Seth, walked back to the desk, and hit the intercom button. "Farnsworth here. Two APs. On the double." Turning his back on Seth, he stared out at a squadron of marching airmen. For a minute, only the cadence count of the squad leader could be heard—*hut two hareep-hor, hut two hareep-hor*—but then the general turned and calmly said, "You're in way over your head, boy."

Seth met his eyes. "Like Murphy was?"

"Your innuendo is insulting and outrageous, Cameron. It happens that Murphy caught a bird in his air scoop. It happens."

"A bird?" said Seth, pointedly gazing at Farnsworth's epaulets. "I'm betting it was an American eagle."

A sudden loud blow to the door caused Seth to jump out of the way as two burly uniformed men powered through it like offensive guards.

"Please come in, gentlemen," Seth said, stepping between them, "I was just on my way out."

SETH WAS AWAKENED BY FAT DOG'S MORNING HEADER OFF THE BED. The mutt had never gotten the hang of backing his way down, and his missing foreleg made a graceful headfirst landing impossible.

Fat Dog was probably supposed to have been a golden retriever, but something had gone wrong—possibly a male basset hound—during mating. Then, not far into life, a car attack left him an orphaned pup with three legs, which is the way Seth found him at the Bakersfield SPCA, just in time to commute his sentence. In Seth's case, after Rosie's departure, Fat Dog wasn't "man's best friend"; he was his only friend.

"We're in trouble, Fats," said Seth as they ate breakfast together. "I just lost my key witness on the statute of limitations and defective manufacture. Treadwell is going to shoot my learned avionics expert down in flames this morning. If things don't pick up, it's beans for me and whatever you can catch for you."

Fat Dog yawned.

"Not that you couldn't afford to lose a few."

Four hours later, Seth and Professor Daimler strolled across Market Street and north into the financial district. The wind rushed down Montgomery Street like an invisible wall, penetrating Seth's suit coat, assailing his damp shirt, and adding to the discomfort of a head aching from fatigue and anxiety.

"Cool here in the city," said the professor.

Seth understood the importance of small talk now—the smaller the better—as they approached the moment of truth. Preparation time was over; it was time to pass or fail.

"These buildings have turned our streets into a series of Boeing wind tunnels," said Seth, indicating an inside-out umbrella to make his point. "Plus they block out the sun, which keeps the air cold. Adds up to an uncomfortable chill factor. Sad."

"Yes," agreed the professor. "Sad."

Seth had been surprised to learn that Treadwell would take the professor's deposition himself. Was it at Traeger's insistence? ConSpace's? Hard to imagine the Great Man taking a deposition, a task usually assigned to a younger lawyer, even in very large cases. Also hard to imagine Treadwell doing anything he didn't want to do. So what was the message?

"Have you been here before?" asked Daimler as Seth deftly guided him into the tower elevator bank without a glance at the directory.

"Used to work here," said Seth, and the professor let it drop.

Seth greeted the penthouse receptionist, who offered them a seat, coffee, and a sympathetic smile. The clock struck ten as they sank deep into a leather couch across from a leather-faced woman whom Seth judged by her machine to be the court reporter. Coffee arrived at five past the hour, but no Treadwell. The minutes passed as they waited for the summons to Treadwell's office.

Just like old times.

At ten minutes past the hour, Seth told the receptionist to inform Mr. Treadwell's secretary they would not wait past ten-fifteen.

The game was on.

At precisely ten-fifteen, Miss Tarkenton quick-stepped into the lobby, proffering apologies for the delay, and escorted them into Treadwell's office. She gave no indication of remembering Seth.

Seth felt a chill as he reentered the senior partner's lair for the first time in months. He quickly scanned the main office, the conference area, the wet-bar area. No Treadwell.

Checkmate.

"He'll be with you momentarily, gentlemen," said Miss Tarkenton as she showed them into the conference wing of the senior partner's huge office. "Another cup of coffee?" Seth fumed and glanced at his watch.

Stay cool, Son. Remember, mind games only work if you let 'em.

At 10:22, the door was flung open, and the senior partner briskly entered, followed closely by two younger lawyers. The sight of Treadwell rocketed Seth's heartbeat. *Must be the coffee,* he rationalized.

"My apologies, gentlemen," said Treadwell in his robust baritone, offering a huge, well-manicured hand to Professor Daimler. As tall as the professor was, Treadwell's height and presence made him seem the taller man, creating the formidable impression of a skyscraper viewed from the street. "Clients pay you four hundred dollars an hour," he added, "and damned if they don't expect to speak with you occasionally."

The associates laughed on cue and introduced themselves. Seth remembered one of the associates—an exceptionally bright lawyer named Jim Woodsen—but not the other. Only a perceptive observer would have noticed that the ritual was completed without Seth and Treadwell shaking hands.

When all were seated and the reporter's fingers were poised over her machine, Treadwell turned his massive head toward Seth for the first time. "Well, now, Cameron," he said, managing a half smile that did little to soften the disdainful tone of his voice, "how do you find life as a Mission Street lawyer?"

Seth met the senior partner's laser gaze. "It's quite different, Mr. Treadwell; you know, with the quill pens and no telephones."

Woodsen unsuccessfully stifled a laugh, drawing a glance from Treadwell.

"The other difference is we represent people there."

"How nice for you. And I take it that this fellow Benjamin Tucker is one of those people. Frightening claim: twenty-five thousand dollars! What's next, Cameron, a small-claims court suit for a broken vase caused by an X-215A sonic boom?"

Woodsen, trying to compensate, laughed a little too loudly.

"Well, Cameron, to show our good faith, we'll stipulate to your request for consolidation of the two cases, assuming you'll produce the plaintiff here in San Francisco for deposition."

"Agreed," said Seth. "Mr. Tucker has suffered a mild heart attack, but we'll produce him as soon as he's out of the hospital."

"Very good. I see you have no statute problem with Tucker's humble claim, since it's only for property damage, but I assure you there is at least one similarity between Montgomery Street and Burritoville: you can't file a wrongful-death lawsuit after the one-year statute of limitations has run."

"And I assure *you*, sir, that I have not done that." Seth picked up his pen. "I believe we're here for a deposition?"

"Just so," said Treadwell, and turned toward the expert witness. "I won't detain you long, Professor. Mrs. Bartholomew, please swear the witness."

The interrogation quickly deteriorated into something between a chess game and a mud-wrestling match as Seth kept Treadwell at a safe distance from his forensically inexperienced witness, making frequent objections to give Daimler time to become more comfortable with the process. Treadwell retaliated with artfully phrased leading questions and frequent threats to seek sanctions for Seth's "obfuscation and obstructionism." Not until three in the afternoon did Seth feel that Daimler was sufficiently ring-wise to allow Treadwell to get to the real issues in the case.

It didn't take the senior partner long to find what he wanted.

"So you really can't say what caused the crash, can you?"

"Only that it was, in all probability, an electronic failure."

"How can you say even that?"

"Because Captain Barton's flaps were up, according to the accident report."

"So?"

"No pilot would intentionally crash-land a high-speed aircraft with flaps up."

"Why not?"

"He would come in too hot—which is probably what happened, according to the available information. The flaps are electronically controlled, thus it's logical to assume that an electronic failure of some kind had occurred."

It won't get us home, Henry, Seth had told the expert earlier, *but if it's the best you can honestly do, then that's what we'll have to go with.*

"So, Professor, you admit at least that Barton was alive when he tried—and obviously failed—to make a safe crash landing in the desert?"

"Objection," interceded Seth in order to give Daimler time to consider the question.

"What possible grounds, Counsel?"

"The question assumes there is such a thing as a safe crash landing, a classic oxymoron. But go ahead and answer, Professor, if you can."

"Alive, perhaps, but not necessarily functional."

"Now there," said Treadwell sarcastically, and glaring at Seth, "is the kind of bullshit response that only Mr. Cameron could have put into your mouth. He *was* alive was he not, Professor? Nothing was wrong with the cockpit life support systems, was there?"

"Objection," said Seth. "Argumentative. Please control your attitude and your language, Mr. Treadwell, or this deposition is finished right now."

Treadwell raised an eyebrow. "My, my, Cameron. Have you had a religious experience since the days when you filled this very office with epithets that would make a stevedore blush?"

Seth nodded toward the reporter. "Never when there was a lady present."

The associates exchanged a snickering glance. Treadwell raised another eyebrow.

"Oh, I see," he said. "Well, then, Professor, what pray do you mean, 'perhaps not functional'?"

"Once the electronics failed, the oxygen mix could be affected, thus impairing the pilot's ability to judge distances and altitudes if he happened to be at a high altitude at the time of failure. So if hypoxia didn't get him in the air, the absence of flaps and other controls got him on the ground. Either way, it was probably an electrical failure of some kind."

Treadwell's eyes flickered between the witness and Seth. He checked his notes, glanced up at his associates, then stared back at the witness with metallic consternation.

"*Of some kind*," he repeated. "You've never seen the plans to the X-215A, have you?"

"Of course not."

"Never flown in one?"

"No."

"Ever so much as seen one?"

"Only pictures."

"And you can't say what the specific failure was?"

"That's true."

"And that's because pinpointing it would require speculation on your part, am I correct, sir?"

"No, sir. It's because you won't let me see the aircraft."

"Well, apart from whether the Air Force should let every Tom, Dick, or Harry come in and examine our nation's number one military secret, *the fact is your conclusions stated here today are based on pure speculation, are they not?"*

Professor Daimler looked hopelessly at Seth, then down at his hands. Everyone in the room knew what his answer had to be and that an affirmative reply on the record would set up a certain summary judgment in favor of ConSpace. Treadwell and Woodsen exchanged a smile, and when Seth looked at Treadwell he was stunned to see the senior partner winking at him.

The secret, kid, is perseverance. Never give up, even when your back is bleeding against the wall. When all else has failed, stall for time. Something might happen. When time runs out, stall some more. Never quit thinking. Never quit trying! Never quit!

"Objection," said Seth. "The question's been asked and answered. I instruct the witness not to answer again."

Treadwell exchanged a laugh with his associates, then sneered at Seth as he spoke to Daimler in a condescending tone. "You may go ahead and answer, Professor. Counsel knows that a judge would severely sanction him for such a frivolous objection, and that even if the objection were valid, he can't instruct a witness not to answer except when the witness is also his own client."

Treadwell's words hung in the electric air as Seth and Henry Daimler exchanged a look.

"Professor Daimler," said Seth in a quiet voice, "you look like a man in serious need of a lawyer."

Daimler innocently raised his eyebrows. "But I *have* a lawyer, Mr. Cameron. *You, of course.*"

Treadwell slammed his hand on the table, and his eyes bulged into white-hot coals. Coming out of his chair, he leaned across the table as if to strike Seth.

"I'll have your ticket for this little prank, Cameron. But first I'll see that Judge Singer sanctions you and that dyke you work for—"

That was as far as he got, for Seth had grabbed his tie and pulled him down to within inches of his own face. "I told you once, podner, to watch your language in the presence of the lady here. Now, you've obviously got a burr under your saddle, but you've got to turn it down a notch right now or this deposition is over. And if you ever say another derogatory word about Allyn Friedlander, I'll have to hurt you."

Woodsen recovered from the shock of the moment and

grabbed the senior partner's tie, together with the attached senior partner, and hauled Treadwell back into his seat, gasping like a grounded bass.

"Let the record show," said Treadwell, swiftly regaining his composure, "that I've been assaulted by this hillbilly gladiator who purports to represent the witness."

"Would you like a recess, Mr. Treadwell?" asked Seth, returning the wink. "Time to reflect on your own decorum? I believe the record will accurately demonstrate your words and actions, including the fact that in lunging at me, you crossed well over the center line of the table."

The court reporter gave Seth a motherly, reassuring nod.

"I need no recess," said Treadwell, straightening his notes and his tie. "First, Professor, let me assure you that I will eventually have my answer to the last question, and I will have substantial monetary sanctions as well. But let us proceed.

"If, hypothetically, Barton's crash was not pilot error, Professor, and your 'theory' about defective electronics is correct, wouldn't ConSpace logically have taken the necessary steps to correct the problem after the first two crashes?"

"It's not that easy, Counselor. Today, almost everything in stealth aircraft is done optoelectronically through fiber-optic, digital data buses. Forty percent of the cost of the X-215A is in fiber-electronics, so—"

"Alright, Professor, that's enough. You've answered the question."

"—if invasive sparking is occurring at critical points along the electrical wire harness that protects the sixteen miles of wiring in the X-215A, God knows where you'd find it."

Treadwell scowled, while the unstoppable Henry Phineas Daimler, Ph.D., professor of avionics and chaos dynamics, and now a confirmed advocate as well, forged ahead.

"You must understand, Mr. Treadwell, that your client *is* undoubtedly troubleshooting. Probably around the clock and probably since the very first crash, but as of October fifteenth, 1993, they obviously hadn't found the problem, had they?"

For no apparent reason, Treadwell suddenly smiled.

"October fifteenth, you say, Professor. I think we've finally found a point of agreement."

Seth shot Daimler a look with the force of a kick under the

table, then tried to think of an objection. Failing that, he decided to testify instead. "Excuse me, Mr. Treadwell, but the time and date of the accident is beyond this witness's knowledge and expertise."

"That's true," said the chastened professor, "I have no evidence concerning the specific time of the crash."

"Nor," said Treadwell, "do you have a *shred* of evidence that it occurred *after* midnight—on October *sixteenth*." It wasn't a question.

"No, sir, I don't."

"The X-215A is not a body on which you can perform an autopsy and pinpoint the time of death, is it?"

"No, sir, it isn't."

"Thank you. Incidentally, while on the subject of things 'entirely beyond your knowledge and expertise,' I have seen confidential Air Force records establishing that crash landings without major incident are quite common in flat areas such as the desert, Professor. Isn't it a fact that our prima donna stealth pilots have simply lost touch with the fundamentals of flying in general and emergency procedures in particular?"

"You're wrong there, sir. I've seen those records. They report on standard jet aircraft crash landings, not stealth aircraft. The X-215A, for example, hurtles through pitch darkness at several hundred miles per hour, fifty feet off the ground. Once a stealth aircraft's electronics fail, the pilot has no instruments to tell him how high he is, no sensors to warn him of what's ahead, and no workable flight controls to allow him to react to what he can't know anyway."

Treadwell slammed his trial book shut. "All right, that's enough! I'm finished with this witness. Would you step outside for a moment, Mr. Cameron?"

Once in the hallway, the senior partner gained control of his anger, but his voice radiated enmity. "All right, hotshot, let's have it. Just what in the hell are you up to anyway?"

"Just a shade under six feet, why?"

"Don't be impertinent with me, you country bumpkin. *What do you think you're doing?*"

Seth chuckled. "Boy, this *is* like old times, isn't it, sir? I had forgotten that having a conversation with you is a lot like driving in heavy fog. You want to be more specific?"

"Don't play games with me, Cameron. *I want to know what in God's name you're after.*"

"Fame and fortune, sir, same as everybody else around here. As concerns this case, I think my complaint on file is pretty clear. It seeks damages in the amount of ten million dollars for Mrs. Barton and twenty-five thousand dollars plus lost rents for Mr. Tucker. I'm afraid Mr. Tucker's claim is set in cement, but I might be able to slide Mrs. Barton's demand down a few dollars, given the fact you're her godfather."

"Is that a fact?" said Treadwell, turning back toward his office. "Well, I suggest you slide right on down Montgomery Street and across Market, back into that boar's nest you call a law office."

"Planned on it, sir. I'll even save a spot for you there—for when the Young Turks do to you what you did to me."

Treadwell spun around and impatiently shook his head. Abruptly, he turned back toward his office, then stopped again. He seemed like a man who couldn't decide whether or not he had left a burner on before leaving his house. Finally, he addressed Seth in a tone of quiet concern. "Is it possible that you don't realize the enormity of this foolish little frolic you've undertaken?"

"The jury will decide if my lawsuit is foolish, Mr. Treadwell."

"You're missing the point, Cameron," said the older man, becoming angry again. "You're not just trying a lawsuit here. *You're trying the patience of the most powerful government in the world!*"

Seth smiled into the senior partner's wrath. "If you want to threaten me, Mr. Treadwell, you'll have to take a number."

Treadwell's reaction was that of a man accosted by a deranged beggar—repugnance mingled with demeaning sympathy. For a few seconds, as he pointed a finger at his tormentor, lips moving wordlessly, his frustration seemed to border on confusion. But then he gathered himself, straightened his shoulders, and strode into his office.

Later, back in Seth's cubicle, the professor sipped his coffee and sympathized with his new lawyer.

"What do you think the judge will do?"

"He'll fine me a thousand bucks or so and order you back to answer the question."

"So why did you do it?"

"Time."

"Time?"

"Time to think. Time to come up with something."

"I hope you do. You know where to find me if that happens."

"Thanks, Henry. Oh, yes. The law requires ConSpace to pay for your time as an expert, but send me a bill for our earlier meeting."

"Not to worry, young man. A man shouldn't start his meter running until he knows where he's going. I'm just sorry I couldn't be of help."

Seth stared out the window after Daimler had left. Fatigue was overwhelming him. He considered some pharmaceutical help, then rejected the idea. What he needed was sleep. And a cigarette. He had quit eight years earlier, but what he wanted was a cigarette.

"Why did you do it?" the professor had asked. Why *had* he done it? *Time. I needed time to come up with something*, had been his glib reply.

He wondered if Ramon had any cigarettes in his desk as he absently thumbed through the sparse notes from his first meeting with the professor. *Flattened fuselage, too many grapes, sparking, improper interfacing, fire, canopy-cockpit area . . .*

Something was nagging at him.

Canopy-cockpit area. What was it? Something trying to resurface.

Then, from a thousand miles away came a memory, formless at first, then clearing into a vision: the flushed face and blustering voice of an overweight tech rep.

BOSTWICK! Yes! Harold Bostwick! It's the fucking canopy! Leviticus and Seth had been so excited about Bostwick's statute-of-limitations revelation, they had forgotten the tech rep's abrupt stonewalling when Lev had brought up the subject of canopy design.

Seth leapt over his desk and raced down the stairs, sprinted up Third Avenue to Market, then down to the Montgomery Street BART station. He got there just as Henry Daimler was about to board a trans-bay car.

"Sir!" gasped Seth, spinning the startled professor around. "Could activating the canopy—the one made by TDA—create friction and damage to the electrical harness?"

The professor's mouth slowly widened into an embarrassed

smile as he reluctantly nodded his head. "Only every time the pilot enters or exits the aircraft."

"Then . . . could that be what's—"

"Come over here and sit down, young man. Catch your breath and pay attention. I've just started my meter running."

Seth nursed his '82 Honda Civic over the Golden Gate early the next morning—he had sold the Porsche to handle the increased cost of Pop Cameron's round-the-clock home nursing care—and took one hand off the steering wheel to rub swollen eyes drawn to a surreal, angry dawn blooming over the Berkeley hills.

He'd need more cash now; Treadwell would ask for at least $3,000 in monetary sanctions, and the judge would probably give him half that. Well, it would be worth every nickel, for now Daimler would be equipped with an answer to the $64,000 question Seth would now allow Treadwell to ask. Most important, he now had a strategy, a theory on how it all happened! And with a jury trial just a few months away, it didn't hurt to have a strategy and a theory.

Midway across the bridge, he reflected on Treadwell's warning at the end of the day. Something about the look of genuine incredulity on the senior partner's face had shaken Seth more than he had shown. *How much does Treadwell know?* Seth shivered and turned the car heater up a notch. He snapped a Joe Silverhound cassette into the tape deck, took a deep breath, and cranked up the volume. The country sounds drifted out across the gray, choppy waters that merged at the horizon with a tortured, Vlaminck-painted sky, all blacks and whites and reds.

> *How strange it now all seems*
> *The way you rearranged all my dreams*
> *In just one day*
> *You staged a matinee*
> *For all our troubled friends to see*
> *That we were soon to be*
> *So all alone, all alone*

Seth reached back down and switched the music off. He didn't want to think about Rosie right now, and that song always put him in mind of Rosie. Songs could do that to a person, even when that person should be celebrating the dawn of a new day and a gut feeling that things were about to turn around. That signs of worry would soon be appearing on Treadwell's pallid face as he realized the tide was turning against him and that his balls were being slowly but firmly squeezed. That he had been wrong about the kid from Bakersfield—the one doing the squeezing. Then, it would only be a matter of time before Anthony Winthrop Treadwell, one of America's leading trial lawyers, would be saying uncle in the soft whisper of an Italian castrato.

Cause for celebration. Cherish the moment and savor the new possibilities. Then along comes some fucking song from out of the past, carrying vague misgivings and themes of where-did-I-go-wrong.

Seth passed through the toll at the south end of the bridge and pushed the little Honda through the Marina, up Lombard, down Van Ness. Green lights all the way, except for those that were orange and a couple on the red side, and ten minutes later he was in his office.

Waiting there was Treadwell's motion seeking $4,000 in sanctions, about $3,000 more than Seth had to his name, and Allyn Friedlander, who looked even worse than he did.

"A woman named Jenkins just called from Bakersfield, Seth. She said to tell you it's Pop and you'd better hurry."

SOMETHING WAS ALREADY GONE.

Seth felt the change as soon as he got out of his car. Not just the bougainvillea needing water, its leaves limp from neglect, nor the presence of outsiders inside the house—Doc Farley, Alice Jenkins, the Hispanic couple from next door—nor even the appearance of the house itself, which had not changed materially since its construction in 1953, when Joe and Ruth had placed their hopes and postwar dreams within its freshly painted walls.

No, the change was not physical, but ethereal, born of the cosmic ether, yet as real to Seth as the concrete steps his legs now wearily mounted. He knew that the heart of a house that had survived Ruth's departure, then his own, would not survive another.

"Hello, Seth," Dr. Farley said, gravely extending his hand. Seth had girded himself for *It's only a matter of time* and was relieved when the doctor smiled reassuringly and said he had called for an ambulance. "I didn't tell him; he won't want to go, though I think he might have a chance in the ICU. He's been asking for you."

Seth's first reaction upon entering the bedroom was relief at Joe's appearance. His skin seemed tighter, the pallor gone. His eyes, though sunken, were clear, even radiant.

"Hi, Pop."

"Glad to see you, Son," said Joe Cameron, his voice crackling like footsteps on dry leaves. "To clear the air, let me say that I know what's going on here, and I'm ready to die."

"No way, Pop, but don't talk now. Are you in pain?"

"Nothing I can't handle for a few more hours."

"Do you want something? Doc's right outside."

"Don't want any more morphine. I've already spent too much of my life in a muddle-headed condition. Enough's enough."

Seth looked around the room, feeling strangely awkward.

Joe broke the silence. "How's Rosie?"

"She's fine, Pop."

"You solve your problem yet? She comes every week, but never talks about you. Don't let that one get away, Son, you—"

The old man was seized by a fit of coughing, which brought Doc Farley to the bedroom door. Seth cradled his father's head— it seemed no larger than a cantaloupe—and held water to his lips.

"Did you just hear a rattle, Seth?" Joe said.

"Not funny, Pop," said Seth, smiling.

A longer silence. Seth had never heard such silence, broken only by traces of whispered conversation from the living room, the hall clock, his own heartbeat. Joe stared straight up at the ceiling and seemed to be falling asleep, or . . .

Where was the damn ambulance? Pop was breathing though,

probably just dozing off. After a few minutes, Seth restlessly returned to the living room.

And there she was.

"Hello, Seth."

"Rosie. I'm glad you're here."

"I don't want to be in the way."

"Pop would want to see you. Come on in."

"Don't think of the sun!" his father's voice blurted out from the bedroom. "It ain't right!"

Seth and Rosie entered the bedroom. "No, Pop," said Seth, stroking the cool bald head, "it surely ain't right. Just rest now."

Pop continued to sleep, and Seth started to call for Doc Farley, but the old man's breathing was strong. When his eyes opened after a few minutes, they were clear again.

"Hi, sweetheart," said Pop. "It's about time you came back. And if it takes me dying to get you two in a room together, it's worth it."

"Hi, Pop," said Rosie, "but you can forget the part about dying. I hear there's an ambulance on its way, and Doc Farley says you're going to be okay."

Joe pushed himself up on his elbows, suddenly furious. "No, damn it, I don't *want* to go back to the hospital. Aren't any of you payin' attention? I don't want to *live* any longer!" Exhausted by the effort, Pop fell back onto his pillows. He turned to Seth and pleaded in a pitiful, hoarse whisper. "Don't let them take me back there! Please, Son."

"Just for a day or two, Pop. Then I promise I'll get you out and back here. Okay?"

Joe Cameron grabbed his son by the arm with surprising force. "I don't have a whole lot of control over decisions right now, Son, but I guarantee you that if I go, I won't be back. So listen up."

"Pop, please—"

"Let me talk. The warden tells me I've been saying terrible things to you on and off for a long time. I wish I could say I don't remember them, but in a funny way I do—like when I was drinking hard and things would crowd into my head the next day, all blurry but unavoidable?"

The old man started coughing again, so hard this time he bounced on the bed as if prodded by a 220-volt current. Seth tried to silence him but he pushed himself up on his elbows again and spoke in a firm voice, looking Seth squarely in the eyes.

"I was all wrong about those things I said about you, kid, and I'm sorry. Truth is, I guess I was envious. All those years watching trial lawyers come and go in my courtroom . . . well, you get to thinking you could be as good as most of 'em, you know? Like maybe I could be one myself? Ruth would probably still be here if I had gone and done it, made something of myself, but by the time I saw what she needed me to be, it was too late. I started night courses when you was a baby. Got through the first year, maybe shoulda tried harder, but there was . . ."

"Me," said Seth.

"I don't blame anyone but myself. All of a sudden I'm forty, I'm married, I got a kid, and well, a man just gets stuck. By the time she left us, I was just too old and busted up. Faced with a choice of trying to pass the bar or just goin' to one . . . hell, it was no contest. You know the rest."

"I had no idea, Pop. I'm sorry."

"Quiet. I'm the one trying to apologize here. See, Doc Farley explained that when that damn tumor shuts down part of my brain, all this bad stuff pours outa my mouth, just like *that.*"

Joe tried to snap his fingers, but could barely rub them together.

"Anyway, they should have taken me out and shot me a long time ago. I wish I could take back all the things I said, like you not having what it takes to make it in the major leagues. You proved me wrong and I'm . . ."

"Pop, listen . . ."

"No, you got the rest of your life to beat your gums. I just want you to know how proud I am that you made it. Miller and McGrath is one of the best and—"

Pop started coughing again and fell back on the bed. Rosie took one hand, and Seth held the other. "Don't say anything more, okay? Please."

"Well, I'm right, aren't I?"

"Miller and McGrath is definitely one of the best, Pop. The major leagues."

Seth felt Rosie's eyes burning into him, so he kept his eyes on his father.

Two paramedics burst through the door and, without a word,

methodically strapped the old man to a gurney. Seth was pushed out of the way as they whisked Joe into the ambulance, then drove off with Doc Farley in the back. Following close behind, Seth was relieved that the hospital was only a few miles away. Rosie said she would need her own car, so she followed with Nurse Jenkins.

They had already taken his father inside by the time he parked. Doc Farley—passive, yet solid as a marble statue—stood waiting at the emergency entry. He didn't have to say a word, but he did anyway.

"He's gone, Seth. He said to tell you to call your mother and tell her no hard feelings."

Seth said he'd contact the hospital later to make arrangements and quickly drove off just as Rosie was pulling up.

Within twenty-four hours, Joe Cameron was laid to rest without fanfare, in accordance with his written instructions. The For Sale sign went back up on the lawn, just in front of the bougainvillea.

Seth was surprised at the number of people who showed up at the memorial service. Ruth, of course, was not among them. Seth had no idea how to locate her and reasoned that thirty-one years of silence communicated its own deafening message.

Tom Huckins was there, and Rosie of course. Tom left without saying a word. Seth had to catch up with Rosie on the front steps of the mortuary.

"Rosie. Can't we just talk for a minute?"

"Sorry, Seth," she said, continuing to walk. "I've got to get back to the bank."

"Can I take you to lunch?"

She picked up her pace. "Not a good idea."

"How about after work?"

"Also not a good idea."

"Rosie, could you slow down to a trot? This is embarrassing."

Rosie stopped, but Seth couldn't get her to look at him.

"Give me a break, will you? In the past year I've been jerked around, fired from my job, abandoned by the woman I love, and had my life threatened. I'm in a case that's like swimming upstream through water moccasins, and I've just lost my father. My brain's burnt toast, and my stomach's thrashing like a lobster in boiling water." He considered taking her by the shoulders, then thought better of it. "Seems like a little slack could be cut here."

Rosie glanced up at him, then brushed her hair back from where the wind had blown it across her pale face.

"I'm sorry, Seth, but everything's different now. My life is changing."

"As in how?"

"Well, for one thing, my parents are gone now, too—Esther died last spring—and this has been a—"

"Jesus, Rosie, I'm sorry. Why didn't you . . ." Seth's voice drifted off. No need to finish that one. As if seeking divine intervention, Seth gazed skyward at some slate-colored stratocumulus formations drifting in from the northwest.

"Nothin' to be sorry about. Mom and I weren't all that close."

"Still."

"Truth is, Seth, Esther Wheeler was sort of a fraud. My grandmother knew it, never said it in so many words, but she knew it."

"That was your Iroquois grandmother?"

"Yes."

"You've never told me about her."

"You never asked."

"I'm asking now."

Rosie gave her shoulders a little shrug and started walking again, but more slowly, encouraging Seth.

"Well, her name was Amelia Moon. I reckon she was the most important person in my life when I was tryin' to grow up."

"She lived in Custer?"

"No. Canada. Lived up on the Six Nations Reservation. I had just picked up scraps of information about her as a kid, seein' as how Esther was embarrassed about havin' an Indian for a mother. Until she got famous in L.A., that is, and saw there was profit in bein' the daughter of an Iroquois shaman."

Seth laughed, and Rosie loosened up. Told him about her Great Adventure as a restless fourteen-year-old whose meager hoard of information about her grandmother had begun to add up to a legend. How she had risen early one morning, told her mother she had a job in town, then hitchhiked all the way to Ontario. Stayed just three days and nights before Amelia Moon put her on a bus back to Custer, but was never the same again. Neither was her bottom, after Esther finished working it over with a three-foot willow branch.

"Told me next time I so much as mentioned my grandmother's name to anyone, I'd be living up there with her on the Six Nations Reservation." Rosie submitted to her mother's wishes, but she would never forget those precious days with Amelia, would protect them in her memory as if they were petals from the last rose on earth. She had learned much from the gray-eyed old shaman—skin the color and texture of a walnut shell, a smile so radiant you didn't notice the missing teeth or the poverty around her. Learned about her grandfather, a practicing Atsina medicine man, and more about her father, Sam Wheeler, a handsome structural steelworker from Oklahoma whom Rosie didn't remember and who was also high on Esther's list of people-we-don't-talk-about. Learned that he had some Mohawk in him, which made Rosie half-Indian herself.

Family secrets.

Sitting cross-legged and wide-eyed, Rosie heard the old men singing to their grandfathers' drums and listened as Amelia told her to harvest dream material before it was lost to the ether, to become "hollow bones" for the spirit to work through, and of the need to live in accordance with the Law of the Great Mystery. Of the need to fear nothing.

But mostly Rosie would remember her last morning at Six Nations. "You must go now," Amelia had said. "Your mother is burning with worry and anger, and my own time in the Earth Walk is now finished." Rosie knew what she meant, knew that her grandmother had visited the dream place the night before and seen the end there. She cried and hugged the old woman, who pressed bus money into her hand then stepped back. As Rosie climbed into the back of a pickup truck that would take her to the bus stop, she heard Amelia's weakened voice say something about protecting the gift—which Rosie took to mean the bus money—and holding the bills high above her head as the truck sped away, her face still wet with tears, she waved her thanks.

Rosie paused, and Seth didn't know what to say.

"Point is, Seth, Esther's passin' freed me up to admit to some stuff I'd been denyin'. You know, take a good look at who I really am, where I come from?"

"Sounds like you've been busy."

Rosie seemed to brighten for the first time. "Well, I guess I have. I've been studyin' on my family history. Learnin' things about my grandparents. Myself. Went back up to Six Nations in Canada for two weeks this summer."

"That's good, Rosie. That's real good. So we've got a lot to talk about."

Rosie gave her head a quick shake. "I'm sorry, Seth, but I'm not ready."

"Ready for what? Jesus, woman, I'm talking about dinner here, not Niagara Falls."

Rosie shrugged, looked past him, through him, toward the darkening horizon. "I'm sorry, Seth, but I'm not ready to risk slippin' back into that person I was when I was with you."

"There wasn't anything wrong with that person."

Rosie took him by the hand. "It's hard to explain, Seth. But when I was with you, I wasn't sure how important I was."

She suddenly dropped his hand. "No," she said, frowning and pooching out her lips, "that's not the right word." Started again.

"I just needed to know if without you or *any* man in my life I was really . . . *valuable.*" She paused, gave Seth a sideways look, and added, "So I guess I'm just not ready to hang out with you right now."

Rosie started walking again, more briskly now to underscore the point. Seth briskly followed.

"Rosie. I'm not sure what all that means, but I've changed, too, lots of things have changed."

"Nothin's changed between us, Seth."

"You're wrong, Rosie." Seth moved ahead of her, put his hands on her shoulders. "If I win this case, I'm back on Montgomery Street—on *our* terms this time, Rosie, I swear to you."

Rosie shook her head in exasperation. "If there's change in you, Seth, I'm afraid I haven't seen it," she said, gently turning out of his grasp, "other than you used to honor the truth more."

Seth winced. "That thing with Pop? Isn't that an inch or two below the belt, Rosie? I had a situation there. A delicate balance, a Hobson's choice."

"Sounds like something your friend Treadwell might say."

You're already as good as Treadwell. In five years you could be even worse.

He started to speak, but Rosie wasn't finished.

"You've chosen to be a raider after some lost ark, Seth. I'm happy just bein' a bank teller in Bakersfield."

"There's nothin' wrong with—"

"But at least I'm becoming a person, not just a reflection of you or some figment of other folks' imaginations like I was in the city."

She started to walk again, but Seth spun her around. "Okay, let's say that's good, but can you look at me and tell me you don't still love me?"

Silence.

"And I've never stopped loving you, Rosie. So what's missing?"

"I don't know, Seth. Maybe just you loving yourself."

"Come again?"

"And believin' you always had my love—without having to earn it."

"That's crazy. Of course I know you loved me. You still do."

"Seth," she said, putting her hand on his, her eyebrows slanted in concern. "Dear Seth."

Seth couldn't remember anybody speaking to him with quite that tone of voice. Or touch. Though he had never had a sister, it seemed a sisterly sort of expression. Which wasn't bad, except that it was coming from Rosie. Now she looked him straight in the eye. "If you really believed I loved you, Seth, then you wouldn't have to swim through poisonous snakes to be happy."

"Slow down, Rosie, you've lost me."

"I know. We've lost each other."

Seth watched her walk away, watched her until she turned the corner at Jefferson Street, then he forced himself back to the vestibule, where a few of his father's old friends—a fellow clerk, two bailiffs, and a superior court judge—continued to visit.

Talking about the good old days.

At the edge of town, Seth stopped at a pay telephone and called Elena. She answered on the first ring and not only accepted his invitation to dinner that night but offered to cook it. That cheered him some, but he hit the freeway in a torrent of emotions, certain of nothing except that he had seen the last of Bakersfield, California.

*   *   *

241

One hour and eighty miles up the road later, mired in anguished thoughts of Pop and his scene with Rosie, he forced his mind to other things and, eventually, the case. With trial nearly upon him, he knew he would need three things to win: support for Daimler's harness-chafing theory, some new evidence to beat the statute of limitations, and protection from whoever was trying to stop him from revealing whatever it was he didn't even know.

He resolved to make Elena accompany him to Washington, D.C., and persuade Senator Traeger to send the boys with the butterfly nets after General Farnsworth. The joy of victory at trial would be considerably dampened should the general kill him before he had a chance to savor it. Surely the government must have a federal funny farm for burnt-out crazies like Farnsworth.

Meanwhile, he had decided to retain one of Daimler's associates, Dr. Alan Millstein, to run a test to simulate the chafing and harness failure. He would have to subpoena the harness and the TDA specs on the activating mechanism, but both were off-the-shelf components and would present no government secrecy problems. Daimler and Millstein were guardedly optimistic that the tests would provide empirical corroboration for the professor's testimony on the proximate cause of Sam's crash.

Things were looking better; he was sure of it.

He was also sure he had never felt worse.

Part 5

"It's definitely not Stars, Seth, but I thought you might like a home-cooked meal after what you've been through."

Harry Cooper had been right about one thing: Elena Barton looked like a movie star. Even in jeans, Reeboks, and a simple blouse, she was a certified knockout. She knew it, too, Seth observed without judgment. She had all the moves. Like giving him her best side for a five count—as if she didn't know his eyes were locked onto her perfect profile, the delicate nose, the full lips—then spinning her head around to face him with a suddenness that framed her face in a flurry of radiant hair as if an off-camera wind machine had sent it flying.

As she cleared Seth's unfinished plate, she kissed him lightly on his cheek, and that soft hair brushed his face like autumn gossamer.

"So what's the verdict from Chef Cameron?"

"The petrale sole was great."

"Just great?"

"With your lemon-caper sauce, it was perfect."

"Just perfect? You didn't finish your pasta. Was my marinara sauce lacking?"

"It was fine."

"What was wrong with it?"

"The truth?"

"You're my lawyer."

"Okay, next time I'll show you a place in North Beach where you can get fresh organic Italian tomatoes. I'd say you were also a little heavy on the oregano—I use just a pinch—and maybe you were a little light on the garlic. Try mincing at least three cloves."

"I used one. Anything else?"

"I prefer Romano over Parmesan. Since you asked."

"I did. And if you're this good with a hobby, I'm glad you're on my side in court."

"I get a little fanatical about things. There's nothing wrong with your cooking. The main reason I didn't finish it was because I'm just too damn tired to enjoy anything."

"Anything?" she said, smiling and stroking his hand.

"Well, I reckon 'anything' was an overstatement. But I do need to talk to you before we . . . relax."

"You're getting that lawyer tone in your voice."

"Sit down, Elena. Turn off the music."

For twenty minutes, Seth reviewed the events of the past several days: Daimler's testimony, the Las Vegas disaster, Farnsworth's threat, Treadwell's warnings, everything. Elena listened without moving except to occasionally bite her lower lip or close her eyes against the force of his words. She cried when he told her that Murphy had died. Probably murdered. Probably Farnsworth.

"On top of all that, Treadwell's budget is unlimited," he concluded. "He's got a support team consisting of the U.S. Air Force, plus two smart associates, two paralegals, and at least one other partner working full-time. I've got *me* working *part*-time with occasional help from Leviticus. I'm burning out, and I need to know what in the hell I'm into. You've got to help me find out."

Elena dried her eyes, then rose and poured them each a cup of coffee.

"Our lawsuit is making everybody look bad, Seth: ConSpace, the Air Force, Daddy, the entire government. If we win, everybody else loses."

Seth shook his head. "It's not just that. This is not the first time a suit like this has been brought. We're not breaking new ground here. No, there's something more. Something . . . really important."

Elena shuddered. "You must be right. Murphy. Dead. Three young kids. What could be that important? *Murder?* It's unthinkable, but . . . scary. If you want to pull out—"

"That's not it. What I want is some protection, and the only man I know who's high enough up in government to provide it happens to be your daddy."

"That's out of the question, Seth. We haven't exchanged a cordial word in years."

"Time to get cordial."

"Impossible." Elena wrapped herself in her arms and fell into a chair across from him. She looked vulnerable, almost childlike. "I don't want to go into it, Seth, but let's just say he loved me a little too much when I was a little girl." Tears formed in her eyes. A hand went to her mouth, as if to keep from saying too much, straying too far into the past. "He . . . things happened. I got away from him as soon as I could. Left home and married Sam."

"Was Sam in the Air Force?"

"Not yet. Junior college, but he got into the aviation cadet program as soon as we were married, and you know the rest. He was a natural, became the youngest astronaut ever. Anyway, we had been neighbors—sort of grew up together—I guess you could call us childhood sweethearts though he was a little older than me.

"Sam was my hero since I was seven. Still is, which is why I've got to clear his name." Elena started to cry again. Seth came up with a cocktail napkin. "My mother stood up to Daddy for the first and only time in her entire life by signing the parental consent. I was sixteen."

"Where's your mother now?"

"He dumped her when he found out that she had signed. She moved back to North Carolina, lived with an old-maid sister, then caught cancer and died. I hate him most of all because of that. And he hates me as well." She laughed a short laugh. "I don't know which he hated the most: the fact that I ran away and embarrassed him at a law firm that doesn't permit runaway daughters, or the fact that I married 'that soldier,' as he always called Sam. He couldn't stand the thought of me being married to a serviceman, even an astronaut who became a top gun. Laudable tolerance coming from a member of the Armed Services Committee, don't you think?"

Seth nodded.

"Now he hates me even more for bringing this suit. He thinks it's my revenge. Maybe he's right, but you can see that there's no way I can ask him to help us."

Seth shook his head. "Find a way. This case is important to both of us—for different reasons. Important, but not to die for."

"I can't do it, Seth."

"Yes, you can and you will," he said, then added as if he meant it, "or I *am* out."

Seth snatched up his coffee as if to signal the discussion had ended, but he could feel her eyes on him as he emptied his cup. After a minute, she delicately blew her nose into the cocktail napkin and went to the kitchen. Seth heard the sound of pots and pans, then ten minutes later the buzz-click from the dishwasher.

Another five minutes passed before she emerged, drying her hands on a monogrammed kitchen towel. "All right, I'll call him in the morning. Now let's go to bed."

Seth lay on his back, waiting. She came out of the bathroom in a white terry robe, which she loosened but kept on as she straddled him. Expertly massaging his chest and neck, she kept her eyes steadily on his. She dug her fingers into his shoulders, then up into his tense neck, gently rocking back and forth, never taking her eyes off him.

Seth reached up with both hands and pulled her head down. Their lips locked together. Elena's tongue explored his mouth while Seth's hands moved inside the robe onto her stomach, then slowly up onto her small, firm breasts. He pulled the robe down over her shoulders so that it pinned her arms to her sides and set his teeth gently around the edges of one rigid nipple—his tongue flicking the tip—then the other. He heard funny little gasps from her as he closed his lips over as much of one of her breasts as he could take in.

Fill my emptiness, Elena. Make me forget that I've lost nearly everyone important to me.

Elena's rocking motion gained intensity. She pressed her vulva into his pelvis and he felt her wetness spreading across his stomach.

The woman I loved.

Elena struggled free of the robe and secured his arms to the bed with surprisingly strong hands. He closed his eyes and felt her satin hair again, caressing his chest now, then lightly whipping against his stomach, surrounding her hot tongue as it moved lower and lower and . . .

Elena's head snapped up as if she had been shot, her eyes blazing.

"You don't want me!"

Seth tried to hold her, to console her—and himself—with whispered reminders that it had not been an easy week. But Elena was implacable.

"I think you'd better leave," she said, pulling on her robe and reentering the bathroom.

Seth dressed, then said goodnight to the bathroom door.

"Wait," said a muffled voice from behind the door, and she came out, hands in the pockets of her robe. She had been crying.

"Blamed my fading beauty. Pretty insensitive, huh?" she said, taking a tentative step toward him.

"Call it what you want. Doubt I was your first disappointment."

"My second. I was married to the first. Sam had been so stressed out during the last year over the X-215A, well ..." She put her arms around his waist and laid her head against his chest. "Damn it, Seth, I've fallen in love with you. But I think we'd better try to keep it professional for now. Too many things going on."

Seth put his arms around her. "Too many things."

"You won't leave me, will you?" she said, the little girl again. "Or the case?"

It was a beautiful, clear night over the Golden Gate Bridge, moon craters visible, the Bay still and shiny as a sheet of foil. But Seth drove home without noticing, utterly defeated.

Six hours later, Seth fed Fat Dog, grabbed a muffin and a Bennie, and hit the road again. For variety, he took the Richmond–San Raphael Bridge across to the East Bay, driving straight into the rising sun, its rays spreading like brushfires down Mount Diablo twenty miles away. At least that's the way it looked to him. A tourist from Des Moines might have seen the bands of blazing light as God's own awakening.

He then turned south, down U.S. 880 to Berkeley and his meeting with Professor Daimler and Dr. Alan Millstein.

The experts had agreed to meet at seven-thirty to accommodate Seth's debtor's hearing in San Francisco Municipal Court at nine, a new-client meeting at ten, a divorce mediation at eleven, and three depositions in the afternoon. Allyn was on the warpath and didn't even know yet about his intention to fly to D.C. with Elena.

"Dr. Millstein is a little quirky," Professor Daimler had warned, "but he's the best failure analyst alive. His Ph.D. is from MIT and his dissertation was on 'The Predictability of Non-Linear Phenomena.' Don't expect 'too many grapes in a bag' clarity from Alan."

Actually, Seth liked the diminutive, thirty-something consultant from the start, except for the fact that he was meeting with the last of the big chain smokers in the smallest office in the University of California system. Not even the reek of sulfuric acid from the labs below was a match for the plumes of noxious smoke issuing from Millstein's lungs. Batting his reddened and glistening eyes, Henry Daimler suggested that Alan explain his role.

The consultant nodded affirmatively, lit another cigarette, and lifted off.

"Okay. First, let's see, uh . . . okay, well there's this subfield of science called chaotic dynamics in which a bunch of smart guys without real jobs but blessed with foundation grants sit in university laboratories and, you know, sweat bullets over such weighty issues as the predictability of physical phenomena, you know, like whether we should wear a raincoat tomorrow? Okay?"

Listening to Millstein was like white-water rafting on the Colorado River. Seth had never heard words propelled so fast from a human mouth.

"See, Newton thought the universe was one big fucking clock—a 'clockwork universe' people called it—but a smart guy named Poincaré came along and said, 'Bullshit: we live in chaos.' He posited that the reason there's no clockwork predictability in nature is because of what he called a 'sensitive dependence on initial conditions.' "

"Which means?" asked Seth.

"Simple example: A foundation-blessed colleague of mine hung a magnet at the end of a short stick which was rigged to swing like a pendulum over a table on which were mounted three randomly fixed magnets. Got it? He pulled back and released the pendulum—which obviously went ape-shit the minute it entered the opposing fields of the magnets beneath it. He then spent a year or so—time you might argue could have been better spent in AIDS research, solving the homeless problem, or trying to get laid—staring bug-eyed at the swinging magnet's erratic path in hopes of tracing some kind of repetitious pattern. Okay?"

"And he found there was order in chaos?"

"Order?" said Millstein, looking surprised. "Fat chance. Order is the dream of lawyers, my friend, but chaos is the law of nature."

"Okay, so he didn't find order in chaos."

"At the risk of sounding like a lawyer, yes and no. Yes, some patterns emerge if one doesn't get hemorrhoids first; but no, he mainly proved that Poincaré's 'sensitive dependence on initial conditions' is still with us. In other words, since you don't know the exact release point of the magnet—the initial condition—you can't predict where the hell it will eventually go. The problem derives from the underlying nonlinearity of the equations describing the motion."

"Alan," interrupted Professor Daimler, "he doesn't like it when you use MIT jargon."

"He's right, Alan," added Seth. "Could you be a little more practical?"

"Practical?" asked Millstein as if confronted with a demand for his passport in a foreign language.

"Practical," said Seth, "as in, what the fuck are you talking about?"

"Sorry. Okay. I can do practical. Here is a practical example of where these birds are coming from. The reason that weathermen fuck up nearly every day on TV is because of—you guessed it—Poincaré's 'sensitive dependence on initial conditions.' They can't predict the speed and direction of wind that will hit Milpitas tomorrow morning *because they can't know exactly how it all got started yesterday.*

"Weatherfolks call this the 'butterfly effect,' meaning that because a weather system can be started or impacted upon by the gentle movement of a butterfly's wings up in Petaluma or Portland or wherever—Poincaré's 'initial conditions'—nobody can accurately predict what it will look like by the time it blows into hapless Milpitas a day later."

"So," said Seth, "you are telling me there can be no predictability of the harness failure unless we know exactly what the initial stresses were?"

"I'm *not* saying that. I'm just giving you a crock of theoretical bullshit so the other side's expert won't be able to tie you in forensic knots. You see, there's another group of smart guys out there—also without real jobs but with a more optimistic slant on all this—who hypothesize that if you plot various elements of chaos in nature long enough, you really *can* observe patterns emerging. Get it? Predictability! Order out of chaos! Brought to you by brilliant theorists who must never have tried commuting during the Christmas shopping season or standing near an elevator in an office building at quitting time or attempting to complete the most simple task at any branch of a U.S. Post Office."

"Given your skepticism about predictability, Alan," said Seth with a wink at Daimler, "can you predict why I'd want to pay you to be involved in this case?"

"First, because I'm cheap. Second because I'm fun. Third, because Poincaré was talking about predictability of 'things in *na-*

ture.' A high-density plastic harness might be a lot of things, but it damn sure ain't nature."

"So you *can* predict failure?"

"But of *course*, monsieur, assuming you can give me the specs on the harness and the canopy activation design. We will then make our own fucking airplane—at least an adequate simulation of the major elements of said fucking airplane—then we'll punish it until it fails. For backup, we can set up a digital computer model. One will corroborate the other. Our brilliant comrade, the good professor here, will then take the witness stand and charm the birds out of the trees without the slightest concern about cross-examination."

"Sounds good, pard," said Seth, looking at his watch. "I'll subpoena the specs today. Meanwhile, thanks for the coffee and the lesson on chaos. Very interesting."

Millstein seemed to drift off for a moment, then gave Seth a look through narrowed eyes that to Seth looked both shrewd and slightly mad. Seth was beginning to sense that Alan might have a few screws loose and others a bit too tight.

"You think *that's* interesting? How about this: If Poincaré is right in insisting that the fundamental cause of chaos of things in nature is a 'sensitive dependence on initial conditions,' what does this tell us about us two-legged representatives of nature? What if there's a 'butterfly effect'—some early trauma—lurking in each of our lives that renders confident predictability of our behavior impossible?"

"Sounds like psychobabble to me, Alan."

"So? I think Freud and Poincaré would have danced to the same cha-cha-cha. You can take it to the bank."

"All right, Alan," said Professor Daimler, seemingly embarrassed. "Seth's got a busy sched—"

Millstein shrugged. "Okay, but think about it, Seth," he added, a small puff of smoke accompanying every word that flew from his mouth. "Isn't it possible that the flapping of destiny's wings in your distant past might have set in motion a nonlinear force that could cause you to do something completely unpredictable at a crucial point in your life, something that could bury you in chaos?"

"I can't remember when I haven't been buried in chaos, Alan," said Seth, smiling, "and I think you've got butterflies on the brain."

"Maybe," said the little man, inhaling deeply, then locking onto Seth's eyes like a heat-seeking missile, "but sometimes, from far back in my past, I hear the rustle of those wings. Don't you?"

SENATOR TRAEGER TURNED OUT TO BE SURPRISINGLY COOPERATIVE. Elena was amazed at his conciliatory tone and his willingness to come out to Dulles International to meet with Seth.

"He was friendly, Seth, almost *fatherly*, for God's sake!"

"I'm not one to get involved in private family matters," said Seth, "but it won't hurt to keep in mind that he wants something from you."

Elena's face hardened. "He always did. But since he won't get it, why do you expect him to be willing to help you?"

"I'm not traveling empty-handed," Seth said, and Elena knew better than to pursue it.

The cease-fire between father and daughter was short-lived. The trio met in the Red Carpet Room and Traeger offered friendly, if somewhat guarded, greetings. Seth thanked him for driving to Dulles and explained that he had to turn around and head back to San Francisco on the red-eye to cover three hearings the next morning.

"I'm happy to help out," said the senator. "Now what's all the mystery about? Elena wouldn't tell me what was important enough to cause the two of you to fly back here. I'm hoping it's got something to do with calling off the dogs."

"That's exactly what it's about, sir, calling off the dogs."

The senator beamed. "*Wonderful*, Seth. You're dismissing your case?"

"No, sir. Different dogs. We're talking different dogs here."

"I'm not understanding you, Counselor," said Traeger, lowering his voice and glancing around to check out the people closest to them. A Japanese couple conversed in Japanese two tables away. Another man sat in a wheelchair, engrossed in *Sports Illustrated* and sipping a martini. None were in hearing distance, but Seth also kept his voice low.

"The reason I'm here is that in the space of a few weeks I've been threatened by an Air Force general, Senator, and ominously warned by your old partner, Anthony Treadwell. I need you to intercede in my behalf. I need you to talk to the secretary of defense about one of his bat-shit base commanders, and I need you to find out from Mr. Treadwell what's got everybody so stirred up."

Traeger's manner changed; his posture, even his face. "I had hoped you had come back here to talk sense, not fantasy."

Traeger looked as if he were going to get up and leave, but then turned to Elena, who had been sitting quietly between the two men. "Elena. Darling. I *beg* you to end this farce. You're not just embarrassing me, your suit could mortally wound the entire Stealth Program, which, for reasons I'm not at liberty to disclose, is going to be desperately important to this country before this decade is out."

Elena stared at him as if he were a total stranger.

"The press will be in a feeding frenzy if this thing gets to trial," he continued, becoming more agitated. "I'd probably have to excuse myself from future hearings on the B-2 and X-215A!"

"Daddy is afraid baby will take away his toys," Elena said to Seth with an iciness Seth had never heard from her.

"Elena—"

"No, Senator," she added scornfully, "I'm no longer a little girl, and I'm not one of your Washington whores who will cater to your every demand, and I'm not my mother, who always just looked the other way. So you can—"

"Give it a rest, Elena," said Seth, "this is not helping."

Too late.

"You go ahead and do your damnedest, you ungrateful little bitch," said Traeger, spitting out the words at a volume that attracted the attention of everyone in the cocktail lounge. The senator glanced around, then lowered both his head and his voice. "The only reason either of you are in this thing is for the publicity and the hope that the Air Force will pressure ConSpace into making a fat settlement with you." Turning on Seth, he added, "Well, it won't work, damn it! I've dealt with opportunists like you and I've dealt with strike suits like this."

"This is no strike suit, Senator, and I'm prepared to prove it to you."

"You're wasting your time, Seth," said Elena. "Even when we get our justice, he won't understand it."

"Justice?" said Traeger with a sardonic laugh as he reached for his coat. "Justice is nothing but a blind woman who mates with the guy who has the best lawyer. And ConSpace has the best lawyer in America."

Seth shrugged, then convinced Elena to wait in the other room. He hadn't flown all the way back east to have a rerun of *Family Feud* preempt his own carrot-and-stick program. Time to summon The Manipulator.

The carrot.

Seth first persuaded the senator to put his coat down and listen for five minutes. He then offered exaggerated affirmations concerning his open-mindedness to the true facts. He offered another drink. He offered apologies for Elena's outburst and listened sympathetically to Traeger's further lamentations on fatherhood. After the senator began to relax somewhat, Seth carefully returned to the matter of the lawsuit.

You know who's the easiest guy in the world to manipulate, kid? A manipulator. You know why? Simple. A manipulator is that way because he's so needy. I've seen it time after time on the witness stand. Just give a con man what he needs, and you can manipulate him right out of his counterfeit soul.

Seth flattered the senator and professed understanding of his concerns, warned him that even Elena could be at risk. Then, to establish his good-faith belief in the merits of his case, Seth gave him a five-minute version of his opening statement.

The senator was impressed and did not try to conceal it. "Daimler will say all that? I usually disagree with everything the man says, of course, but his reputation is beyond question. See here, Cameron, strictly off the record. Suppose I personally looked into that harness and canopy situation. Hypothetically speaking, suppose further there was something to your theory and that ConSpace converted to another canopy system and re-placed the harnesses. Pronto. Would you agree to drop your suit?"

"Sure, so long as they would also bring Sam Barton back to life. You were a trial lawyer yourself, Senator, one of the best in the city from what I hear. You know I can't just walk away from this."

The stick.

"What I *will* do, sir, is agree not to hand you this deposition subpoena. I have no desire to embarrass you further. All I ask in return is that you try to keep me alive, at least until this thing is resolved one way or another."

The senator's eyes darted between Seth's face and the sub-poena in his hand.

"After all," Seth added with a half smile, "I *am* one of your constituents."

"Of course, I'll look into it," said Traeger at last. "Farnsworth you say? Hell, he's heading up the whole X-215A test program at Symington. I *have* heard he's a bit erratic; sees himself as the new Ollie North."

"Will you talk with him?"

"Damn right I will, and I'll talk to the secretary of defense as well. I'll do it tonight. Frankly, Cameron, I can't say I've liked you, but this goes beyond personalities. I can't have my program in the hands of some self-styled Rambo if what you say is even half-true. I'll also chat with Tony. Maybe I could influence him to make you an acceptable offer."

"Always willing to listen to acceptable offers."

They shook hands and parted.

Outside the cocktail area, while the senator was paying the bill and putting on his coat, Seth swept Elena out of her chair and guided her toward the opposite end of the terminal. "I've got the wheels greased, Elena. I don't want you to go throwing sand in them."

"He'll help?"

"He said he'd get on the telephone right away."

True to his word, Sen. Stanford Traeger stopped at the very first bank of telephones and placed a call.

"Aubrey? Father here. We've got a problem."

SETH AWOKE TO A TYPICALLY CRISP AND LONELY LATE-NOVEMBER
morning and prepared a gourmet breakfast for himself and Fat
Dog. Since Rosie's departure, Fats had become his dining companion whenever he had time to practice his secret passion.
Today, they would indulge in Seth's version of a Denver omelet—using the milder Gruyère cheese and only Maui onions (he
had found a reliable supplier)—and macadamia-banana waffles,
Fat Dog's personal favorite.

After breakfast, they headed to the small park nearby for a
Frisbee workout. The mutt was not much of a jumper—particularly after an omelet and two Belgian waffles—but compensated
for his disabilities with passionate determination and the timing
of a mongoose. Tears blurred Seth's vision as he watched the
game little pooch slip and stumble in the damp, thick leaves that
blanketed the grass. Cold air could do that to a person's eyes.

Fat Dog signaled his weariness in the usual manner: caught
the plastic sphere with a perfect grab—he always ended on a
high note—then careened straight for home, his rear end oscillat-
ing wildly from the eccentric forces imposed by the missing
front leg.

We're alike, Fat and me, Seth thought, *a couple of beat-up junkyard
dogs, too dumb to quit.* He walked slowly, past awakening houses
with wood-burning stoves already sending up sweet-smelling
fingers of smoke against the silent majesty of Mount Tamalpais,
which, with its crown of rare, fresh snow, looked like a torch
created to brighten the lead sky. He walked slowly because his
energy was failing him. At nine in the morning he was already
fatigued to his bones.

He resolved to whip himself into shape after the trial. He'd
start jogging alongside Richardson Bay as he had done with Rosie

once long ago, when they had sent the feeding egrets scurrying off to deeper water, sucked steam fog off the bay into their bursting lungs, laughed back at the gulls, rejoiced at the sun's arrival. Long ago.

He forced his thoughts back to the case, to the statutory wall standing between him and a jury trial. Was Crispie telling everything he knew? Perhaps Bostwick would come around. Maybe they could find somebody else at Symington who had witnessed the takeoff. Funny that the only people on the flight line that night were—according to the Air Force anyway—either dead, transferred to a "high-security overseas theater," or, like Bostwick, just plain lying. He had to find somebody willing to tell the truth. Somebody in New Mexico, where it all began.

Conning his way into Symington Air Force Base a second time turned out to be another one of those pretrial challenges for which there had been no preparation at law school—not as daring and heart-stopping as his first incursion with Leviticus, but requiring more skill and patience.

First, Seth had to persuade Allyn to advance $2,800 and expenses for a trip she had characterized as "an epic waste of time" and "a fool's errand even by your standards, Seth." She had finally reached for her checkbook, but Seth knew he had exhausted any residual credit from the Pacific Sigma windfall. Worse, Seth saw that Allyn had lost her enthusiasm for the case, and like a priest whose bishop has renounced his faith, he would find it harder to sustain his own.

With the money secured, he had to figure a way to get inside the base. He decided to have Elena convince Crispie to grant Seth an interview. This turned out to be harder than he had expected.

"Please don't ask me to do this," she had said, her eyes pleading. "He's just going to say no. He thinks you're a little pushy, Seth, and now with Jerry Murphy getting killed—"

Seth bristled. "I'm sure he's said worse than that about me. But now it's your turn, Elena. It *is* your case, remember?"

Their discussion began as they walked down Divisadero from her Pacific Heights apartment, toward Union Street in San Francisco's Cow Hollow district. He had arranged a special lunch, knowing this would not be easy.

"But what can you hope to accomplish," she asked, "even if he did agree to see you?"

"Jesus, Elena, I won't know until I've accomplished it." He always felt awkward, walking beside her; as if he should be holding her hand or she should be taking his arm. Made him irritable somehow as he shuffled along, hands in pockets, kicking at sticks and rocks on the sidewalk.

"That's the way this business works," he added, his breath scalding the crystal December air as he spoke. "Winning trial lawyers shoot until they run out of ammunition, then they keep on shooting. I'm not quitting on you just because we're out of bullets, but now it's your turn, damn it."

An uncomfortable silence consumed their thoughts. Seth was seeing a vacillation he didn't admire in anyone, let alone the woman of his dreams and an otherwise gutsy person who had the most to gain from his success and nearly the most to lose from his failure. He tried not to expect others to share his take-no-prisoners approach to problem-solving, but hated it when his clients drained energy he preferred to save for the enemy.

"Look, Elena," he said, taking her by the arm, "this case is history if we don't find something before the hearing on Treadwell's motion to dismiss under the statute of limitations."

That got her attention. "When is the hearing?"

"Two weeks from now. The declaration of Symington's base commander swears the crash occurred before midnight. With no counterdeclaration, the court will have to deem the fact admitted."

"What about that tech rep? Bostwick."

"Good ol' Bullshit Bostwick. He probably told us the truth when he talked about rumors of a late takeoff, but he stonewalled me at his deposition. Getting back on that base and finding someone or something else is our last hope."

They surrendered to another long silence before she agreed to try, but not without questioning how he expected to accomplish anything.

"I have a secret weapon."

"As in?"

"I'm going to talk Lev into going with me again."

"Oh," Elena had said, unimpressed. Nonetheless, she did her part, and a week later, Crispie agreed to a "final and very brief" meeting. His terms—which did not inspire confidence in the outcome—required that Seth first agree in writing not to inquire into any matters pertaining to the "national interest."

That, thought Seth, *will probably include everything from the price of drinks at the Officers' Club to his shoe size.*

But Seth had reason to smile as he and Leviticus boarded Southwest Airlines flight 642 to Albuquerque. At least he had accomplished steps one and two—getting there and getting through the gate—now he just had to figure out what to do once they were inside.

"What's our strategy, Cowboy?" Lev asked as they settled in their seats. Seth told him that Alan Millstein had succeeded in constructing a nearly identical model of TDA components, plus an interfacing with a three-meter section of electrical wiring protected by the same harness that was used in the X-215A.

"That's good," said Lev, noticing the look exchanged between Seth and a petite flight attendant, "but what's our strategy today?"

"No different than yesterday," said Seth, buckling his seat belt, and Lev let it go until they were at cruising altitude.

"Refresh me, Seth, what was our strategy yesterday?"

Seth took a deep breath. "Okay, first we'll contrast Sam Barton's record of proficiency with the X-215A's record of failure, then bring in Henry Daimler—hopefully supported by a failure in Millstein's model—to lay out his harness theory. We'll wrap it up by having the widow Barton shed a few salty ones, then count on the jury's sympathy and traditional distrust of government contractors. Of course, we have to get past the statute."

"I believe," said Lev dryly, "that's why we're on this airplane?"

"Right. We'll beat the statute by persuading either Bostwick or Christopher to tell the truth. If that doesn't work, we'll have to find somebody who saw the late takeoff."

"And our strategy for doing that is what I'm asking."

Seth glared at Lev. "I'm working on it."

Lev shrugged, tilted back, and drifted into sleep.

Seth doodled on a pad and sipped coffee he really didn't need from a flight attendant who leaned in across the sleeping Lev in a way that revealed her interest and a pair of promising breasts.

Lev was awakened an hour later by rough air and noticed that Seth appeared to be finished glaring at him.

"You have a strategy."

"I do," said Seth, and summarized what he called Plan A and Plan B. Lev listened quietly, his intelligent eyes unblinking, his expression inscrutable.

"So," said Seth as he finished, "what do you think?"

Lev pinched the bridge of his nose and considered for a moment what he had heard. "I think you should give some thought to having someone check out the soundness of your mind."

By the time they were on the ground at Albuquerque International, however, Lev agreed that though the plan was flawed, he couldn't come up with a better one.

"It'll work," said Seth.

"It should work," said Lev, looking straight ahead so Seth couldn't see his eyes.

They picked up a rental compact and headed toward the base, past mesas that rose several stories above the mesquite-blanketed prairie, then flattened out so level a football game could be played on top. Seth had no problem finding good country-music stations, and Lev had given up insisting there was no such thing. Both men's thoughts were turned inward, tense and expectant. Later, they exchanged some small talk—the 49ers' newly constructed team, Lev's wife's decision that it was time for them to start a family. Seth's admission he had obtained the flight attendant's telephone number—then they turned quiet again. As they approached the base, Lev broke the silence.

"Yeah, it's bound to work."

"It'll work."

"But why do I always have to do the hard part?" Lev asked.

"Because you're bigger."

"Did you say because I'm a nigger?"

"No, I said because you're smarter. And more handsome."

"You left out debonair."

They were swiftly escorted through Gate 6, the same one they had entered before. The only delay this time was waiting for their assigned "drivers," a staff sergeant named Grover Draper—who looked as if he could bench-press the Ford staff car he was driving—and a hard-looking airman first class who did not bother to introduce himself. Both wore the white arm-bands of air policemen as well as sidearms—conveying a message in typically subtle military fashion: *Don't try anything funny.*

Five blocks and two right turns later, Seth recognized the ConSpace headquarters Quonset and leaned forward. "Would you mind stopping here for a second, Sarge? I'd like to say hello to an old friend."

"Sir?" said the sergeant with no perceptible slowing of the vehicle. The airman riding shotgun suppressed a smile.

"Hal Bostwick. Works for ConSpace. Great guy. Works right inside that building there—"

"Sorry, sir."

"—the one we just passed at the speed of light."

Sergeant Draper's eyes, reflected in the rearview mirror, betrayed no reaction to Seth's sarcasm.

So much for Part A of the Great Plan.

"My orders are to take you directly to the Officers' Club, gentlemen. No exceptions. Sir."

"No exceptions," said Seth, then asked the sergeant if he would be more at ease if they submitted to leg irons. This remark drew no reaction at all from the stoic aircop, though the jaw of the hard-eyed airman first class began to twitch with a noisy click that reminded Seth of the warning sound of a rattlesnake.

"That won't be necessary, sir."

Five minutes later, Sergeant Draper turned them over to a master sergeant, who escorted them to a small conference room where, he assured them, the major would join them in just a few minutes. The airman first class's jaw had stopped clicking, but he gave Seth a final hard look as he followed Grover Draper out the door. Seth nudged Lev, who asked the master sergeant where the men's room was, then headed off rapidly down the hall.

Plan B was under way.

"I thought there were two of you," said Christopher as he came into the room a few minutes later and offered one of his guarded, below-the-eyes smiles. "Where's Mr. Heywood?"

"I'm afraid he's a little under the weather, Major. He's in the head disposing of the last of his airline lunch. Doesn't travel well. He'll be back in a minute, but we can begin without him."

*   *   *

263

While Seth was getting the anticipated party-line responses from Crispie, Lev was scrambling outside the Officers' Club, randomly approaching anyone who looked as if they might know something about the crash. After several failed attempts, he spotted two enlisted men raking leaves behind the club. One of them turned out to be from Los Angeles and recalled Lev's short-lived career with the 49ers.

"Hell, I remember you," said Airman Second Class Bobby Baxter, whom Lev sized up as one of those characters one meets in the service who makes it his business to know everybody else's. "Fucked up your back, right?"

"Knee," said Lev, giving it a whack. "Second year."

"Oh, maaan? And after bein' Rookie of the Year? Shee-it!"

"Runner-up."

"Still." Baxter turned to his partner, displaying a formidable set of teeth. "This man was bad. Verrry bad."

"The older I get," said Lev, quoting Connie Hawkins, "the better I used to be. I'm just a mule for the government now, boys, like you, but without the uniform and the glory. I'm looking into how we can improve the safety record around here."

One thing led to another, and Lev was soon on his way back inside the club looking for a Corp. Mitchell Simmons, described by Airman Baxter as a club bartender who was one of the last people to see Sam Barton alive. Lev found Simmons setting up the bar.

"Yes, sir, I knew Captain Barton," said Simmons, a pleasant, light-skinned black man with freckles and reddish hair. "He didn't come in much, but everybody knew who he was. The captain was considered a troublemaker—kinda like me."

"Troublemakers don't land jobs working at the Officers' Club, Mitch."

"Oh, I ain't a fuck-up while I'm here pickin' the white man's cotton, Mr. Heywood. I'm Mr. Personality. Corporal Straight Fucking Arrow. You can put it down right there in your notes and take it back to the Pentagon: 'Mitchell—that's two l's—Simmons. A credit to his race and to the Air Force he so courageously and unselfishly serves. Got that?"

"Got it," said Lev, smiling. "Anything else?"

"Yeah. I'm overdue for promotion to staff sergeant. Where the fuck's the guy cuttin' the papers?"

"I'll check it out," said Lev. "Now tell me about the last time you saw Captain Barton."

In another wing of the Officers' Mess, Seth was getting nothing out of Jack Christopher.

"Look, Seth, you know I'd do anything for Elena. Anything. But you're putting me in a hell of a bind here."

"You told me before that Sam was the best pilot in the unit."

Christopher squirmed in his seat. "All right, I'll testify to how great he was, but just between you and me? The fact that he was a hotshot astronaut didn't make him any better than the rest of us. Walking in space didn't mean he could walk on water."

"Did he think he could?"

Crispie shrugged uncomfortably and looked out the window. "He thought he knew a lot of things he didn't. He was a shit-disturber and a lot of people were listening. He was getting a little messianic."

"Sounds like he was carting his balls around in a wheelbarrow," said Seth, hearing the resentment in Crispie's words, and giving him some rope to see what he'd do with it. "But that doesn't make friends. Power always engenders envy."

"*I* was his friend."

Seth relaxed. "Good. You'll have a chance to prove it. Now, what about the takeoff time? That's where we really need you, Crispie, and I think you could help if you wanted to."

Crispie glared at him. "I've told you I wasn't there. I don't know!"

Seth tapped his pen on the table, out of ideas, and hoping Lev was doing better than he was. "I guess," he said, laying his pen down, and summoning a tone of sympathetic understanding, "that what happened to Gerald Murphy out in Vegas has everybody a little on edge."

Christopher reddened at the implication. "You've got an attitude, Cameron, and I'm fed up with it. I'm not afraid of some fantasy repercussions your mind has concocted. I'm a stand-up guy. As for Murph, hell, anybody can buy a bird in the air scoop, it happens—"

"—all the time," finished Seth, wondering if his sarcasm had slipped through.

"That's it, Counselor," said the major, pushing himself away from the table. Seth's sarcasm had slipped through. "And by the way, where the hell's your associate? Flush himself down the toilet?"

"Probably down on his knees in the head, praying to the White Ceramic Goddess. Dry heaves. Look, Jack, I'm sorry if I got out of line." The apology was rendered with a lowered head, a trick Seth had picked up watching male elk battling for supremacy on *The Wild Kingdom*.

"I'm trying to help Elena, too," Seth continued. "I get carried away. Maybe you could fill in just a few last blanks about Sam's skill as a pilot." Seth was not at his best when he was begging, but he noted that Crispie's shoulders relaxed and the skin around his eyes was not stretched quite so thin against his protruding cheekbones.

"For Elena, okay?" Seth added, hating himself almost as much as he did Christopher. "Then I promise I'm out of your hair for good."

Meanwhile, Lev tried to stay calm in the face of news so astonishing he could scarcely believe it.

"You're sure about this, Mitch? Barton and some other commissioned dude walked out of here the night of the fifteenth around eleven-thirty P.M.?"

"Exactly eleven-thirty P.M. I don't know what the date was, but I know it was the night he crashed."

"But if you don't know the date, how do you know the time?"

"Simple. That's what time I always close the bar."

Lev's jaw tightened and his pen froze against the yellow pad. "Barton was here until you closed the bar?"

"The two of them left same time I did."

"And you can't remember," asked Lev, temporarily forestalling the question to which he most feared the answer, "who the other guy was?"

"I can picture the guy—seen him a couple a times—but don't know his name. I think he was a captain, but I'm not sure. Didn't hang out here."

Lev took a detailed description of Barton's companion, then affected the most casual manner he could muster as he asked, "Did either of them have anything to drink that night?"

"One of them was loaded," said Mitchell Simmons without hesitation, "but the other one wasn't drinking."

Lev took a deep breath. "Which one was drinking?"

"Listen, Cameron," said Christopher, rising to his feet. "I've answered that and all your other questions two or three times now. I don't know what the hell you're up to, but I want to know where your man is."

"Crispie, just one more minute and I'll be—"

But the major was grabbing a phone. "Christopher here. Send two men to the men's head and bring me a black man you'll find in there. If he's not there, call the APs and have them surround the building. Find him! Yeah, black and in civilian clothes. Probably big. *On the double!*"

Seth started to rise.

"Stay right there, Cameron. We're going to wait here for your partner."

Lev watched Corporal Simmons scan the handwritten statement. *Just sign it, Simmons,* Lev thought to himself, *you don't have to fucking memorize it!* He had drafted the statement meticulously, even using the bartender's own words, but Simmons was studying the single sheet of paper as if it were a property settlement agreement. Lev glanced at his watch and surreptitiously swept away beads of sweat that were erupting on his forehead. Crunch time. Getting the signature on the page. Closing the sale.

He glanced at the clock. Twenty past the hour. They'd be looking for him by now. *Sign it, Mitch, for Christ's sake! Make my day.*

Simmons looked up sheepishly. "I don't think I can sign this, Mr. Heywood."

Shit! Sweat broke across his brow again. "What's the problem, man? I laid it down just like you told me."

"No, sir. You say here that the two guys left 'around eleven-thirty P.M.' "

"Hell, Mitch, that's what you told me. I didn't put in there about the call you took from the base commander for the other guy 'cause it didn't fit in anywhere, but otherwise, it's just like you gave it to me."

"Wrong, Mr. Heywood. My orders are to close at *exactly*

eleven-thirty P.M., not *'around'* eleven-thirty P.M. I'd be crazy to leave a minute sooner, and even crazier to stay a minute later."

Lev started breathing again, at least until he glanced through the north window and saw four air police scanning the courtyard outside, moving toward the bar. He also heard loud voices and doors slamming down the hall. Sounds rumbling closer.

"No problem, Mitch. Here, I'll take out 'around' and put in 'exactly.' Okay now?"

Lev saw one of the outside AP's moving toward a doorway into the club. Another one was trying to peer into the bar through the tinted glass. Footsteps were approaching fast from down the hall. Simmons seemed oblivious to the voices all around them.

"Looks cool to me," said the corporal, initialing the change and signing his name to the end of the statement.

Lev eyed the paper, but suppressed the impulse to snatch it out of the bartender's hand.

"So," said Simmons, sliding the paper back across the bar to Lev, "do you miss the action? You know, bein' out on the field."

"I get all the action I need," said Lev, quickly folding and pocketing the statement. "Sometimes more."

"Anything else I can do for you, Mr. Heywood?"

"Matter of fact, I could use a drink."

"Sorry, my man, that's the one thing I can't do for you. We ain't open till four. Can't serve civilians anyways 'less they got a commissioned chaperon."

An outer door crashed open and Corporal Simmons's head snapped up. "What the hell?"

Lev leaned in close to the bartender and grabbed him by the arm. "Listen, Mitch. I'm in a situation here. You got to make a choice right here and now between me and the Man. As for the whiskey," he added, reaching over the bar for a bottle of Early Times bourbon, "I don't want to drink it, I'm gonna wear it."

"Simmons's confusion froze him in place behind the bar as Lev sprinkled the bourbon across his chest, rubbed some on his face as if it were shaving lotion, then took a quick shot right out of the bottle. "You don't know me, Mitch. You've been working in back. *Got it?* You just came out here and found one drunk nigger demanding more booze. Here's your chance to take care of business and be a fuck-up at the same time."

Lev watched as the bartender's mind assimiliated this radical turn of events. "You been shuckin' me, Mr. Heywood?"

"Only about the government credentials. Four guys been killed already in that flying coffin, Mitch. Barton was the third. I'm just a working man trying to save number five. Help me out here, brother."

A small, intense-looking AP burst through the door, followed by a gangling, freckle-faced kid who looked sadly miscast as an air cop. Before they could speak, Lev began shouting in a slurred, angry voice.

"Who shays you can't find a cop when you need one? Thank God you're here, Officer. Explain to thish poor excuse for a bartender that I'm a tax-payin' citizen. A citizen in serious need of another little taste."

"Come with us, sir."

Mitch Simmons extended his hands, shrugged his shoulders, and had no trouble manifesting total surprise and confusion.

Lev slapped a twenty down on the bar. "Can't do it, Ossifer. Got to go see Major Chrishtopher. Know him?"

"He wants to see you, too, sir," said the shorter air cop, stuffing the twenty back in Lev's coat pocket as they each grabbed one of his arms.

"Found him drunk in the bar, sir. He's apparently been helping himself."

"So it smells," said Christopher, displaying a rare trace of wit.

"I trust," said Leviticus, mustering the appearance of indignation as he shook his arms free of the AP's grasp, "that I've not incon . . . inconvenienshed you. Felt a little shaky after I got sick and—"

"And got drunk again," said Seth in a disgusted tone.

"Ash a matter of fact," added Lev, scanning the room dizzily, "I think I'm gonna get *sick* again."

"Escort these men out of here," said Christopher. "Take them directly to their car. Then find out who was supposed to be on duty in the bar."

"There's good news and bad news," said Lev as he accelerated the rental car out of the base parking lot, all windows down. He removed a folded paper from his inside coat pocket. "Here's the good news."

Seth devoured the contents of Simmons's statement without taking a breath, then let out a *hooo-ahh* that turned heads along the service road as he planted a kiss on Leviticus's cheek, nearly sending them into a construction trench off to their right.

"Shit, Cowboy, knock it off! I can't keep this car on the road with you tryin' to romance me."

"How the hell did you do it?"

"Luck and patience, though the sphincter factor got pretty extreme there for a few minutes."

"It's almost too good to be true. This means Barton *couldn't* have left the ground before midnight on the fifteenth, let alone die before then. The affidavit version of this statement will kill Treadwell's statute defense!"

Seth leaned back in the passenger seat and took a deep breath, oblivious to Lev's sudden brooding silence.

"Now I can get to a jury," Seth continued. "How will this Simmons be as a trial witness."

"Couldn't ask for better. He's a good kid. Conscientious, sharp, likable."

"Now all that's left is proving that Sam crashed because of a defect in the X-215A."

"Well," said Lev, eyes fixed straight ahead, "that brings me to the bad news. The too-good-to-be-true part?"

"What?"

"Your man was flying high long before midnight, Seth."

"But this statement says—"

"I'm talkin' what it *doesn't* say, Cowboy. Barton had sucked up at least three vodkas and some wine before he left the club at eleven-thirty."

Seth's eyes closed as his mind reluctantly digested the unwanted news. He knew Lev too well to hope he might be kidding.

"He was drunk," Seth whispered through clenched teeth.

"Well, he was drinking all right," said Lev, grasping at straws.

"We're fucked," Seth whispered.

"Yeah, we're fucked," agreed Lev, his natural optimism succumbing to the weight of reality.

SETH WEARILY CLIMBED THE TWO FLIGHTS OF WORN STAIRS TO CHECK his mail before heading home to Mill Valley. Nothing important. He listened to his telephone messages. Routine, until the last one, recorded at 11:30 PM., an hour earlier. It sounded like Huckins— a very drunk Tom Huckins.

> "Hey, Cameron, how're they hangin'? Hope you're gettin' rich and famous there in the big fuckin' city with all those big fuckin' clients, includin' the ones you stole from me. Well, me and ol' Lo-Ball was just sittin' here havin' a few and thought you'd like to know what a great piece of ass you passed up when you decided you were too good for the rest of us. Yep, she's somethin' special all right. Best I ever had. Ha, ha, ooh-yes! Well, you fucked me good when you bailed out of town, Cameron, but I fucked your ex–old lady good tonight so maybe we're close to even. Well, keep on keepin' on, old son. Ha, ha, heeeeooo—"

Seth continued to stare at the phone long after he had dropped it into the cradle. He felt dead, immobilized. He tried to see it as one of Tom's childish pranks, but fatigue fueled his fantasies, and he cleared his desk with a sweep of his arm, then drove his foot through a wall. He fell into his chair, then pushed himself right back out of it and began to pace the small office like a caged animal. *Rosie? Tom? Ridiculous.* Finally, his immediate anger spent, he resolved to put the cruel joke out of his mind and head for home. A good night's sleep would put everything back into perspective. But already his mind was plotting revenge, formulating responses. A letter? Tit for tat on Huckins's own message machine? *Your ex-wife wasn't so bad, either, Tom, except*

*for the fact that I was the last guy in town to fuck her and she gave
me the clap.*

No, damn it! He wouldn't give the son of a bitch the satisfaction of taking him seriously.

He turned the lights off and headed down the stairs. But as he reached the landing at the first floor, he spun around and stumbled back up the creaking stairway.

"Rosie?"

"Yes?" came a whisper, followed by a sleepy "Who's this?"

The sound of Rosie's voice sent a sharp pain into Seth's stomach. *This is crazy*, he thought. Static in the phone line didn't help. A bad connection. Probably a sign, but there was no turning back or starting over.

"It's Seth, Rosie."

"*Seth!* My God, it's one-thirty in the morning! Are you all right? What's happened?"

He imagined her at the other end, could almost see her propped up on one elbow—she'd be on the left side of the queen-size bed they had bought together—tossing her thick black hair over her right shoulder so the phone could be pressed against her left ear. He pictured the beginning of white softness showing just above the open neck of the T-shirt she liked to sleep in, the lower breast straining against the cotton material through which he could imagine the faint outline of the pink areola and nipple.

The soft, pale skin around the dark eyes would be creased now into crow's-feet as her gentle features strained toward consciousness and comprehension of the meaning of this abrupt interruption. *Do you still sleep in a T-shirt?* he wanted to ask her.

"What *is* it, Seth?"

From behind her, his imagining eyes took in her back, traced the curve from her upper shoulder as it glided down to her shallow waist, then flowed up over her right hip before descending again into the secrecy of her bedcovers.

"I'm all right, I guess," he said lamely, suddenly aware that he had no plan. "Sorry about the hour."

She accepted his apology and politely asked if she could go back to sleep now that it had been established that he was sorry but otherwise all right. The way she put it made Seth feel so ridiculous that he came right out with it.

"I just had a message from Tom Huckins. Claims he ... says that the two of you, well—"

"He said what?"

"Slept together."

"He told you we slept together?"

Seth felt his anxiety diminish in inverse relation to the volume of her expressed anger, and already another compartment of his mind resumed plotting revenge against the drunken bastard. The ex-wife-and-clap message was too good for him. More direct action was called for.

"I can't believe," she said, sounding more controlled, "that Tom would tell you that."

Through the static, Seth's trial-lawyer's radar picked up an ambiguity in her words—not a red flag exactly, but a flag nonetheless. Now he'd have to test his instincts. Prove them wrong.

"I'm sorry I bothered you with it, Rosie," he said, pacing to the limit of his telephone cord. "Tom's never been all that intimate with the truth."

Silence.

"None of my business anyway." He switched the phone to his left hand, dried the right one on his pants leg.

More silence. "That's true," she said at last, "so why are we having this conversation at one-thirty in the morning?"

"I needed to know it wasn't true."

The empty sound of distance between them and the occasional burst of static was wearing thin, and he suddenly heard himself shouting into the phone.

"For Christ's sake, Rosie, just tell me it isn't true!"

"I can't tell you that, Seth. I'm sorry."

Seth stared at the offensive instrument in his hand, then jammed it against his chest and slowly collapsed into his chair. A low groan issued from between clenched teeth, and his head banged into the wall behind him.

"Seth?" came a small voice from a million miles away.

He clamped his eyes shut as if he were about to be hit by something. His head rolled slowly back and forth against the wall.

"Seth?"

"Oh, Rosie," he whispered. *"Rosie . . ."*

Straightening, he fought for control. He wanted to throw the telephone through the window and himself behind it, but he held on to it with white-tipped fingers, held on for dear life.

"The son of a bitch did it to get even with me," he said. "He used you to get even with me."

"No, Seth," she said after another intolerable silence. "*I* used *him* to get even with *you*."

Seth would later recall Ken tactfully cutting him off after he had inhaled four shooters at Stars. He miraculously located his car and began to creep up Franklin Street, where he thought he'd see fewer traffic cops than on Van Ness. The country music station blared a Joe Silverhound tune that pretty much summed things up.

> I got into my car, headed straight for the City
> Driven by self-pity, wonder'n why,
> And right there at my side, rode that demon called Pride
> Talkin' 'bout fallen angels and an eye for an eye
>
> Well, I turned on my radio, I tried to find
> Some music to drown out the noise in my mind
> I should have taken my time
> Now my time's been taken from me.

Seth snapped the radio off to better concentrate on staying between a pair of white lines that kept moving on him. He managed to find his way out to Union Street and into a friendly bar, where he proposed marriage to a waitress who accepted his order for an Irish coffee, but he was then eighty-sixed by the bartender to whom she was already married. At some point after he left Union Street—or perhaps it was later, after the pepper vodkas at the Washington Square Bar and Grill—a gray wave moved in, and he gratefully sank beneath it, leaving the demons to languish harmlessly on the surface of his consciousness.

Still later, after he had thrown up in the tiny men's room and washed his face, he saw a man in the mirror he barely recognized. From somewhere behind the dark-circled eyes, he heard a voice asking him how long he thought he could keep this up.

He closed the toilet seat—the smell of his own vomit was making him sick again—and sat down hard on it. His head was already starting to spin again, and he knew he'd better stay put. Piano sounds drifted in, intermittent vocals slipping through the filter of bar chatter. *"It had to be you, it . . . be you . . ."* He let his head sink into his hands. *". . . wandered around, finally found, somebody who, could make me feel blue . . ."* Inexplicably, thoughts of warm Valley nights in Bakersfield entered his fevered mind, temporarily soothing the turbulence, a fanciful fleeting memory, comforting as a mother's embrace, but light-years away and heading in the opposite direction.

THE SHRILL RING OF THE TELEPHONE PIERCED THE SILENCE OF THE DAWN and sent Fat Dog plunging off the bed in a graceless clump. The mutt gathered himself, then expectantly rested his chin on the edge of the bed. But Seth slumbered on, corneas darting and rolling under fluttering lids while his restless unconscious integrated the first few rings of the phone into a nightmare in which he was boxing a man twice his size. The giant kept hammering the side of his head even though the bell was signaling the end of round one. An indifferent, black-robed referee gazed the other way over at a hockey match in which Seth's head appeared again, shrunken and dismembered, and cast this time in the role of the puck.

Fat Dog lost interest and gimped out of the room in quest of water. The ringing persisted until it penetrated Seth's skull like a pair of ice tongs and sent his hand groping for the source of the invasive instrument. Round two.

"Yeah," he gasped into the receiver.

"Seth Cameron?"

"I think so." His mind struggled toward the surface of consciousness. He was drenched in sweat. "Sounds familiar."

"This is Barbara Heywood."

Seth opened one red-rimmed eye and pointed it toward a clock that read six-thirty. He winced from the fulgurant pain lacerating his temples, then eased his back into an upright position against the cold plastic headboard. It smelled like someone was burning rubbish next door, but his window was closed and nobody lived next door. His mouth was so dry he could barely swallow, let alone talk. He forced the other eye open and stared across the room into a mirror above the dresser. Reflected there was forlorn but unassailable evidence that he was indeed Seth Cameron.

"Heywood," he grunted. "That one sounds familiar, too."

"Lev's wife," came the shaky voice. Seth's head was too muddled to tell if the woman was angry or frightened. "I met you once in the city."

"Sure, I remember," he lied. "Sorry. What can I do for you?" He wondered why he was apologizing to someone who was calling him at six-thirty in the morning.

"They've got Lev!" she said with an intensity that slapped Seth into consciousness. "He's in *jail!*"

"What?" Seth's feet hit the floor. "Who's got him? What jail?"

The story came out in fragmented bits and pieces, but added up to something about a pair of federal marshals waiting for Lev to come home the night before.

"They waited out front for hours. Lev got home one o'clock in the morning and parked in the carport. I heard him drive up so I ran to the door, but they came right out of their car and grabbed him as he was walking toward me."

"Did they identify themselves?"

"They had shown me badges earlier, but not him. Just started beating him up. I rushed out and started screaming, but one of them grabbed me while the other one—Lev was down by then—kept on kicking him in the side. I think they hurt him pretty bad."

"Where is he now?" Seth was already clumsily trying to dress himself with one hand.

"He just called me from the Federal Building. I've been half-crazy all night." Seth heard the voice give way to heartbreaking sobs. "He said to call you, tell you they must have planted the coke on him while he was on the ground."

"Cocaine?"

"They've also charged him with resisting. He broke one of the guys' nose and some ribs."

Seth hung up, grabbed a handful of uppers, rinsed the taste of rubbish out of his mouth, and stumbled to what was left of his car. He had no memory of an early-morning confrontation with the corner of his garage at the end of his unaccountably successful drive home. The left fender was crumpled like a discarded candy wrapper. Worse, the Honda wobbled badly on a misaligned right front wheel, the result of a detour onto a high curb as Seth was trying to drive away from the Washington Square Bar and Grill.

By the time he crossed Richardson Bay, the sun was starting to burn off the fog, and the reds were consuming the last cobwebs inside his head. Although the amphetamines had hit his heart like a cattle prod, he kept a light foot on the accelerator as he lurched down 101. He glanced at the hills off to his right, taking in the patchwork quilt of pastel greens, mustard, taupes, and deep blues, unrolled like a carpet against the tangerine sky. His head was completely clear by the time he hit the bridge, and he became conscious of tankers beneath him, honking and blaring as if to scare away the last stubborn fingers of low-lying fog obscuring their vision. The mist had already lifted to the northeast, where bands of circling gulls hovered over a fleet of herring boats clustered in the choppy black and white waters near Sausalito. Across the bay, smoke from the petroleum complex at Richmond curved up over the red horizon in pursuit of the rising sun. Another day in paradise.

As Seth approached the tollbooth, he shifted his attention to passing through the gate without having his car impounded as a road hazard. The bored operator paid him no attention, however, other than to demand the toll, which was when Seth found that his wallet was completely empty. Which was when he also remembered stopping on the way home at Stella's on Caledonia Street in Sausalito—something about a game of pool and throwing bills and change at somebody, the bartender maybe. He couldn't remember why he had done it, but suspected a connection between that event and the kaleidoscope bruise already splotching its way across his left cheek.

He turned right into the bridge parking lot, paid the $3 toll at the office with his Visa card, and aimed the Honda back onto

Doyle Drive, over to Lombard, then south toward the Federal Building. He felt uncomfortably wired now and even behind sunglasses had to squint against the blinding glare. Every traffic light he approached seemed to turn red, and every lane he chose was slower than the one he had just wobbled out of. The world outside his rolled-up windows seemed to bristle with air-raid intensity, and the street din blasting his ears became indistinguishable from the blazing visual bedlam around him; the blare and the glare had become one, and he was getting sick again. Too many reds, too little sleep, and rogue thoughts of Rosie crowding into his head like floodwaters through a damaged levee.

He slipped into the slow lane, but his heart was pounding up through his throat, gushing like an errant oil rig, sending torrents of blood northward to batter his temples and collide with more images of Rosie, often in various forms of undress with Tom Huckins.

And positions.

He started hyperventilating and had to pull into the Standard station at Van Ness and Pine. He skidded to a stop, waved away a black dude wanting to wash his windshield for change, lurched into the cashier's station, bought some candy in a paper bag, then threw away the candy and started blowing into the bag, a trick he had learned from an associate at M&M.

Back on Van Ness, he ignored the curious looks of other drivers as he tried to steer the defiant Civic with an elbow, holding the top of the bag with one hand and shifting gears with the other. At a long stoplight at Ellis, he had a chance to blow several times into the bag and began feeling better—until he heard shouting from the car next to him and saw the two skinheads laughing at him.

"Hey, Dizzy," shouted the driver, leaning forward in his seat, "play 'Misty' for me, okay?" More laughter.

"When you finish with the bag, fuck-face," shouted the passenger, "I got something else here you can blow on."

That almost cooked it for Seth, but luckily the light turned green, and Seth—reminding himself he was on his way to solve a problem, not become part of one—let the freaks take off ahead of him in the fast lane. He watched as carbon smoke surged from the exhaust pipe of the ancient Chrysler New Yorker, almost obscuring the messages, AMERICA FOR AMERICANS, WHITE IS RIGHT!

and several other antiblack slogans displayed on the rusted-out rear bumper.

As he continued to blow into the bag, his breathing became more regular, at least until he saw the traffic light turn red at the next intersection. The freaks had the yellow but didn't take it. They weren't finished with him.

He felt his anger rising again, but was in no condition for a confrontation and tried to make his way out of the middle lane. No luck. He had become a link in the chain of commuter traffic that crowded all three lanes of Van Ness Avenue every morning. He dropped the sack on the floor, rolled the window all the way up, and resolved to ignore them.

"Hey, man, what happened to the bag?" shouted the driver over the booming bass line from his radio. "Did it go pop?"

Seth rolled his window down and tried to smile. "Don't rile me, boys. Let's be cool, okay?"

This drew derisive laughter from the passenger. "We're cool, man. We just miss the bag. You keep your brains in there?"

"Or your balls," shouted the driver, "if you got any, that is."

More laughter and gunning of the Chrysler's engine.

Seth turned again and took in their taunting faces, holding on to rationality, holding off the orange fog that was slipping in at the edges of his blurred vision. The bald passenger was midtwenties and wore some kind of sleeveless leather vest out of which bulged a white shoulder emblazoned with an iron-cross tattoo. He also wore a tiny gold or brass nose-ring and an expression forged in hatred. Cruel eyes under thin white eyebrows, set in a fleshy, pale face. Seth couldn't get a good look at the driver except to see that his misshapen head needed a fresh shave and that he displayed an unusually long middle finger. Seth tried to look away from the grinning, maniacal faces—*Just let it go*—but a magnetic revulsion drew his eyes back, inspiring additional creative remonstrations from his tormentors. He felt his mind racing away from him, like a runaway train hurtling into a dark tunnel.

"What you lookin' at, asshole?" shouted the driver. "You want a piece of us?"

"Hell, no, he's too chicken-shit," answered his passenger, drumming loudly on his car door with the flat of his right hand

and now turning his attention to a woman driving a Mercedes behind Seth. "Hey, pussy," he shouted at her. "Wanna party?"

The woman cringed, looked down, stung mostly by the cruel hand motions that accompanied the words. Seth, watching her in the rearview mirror, felt helpless and impotent. As if he were watching the unfolding incident through one-way glass. Something fluttered across his memory, rising out of the deadly nightshade shadows of his childhood.

Watching. Cold glass.

"Come on, cunt," the passenger continued. "Bet you'd like to come in here and taste about eight inches of white power and . . . *holy shit!*"

The passenger was interrupted in midinsult by a hand clamped across his face, then sliding down under his chin. He stabbed at the door lock, but not quickly enough, and suddenly found himself being dragged from the car. In what appeared to be a single motion, Seth had leapt from his car, snatched the right front door of the Chrysler open, and seized the wide-eyed man's face and leather vest in an iron grip.

"Jesus!" said the driver as he slammed his foot against the accelerator, preferring the risk of running a red light to dealing with this weirdo. Not until he was fifteen feet into the intersection did he realize he had lost his passenger.

The passenger punk turned out to be considerably bigger than Seth, but was never in it. Experienced street-fighters know that size and skill often mean little against wild aggression and the first devastating punch, which Seth delivered hard into the skinhead's surprised face. The blow sent him flying backward, but Seth held on to the vest to keep him from falling to the pavement so he could hit him again. The next blow drove the freak backward into the woman's Mercedes, still idling behind Seth's Honda. As the skinhead started to slide down toward the pavement, Seth caught him and buried his fist deep into his gut, followed by an uppercut that shattered the punk's jaw. Blood splattered from his mouth as he fell to the asphalt street.

Less than ten seconds had passed. The light was just now turning green.

The driver abandoned his car in the middle of the intersection and raced toward the melee, but not before Seth had delivered a savage kick to the fallen passenger's side.

"Are you *crazy*, man?" shouted the driver, jumping Seth from behind and pinning his arms to his side. But Seth didn't need his arms to continue delivering kicks to the passenger or to throw his head back into the face of the driver, fracturing his nose with a dull, crunching sound. The driver staggered backward, and Seth turned his attention back to the passenger, who had managed to crawl halfway under the Mercedes. Seth grabbed his feet and began pulling him back out.

Horns were honking all the way back to Ellis Street. A small crowd gathered in the crosswalk at Van Ness and Eddy, but they were immobilized, transfixed by the horror they were witnessing. Seth noticed none of this. His disembodied mind was deep in the tunnel now, where nothing existed but the violent orange haze, shot through with flashing bolts of fiery red, and the leering face of the skinhead.

The driver started back toward Seth, holding his hand to his bleeding nose. *"Help me, you fucking idiots!"* he shouted over his shoulder to the bystanders. *"The crazy bastard is killing him!"*

Seth turned back in the direction of the voice, and the driver quickly took refuge behind the two people closest to him.

The passenger rolled over and groaned, and Seth started back to finish him, but the fragile-looking young woman had stepped out of the Mercedes and was bending over him.

She looked up at Seth through dark eyes that were shocked but unafraid. His raging mind's eye took her in, trying to program the impact of this unexpected obstacle confronting his body's unfinished business.

"Please," she said. "Stop this. I heard the things they were saying, but nothing justifies this."

She put a sweater under the punk's head and added, "You really *are* killing him."

Her words reverberated in his head, momentarily immobilizing him like bullets from a stun gun. He became aware of people around them, people staring at him. His mind was reconnecting with his body, and he began to identify several alien sensations: a stabbing pain in his left hand, a taste like diesel oil in a mouth so dry he couldn't swallow, a runaway heart pounding in his temples, a heaving chest partially exposed through a torn shirt. His mind's eye surveyed the damage his body had done, and he shivered as a cold wind slashed at his soaked shirt. Wiping his mouth, he turned toward the bystanders. They drew back from his gaze as if blown by a heavy gale.

He became aware of the sound of horns from cars now stacked all the way back to California Street. He looked again at the dark-eyed woman, who had turned her attention back to the passenger. She pulled her long black hair back over her shoulder to keep it out of the punk's eyes. *Just like Rosie would do.* Behind him, Seth saw that two people were now ministering to the driver, who was down on his knees in the pedestrian crosswalk. Others took advantage of Seth's hesitation to join the dark-haired woman helping the passenger. They warily circled around the other side of Seth's car or up onto the traffic island to avoid walking too close to him.

The intersection looked like an automobile crash scene. People were moving everywhere now, as if someone had shouted, "Action on the set!" Somebody shouted, "Call an ambulance," sending bystanders in different directions. Others, seeing the excitement was over, drifted away, not wanting to become involved in any aftermath.

Seth took advantage of the confusion to walk to his car and simply drive away.

Later, when the police asked for a license number, only one citizen had thought to try to get it, and he was an old man who had forgotten the last two numbers and wasn't so sure about the three letters either. But when one of the officers asked for a description of the car, two men confidently obliged.

"Yessuh, Officer, it were a 1988 or '89 Oldsmobile," offered the first bystander.

"You right, Clifford, it surely were an Oldsmobile, all right," agreed his companion, "but I'd put it at an '87."

Seth parked his crippled Honda a block from the Federal Building and dropped his head onto the steering wheel. He noticed blood on his shirt, but his coat would cover up most of it. After a minute, he reached into the glove compartment, removed an amber-colored plastic container, and got out of the car, slamming the door so hard the window nearly broke. He lost his balance and fell against the side of the car as if he were drunk. He grabbed at a stabbing pain in his stomach, and his entire body tightened like a fist around his burning gut.

He was still angry, but now only at himself. He shook three bennies into his mouth and tried to summon enough saliva to get them down. A couple of pills spilled on the sidewalk because he had lost the use of his left hand, which now hung limp and broken at his side. It was beginning to hurt, and he looked at it with disgust, then spit the pills out of his mouth and sent the rest scattering out into the street. Remembering some in his pocket, he awkwardly fished the red bullets out with his good hand and threw them into the street, too. This attracted the attention of a few onlookers, seemingly his fate today.

"What the hell are you looking at, boy?" he said to a particularly nosy kid.

"You shouldn't waste good drugs like that, man," said the kid.

"Better them than me," he said, and headed for the Federal Building.

He had Lev out on bail by ten, thanks to Allyn Friedlander's checking account and Seth's impulsive bullshit bluff about Lev's wife owning a video camera.

While he had been practicing his craft inside City Hall, the sky had turned slate colored—like his face. Menacing clouds were leaking inkblots on the northern horizon. The rain would soon hit San Francisco. He could smell it.

"You don't look so good, Lev," said Seth as they drove away from the Federal Building. The amphetamines had mercifully worn off, but had left him even more ragged than when he had first awakened. *A. P. Giannini was right, kid, but he didn't go far enough. There's no such thing as a free* anything. "You want me to take you to Emergency?"

"I'm okay."

"You don't look it."

"You said that twice now," said Lev sullenly. "It's been a long night."

"It's about the case, isn't it."

Lev took in a deep breath of fresh air, then exhaled noisily. "The bastards were cagey. Nearest they came to it was when the honkie said, 'You better stay closer to home, boy.' Then the black guy starts to laughin' about the 'homeboy' bit, and while the white guy's trying to figure out what he had said that was so funny, I took the opportunity to bust up his ribs a little."

"I heard."

"Which he didn't much care for."

"I can imagine."

They rode in silence for a few minutes, then Lev took a good look at Seth.

"You don't look so pretty yourself, Cowboy."

"Had a few last night."

"What's the matter with your hand there?"

"Nothing serious."

Lev was silent for a minute. "You're drinking lately like a man just out of prison," he said, slowly shaking his head. "And your fly's open."

"Alcohol-abuse counseling," said Seth, zipping up as he waited for a light to change, "from a guy charged with cocaine possession."

Lev suddenly flared. "I thought you were going straight to the office last night to turn my statement into an affidavit." His bloodshot eyes were flashing. "Instead, you go out fucking around while I'm getting my kidneys bent."

"You're right. You're going to drop me off up there at the office and take my car home. But stop by Doc McKuen's office. She'll check you out, take some gory photos so we can make a good plea-bargain, and—"

"I know the drill, Cowboy. I'm *in* this business, remember?"

"Right. Sorry." There he was, apologizing again. "I'll draft the affidavit today, I promise."

"You best draft it *now*, Cowboy. If they'll do this to a guy who turns up a key witness, think what they'd do to the key witness hisself. As for your car, no thanks. This thing's in worse condition than either one of us."

"Jesus, Seth," said Allyn as he dragged himself onto the landing, "you look awful."

"So I've been told."

Ramon moved back as if confronted by a leper.

"Did you get Lev out?" Allyn asked.

Seth said, "Yeah, he's out," grabbed some coffee, and gave her a sanitized version of what had happened on Van Ness Avenue. She gave him the name of a good hand specialist, followed by a stern lecture.

"A man who can't control his temper," she concluded, "can't hope to control a courtroom."

"Thanks for the doc's name," he said, looking at the ceiling.

"Okay, end of speech. More bad news. Tucker died yesterday. Heart."

"How did you find out?"

"Turns out he had a daughter. She'd like you to continue on, representing his estate."

"Estate?"

"Well, all that's in it is what's left of the motel and the lawsuit. I told Ramon to go ahead and prepare the paperwork."

"Thanks. Poor bastard never had a decent break, but not even bad luck will be able to find him now."

Allyn shrugged, and Seth locked himself in his office with Mitch Simmons's statement. He scanned Lev's handwriting for a few minutes, then began to draft Simmons's declaration in longhand:

I, Mitchell Simmons, declare under penalty of perjury that the following is true and correct. That I am a corporal in the United States Air Force and that at all times relevant hereto, my primary duty assignment was bartender and food service manager attached to the Symington Air Force Base Officers' Club, located in the State of New Mexico. I was on duty in this capacity on the night of October 15, 1992.

Seth paused for a moment. Despite everything that had happened during the past twelve hours—Rosie, Leviticus, his broken car, his bruised face, the pain in his left hand—he couldn't help but smile with satisfaction at the thought of Treadwell opening his mail and seeing that his motion for summary judgment had been shot down.

New Mexico. The key to ending the statute-of-limitations threat had been waiting there right where it had all begun.

In New Mexico.

SETH SIPPED HIS COCKTAIL AND STUDIED ELENA BARTON WHILE SHE, her lips parted in a beguiling half-smile, scanned a copy of the Simmons declaration and pretended she wasn't conscious of being studied. They were seated together on her living room couch, one of those sand-colored wraparound jobs featured in magazines and on *Lifestyles of the Rich and Famous*.

Seth had thought twice—several times in fact—before inviting himself over. He wanted to celebrate the imminent defeat of Treadwell's motion with someone, but Allyn was busy, Lev was home nursing his cuts and bruises, Rosie was out of his life, and Harry Cooper had become a pain in the ass with whom he would just end up crazy drunk in some sleazy south-of-Market singles bar. God knows there had been few occasions for celebration in this crazy case, and though Stars' renaissance bartender Ken was a good listener, Seth was tired of drinking alone.

So he had called Elena Barton, using his hot new evidence as bait. He was astonished to find her at home, and eager to see him.

He was also uneasy. It wasn't just that Elena was untouchable again (under his renewed commitment to start behaving like an attorney with his client); after their last sexual debacle, that was grounds for relief, not anxiety. It was more basic than that—even that. The debacle was just the effect, not the cause. The cause was what Allyn had seen from the beginning. He was a man in love, but he was also a man in way over his head.

Elena Barton was beautiful, wealthy, and refined. He was a Bakersfield refugee, a Montgomery Street reject with a foul temper and a cast on his hand to prove it; a south-of-Market lawyer with an overdrawn checking account, working for peanuts in a

Mission Street firetrap. He was, to put it bluntly, unworthy of Elena Barton's attention, let alone her love.

For now at least.

As he watched her reading the affidavit, he could tell by the sudden swell of her breasts that she must have come to the part about Sam's not leaving the club until 11:30 P.M. She met his eyes, smiled, leaned forward on the couch, and kissed him on the cheek. A client's kiss, to be sure, but a kiss that shot a burning sensation through his confused groin.

But as Elena read on, a small, V-shaped worry crease appeared between her eyes. The eyes swept back to the top of the document, then down again.

"But can we prove," she asked, "that Sam was drinking Shirley Temples the whole time he was at the club?"

Seth was not surprised at her perceptiveness, although in a perfect world he would have preferred her unquestioning joy and approbation.

"And," she added before he could answer, "doesn't this give us more than we really wanted? Didn't Bostwick suggest that the takeoff was around the time Simmons now says Sam was still at the club?"

Seth started to respond, but Elena wasn't finished.

"After leaving, Sam would have had to change clothes, then preflight the X-215A. Then there's the flight plan, tower clearance—"

"Mice," Seth said quietly, "not elephants."

"Pardon me?"

"Every case that makes it to trial is full of these kinds of inconsistencies. They aren't trivial, but they're not decisive either. We call them mice." Seth paused, swirled the ice in his empty drink, and added, "We *had* an elephant—the statute of limitations— now we've got mice."

"Oh."

"We can live with mice," he added, regaining the initiative— a slippery thing to hold on to with a woman like Elena. "With the statute out of the case, the judge will have to let it go to the jury, and once they hear your story, the sky's the limit."

"*Oh*. Well, then," she said, the worry lines erased with a smile, "another kiss for my conquering hero."

It started innocently enough—a kiss on Seth's other cheek—

but Seth reached up and touched her hair, then her face. She didn't pull back, just stared at him through wide, questioning eyes, like a deer looking into headlights.

"Seth?" she whispered, her hands against his chest. "Our . . . arrangement."

But Seth gently kissed her unyielding lips. Then again, and again, until her lips slowly softened and began to press back against his. She closed her eyes as Seth slid a hand up under her sweater, and barely audible animal sounds escaped her lips as he lightly caressed her bare breasts.

Both aroused, their kisses became ravenous—probing tongues amidst colliding teeth between fused lips as Elena now clawed at his back with one hand and pushed against his erection with the other.

Suddenly, Seth was upon her—her skirt bunched up under his chest, her panties pulled to one side—thrusting himself inside her. Even in the deranged passion of the moment, Seth could not take his eyes off Elena's face, her perfect features now contorted with the imminency of orgasm, wildly beautiful. He, too, was aware of a pressure that would not wait. He didn't care, because he felt her body tighten against his and saw that her eyes were suddenly open again and burning into his.

"Seth, *Seth!* I . . . oh, Seth . . . love . . . you, love . . ."

Their bodies shuddered together, then collapsed into the couch.

Little more than a minute had elapsed since her friendly kiss on his cheek.

Lifting himself into a sitting position, Seth watched Elena smooth her skirt down, then disappear into the upstairs bathroom. Seth awkwardly pulled up his trousers with his one functional hand and stumbled into the kitchen to pour himself a fresh JD over ice. He returned to the couch and tried to take it all in. The suddenness of what had happened amazed him, the violence of it. Like the 7.2 earthquake in '89, only nobody got hurt in this one.

Not yet, anyway.

Fifteen minutes later, Elena rejoined him, barefoot, in fresh shorts and blouse. Her embarrassment was out of character, but it suited her for a change and helped him to feel relaxed with her. She poured herself a drink and sat down beside him. She put a hand on his and started to speak, stopped, then started again.

"I hope you don't think—"

"That you meant what you said?"

"No," she said, resting her head against his chest, "for better or for worse, I meant it. I do love you, Seth. But until this is behind us . . ."

This was a day full of surprises. "You're probably right," he said, trying to fill the silence, yet not betray his utter amazement at her casual declaration of love. "Loving you would be a full-time job and the damn case might get in the way."

"Then let's get the case—the damn case—finished. Meanwhile, Seth, I'll try harder to stick with the attorney-client relationship until then. Otherwise, I'm afraid I'd be attacking you at every recess."

"It would give the bailiff something to do."

She kissed him again, softly, but not a client's kiss. He put his arms around her, hungry again. Her eyes still seemed strangely vulnerable, yet shone bright as those green marbles you see at the bottom of a lighted fish tank. She sighed and flattened her body against his renewed hardness.

"I think we need the bailiff right now," she said.

"Yeah," he whispered into her lips, "I'm afraid we've got ourselves a problem here."

"As in mouse or elephant?" she said, taking his hand and leading him upstairs.

In the morning, Seth dropped his Honda off at the shop for realignment of the right front wheel—the battered fender would have to await his next paycheck—and caught a bus to the office via San Francisco's notorious Tenderloin, passing the Elk Hotel, the Hotel Jefferson, the Hotel California. He stared out the window as the bus went past Aunt Pearl's Jam House—haven to the hip and the yup who crowded into the bar each day after work, past Boeddeker Park—haven to pimps and drug dealers who crowded into the park each night after dark. Past the Tea Room Theatre ("All Male Movies!"). Watched the stream of lonely denizens as they filed up Taylor Street toward St. Anthony's Kitchen and Cecil Williams's famed Glide Memorial Church, at black prostitutes and other survivors of this open-doored prison jammed by people down on their luck. No tourists here. Even locals bypassed the Tenderloin—never know when somebody with nothing left to lose might try a car-jacking, or just jump in front of the car to collect insurance money. The Tenderloin was a place where dreams came to die.

Other parts of the city had changed from the days when he and other reckless high school youths had driven up from Bakersfield to try to catch sparks from the embers of the fiery, romantic sixties. The Haight-Ashbury, once the center of "sex, drugs, and rock 'n' roll," was now a gentrified community where it was easier to buy a good cross-training shoe than LSD. One of the last gay bathhouses at Eighth and Howard now housed the Episcopal Sanctuary for the Homeless, where gaiety was notably absent. Where was Sister Boom-Boom now? Fee Waybill and The Tubes? Acid rock had long since given way to acid-tongued rappers, while beatniks-cum-hippies-cum-yuppies were now parents, even grandparents, decrying the excesses of the young.

Seth left the bus at Market, elbowed past street hustlers, and headed south toward the Mission. Anthony Treadwell would be surprised to know that this area was changing, too, with several Establishment law firms moving into luxurious high-rise buildings at the east end of the Mission. Calling someone a "south of Market Street lawyer" was no longer an insult calling for a challenge to a duel.

"My, don't we look cheery," said Ramon, greeting him at the head of the stairs. "Did we win the lottery?"

"Bingo."

"That, too? You've been busy."

"As a bee. Do I smell coffee?"

"Coming right up. Queen Mother ran over to Oakland on a show-cause matter; wanted me to remind you about the Lopez hearing at ten. The file is on your desk. Toward the top of the stack on the right."

Seth looked at his watch: 9:10. Fifteen minutes by bus to City Hall; another fifteen plus bus time to organize his argument in Lopez; time to slip in a call to either Elena or Alan Millstein.

"Hello, Seth!" said the expert witness. "Yes, it's going beautifully. I was at the lab last night, saw the first signs of fatigue in the harness. Textbook fraying over an oval-shaped area approximately one centimeter." He paused, and Seth could picture the little guy lighting up a new cigarette off an old one, seemingly inhaling and making sounds at the same time like a bagpipe player. Seth swore he could smell the tar through the telephone.

"Should see a breakthrough—breakthrough, get it?—any day now. Then the fun begins. Fourth of July. Bring your marshmallows."

"You still think it'll spark?"

"Did you happen to see the closing ceremonies at the L.A. Olympics?"

"I'll settle for a spark or two. When do you think it'll happen—if it happens?"

"Hard to say. Maybe tomorrow, maybe next year."

"The trial starts in less than six weeks."

"Oh, yes, the trial."

"That's why we're doing this, Alan. Remember?"

"Just kidding, old boy. A little forensic humor. Not to worry. Any day now. Fingers crossed."

Seth smiled as he replaced the phone in its cradle. He had not felt so good in months. Full of energy again despite limited sleep and the absence of pharmaceutical support. Controlling the energy was the problem. His mind seemed hot-wired, his thoughts undisciplined.

Where's that Lopez file? Maybe meet Elena after the hearing for lunch at Stars. Bad idea—just enough cash left to get the car out of hock. Better start drafting my witness list, then prepare for the hearing on Treadwell's motion. Express mail with Simmons's declaration should be here by the time I'm back from City Hall. Got to see her tonight. I'll hit Allyn up for an advance. Better start working on Daimler's direct examination when I get back. Said she's been as lonely as I have. No one else since our last time together and before that no one since Sam. Explains why my back looks like I slept on a cat-o'-nine-tails. Shouldn't take long to draft a supplemental memorandum of points and authorities incorporating Simmons's declaration. Got to give Lev a call, see if I can drop something off for him on the way to Elena's tonight. Bet Barbara is pissed at me for involving him. Better take her some flowers. Send some to Elena, too.

Seth bounded up the stairs at noon after his hearing and was greeted again by Ramon. This time, his perfect white teeth flashed a wide smile. "Looking for this?"

Seth snatched the express envelope from the secretary's hands and raced into his office. Tearing it open, he pulled the declaration out, skipping to page two and the signature line.

Blank. Unsigned.

His heart pounded against his rib cage, and his legs began to give way beneath him. He collapsed into his chair and forced himself to take a deep breath as he glanced at the cover letter from Symington's public information officer on top of the declaration.

The letter reported the "untimely death" of Mitch Simmons, returned his document "with apologies for whatever inconvenience this regrettable event may have caused," then made reference to an attached newspaper article, which the writer observed was "self-explanatory."

Airman Falls to His Death
Associated Press

The body of Air Force Corporal Mitchell Joe Simmons was found early this morning by employees of the Albuquerque Continental Hotel where the decedent was staying. The victim had fallen or jumped from his hotel room on the fourteenth floor.

Corporal Simmons, stationed at nearby Symington Air Force Base, was due to be discharged in August. Officials there could not speculate as to why Simmons had reserved the room earlier yesterday using his credit card number, but one informed source revealed that he had recently seemed moody and depressed.

An autopsy revealed a blood-alcohol level of .24, nearly lethal in itself.

The decedent is survived by his parents, Mr. and Mrs. Everett Simmons of Moultrie, Georgia. Despite the circumstances of his death, a spokesman from the base commander's office informed the *Times* that Corporal Simmons would be buried with full military honors.

THE LEGAL STAFF OF ALLYN FRIEDLANDER AND ASSOCIATES SAT STARing at each other on the second floor at 618 Mission Street, drinking high-octane coffee laced with cheap brandy as late-afternoon shadows played across the office. A chatter of voices rose from across the alley as employees of the department store next door headed for the warm security of home or the noisy hope of a singles bar, then gradually died out and gave way to the sounds of car engines and air brakes. Someone was cooking a chicken upstairs, probably the Avon lady who kept them in new toothbrushes.

"So," Allyn said, "I see you've added smoking to your growing list of vices."

"A temporary lapse," said Seth with a shrug. "My discipline is in sharp decline at the moment. Also my hopes for getting this case to a jury."

"Don't you think you should try to settle now?"

"Treadwell will come up with some decent money when we get to the courthouse steps."

"I thought he said he wouldn't," she said.

"That's right."

"He might be telling the truth."

"I guess it happens."

A quiet darkness settled in the office, but neither Allyn nor Seth reached for a light switch. Ramon had left an hour earlier as had the small building's other second-floor tenants.

"What about the finish of Bostwick's deposition yesterday?"

"He continued to deny everything but his name. Parroted the official statement that Sam crashed around ten-thirty the night of the fifteenth. Denied telling Lev and me otherwise."

"Can't say I blame him, given the fact that everybody who tries to tell the truth in this case ends up seriously dead."

"I can blame him."

"How's Leviticus?"

Seth's video bluff had not held up, and Lev had been arraigned on charges of possession and resisting arrest. Trial was set for next month and bail had been set at $20,000, requiring an unusually high bond.

"He's back at work, thanks to you and your bottomless bank account," said Seth. "Said he might pop in this evening to consult with his lawyer."

"And who might that be? You don't know shit about criminal defense."

"I was hoping you'd do it."

"And I," she said, smiling, "was hoping for Lev's sake you *wouldn't*." She grunted as she lifted a black-stockinged foot up onto her desk. "Sure, I'll do it, though it looks to me like you'll have plenty of time to give me a hand—once Treadwell's motion for summary judgment is granted next week."

They drank and smoked in silence. The cigarette was making Seth dizzy, but he smoked it anyway.

"Too bad about Simmons and your affidavit," said Allyn. "My TDA stockholders' suit request just produced two boxes full of files on Tellman Design Associates from your pal at the tax division."

"Save your eyes. We're dead."

Allyn lit a cigar, poured fresh coffee and brandy, then turned her head toward a creaking sound from the stairwell. "Must be Lev," said Allyn.

"That's not Lev," said Seth, easing out of his chair. "You expecting anyone?"

"No."

"Got a gun in here anywhere?"

"Shit, no. I would've killed Ramon years ago if I had a gun. Why?"

"Like you said, people seem to be dying like flies around this case."

"Hello? Anybody here?" came a voice decidedly not Lev's.

"*Jesus*," said Seth. "Just what I need right now."

A gaunt face appeared in the doorway. "Hi, guys."

"Hello, Harry," said Seth. "Allyn, you remember Harry Cooper?"

"Hi, Harry. How're things at the Big Uneasy?"

"M and M? Same old shit, Allyn," said Harry, eyeing the brandy. "Bum a cup of coffee?"

"Help yourself."

They watched as Harry laced his brandy with a shot of coffee.

A few minutes of small talk, carefully avoiding any mention of the ConSpace matter, then Harry came out with it: big case, big client, dispositive motion, reply brief due tomorrow, long story, big trouble. Déjà vu.

"So," he concluded, "I need a little help."

"Hell, Harry," said Seth, "you're a partner now. You got twenty, thirty ex–U.S. Supreme Court clerks at M and M sittin' on their fat asses, every damn one of 'em a hell of a lot smarter than me."

"You don't understand, Seth. The kid I assigned blew it, and I've been traveling a lot lately, and, well . . . I've been a little under the weather. I've tried to pull the brief together, but nothing's working. Now I'm out of time. It's a bet-the-ranch motion, Seth. But you and I working together like we used to—"

"Sorry, Harry. Got my own load right now."

"No, Seth, you're not hearing me. I've got big trouble here." Harry leapt to his feet, poured another shot of brandy into his empty cup. Forget the coffee. "I'll pay you. Full rates." He looked at Allyn for support, but she was looking out the window.

"I'm not looking for any favors," he added, then slugged down the brandy. "*Double* your full rates. *Whatever!*"

Seth stood, too, then reached out and took the cup from Harry's hand. "No, *you* listen for a change, pardner. First place, I told you last time I bailed you out it *was* the last time. Second place, I've never been one for asking favors, nor giving 'em out either. Every time I get involved in someone else's problems, I'm asking for trouble, which I don't need more of right now. Third place, you don't need a lawyer, old son, you need a doctor. Now we're a little busy here, so—"

"So just buzz the fuck off, is that it? Just go see Treadwell in the morning with my hat in my hand and admit I'm too fucked up to be a partner at Miller and McGrath?"

"Harry," said Allyn, interceding with as soothing a voice as she could muster, "why don't you just get a continuance?"

"Don't you think I've tried?" said Harry angrily. "I've got Caldwell and Shaw on the other side. Need I say more? They know they've got me by the balls."

"Then move the court for a continuance tomorrow."

"Jesus, lady, do you think I came in on the last load of West's Law Digest? *I've had two already!"*

"That's enough, Harry," said Seth, "I'm asking you to leave now."

"Well, fuck you very much, too, old pal. I won't forget this."

"Neither will I, Harry. Good night."

Allyn and Seth listened to the retreating footsteps, heard the door slam downstairs.

"He seems pretty upset," said Allyn.

"That wasn't talcum powder on his tie."

"So?" Allyn said cautiously. "that's not aspirin you've been taking."

Seth reddened. "I'm clean now, Allyn. Besides, I was taking what I took to stay in the game. Harry takes what he takes to escape it."

"I understand, but—"

"And to say Harry's a coke freak who's squandered a brilliant mind is to give him the benefit of the doubt."

"Okay, but you were pretty rough on him."

Seth stared down at his hands as if he wanted to use them. "There's a history," he said, then walked across the hall and into his office.

Though it was cold, Allyn opened a window.

Seth stared at his dictating machine, trying to think of something to say in his brief, something to head off the inevitable disaster.

Nothing came to mind.

He had already broken the news to Elena, who dealt with it by the simple expedient of denial.

"You'll find a way to win," she had said. "I know you will."

Her refusal to deal with the message—except by putting more pressure on the messenger—irritated him, and the conversation had not ended well. He had hung up the phone, picked up the unsigned declaration, and torn it to shreds.

Twenty minutes later he still had not dictated a word and almost welcomed the sounds of footsteps on the stairway, heralding the prospect of an interruption. He turned off the recorder and looked up to see his open doorway nearly filled by Leviticus Heywood.

"Is the lawyer in?"

"Depends. You some kind of dope fiend? You look like one."

"Maybe I'll take my business to Miller and McGrath," said Lev. "I hear they really take care of their people."

"They took care of me, all right. How's it going, pard?"

"Okay. I just heard about my man Simmons."

"Yeah. Pretty unsporting of the kid to get murdered and fuck up my case."

"You probably would have managed it on your own anyway."

Lev lumbered in and overstressed Seth's client chair, then sat there rubbing his hands together. Seth could see he was troubled.

"Allyn's going to beat this rap for you. Don't worry. She's damn good."

"That's not what's buggin' me, Cowboy." Lev rubbed one of the huge hands across his face. "You know I good as wrote that kid's death warrant."

Seth couldn't think of a consoling word that held water. It was painfully true.

"The kid was a talker," he offered lamely. "All you did was listen."

Lev grunted.

Allyn stuck her head in and suggested they move over to her office where they could all sit down at the same time.

"What's wrong with my lap?" said Lev.

"Thanks, good looking," she said, then with a mocking wink at Seth, added, "but it would be unethical for us to get romantically involved if I'm going to be your lawyer."

"Don't give me that," Lev said. "You're just like all them other Jews; can't stand us black people."

They all laughed and moved across the hall where, after they had devised a strategy for defending Lev, Allyn handed Seth a document.

"What's this?"

"You better read it."

Seth scanned the three pages, then looked up at Allyn through red-rimmed eyes. "Where did you find it?"

"I couldn't resist looking in those tax-division boxes."

Seth fell into a chair. "Jesus."

"I almost didn't show it to you."

"I almost wish you hadn't."

"What's goin' on?" asked Lev.

Seth held up the document. "It looks to be an in-house Con-Space memo. Here's a paragraph from page two:

" 'The TDA system is an ingenious compilation of three independent off-the-shelf components. The canopy itself is made of standard high heat-resistant—five-hundred-degrees Fahrenheit—Plexiglas with an Austin-designed activation mechanism and a Stellar Electronic Array. The problems we are encountering could be a function of incompatibility of the Stellar electrical system and the Austin activating mechanism. Components of the latter could be implicated during opening and closing of the canopy in a chafing action with elements of the former, resulting in compromise to the integrity of the protective wiring harness.' "

"So your guy Daimler was right-on."

"In the margin of what I just read," continued Seth, lighting a cigarette with a match that wouldn't sit still, "are some handwritten notes, probably somebody from Justice: 'Why did Con accept TDA's system? Pressure? Time? Political? Does Father fit in here somewhere?' "

"This is *terrific!*" said Lev. "So what's with the long faces?"

They just stared at him.

"Oh, yeah," he said. "Sorry. Slow reading group."

A siren from an ambulance over on Market broke the silence in the room as the friends stared into their coffee mugs. Seth closed the window. Every sound was an irritant.

"When's your reply brief due?" said Lev.

"Tomorrow," said Seth, adding a dash more brandy to his coffee.

The siren sound died.

Lev sniffed, fanned the smoke from his face, opened the window. In the alley below, a pair of cats were mating, fighting, or both.

"I busted my ass to get that statement," said Lev.

"You did good," said Allyn.

"I can picture the boy like he was in the room here. Good kid. Smart-ass, but hell, he was young. What a waste."

Seth suddenly jammed his cigarette into an ashtray and jumped to his feet. "Maybe it doesn't have to be a waste."

"What?" said Allyn.

"Instead of Simmons's declaration, how about we use his statement, then have Lev sign a declaration which attests to the accuracy of the statement?"

"You'd never get it into evidence," said Allyn.

"Not at trial. But the judge would have to read it at the hearing on Treadwell's motion. He'd see the problem."

"Hell," said Lev. "I'm just a step ahead of jailbird status, but I'll sign anything you put in front of me if you think it'll do any good."

"You'd just be delaying the inevitable," said Allyn, wagging a nicotine-stained finger at Seth.

"Yeah?" he said, heading for his office. "So what's your point?"

"MR. CAMERON'S OPPOSITION PAPERS ARE AN AFFRONT TO THIS COURT, Your Honor!" said a vexed and irate Anthony Treadwell, coming out of his chair on the heels of Seth's argument, "and I move that Mr. Heywood's double-hearsay declaration be stricken from the court's file." Treadwell looked elegant, as usual, in a Gianfranco double-breasted wool suit, a $400 Borrelli shirt, and one of his trademark Hermès ties with matching silk pocket square. He commanded attention—even when he wasn't obviously vexed and irate—one of those gaunt, small-boned men who somehow conveyed the inner force of a supercollider. Seth hated this attribute, not just because Treadwell possessed it, but because he didn't.

Judge Singer raised his glasses to his forehead and peered

down at Seth. "Mr. Cameron, while I prefer that cases be resolved on their merits before a jury, I'm disposed to grant Mr.
Treadwell's motion. I'm simply unable to comprehend your
argument."

"Let me try to be more clear with Your Honor," said Seth,
rising again in his own finest, a decent Brioni knockoff from
the local factory outlet. "I'm afraid we're passing like ships in
the night."

"That may be true, Counsel," said the judge with a kindly
smile, "but mine is sailing into harbor, and I'm afraid yours is
heading out to sea."

"I'll try to come about, Your Honor," said Seth, gathering himself for another attempt. "As I said before, Mr. Heywood's declaration is not really hearsay. It's a declaration concerning facts
within his direct knowledge, raising a clear factual issue for the
jury as to whether the crash occurred the night of the fifteenth
or the early-morning hours of the sixteenth."

"I believe," said the judge, wearily rubbing his eyes, "that it's
the attached statement of Corporal Simmons with which Mr.
Treadwell takes most vigorous issue."

"But the statement," said Seth, steadily meeting the judge's
gaze, "is but a part of the declaration, incorporated therein as if
set forth in full. In short, Your Honor, Mr. Heywood is simply
declaring under penalty of perjury that this is precisely what he
heard the corporal say to him. Thus, apart from the statement—
which you will note was indeed signed by the decedent—you
have the word of a licensed private investigator."

Treadwell snickered at this and triumphantly waved a document in his extended hand. "Precisely, Your Honor! The word
of a private investigator who has recently been indicted—as this
certified minute order will show—on counts of cocaine possession and resisting arrest!"

"Objection, Your Honor!" said Seth. "Documentary impeach-
ment of a declarant is not only inappropriate, but too late. This
is the first I've seen of this document."

But Judge Singer was already studying the order. Treadwell
flashed Seth a contemptuous smile and said, "You don't mean
to tell the court that you're surprised, do you, Counsel? As a
matter of fact, your office represents the man, doesn't it?"

Seth stared back at the senior partner and could think of nothing to say or do that would not get him fined for contempt of court or busted for assault and battery.

Be prepared for a life of uncertainty and devastating surprises, his father had cautioned when Seth finished his first year in law school and proudly announced he would become a trial lawyer after winning the school's moot court competition. *A trial lawyer? No, no, anything but that, Seth. A trial lawyer lives his life dancing on the edge of contingency. The only two things he knows for sure when he sets foot in a courtroom are that he doesn't know enough and that something will go wrong. He just won't know what or when.* Young Seth had laughed and said that must be what makes it so exciting. *Exciting? Tell me what's so exciting about a bleeding gut and a liver like a rubber doorstop.*

"Is that true, Counsel?" said the judge as he perused the minute order. "Your firm represents the declarant, Mr. Heywood, in a pending criminal case?"

"Yes, Your Honor, but—"

"Never mind, Counsel," said Judge Singer, removing his glasses and giving Seth a stern look. "Although I am deeply troubled by this unseemly coincidence, it's not my province at this time to rule on such matters as possible bias or improper influence. On its face, the declaration is admissible and requires that I deny your motion, Mr. Treadwell."

The judge then turned to glare at Seth. "I do so with great reluctance, however, and warn you, Mr. Cameron, that this just gets you past this motion, bound as I am to resolve all doubts in favor of a trial on the merits. Come trial later this month, however, the standards for admissibility change, and you had better come up with clear evidence that the crash occurred on the sixteenth. If not, I'll gladly grant Mr. Treadwell's motion for nonsuit and move on to other pressing matters on my calendar."

"Understood, Your Honor," said Seth, starting to breathe again.

As the judge left the bench, Treadwell scowled and shoved his notes and case authorities into his briefcase. As he started toward the rail, he gave Seth a hard look and said, "Surely you must have a paying divorce client or some equally worthy matter to attend to, Cameron. It's clear to everybody but you that your pathetic little case is dead."

"You don't say."

"Seriously, Cameron, do you think Judge Singer will allow this case to fall into the hands of a jury? I know that's what you're counting on, but it won't happen. Give it up now, for God's sake, and I might be able to get you twenty-five, maybe thirty thousand."

Seth snapped his trial bag shut.

"Add a zero," he said without looking up, "and we can talk."

"There will be no zeros, Cameron, and no further settlement discussions after today. ConSpace can't risk the publicity of paying you one cent more than nuisance value. On the other hand, they'll pay me millions to see that this case never reaches that gaggle of emotional idiots we call a jury."

"And you don't mind taking the money."

Treadwell's features compressed into a scowl.

"You just don't get it, do you?" he said, slamming his briefcase down on the table in front of Seth. "These people are . . ."

Treadwell stopped himself, and Seth thought he saw a trace of desperation hidden inside the anger.

"Let me put it to you this way, Cameron, and you can make of it what you will. The pressure they're putting on me to win is *nothing* compared to what they'll put on you to lose."

"You don't say."

"I do say, and I wish to hell you would listen while there's still time."

Seth thought he had become immune to threats, yet Treadwell's words, and the despairing way he uttered them, reverberated in his head, then dropped into his gut where they smoldered like particles of nuclear waste. The two men stood in the silence of the empty courtroom, their eyes locked together.

"I'm not sure who 'they' are, Mr. Treadwell, but if *you* know, perhaps you could tell them for me to go fuck themselves."

Treadwell shook his head despairingly. "I think you would do well to reconsider your situation here, Cameron—as well as your mode of expressing yourself."

"Mr. Treadwell, I think you're confusing me with someone who gives a rat's ass about your opinions."

The senior partner reached for the handle of his briefcase. "You're being childish."

"I'm really glad we're having this exchange of ideas."

"Is that all you have to say to my offer?"

"No. I have a question. How did you find out that Heywood had been busted?"

Treadwell snatched up his briefcase and reached for the swinging gate leading out into the courtroom gallery, but Seth grabbed him by the arm. "Or maybe you knew it was going to happen ahead of time. Maybe *they* is *you*."

Treadwell snorted as he tried to twist out of Seth's grasp. "For that typically subtle demonstration of innuendo, Cameron, I'll have you back on a nag in Bakersfield punching plastic flamingos for a living!"

Seth's cobalt blue eyes bore into Treadwell as he tightened his grip on the senior partner's arm. "Do your worst, but if I find out you knew in advance what those federal meatballs were up to, you'll wish I had never left Bakersfield in the first place."

Treadwell slammed the gate open with his briefcase and stormed out.

The gate swung back and whacked Seth above the knees, but he didn't even feel it. In fact, he felt nothing at all, except for the realization that for better or worse, he was going to get his trial.

Now all he needed was some evidence.

"Now all you need is some evidence," said Allyn an hour later after he had dragged himself to the top of the stairs and given her a thumbs-up. "I bet Treadwell went ape-shit."

"Ballistically ape-shit," said Seth, and told her everything, except for his latest threat.

"Sit down, Cowboy. I couldn't resist going through the rest of the tax division's file. Look what else I found."

She handed him a police accident report from Destry, Arizona, a small town forty miles from the crash site. Seth quickly scanned the routine entries in a sketchy report and chuckled as he saw, beneath *Description of Vehicle 1*, the entry *USAF airplane*. There was a blank, of course, under *Description of Vehicle 2*, as well as under *Estimated time of collision*.

"Tell me there's more."

"Shut up and keep reading."

The shocker was at the bottom of the last page in a square labeled *Witnesses*. Seth had to strain to make out the names there. "Can you make it out? Looks like Thomas and Ruth Lochers or Luckens or something."

"It's hard to read," said Allyn. "What's more puzzling is that there's no explanation as to what the hell the witnesses were supposed to have witnessed. The dumb cop didn't even put down their addresses."

"But these reports are typed off notes. His notes would have more information!"

"Brilliant," said Allyn, blowing smoke in his face.

"I'm out of here."

"Slow down, Cowboy. You've got the Jensen trial starting tomorrow, remember?"

"You could cover me."

"And who would cover me on the Lansing divorce case starting day after tomorrow?"

They sat in silence for no more than a minute before the obvious solution came to them.

An hour later, Seth pulled up in front of Lev's house. Allyn had flat-out refused to accompany him to help deal with Barbara Heywood. "No way," Allyn had said. "I'd feel the same way if I had a husband who had been beaten, framed, and was about to be convicted of a felony."

His heart sank when a hostile Barbara Heywood answered the door and informed him that Lev was out of town on an assignment. Seth was leaving when a familiar voice boomed out from behind her, "Hey, Cowboy, what brings you out to the fog belt?"

"Hi, Lev. I tried to call—"

"I've been on the phone. Trying to dig up some work."

Barbara played with her hands and started to leave as her husband swung the door open, saying, "Don't just stand there, Cowboy. Like a beer? Cup of coffee?"

"No thanks, but I need to talk to you. Both of you."

Seth explained what Allyn had found, how important it might be if they could find the witnesses, and why he couldn't do it himself or trust anyone but Lev to do it. Lev was silent, stealing an occasional glance at his wife, while Barbara's narrowed eyes shot back and forth between the two men. When Seth was finished, both Lev and his wife sat gazing straight ahead into the heavy silence. When it was obvious that Lev would not speak first, Barbara did.

"A man under indictment can't leave the state," she said without looking up at Seth. "Even if he wanted to," she added pointedly with a sharp glance at her husband.

But Seth was prepared for that one, remembering that Barbara had been a legal secretary for the San Francisco public defender's office. "I've called the U.S. Attorney. He'll clear it."

"Will he also clear any medical and/or funeral expenses resulting from the trip?"

"Now, honey—"

"Lev, damn it, you *promised!*"

"But this is a piece of cake, honey. I find the cop whose name's on the report and sweet-talk my way into his notes. If I'm lucky, I catch up with those nice folks and find out once and for all exactly when this bird went down."

"I don't give a damn if you're going to meet the Grand Mufti of Jerusalem surrounded by U.N. peacekeepers!" she shouted. "You're finished with this case . . . *or I'm finished with you!*"

Lev winced at the stinging words. Nobody moved. Nobody spoke. Seth knew that the only decent thing for him to do at this point was to apologize and walk out the door.

Instead, he planted himself directly in front of her and looked her squarely in the eye. "Hear me out, Barbara. Our trial starts in two weeks and these people are our last hope for getting this case to a jury. They're also Elena Barton's only hope for clearing her husband's name, and my only hope for exposing this airborne killing machine for what it is."

"And what about *my* hopes, Mr. Silver Tongue? Hopes for having a husband who's all in one piece. Did he tell you the doctor says he may lose his *kidney?* And how about our hopes for having a family?" She turned back to Lev and seemed about to break up as she added through trembling lips, "How about our hopes for being able to . . . to love like we used to—"

"*That's enough, Barbara,*" said Lev, rising and taking her by the shoulders. "Listen, honey, I know what I promised, but hell, woman, I can't spend my life shadowing cheating husbands. How can I be a man for you when I don't see one looking back at me in the mirror when I shave in the morning?"

They seemed to have forgotten Seth was in the room, and Seth earnestly wished he weren't. He felt like a motorist standing over the body of someone he had run down in a car.

"Lev," he said, turning to leave, "thanks, ol' son, but you don't owe me anything."

"You right about that, Cowboy, but I owe them feds big time, and I'm gonna help you pay 'em back."

Barbara's anger and pain overtook her and she began to sob. "They . . . they're going to . . . kill you next time," she stammered.

Lev put his big arms around her and pulled her close to him. "I'm an investigator, honey, not some goddamn second-story snoop. If I keep doing this shit, I'm gonna die anyway."

Barbara Heywood wiped away her tears of anger and uttered her final words on the subject with frightening intensity.

"You promised me."

Leviticus sadly nodded his head, then told Seth to wait in the car while he packed some things. "I'll need a ride. The damn feds impounded my car." He then marched into the bedroom, leaving Barbara Heywood alone with the man who had come to disrupt their lives.

Leviticus's flight did not leave for several hours, so they went back to the office. Allyn heard them pounding up the stairs and was waiting at the top.

"Where you been all week, you big bear?" she said.

"Hibernatin'," said Lev.

"Come to save our unworthy asses one more time, huh?"

"A trained seal could do this gig," said Lev, smiling, "but Cowboy here reckons he's down to his last roundup." He glanced through Seth's open office door at a blackboard mounted on an easel and asked, "That your witness list?"

"Such as it is," said Seth.

"That's *it?*"

"Yep."

"If that was a menu, I'd eat somewhere else. Where the hell's all your witnesses, man?"

"We're going in lean and mean." Seth then explained that he would first call either Crispie to talk about Sam's skill, or Henry Daimler to review problems the X-215A had experienced before the crash, and to give his opinion, hopefully supported by Alan Millstein's lab work, that chafing against the protective harness had caused the failures. He would try to get the incriminating internal ConSpace document into evidence through his expert, but knew he would fail, as he had been unable to authenticate it. No names anywhere on it. Not even a date. Torville hadn't a clue how the tax division had got it. Seth's one smoking gun had never been loaded.

Next, he would call Harold Bostwick as an adverse witness and work him over with a series of questions Professor Daimler had prepared. Then he'd take one last fling at getting Bostwick to repeat what he had said at Symington about the late-night takeoff.

"Fat chance," interceded Allyn.

"Right now, he's all I've got," said Seth with a shrug.

"What about the subpoenas in your stockholders' suit, Allyn?" asked Lev. "Catch anything?"

Allyn explained how she had finally tracked down Dr. Ivor Tellman—the genius behind the TDA canopy system—in a cemetery outside Cambridge. "According to Olmstead, Tellman's final mean-spirited act before 'committing suicide' was to destroy all the company records. Olmstead's answers to my interrogatory described it as 'the final, inexplicable act of a mad genius in the grip of alcoholic paranoia.' Dramatic, huh?"

Lev grunted and rolled his eyes. "Poetic."

"And convenient," added Seth. "Olmstead's lawyer convinced the court on the basis of affidavits and his answers to interrogatories that his client's scientific competence did not extend to hammering a nail. Said we were just harassing him, and Judge Singer bought it. Denied me his deposition."

"Do you think the feds have gotten to the judge, too?" asked Lev.

"I doubt it. Singer's a state-court judge and a reputable one. He just doesn't like witch-hunts or drawn-out fishing expeditions, which is what he thinks we're up to. He'll come around."

"Not," said Allyn, "if *you* don't come around with some evidence."

"I plan to spring the so-called 42-W flight plan on Crispie. He's already mad at me, but I might be able to get him to say that the crash site was at the end of the standard test route to bolster our theory that the crash was after midnight."

"Lots of luck," said Allyn. "Didn't you say the Defense or State Department was going to have people monitoring the trial to file motions to suppress testimony whenever matters of 'national security' were involved—like they did in the Ollie North hearings?''

Seth shrugged. "The jury will see that something big is involved here. I'll turn it around to my advantage."

"What brand of blind faith you smokin' these days, Cowboy?" said Lev. "I think we should call Ripley, Allyn. Got a guy here who turns sows' ears into silk purses!"

Allyn smiled. "Seth was the kid in the joke whose parents gave him a roomful of horseshit for Christmas to try to dampen his overly optimistic view of life."

"I know that one," said Lev, chuckling. "Parents come in and see the kid all smiles and excitement, throwing shit all around the room, shouting he's sure there's got to be a pony in here somewhere."

"Cute," said Seth as their laughter died. "You guys would have killed 'em on *Hee Haw*. Anyway, that's my case."

"That's it?" said Lev.

"I'll end with Elena, of course, but yeah, that's it."

"That's it," repeated Lev, deciding not to mention Sam's drinking.

"Where is she, by the way?" asked Allyn. "I haven't seen her lately."

Seth jammed his hands deep into his pockets and shrugged his shoulders. "I haven't either. Her service says she's out of town."

Allyn knitted her brow. "Out of town? With trial starting in two weeks?"

Seth grabbed a cigarette and irritably snatched Allyn's lighter off her desk. "The message says she'll be back next week, *okay?* No problem."

Allyn and Lev exchanged a look. "Why would I think there's a problem?" she said calmly. "Okay, so you're missing a client—"

"In more ways than one I'll bet," interrupted Lev, drawing a scowl from Seth.

"Your client's missing," Allyn continued, peeling the cellophane off a cigar. "But that's no problem because the judge will dismiss the case on the statute before you get to her part in the trial anyway."

"Lev might get lucky in Arizona," said Seth. "Or maybe the other officer who left the club that night with Sam will come forward."

"And maybe," said Allyn, "all the frogs in Marin County will grow wings and fly to Dover."

"Or there'll be a pony under all that horseshit," added Lev.

Seth rose and turned toward his office. "This is not a useful conversation, folks."

"Then there's that other little problem," said Allyn as if she had not heard him, "that your technical causation case is so flimsy Treadwell will shred it like a piece of Kleenex. But maybe that's not really a problem either, given the further fact that Sam was flying drunk and the way you look right now, you probably won't live long enough to see the trial anyway."

Seth started to reply, but he was suddenly too tired to deal with her. Besides, deep down he knew she was right: his dog of a case was barking louder every day.

Across the continent in Vero Beach, Florida, Aubrey Olmstead and Senator Traeger met in a motel room as ugly as their moods.

"This had better be important, Aubrey," said Traeger, placing his cellular phone on a green plastic table with wrought-iron legs. He was momentarily distracted by the dissonance of noisy colors in the room. Wondered what manner of person would decorate a plaid couch with striped pillows. Sniffing with distaste, he added, "I'm missing a high-profile vote in the Senate today."

Olmstead cracked his knuckles and his red balloon of a face went to purple.

"Is staying out of federal prison still important to United States senators?" he said, the folds of his neck shaking with each word spoken.

Traeger's features puckered in disgust, but he took a deep breath and returned Olmstead's serve with a soft lob. "I'd say that most of us consider that to be a valid working principle. So can we get on with it please?"

The senator no longer tried to conceal his revulsion at the sight of Olmstead's obesity. Olmstead was just as obviously appalled at having to look at Traeger, whose bulging fishbowl eyes and harpoon nose combined to create the impression of a person mugging too close to a camera lens. In short, they were murderously sick of one another, and like many people locked together by business or marriage or some other cheerless enterprise, their Siamese dependency had risen to that level of resentment where nothing penetrated the cornea of one partner's eye but the physical flaws of the other.

Olmstead watched as Traeger rose from the discordant couch as if fearful of contracting something, then slowly patrolled the garish room, picking at one of the pillows, straightening a Keane print in a yellow frame, pinching the floral-patterned drapes. Olmstead knew that the persnickety senator was somehow blaming him for the room's blazing cacophony of bad taste.

"I've had enough of your arrogance, Stanford," he said at last, "and I'll thank you to sit down, turn off your goddamn cellular phone, and quit glancing at your Rolex President. I'm not impressed. I give them out for Christmas presents."

Traeger looked at his corpulent partner with new interest. "My, my. Have we been taking a course in assertiveness training, Aubrey? All right, I'm sitting. Now, what's the problem, old sport?"

"The problem, you pompous bastard, is your daughter, specifically your inability to control her actions. Are you aware that she and her maverick lawyer start trial in fourteen days?"

"Twelve," said Traeger, glancing at his Rolex President. "Trial starts, to be precise, on the eighteenth. A Wednesday."

"Oh, for God's sake, Traeger, stop being so goddamn arrogant!"

Father raised an eyebrow. "Is it arrogant to be precise? If you and your inept professor had been more precise, we wouldn't have this . . . situation. People like Tellman give fools and bunglers a bad name."

"Let's stop this, Stanford," said Olmstead, flapping his arms in the air with obvious effort. "Trading recriminations is getting us nowhere. The fact is, we *do* have a situation on our hands. I barely escaped having to testify, and if Ivor Tellman hadn't been . . . hadn't killed himself, he would have killed *us* at trial."

"But he *is* dead, so stop being so damn paranoid. Farnsworth and his aide-de-camp are thoroughly secure, and Cameron isn't onto anything but my daughter, who knows even less than he does."

Prurience overcoming anxiety, Olmstead's eyes brightened. "So your formidable daughter has been mastered at last. The shrew has been tamed!"

"Hardly. If curiosity doesn't get Cameron killed, my bitch daughter will finish him off. Poor bastard has figured out even less about Elena than he has about what happened the night of October fifteenth. I've done all I can, short of dropping a hydrogen bomb on San Francisco." Traeger handed Olmstead an Albuquerque newspaper. "Here, you may have missed this. This Simmons fellow blabbed to an investigator, but we got him before he could testify. What the hell more do you want from me?"

Olmstead studied the paper, then neatly folded it and put it down. "This is reassuring," he said coldly, "but I note that this occurred *before* I received a telephone call from your daughter's lawyer asking me to meet with him."

"So?"

"So Cameron is still not getting the message. Surely you know, Father, that to kill a snake, you don't cut off his tail; you go for the head."

"SHOWTIME, BIG GUY," SAID SETH. LEVITICUS WAS DOZING ON A COT in the file room. He yawned and stretched his huge arms.

"Is it time already?"

"Almost. Here's your copy of the police report, round-trip tickets to Phoenix, five hundred in cash, some subpoena forms, and a few thoughts I had in case you find the Lukens or Lockhorns or whoever the hell they are."

"I'll find them if they're still alive."

"I know you will, and try to keep 'em that way. The average life span of witnesses in this case is on a downward trend."

The phone rang and Seth heard Allyn's booming *"Friedlander here."* After a short pause, her next words caused his heart rate to jump. "Yes, Mrs. Barton, he's here. *Seth?* It's for you."

He took a calming deep breath, noticing how she always did this to him. "Hi, Elena. Back in town?"

"No, darling, I'm job-hunting—in *Albuquerque* if you can imagine it. I still have some connections back here and decided I'd better start finding a way to keep myself busy after all this is behind me."

Including me, he thought, but said nothing. She picked up on his silence.

"I'd be working in the San Francisco branch of a company headquartered here, so don't think finishing the case means I'm finished with my lawyer."

Seth's shoulders relaxed, but as he shuffled his emotions—frustration, loneliness, irritation, and lust—it was distrust that rested on top of the deck.

"You've been gone two weeks."

"I've been visiting friends for the holidays."

Friends. Another silence ensued that struck Seth as crucial to whatever future they might have together, but a silence he couldn't bring himself to break. The ball was still in her court.

"I do believe, Counselor," she said finally, "that you're missing me. Well, I'm missing you, too, darling, but I felt the need to get away for a while, see some of the girls again. They're all rooting for us."

"I guess I'm a little tired, Elena. It's good to hear your voice." He heard the uneasiness in his voice, a grudging tone that bordered on whining, like some disappointed kid. He tried to snap out of it. "I do miss you. When you coming back?"

She told him she'd be back soon and a few other reassuring things. He told her about the police report and Lev's trip, which reminded him they'd better be heading for the airport. She said good-bye, then told him she loved him—the first time she had said the words since that night.

He said hurry back and hung up. As he stared at the dead phone, it occurred to him he had never told Elena he loved her. Had he ever told Rosie? Anyone?

"Good news from our patron goddess?" asked Allyn, putting on her coat. "Has she deigned to make a cameo appearance at her trial?"

"You never liked Elena, Allyn. Why?"

"I don't trust her."

"Okay, you never trusted her either. Why?"

"We're not talking the mystery of Stonehenge or the Shroud of Turin here, Seth. All you got to do is look beneath the layers of Max Factor to see the truth about Elena Barton. She's using you, kid."

Seth dismissed her remark with a wave of his hand. "She said I shouldn't forget to pass on her profound admiration and respect for you."

"Yeah, well, fuck her, too," said Allyn, smiling.

"She'll be back in time. She's ready to testify. I've already put her through a mock cross-exam. She held up well and I worked her over real good."

"I'll bet you did," said Allyn, provoking a lusty *hoo-ahh* from Lev.

"Seriously, Seth," she continued. "You might as well hear this, too, Lev. This is the last check I write. Something about this case has pitted us against the government, a very powerful corporation, and the entire U.S. Air Force."

"You want out right now, Allyn?"

"I didn't say that. I'm just finished underwriting your suicidal tendencies."

"How about you, Lev?" said Seth.

"Lucky for you, I'm not as smart as I am pretty. I'm still in."

"Then," said Seth, putting a hand on each of their shoulders, "it shapes up to be a fair fight."

LATE THE NEXT AFTERNOON, SETH RECEIVED A CALL FROM ALAN Millstein.

"Seth? We've got wiring!" he shouted, followed by an incomprehensible waterfall of words, which, when played back and sorted out, told Seth that the X-215A mock-up had produced a worn patch in the protective harness through which Millstein had spotted—as shiny and welcome as a lost wedding ring—an exposed piece of copper wiring.

"Good work, Alan! Any sparking yet?"

No, there had been no sparking, and to Seth's dismay, Alan was not hopeful there would be any by the start of trial. Still, it was a breakthrough, and they agreed to meet at the North Beach Cafe for a late dinner to go over a revised draft of his testimony.

Three hours later, Seth hurriedly crossed Market Street, dodging electric streetcars and eccentric street people, then threaded his way up Montgomery through the day's cold leftovers: beggars, overtime white-collar workers racing for the last bus home, and a few disoriented tourists.

He angled up Columbus and into North Beach. Glancing at his watch as he passed Tosca, he wondered if he had time to slip in a quick white nun.

He looked through the window at the people inside, a different crowd from in the old days, when Jeanette Etheridge welcomed ballet dancers, actors, and opera singers to her salon of a saloon. Now her clientele was younger, noisier, and more brash, but still drawn in part by the prospect of seeing local celebrities or being mistaken for one. They looked warm and full of themselves, bathed in the boisterous, smoky light. Seth felt a twinge of envy, an urge to forget everything and become one of them, even if just for an evening. Besides, his stomach had begun to trouble him again, and a white nun might settle it down.

He found a seat at the far end of the bar next to a slightly drunk but reasonably well-dressed old man who looked vaguely familiar. He also looked dead, sitting there so still his body lacked dimension. He looked like a photograph of himself.

"Can't understand the popularity of those things," the old man said, turning his head no more than necessary to eye Seth's drink. He wore a sparse beard that did little to conceal a weak chin or soften a nose that loomed ahead of him like a hood ornament. The skin surrounding the failed beard was sallow and thin as paper.

"Might settle my stomach," said Seth.

"That's a good one, kid," he said with a derisive cackle. Seth glanced sideways and looked into eyes cold as metal and a smile like lingering death. "White nuns can do a lot of things, but settling a stomach surely ain't one of them. For that, you need what I'm drinking—moose-milk."

"Which is?"

"Scotch whiskey and whole milk."

"Haven't we met?"

"Don't think so. I'm fairly new to these parts," he said, lifting his glass slowly to his lips. He put the glass down on the bar just as slowly, then raised his cigarette to his mouth with the same deliberate movement. Watching him was like watching a candle burn. "I'm also open," he added, giving his empty glass a single shake, "to the hospitality of strangers ... should you be so inclined."

Against his instincts, even his will, Seth bought him a drink.

"Them nuns like you're drinkin' there was invented in the late sixties just around the corner in a place called Swiss Louie's, across from Finocchio's." At least the guy had shed his hostility, thought Seth. Maybe it was worth five bucks.

"Louie had some *tuaca* demi-sec he'd got from Italy—this was even before it showed up in U.S. liquor stores—and a spankin' new nickel-plated cappuccino machine. He poured some of that *tuaca* into a glass of steamed milk, and his friend's daughter— named Spawn as I recall—told Louie he should call it a white nun and he did."

Seth grunted to be polite, but his attention had been drawn to a beauty at the bar who was eyeing him over the shoulder of her date.

Undaunted, the old man added, "I was there that night."

"I thought you said you were new to these parts."

The old man swung around on his stool, revealing a stub of an arm. "I don't recollect sayin' I ain't never been here before. I lived here for as long as you've lived anywhere, boy." He took so long to get the drink to his lips, Seth wasn't sure he was finished talking.

He wasn't, adding he had been living in Athens, Georgia, hated Jimmy Carter, and felt sorry for his brother, Billy, who couldn't even take a quiet piss in public without making the front pages. Didn't seem fair.

Whoever put a quarter in this guy should be shot, thought Seth, then realized it had been himself. He wondered if the girl was as nice as she was pretty.

"Gettin' back to them nuns, young man, the problem is they go down too fast, too easy. Next day you got to improve to die."

"Well, sir," said Seth, watching the girl leave with her date, "I guess I can't blame the nuns for a bad habit."

To his surprise, the old man let out a roar of approval and said, "That's a good one, son, but I stand on my recommendation of moose-milk."

"I've seen you before," said Seth, taking a close look for the first time. Then it hit him. This was the old man who had accosted him outside Treadwell's office and sent Miss Tarkenton into a frenzy. "I know you."

"Well, I don't know you."

"It's funny. The last time I saw you, I felt the same way, like I'd seen you before somewhere."

"Where was that?"

"Going into the office of a guy I used to work for named Anthony Treadwell."

"Never heard of him," said the old man, looking past him with a vacant stare and tossing off his drink with an uncharacteristically quick motion, "and I ain't never seen you before neither." With that, he slid off his stool and lurched toward the door, his shoulders tilted downward at a sharp angle, favoring the withered arm, yet thrown back so rigidly it looked as if he might have forgotten to take the hanger out of his coat. The man was a true walking antique. An original.

"Comes in a lot," said the bartender in answer to Seth's question. "Gets drunk and brags about his son being the biggest hotshot lawyer in the country. Pays his bills and doesn't bother anyone."

Of course! *He had been talking to Anthony Treadwell's father.*

Seth spun out of his seat and hit the door, but the old man had already been swallowed up in the tidal wave of people jamming the area that had once proudly called itself the Barbary Coast. Thirty-two years before, just up the street at the Condor, a then tiny-breasted girl named Carol Doda had descended out of the Condor's musty ceiling on a hydraulically powered piano, and topless dancing was born in San Francisco. Later, that same piano would ascend one night after hours, crushing its copulating victims against the ceiling like something out of *The Twilight Zone.* Coitus interruptus. Those were the days.

Two tough-looking street bums stood near the doorway, and Seth started to ask them if they had seen which way the man went, but they quickly averted their eyes, jammed their hands in their pockets, and shuffled off toward the curb. The sight of them set off an alarm in Seth; deep inside, somewhere in the vicinity of the white nun.

What was bothering him?

Of course. Real street bums don't look away, they look straight at you and demand "spare change," "a little help," "bus fare," or whatever con is working best that night. So why would these tough-looking characters dress up like street people? Halloween was over.

But not his paranoia, he concluded, and resumed his walk up Columbus. When he reached Broadway, he started to heed the Don't Walk sign, then broke into a run at the last minute and narrowly missed getting flattened by a pickup whose driver informed him—and everyone within shouting distance—that he was a flaming asshole. As Seth turned back to flip him the mandatory bird, he spotted the same two men, artfully dodging through heavy traffic against the light.

These were not street bums.

He glanced both ways, but as he was neither speeding nor shooting a stop sign, there was no sign of a cop anywhere. What he did see was that his pursuers had now shed all pretext and that both of them—one a lanky black man who moved with frightening speed and grace; the other a stocky fellow with an innocent face and red hair spilling from a black baseball cap worn backward—were closing on him rapidly.

He hurried up Broadway, threading his way through the wall of tourists, cripples, self-conscious-looking men in three-piece suits, assorted derelicts of all colors, races, and persuasions, and big-titted dancers catching a smoke in doorways next to smarmy sex-spielers under signs that announced "Topless-Bottomless" and "Man-Woman Sex Act." He wondered if any of these places had back doors, not relishing the thought of ending up trapped and bleeding in a filthy men's room stall next to some masturbating wino. He was hit with the crazy thought of Rosie Wheeler reading about a San Francisco lawyer found dead in a strip joint on Broadway.

He kept walking.

Halfway up the block he glanced around and saw that only the baseball cap was behind him now. *Where did the tall one go?* A horn honked up ahead, and Seth turned back in time to see the black man caroming off the hood of a Yellow Cab and gracefully rebounding onto the sidewalk in front of Finocchio's, where the usual long line of tourists awaited their turn to enter the national mecca of female impersonators. The tall man had apparently crossed Broadway and back and now stood calmly staring at Seth from less than fifty feet away.

Seth considered his options, now limited to taking his chances in one of the strip joints or racing out into the Broadway traffic to attract a cop. Both were ruled out by a sharp pain in his back. The redhead had quickly closed the distance and was shoving a pistol barrel deep into his ribs.

"Into the car there, Cameron," said the voice behind him, adding in a soft tone completely lacking in malice, "or your guts will fly down Broadway like smoke from a train."

They know my name, thought Seth, noticing the black Ford for the first time, double-parked just in front of a tour bus discharging laughing, middle-aged midwesterners. The tall man jogged toward Seth along the line of tourists waiting to enter Finocchio's, then bounded off the curb and opened the rear door of the waiting car. *So it's my turn now.*

"*In!*" said the redhead with another jab for emphasis. His breath was so musty Seth could have picked him out of a lineup blindfolded.

"Who are you?" asked Seth, holding his ground, buying time.

"I'm the guy who shot you through the heart in front of Enrico's if you don't get your ass in the car. *Now!*"

Despite his anxiety, Seth marveled at the indifference of the people all around him. *Do people seem to ignore you?* he had heard a self-improvement hypester ask on a TV commercial. *Perhaps it's because you haven't made a sufficient effort to get their attention.*

"Well, *hello!*" he said, noisily greeting a couple at the end of the Finocchio's line, now just a few feet from him. "Don't you remember me?" he said, holding out his hand. "Seth Cameron. And say hello to my friend, Red."

The gray-haired couple stared at them with looks of confused goodwill. The gunman appeared equally confounded as he jammed the .38 between his belt and his back and accepted the proffered handshake of the grinning gray-haired man.

"You're gonna *love* this show," Seth said enthusiastically, "won't they, Red?"

"Red" agreed they'd love the show, then sternly reminded Seth they were late for their meeting. Seth took a good look at his assailant and saw the malevolent spark in cold eyes set in an otherwise innocent face. The kid couldn't be more than twenty-five, but those eyes had seen it all.

"The hell with the meeting, Red, let's see the show with these good people, have some laughs."

The redhead smiled and took Seth by the arm with a grip of unmistakable strength and meaning. "If you saw this show again, Seth," he said, his boyish face beaming with innocence, "you could die laughing—like a lot of these other 'good people.' "

Something in the kid's voice convinced Seth that he was not bluffing, so he took a step toward the car and waved a cheery goodnight to his "friends" in line, then jerked his extended arm back hard into the profusion of red hair and felt his elbow connect with flesh and bone. Red groaned as his head snapped back, and Seth bolted into Enrico's.

"Sorry, sir—" said the maître d' at the door, but Seth shoved his way past him, skirted the short bar to his right, then darted into the kitchen before Ward, Enrico's famous three-hundred-pound, six-foot-three-inch bartender, could grab him. Seth glanced back as Red hurdled headlong into Ward's chest, but then rebounded and skillfully spun out of the big man's grasp. Seth paused at one of the huge Wolf stoves, dumped a large pan of oil onto the floor, then flew out the rear kitchen door amid sounds of bodies crashing into walls, counters, and one another. He spun around onto Kearny and began taking the steep steps toward Vallejo Street, three at a time.

At the twentieth step, he heard a shot, followed by a rush of compressed air near his ear. *Jesus!* He'd never make Vallejo, can't outrun a bullet. Must be the tall guy. Five more steps, an open door to his left. Could get himself cornered, but options are limited. Chest heaving, bursting with adrenaline, *go for it*. Another shot whistled passed his head and thudded into the doorjamb as he raced through the opening. Slamming the door shut behind him, he was relieved to see a dead bolt and that the door appeared to be solidly constructed. As he struggled for air, the sound of applause, laughter, and live music greeted him. *Where the fuck am I?* He must be directly over Enrico's now, but where's the singing coming from? He slid forward along the wall, peered around the corner. *He was backstage at Finocchio's!*

The thugs would be breaking through the back door within

minutes; his only hope would be to get to the front door and back out onto Broadway. There was no one in the dressing room—everyone was onstage for the finale.

He checked the lock on the back door again, then moved forward as casually as he could into the main room toward the front door at the rear of the theater. But his heart sank as he saw the driver of the Ford standing at the counter near the front door, one hand inside his coat.

Seth looked around. Not a window in sight. He turned around and hurried back toward the stage. When he reached the dressing room, he could hear Red or the tall man or both forcing the back door and knew it wouldn't hold them for long. His only hope was a window inside the dressing room.

But there was no window. No skylight. No side door. Nothing but four walls; walls through which drifted the sounds of music, laughter . . . and the splintering of the back door.

Red left the tall man to stand guard at the shattered door, searched the dressing room and found it empty, then headed back to the front door to alert the driver that they had their prey trapped somewhere in the building. Returning to the stage area, he began to move through the crowd, front to back, a row at a time, his dull blue eyes scrutinizing every patron.

Halfway through, Red spotted his man, huddled in the rear north corner of the theater, three rows up in a modified balcony area, trying to make himself invisible. Red strode quickly to the front door.

"I've got him," he said to the driver, indicating Cameron's location with a jerk of his head. "There. Right in the corner. The guy who keeps stroking his forehead to cover his face."

"Then get him the fuck out of here," said the driver. "This place gives me the willies."

"Relax."

"They're fucking crazy! All of 'em."

"Haven't you seen actors before? It's just a show, man."

"I don't mean the actors," said the driver. "I mean the audience. Weird fuckers."

"Cameron's weird, too, so watch out."

"Watch out yourself. He's already aced you once tonight."

Red's chin jerked up defiantly. "Big talk for a guy jackin' off in the car while Ernie and I do the heavy work. What did you want, asshole, a public massacre?"

"Just get him out of here, okay?"

Red slipped back into the theater, then made his way along the rear wall until he was behind his man. He bent down until his face was within inches of the man's ear.

"Don't move. Don't turn around. And don't get cute again, or I'll blow away everyone in this fucking theater if I have to."

The man didn't move.

"Now get up and move to the front door, and nobody gets hurt."

The man moved.

At the door the man broke his silence, saying, "Please don't hurt me. My wallet's in my back pocket. Take it, it's all I have."

"*Shit!*" said Red.

"Who the fuck is this?" shouted the driver.

Red flashed a badge and apologized to the terrified man, explaining that they were searching for a dangerous murderer. "It was a case of mistaken identity. I'm very sorry, sir. Okay?"

The shaken man nodded and took off down the stairs to the sidewalk, having had enough excitement for one night.

"So where the hell's Cameron?" said the driver.

Red snapped his fingers. "Only one place left. The head!"

"Think you can handle it, Kelly?"

"Fuck you, Johnson. I'd like to vaporize the bastard and you, too."

There were two rest rooms. Neither was gender defined, in keeping with the current trend, so he tried the one on the right first. Nothing but empty stalls.

He then quietly entered the one on the left. *Bingo!* Red bent down and saw the identical loafers he had seen on Seth—burgundy Ferragamos, just like a pair he had at home—and the same teal-colored, cuffed trousers that had caught his eye at Tosca. Taking no chances this time, he took out his gun, kicked the stall door open with his foot, and leveled the weapon at . . . trousers draped from the toilet bowl and a pair of empty shoes.

Meanwhile, hearing the commotion, the driver raced up the front steps and into the room to provide backup.

"What the fuck?"

The driver started laughing. "Yeah, Kelly," he said, jamming his own .38 back into a shoulder holster, "you vaporized him, all right. Bet the poor fucker didn't even have time to wipe his ass before he disappeared up inside it."

Red was not amused. He checked the other stall, then glided over to the door of an adjacent supply closet. Even in his rage he was all professional—knees slightly bent for balance, gun arm extended and steady, hammer cocked—as he grasped the doorknob, then yanked it open with his left hand.

Nothing.

Turning, he seemed to notice the driver for the first time.

"What the fuck you doing in here?"

The driver winced. "I thought—"

But Red was already running for the front door, only to see a woman in an ill-fitting skirt, blond wig askew, wobbling off the curb into a cab on well-muscled legs. Her tray of empty glasses had been left in the doorway at the top of the entry stairs, and an angry floor manager was shouting after her.

"Seth," said Allyn the next morning. "This thing's gone far enough. Nothing's worth getting killed for."

Seth, still as granite, peered at her through blood-splotched eyes and said nothing.

"I've seen you play Russian roulette before, Seth, but never with five bullets in the chamber. Are you *trying* to get yourself killed?"

"They weren't out to kill me," he said softly.

"Oh, *really!* Then it's my duty to inform you that whatever's been keeping you tethered to reality has now been completely severed."

Seth slowly shook his head. "Guys this good could have taken me out on the sidewalk and gotten away clean. They were sent to scare me, not kill me. Killing witnesses is one thing, but killing either Elena or her lawyer would be too damn obvious. They just want to scare us enough to force a quick settlement."

"Well, I'm sorry, but I hope to God they succeeded."

Seth said nothing.

"You got heart, kid," she said with a wry grin that turned down at the corners of her mouth, "I gotta give it to you."

Allyn poured them both a cup of coffee, and they sat quietly for a few minutes. Seth could feel her eyes searching his face.

"Yeah, you got heart," she repeated, "but is winning so fucking crucial to your life plan? Ending up a Treadwell clone? Or like Austin Barrington did over at SP and M? Is 'making it' back on Montgomery Street so goddamn important?"

Seth flashed her a wry smile. "It's one of the two most important things in life," he said, blowing into his coffee. "And the other one's slipped my mind."

Allyn smashed her half-smoked cigar into an empty coffee cup. "That's real funny, Cowboy. You may not have noticed, but people are being murdered! Remember? This ain't a food fight, kid. Lev's been beaten up and may go to prison! *Remember?*"

"I ran into an old friend last night at Tosca. I think I have an idea that will buy us some added protection insurance."

"*You think! Jesus, Seth, listen to yourself!*"

Silence, a swollen silence badly in need of aspiration. Allyn fuming. Now a fire truck going so fast up Market it's rattling every window in the place.

"*Just who,*" said Allyn, unrelenting and on her feet again, "*appointed you legal gatekeeper of the fucking planet?*"

"I'm just trying to—"

"I know what you're trying to do, maybe better than you do."

"Seems I'm surrounded lately by clairvoyant women."

"And I by smart-ass men who need to prove themselves. Let me tell you something, kid. I was married once, and—"

Seth's eyebrows shot up. "What?"

"You're surprised, I guess. Because I talk like a sailor on shore leave and walk like a stevedore? Because I'm the toughest divorce lawyer west of the Pecos?"

Seth smiled, shook his head. "I know your heart, Allyn. And nothing you do or ever did could surprise me."

She sat down again, relit her cigar. Seth watched her, wondering if she was going to say more about her ex.

"It was twenty-five years ago," she continued after filling the small room with the cheroot's pungent aroma. "He was a little younger than me—a headstrong devil, God help him, a little bit like you, God help me. He was past draft age, but managed to volunteer his way into the army just in time to be one of the last soldiers killed in Nam. I couldn't talk him out of it. I shoulda been able to."

"Like you said, Allyn, sometimes—"

"He was MIA for a while, which was the hardest part."

"Sorry."

"Yeah, well, fuck it. My point is that macho may be harmful to your health. They should brand boy babies with a warning label instead of circumcising them." She coughed, then took another deep puff on her cigar.

"So I'm saying this for your own good, Cowboy. You may think you're bulletproof and I hope you're right, but you take the thirty Treadwell offered . . . or you're on your own from now on."

Seth's head jerked up. "Afraid I can't do that, Allyn."

"*Bullshit!*" she said, mutilating the tip of the cigar in an ashtray. "You *can* do it but you *won't* do it! Hell, you wouldn't take sixty either, or even a hundred and sixty! Do you know why?"

"I know why."

"Because you want that son of a bitch in a courtroom, right? You want to prove you're a better man than he is—am I right, Gunga Din?" She took a deep breath and shook her head in disgust, then straightened the bent tip of her cigar and relit it.

"You'd like to kill the son of a bitch in cold blood is what you'd really like," she went on after exhaling a stream of smoke in his direction. "Beating him in court is just the next-worse thing you can get away with doing to him."

"No," said Seth solemnly, "it's the *worst* thing. Treadwell would choose dying in an anthill over losing to me in a courtroom."

"And you're willing to risk dying just for a chance at him!"

Seth slowly rose from his chair, looked out the window. The fire trucks were starting to return to their stations. False alarm.

"That airplane is dangerous," he said. "It needs grounding."

"Save that line of bullshit for Barbara Heywood. I know *your* heart, too, Seth Cameron."

Seth turned, planted his hands flat on her desk, and leaned in close.

"We're almost there. I never thought of you as a quitter, Allyn."

"Don't try to manipulate me, kid. I'm too smart for you. You've used me, my office, and my bank account, but it's over now. I think it would be best if you moved on. I'm serious about this, Seth. Take the thirty tomorrow or clear your office."

Seth straightened as if he'd been hit from behind.

"And don't give me that hurt look. People like you do okay no matter where they land. Truth is, Seth, you're a user."

"I pay my way."

"Like the nickels out of my bank account you've been paying Lev to risk his life for you?"

"I'll pay you back every cent I've borrowed, and I'll take care of Lev soon as I'm able."

"Like you took care of Rosie Wheeler?"

"You never even knew Rosie."

"True, but I'll bet she's got a view on whether you'd rather spend your time loving her or killing Anthony Treadwell."

"Rosie never complained," he said, a little too quickly, "at least not until the end."

"That's a testament to her perseverance, not your nobility."

"Nobody made her come, and nobody made her stay."

"Maybe, but your anger and ambition made her leave. Not to mention that hormonal attack that seized you every time you got within shouting distance of Elena Barton."

"I suppose you think I'm using her, too?"

"Of course. She's your ticket to ride back to Montgomery Street. Plus you think she's going to fill some empty room in your life."

"Meaning?"

"You think she's so hot that if *she* believes in you, you might be able to believe in yourself. Like Annie Hall in reverse."

Seth gave her a look that said, "Thank you, Doctor."

"At least that's the way I see it," she added.

"You said once you thought *she* was using *me*."

"Let's just call it the Battle of the Titans," she said, pouring herself a cup of coffee. "Oh, what the hell do I know. You were both looking for somebody to spare you from ever having to change. Maybe it's a match made in heaven."

"Sure you're not leaving anything out? I got busted for shoplifting when I was twelve."

"Actually there is just one more thing. I think it might be better if you found your new quarters as soon as possible. I've got the safety of Ramon and myself to think about here."

Seth's face showed nothing as he processed this new reality, though his heart was pounding against the walls of his chest, making his breath forced and uneven. His legs were turning to rubber. But his trial lawyer's face showed nothing.

"Sure, if that's the way you want it."

Allyn looked away. "I think it's best."

"I'll be out of here tomorrow."

"Thank you. No hard feelings?"

Seth picked up his coat and headed for the door. Then he turned and said, "Don't worry about your money. You'll get it back, along with half the fee after I win."

"Sure, kid."

Seth started to walk out the door.

"Cowboy?"

He turned again. First time he had ever seen her tears.

"Please give it up. Don't you see? They know *who* you are and *where* you are. They've *got* you!"

"They've got me right where I want them, and come next Monday morning, I'll have a jury to help me finish them off."

"HELLO, COWBOY," ALLYN SAID, NOT EVEN LOOKING UP. "COME BACK to collect your gear?"

She was cool all right. Must have recognized the rhythm of his footsteps on the stairs. She never seemed to lose that cool either, except maybe a little toward the end of his Pacific Sigma Insurance bluff. Seth admired that attribute, mainly because he seemed to be losing his own poise lately with the regularity of the sun's rising. Well, he was about to test the constancy of her cool again. He wasn't here to pick up his gear.

"I came back because I need to make a phone call."

"Two days on your own and you can't afford a phone call."

"I want you to listen in on this one," said Seth, then walked straight to Ramon's desk and dialed a number from memory. "Pick up your extension, Allyn."

Allyn shrugged, then lifted the receiver just as a mellifluous voice announced, "Good morning, Mr. Treadwell's office."

"Put him on, please. This is Seth Cameron."

The pendulum on the wall clock over Ramon's desk ticked off a half dozen round-trips before Miss Tarkenton sputtered a response in a new voice, the sycophantic singsong suddenly gone. "I'll see if Mr. Treadwell is in." The new voice then crackled cold as dry ice and fragmented into shards of disdain as it added, "For *you*, Mr. Cameron."

A longer pause, then Treadwell's baritone voice came booming through the line, surprisingly cordial. "Well, Cameron. Calling to reopen settlement discussions?"

"No, Mr. Treadwell, I'm calling to reopen your past; your aristocratic background, your treasured lineage."

"Cameron, are you drunk? Isn't it a bit early—even for you?"

"I haven't been drunk since last night," said Seth, winking through the open door to the puzzled Allyn Friedlander. "Had a few drinks with a mean old bird with one wing and a bad stomach. About six feet two, one hundred and fifty pounds, eighty years old or maybe more, straight gray hair brushed back, stubble beard. A real Okie from Muskogee. You know anybody like that?"

Allyn's brow was sculpted in creases as she listened to the silence at the other end.

"I'm hanging up, Cameron," said Treadwell. "You're making no sense whatsoever."

"Yep, this old guy's a real embarrassment," continued Seth. "Got us thrown out of two bars. No class at all. Ugly temperament. Resembles you in other ways, too."

Allyn's eyes widened, and her lips mouthed, *"My God!"*

"Even so," continued Seth, "he looks better now than the first day I saw him. In your office, Mr. Treadwell."

Silence.

"Maybe it's the moose-milk. That's his drink, right?"

Seth nodded a yes-it's-true to Allyn. Nothing but Treadwell's forced breathing broke the deathly silence on the line.

"You bastard."

"Boy, talk about the literal pot calling the figurative kettle—"

"Stop all this mumbo jumbo, Cameron! Let's assume the purpose of this call is to inquire whether the thirty thousand is still on the table. I can get it there, perhaps a little more."

Silence.

"Maybe even fifty," Treadwell added, breaking the trial lawyer's first rule of negotiation: Never bid against yourself.

Excited now, Allyn nodded her head furiously and gave Seth a thumbs-up, but Seth swiveled Ramon's chair away from her and told the senior partner that he hadn't called to negotiate for money.

"There won't be a settlement, Mr. Treadwell. We're going to the mat together on this one, all the way to a verdict. The only thing I want from you is assurance that I'll be alive to hear what it is."

"I don't get—"

"Call off the apes, Treadwell! I want them off me, off Leviticus Heywood, and off everybody I know." Seth swiveled around to face Allyn. "I particularly want assurances concerning the safety of my client and my boss, Allyn Friedlander."

"Cameron, I honestly do not know what you're talking about."

"Let's assume that's true—solely for purposes of discussion. Three nights ago I was chased all over North Beach by federal goons who apparently consider witnesses in this case to be fair game. At least two innocent men have been murdered to keep them quiet. The guys who chased me are probably the same toads who beat up Leviticus Heywood and arranged the phony indictment that you're now going to arrange to have dropped as part of *our* new arrangement."

"You've seen too many Oliver Stone movies, Cameron. You've become a conspiracy whacko."

"Yeah? Then why don't you have a chat with your key witness, General Farnsworth—if he can take time away from his grassy knoll."

"Let's assume all this is true," said Treadwell, " 'solely for purposes of discussion.' What makes you think I could do anything about it?"

Seth considered the question for a few seconds, then said, "I've never liked you, Mr. Treadwell, but I've never underestimated you either. We start trial in four days, and you're their last hope for stopping me now. They—whoever the hell *they* are—are counting on you to do in the courtroom what they couldn't do on the streets."

"Well, I want it understood for the record that I deny the truth of any of your allegations—"

"Spare me the legal bullshit, okay? There's no court reporter here, and I know it's illegal to record a telephone call."

"I was about to say I'd look into it."

"Do that. Then do more. I want you to stop them. *Now!* You were smart enough to get rid of me, now get rid of them. If you can't, I've arranged to have the revised standard version of your family tree sent to Herb Caen at the *Chronicle*, with copies to your fellow board members at the President's Club and to the officers of both the Pacific Union and Bohemian clubs. I can even picture Caen's description in the *Chronicle*: 'The Lyin' Scion of Miller and McGrath.' "

Allyn was smiling now. They could hear Treadwell tapping his pen on his desk.

"I said I'd look into it," he said quietly.

"I appreciate it," said Seth, and hung up.

Allyn hung up, too, then ran through her doorway and nearly twisted Seth's head off in a mighty bear hug. "How did you . . . ? What in the hell . . . ?"

"Dumb luck. Plain dumb luck. Turns out Treadwell's the bastard son of a decent, but hardly aristocratic, family in White Plains, New York. His biological papa is this guy Robert Soames."

"You're losing me."

"More than sixty years ago, a young woman named Marian Treadwell had a brief affair with a drifter named Robert Soames. Got pregnant and had the kid, but old man Treadwell found out it wasn't his. He put baby Anthony up for adoption, then took after Soames with a twelve gauge and blew off his arm. Little Tony ended up in good hands—very wealthy hands—but when old man Treadwell died five years later—one of them spent in county jail—Esther brought a lawsuit and got the kid back. The adoptive parents were desperate, made a deal with Esther that allowed them visitation privileges, and little Tony ended up getting a prep school education. After that, he went on to Harvard and Yale Law on a testamentary trust fund, with a Navy hitch in between—ship's officer, of course.

"Everyone involved is dead now except for old bad-penny Robert, who knows the whole story. I got him good and drunk. Learned a lot."

"Like?"

"Like he's a loose cannon. Studied penology from the inside. Convenience-store robbery. I suspect he's extorting our friend Treadwell from time to time."

"Like you're about to do?"

"If it'll keep us all alive? Damn right."

"He's figured out how much of Treadwell's psyche is invested in the patrician bullshit he's sold everybody?"

"Exactamundo."

"Do you think Treadwell knows the truth about what's going on in this case?"

"I honestly don't know and I don't care, as long as he can *stop* what's going on—and I think he can. Nobody's got more clout with his client than a trial lawyer on the eve of trial unless it's a brain surgeon on the eve of surgery. They'll have to do what he wants."

"Speaking of the eve of trial, is your client back in town?"

"Tucker? Afraid not."

"Very funny. You know who I mean."

"She's returning tomorrow. Has Lev called in here?"

"Not a peep," said Allyn. "You think he's safe?"

"I told him to keep it local, stay away from anyone remotely federal or military. He knows I start trial on Monday. He'll either call or show up by then. He should be okay."

"How about Seth Cameron? Is he okay?"

"I reckon he's okay, except for being unemployed at the moment."

"Well," said Allyn, frowning, "I had committed your suite to the president of Kaiser Steel, but I guess it's still yours if you want it."

"Good. Where the hell's Ramon? I've got to file my jury instructions by four this afternoon. I also need an advance on next month's salary. Landlord's going ape-shit."

"It's great having you back, kid."

Part 6

THE FIRST DAY OF TRIAL IS LIKE NO OTHER DAY IN THE LIFE OF A TRIAL attorney. It's curtain up without a script and the first step onto the high wire without a net. The lawyer can't know all the things that will go wrong; he just knows they're all ahead of him. Waiting for him to drop his guard. Waiting for him to relax.

This angst is compounded for the leadoff plaintiff's lawyer, who also must function as his own stage manager (getting the exhibits and witnesses to the courtroom at the right time); director (ensuring that the witnesses know what to say when they get there); psychiatrist (coping with his client's inevitable nervousness while artfully concealing his own); mind reader (the better to pick a favorable jury); and spellbinder, for research shows that eight out of ten jurors never change their mind after the opening statement, no matter how long the trial goes on afterward.

The case of *Barton and Tucker vs. InterContinental Aerospace* involved an additional element, adding to the anxiety level: a daily *Examiner* newspaper series that had aroused national interest in the case and threatened to stir up yet another media feeding frenzy. The articles had traced the widow Barton's struggle to erase the stigma of "pilot error" from her deceased husband's name and had engendered outpourings of sympathy that were creating a circus atmosphere in the Honorable Jerome Singer's usually staid Department 16. As a result, everybody was on edge: the judge, whose control of the courtroom would be under constant siege by the sparring attorneys; the jurors, who would be the center of national attention—Court TV was covering the trial—during their terrifying fifteen minutes of fame on individual voir dire examination; the lawyers, of course, working under the hot glare of public scrutiny, and the critical eye of pseudo-experts hired by the media to second-guess their every move. Even the bailiff was jumpy today, unused to having to deal with a packed gallery—an unexpected influx of reporters, artists, and curiosity seekers in addition to the usual courtroom habitués.

The first thing an observer noticed upon gaining a treasured seat inside the courtroom was the imbalance at counsel table. Miller and McGrath's support team, consisting of client representatives, jury consultants, and two younger lawyers, took up the entire row of seats inside the rail just behind the counsel table where Anthony Treadwell sat sorting through documents, flanked by Herbert Leffingwell—CEO of InterContinental Aerospace—and Clayton Bingham, known to Seth as an ex–U.S. Supreme Court clerk and the smartest young partner at M&M.

Herbert Leffingwell was a handsome man of small stature, equally at ease with a gavel at a board meeting or a pitching wedge on the Olympic Club's Lake Course. During Leffingwell's deposition, Seth had tried without success to erode the man's calm aura of control and knew he would be a formidable witness on behalf of his company. Bingham sat behind a computer terminal connected by modem to the Miller and McGrath office mainframe, providing him direct access to Lexis and Westlaw, pleading files, and deposition summaries—everything but a hand job.

At the other end of the counsel table—closest to the jury—Seth Cameron sat alone, the way he liked it. An austere widow Barton sat behind him. That was it. No file cabinets to house massive documentary evidence; no computers to spit out arcane case citations on demand; no paralegals to retrieve a devastating exhibit for use on a surprise witness; no investigator to unobtrusively lean close to counsel, then casually stride from the courtroom, don dark glasses, and locate the perfect rebuttal witness.

Seth sat, seemingly calm, with nothing in front of him but a yellow pad, the first page of which contained a half dozen questions to ask prospective jurors. He had no money for a jury consultant and couldn't bring himself to ask Dr. Mitsui for another freebie. He would have to rely solely on his instincts, experience, and the luck of the draw.

On the second page of his pad was a list of five subject areas he would cover with Harold Bostwick, whom he had subpoenaed as a hostile second witness. He needed no notes for Jack Christopher, his first witness, and as usual, he had memorized his opening statement.

This would get him through the first day. If Bostwick wouldn't come clean on the true time of Sam's takeoff, or if Lev failed to come up with something in Arizona, one day's preparation would be enough. The case would be dismissed on the statute.

Sitting rigidly behind him, Elena looked appropriately plain and stricken, not easy work for a drop-dead gorgeous woman who was experiencing difficulty lately calling up a clear image of her husband's face and whose womb even now carried traces of her lawyer's semen from the night before.

This most recent fiery departure from their attorney-client "arrangement" had been fueled as Seth was selecting her wardrobe for the trial. He was good at this—surprising for a guy from Bakersfield whose idea of women's high fashion was a tank top. He didn't know Donna Karan from Ann Taylor, but he knew how juries expected a devastated widow to look, and he had spent the previous afternoon inspecting everything in Elena's wardrobe closet. Then he had inspected Elena herself from the hallway as she was changing out of a navy business suit. Like a Peeping Tom, he watched her reflection in the mirror over her dresser, wondering if women always changed bras whenever they changed outfits. Then those incredible eyes—even more compelling than the reflected incredible breasts—caught him catching her act—yes, an act, for even before he had time to be embarrassed, her catlike smile told him it had all been a show for him, the ultimate voyeur tease. He entered the room and then he entered her, right there against the wall near the closet while she ripped his shirt open and bit his chest and told him how much she loved him.

When this thing is over, Attila, she had said later, *we've got to try to make this last longer than it takes to cook a three-minute egg.* He knew that what she meant by this "thing" being "over" was after they had won the case and he was back on Montgomery Street. Otherwise, he knew there was no future with a woman like Elena Barton.

Tensions relieved, the fashion show had resumed. Seth had tried to make her understand the importance of physical appearance; how jurors respond emotionally to the parties before they start functioning on a cognitive level. He knew that women jurors would not relate well to Elena unless he toned her down into loose-fitting and inexpensive clothes—no Hermès bag, forget the Calvin Klein dress—accenting instead mid-calf skirts, medium heels, and long-sleeved blouses up to the neck. Presto! The wholesome and sympathetic victim.

She had saved her most vigorous protest for Seth's ban on makeup, and Seth ultimately accepted a compromise—allowing a light lipstick—to stave off a mutiny. He stood his ground, however, on the need to slash her long, soft-curled hair, transforming her from what he facetiously described as the "Barbie" look, into what she bitterly described as the "Ken" look. Seth then turned to her eyes.

"I thought you liked my eyes," she said, pouting.

"Of course I like them. That's the problem. They're too distracting. They could engender envy in women jurors."

"I'll wear sunglasses."

Seth laughed until he realized she was serious, that she understood almost nothing about how his game was played. "That would be great," he said, trying to keep it light. "And I'll wear a gold medallion on my bare chest. They'll love us."

When she reluctantly produced a pair of clear driving glasses, Seth asked if she had any Pam in her kitchen. Then he carefully sprayed each lens with a thin gloss and blew it dry. When she put the glasses back on, she was surprised to find that she could still see out of them, though Seth assured her that the stunning glow of her eyes had been dulled to a lackluster finish, evocative of a tragic widow's sorrow. Finally, he told her to cut her sleep back during the trial. He wanted her tired and sad-eyed.

"Well?" she had said earlier that morning when he picked her up at her Nob Hill condo. Unmasked and never more vulnerable, she could hardly meet Seth's eyes. "How do I look?"

"Your uncle Anthony will hardly recognize you," said Seth, pleased that Treadwell would know from the moment he laid eyes on the new Elena Barton that he was in for a dogfight.

"You didn't answer me."

The truth is she looked like her less attractive and considerable older sister—if she had had one—but Seth told her she looked perfect.

"That bad, huh?" she said, reading his meaning.

* * *

Seated in court now, Elena looked dispirited, her vanity in ruins. Seth, also miserable from the pain nagging in his stomach, managed a reassuring smile, then looked past her to size up the panel of prospective jurors.

What caught his attention was the tall man with one white eyebrow seated in the rear of the courtroom. Although he wore civilian clothes, Gen. Clement Farnsworth could not conceal his military bearing. The memory of their confrontation at Nellis sent a shiver through Seth, though he was sure the temperature in the courtroom was over seventy degrees. Two rows forward, on the other side of the aisle, sat Sen. Stanford Traeger with some other gray-suits Seth didn't recognize. Was the senator there to protect Elena or to unnerve her?

He then stole another casual glance at the defense armada. Seth envied Treadwell's support team, but tried to convince himself that the obviously disparate horsepower would help him with the jury. Cheering for the underdog was the American Way. David versus Goliath.

But the gallant effort at rationalizing his situation didn't extinguish the fire that had returned to his stomach, nor did it fool his parched throat or his bloodless face. Nor could he bullshit his rubber legs as he passed behind Treadwell on his way to the watercooler, nor still the trembling hand that held the paper cup to his lips once he got there—curling the upper part of his body around his right hand to conceal it. Adrenaline had him dancing on invisible strings.

Seth looked back at the defense table, wondering if Treadwell could smell his fear and would somehow find a way to expose him in opening statement. *What was happening to him? When it came time for his own opening statement, would his voice betray him?* He quietly cleared his throat, then repeated it, louder this time, to reassure himself. Seth had not spoken to the senior partner since the telephone conversation on which Allyn had eavesdropped, nor had they exchanged so much as a glance today. Seth had nodded a greeting to Bingham earlier, but Treadwell was completely ignoring him. The games had begun. Well, fuck him and fuck Bingham, too, and the general and the senator and the jury consultants and all the horses they rode into town on. Fuck 'em all.

It calmed Seth to remind himself that Treadwell had kept his end of their tacit bargain so far—charges against Lev had been dropped and the threats had ended. Now they would finish it right here in a courtroom, *mano a mano.*

A hush fell over the room as the court reporter and clerk entered and took their seats. Everyone knew the judge could not be far behind, and the room seemed to swell with a morbid anticipation. As the bailiff rose to announce the entrance of the judge, the imminency of the contest charged the room with an even higher level of tension, as palpable as static electricity. It seemed as if the slightest noise or movement now might cause a spark that could set the whole room ablaze.

Seth felt a burning sensation on the left side of his face and turned to find himself looking into Treadwell's fierce, dark eyes; eyes glowing like coals, set deep in his elongated skull. He looked angry, and Seth would have given the world to be able to read his thoughts.

Treadwell was angry, all right, but not just at Seth Cameron. His fevered mind raged at everyone, including himself. Mostly himself. He had made fewer than a dozen mistakes in his professional life, and more than half of them had been made in the last three years, all having to do with that bumpkin from Bakersfield, sitting there looking like he was about to shit his pants.

He should have fired the maverick on the spot—excised the cancer before it could spread. Yet another error was in allowing Traeger and Herb Leffingwell to bully and flatter him into personally trying this two-bit case, which, by virtue of his mere presence, had gained undeserved credibility and now, notoriety as well. Why hadn't they understood this? Well, that mistake would be on their heads, not his.

Still, here he was, in the winter of a distinguished career, matched against a nobody in the most publicized case of his life—and it wasn't even a major antitrust or securities conflict—a stinking personal-injury case. Thank God for the statute of limitations, which, if Judge Singer was true to his word, would make short shrift of this mess he had been drawn into.

The power and anger in Treadwell's eyes forced Seth's head to rotate away, leaving him flushed with shame. He grabbed a pen and scribbled purposefully to cover his embarrassment, then made himself look back. Treadwell's thin lips curled into a malicious smile as he elbowed Bingham, who rose and approached Seth with the sad eyes of a basset hound.

"Hello, Seth," he said. "Here is the supplemental motion to dismiss that was invited by Judge Singer. We'll argue it as soon as you've put on your statute-of-limitation witnesses."

Seth nodded and took the document. Clayton Bingham started back to the defense table, then turned and whispered, "I wish to hell you had taken the thirty thousand, Seth. I'm sorry about this."

But Seth smiled radiantly at Bingham and gave him a hearty handshake and a "thank you" that seemed to confuse the cheerless partner as he headed back to his chair. Seth then flashed another smile toward Treadwell, waving the motion as if it were a winning lottery ticket. Obviously, Treadwell had picked this precise moment to serve the motion, hoping to fluster him. But Seth knew the eyes of every prospective juror were on the lawyers now—there was little else on the stage to look at for the moment—and that a juror's verdict was rarely arrived at on a single point, but on a composite picture made up of nuance and cumulative impressions. Winning trial lawyers knew it was never too early to start forming those impressions, so Seth's manner suggested to the panel's observing eyes that the defense had just made a major concession, the first of many to come! Hell yes!

"*All rise!*" shouted the bailiff at last as Judge Singer entered the courtroom from stage left and charged the bench as if shot from a cannon. He, too, was making an early statement: *Don't mistake my gray hair for a lack of vigor. I'm in charge here.*

"Call the case," said Judge Singer, and the clerk rose for his own fifteen seconds of fame.

"*Number 15397*—Elena Barton and the Estate of Benjamin A. Tucker versus InterContinental Aerospace! *Counsel, state your appearances!*"

After Seth had risen and announced his appearance in behalf of the plaintiffs, he stole a glance toward the rear of the courtroom. Whom did he expect to see there? Allyn was handling a major custody battle in Marin County Superior Court. Lev was somewhere in Arizona. His first witnesses—Crispie and Bostwick—were in the corridor waiting to be summoned into the courtroom by the bailiff. Elena—at least someone who looked like Elena—was right behind him. He felt a pang of loneliness—*aloneness*—but was shaken out of it by the judge's voice as he signaled the clerk to spin the cage and start picking out the names of the first twelve prospective jurors.

Like bingo, but with more than a canned ham at stake.

Seven of the first twelve randomly selected candidates were women. Good, thought Seth. Women tend to function from the right side of the brain—the emotional side—less likely to be in sympathy with the military than their male counterparts, and more likely to vote their hearts if they should take a liking to the reinvented widow Barton. Ditto the gay guy, Knowlton, and maybe the supercool black dude, Spinner. That's nine out of twelve—all he needed for a verdict.

Who am I kidding? Treadwell has six peremptory challenges and research data to ensure that he can use them wisely.

Seth would be on his own in the process of jury selection—*de-selection*, actually, for the trial lawyer's job was to use his precious peremptory challenges to eliminate those prospective jurors who appeared to have the sociopsychological traits least amenable to his clients' side of the case. The trick was in accurately identifying those traits, knowing there was no way he could combat Treadwell's invaluable community-attitude surveys, focus-group analysis, and courtroom assessment of the jury candidates by his high-paid consultants.

The lead psychologist for the defense's jury consulting group sat immediately behind Treadwell, and Seth was somewhat consoled to see a concerned look on her face as she studied each juror's persona—clothing, posture, and other body language. Seth watched her glance from time to time at a three-ring binder and knew she was correlating her observations with objective data from her field people: home address to ascertain general income level, voter registration, prior service on other juries and how each had voted, details of employment, and so on. Her job was to advise Treadwell on whether to accept or challenge a potential juror.

He looked at the names of the first twelve people called.

Joseph Velasquez. Midtwenties, bad haircut, and heels worn down at a sharp angle. A victim of the recession. Velasquez would try hard to get chosen for the five bucks a day plus a good lunch when deliberations started. Probably little sympathy for a big company with a net worth of a $100 billion. If a layoff victim, might also be angry behind that stoic countenance. Seth knew that angry jurors were most likely to render punitive verdicts.

Mary Nance. A real Lady Rolex on that withered wrist. She'll turn out to be the wife of a banker or retired CEO of a big company. Not good. The question is whether her advanced years might trigger a maternal sympathy for Elena that could neutralize her conservative background. So far, two sheep, no leaders.

Karen Fountain. Layers of grunge. Our token hippie. Treadwell will nail her right away. Loud, but still a sheep.

Ronald Knowlton. Looks intelligent, probably gay. Perfect. Could turn out to be a leader.

Edward Stanton. Big trouble and definitely foreperson material. Three-piece executive type. Wing tips. The works. Could be Herbert Leffingwell's twin. Probably sits around the club at lunch bitching about how all this litigation is crippling our American corporations' efforts to compete internationally. Hard eyes. Probably views death as a risk that test pilots get goddamn well-paid to take. Horny old bastard keeps staring at Elena, trying to catch her eye. I'll make sure he does.

Thomas Brown. Probably our mandatory retired postal worker. Looks like a softie. He'll feel sorry for Elena but will follow the herd.

Sophie Byers. Good-looking in a peroxide sort of way, early thirties, charmable. She won't be drawn to Elena, but will tolerate her in her current drab incarnation. She'll like me more than Treadwell.

Maurine Stengler. Possible trouble. Eats nails for breakfast. Hard to read which way this will cut: could be a Rush Limbaugh conservative, but her obvious mean streak might cause her to punish ConSpace with big punies if she did go plaintiff. Possible plus: she's old enough to have a daughter Elena's age.

Ruth Jackson. Looks like a graduate student at S.F. State. Smart. Black. Angry? Perfect.

Barbara Bateman. Executive suit, expensive shoes, no-nonsense walk. Won't like Elena, might even see through the disguise— but might also see her as a victim of the male-dominated military complex. A leader, could vie with Stanton for foreperson honors.

Susan Wanger. Boozer. Hard times. Surprised she's registered to vote. Treadwell will have to dump her. Another sheep.

Calvin Spinner. Black man, blue-collar. Got the cool walk. Wedding band. Solid citizen. Looks smart and may be resentful that he's underutilized, i.e., potentially punitive juror. Good.

All in all, a pretty typical San Francisco jury. No wonder Treadwell's jury consultant looks worried.

Seth would give a year off his life for a five-minute peek at the three-ring binder she was studying. No chance. ConSpace had probably shelled out over $300,000 for the total project, including focus groups, mock trials, community surveys, video witness analysis, issue focusing, an investigation of all prospective jurors, and maybe a shadow jury hiding somewhere back there in the crowd. *Why couldn't they have just given the money to us instead and we would have gone away. Fucking corporations.*

Seth knew that the jury consultants gave ConSpace a tremendous edge, first in knowing what kind of approach would work best in this particular community, then refocusing their approach to the issues and presenting arguments in a way most harmonious with the local folkways and mores, then eliminating any prospective jurors whose background and emotional baggage might generate "cognitive dissonance" with the recast arguments.

So much to know. Seth fought off a panic attack. His instincts, though good, were nothing against the team of sociologists and psychologists plotting at the other end of the table.

"Mr. Cameron, you may commence your examination of the prospective jurors."

"Thank you, Your Honor. Just one moment, please."

Seth checked his notes, realized he could talk to these people forever and never know their true hearts and minds. For that, he'd have to start with hard information he didn't have. He'd need to know how they voted, what magazines they subscribed to, what their bumper stickers proclaimed; need to know the kind of information sitting at the other end of the table in that black, three-ring binder.

He turned to Elena, not to ask her opinion, but to create the appearance that she was involved, to remind the onlookers that this was her case, not his. They might not like him by the end of the trial, but they damn sure had better like her, and care about the fact that when the trial was over and they had returned to their lives, she would have to live with their decision for the rest of hers.

"I'm about to do something weird," Seth told her. "I just wanted to let you know so you won't appear shocked."

"What are you going to do?"

"Something weird. Something to try to show these people our case is so good, anyone in their right mind would see it." He turned back around, took a deep breath, and rose to his feet. He looked each juror dead in the eyes—one by one—and when he had finished, turned back to the judge.

"Your Honor. My client and I have no questions for these good people, and we accept them just as they sit. As far as we're concerned, you can swear them and we can get on with the trial."

Treadwell and Bingham exchanged a look of incredulity. Seth saw a rare shadow of confusion cloud the senior partner's expression and knew he was trying to think of a way to object to a maneuver he had neither seen nor heard of in over thirty years of trial practice.

"Mr. Treadwell," said Judge Singer in a manner that told Seth he had never seen the ploy either and didn't much like it, "please feel free to question the prospective jurors and to exercise your legitimate right to any peremptory challenges you may wish to make."

"Yes," sputtered Treadwell gratefully, "if you will just give us a moment or two."

Seth stole a look at the jurors in the box. Most were quietly observing the confusion at the defense end, but several others gave him a look that suggested relief and gratitude.

Finally Treadwell rose, his poise and gracious facade restored. "Your Honor," he said, looking at the jury, "the defense is likewise quite satisfied with every person in the box."

As the jury was sworn, Seth whispered to Elena, "Look at the steam coming off old Leffingwell! I didn't think anything could shake him up like that."

"What's the reason for it?"

"About three hundred thousand of them, swirling right down the toilet. Plus he knows we've now got ourselves a reasonably level playing field."

"What happens next?"

"Now," said Seth, smiling his first genuine smile of the day, "we play the game."

Opening statements contained no surprises from either side. Seth conveyed the impression that he was dealing in hard facts: previous X-215A failures, Sam Barton's safety record and unquestioned skill as a pilot, the TDA canopy system and its cramped juxtapositioning of components too close to a wiring harness that contained the electrical nerve system of the entire aircraft.

But what he was really doing was working the jurors' emotions, speaking in a hushed voice about the terror of Sam's last few seconds of life as he realized the certainty of his imminent, fiery death; how he must have thought about his beloved wife and the children he would never know. Then Seth spoke about the early-morning knock on Elena Barton's door by the squadron CO, confirming her worst fears before a word had left his tightly pursed lips; about the widow's subsequent isolation, loneliness, and fear; about her determined but frustrated efforts to clear her husband's name of the stigma of "pilot error" and the cold intransigence with which the Air Force had stonewalled her modest plea; on and on until even juror number five—executive Edward Stanton—was involuntarily signaling Seth that he was moved by Elena's situation, and angry at whoever was responsible for it.

Then it was Treadwell's turn, and within minutes, he neutralized Seth's subtle emotional pitch by revealing it to be just that.

"Mr. Cameron will urge you to engage in rank speculation," he said, then explained the plaintiffs must prove their case to a preponderance of the evidence, "*real* evidence, as you will be instructed by Judge Singer, ladies and gentlemen—*real* evidence, not emotion, nor passion, nor even sympathy." He characterized Seth as a master of psychology, then proved himself one as well by challenging them to resist the pull of soap-opera emotion and to base their verdict on the evidence, evidence that would fail to establish a single flaw in the X-215A.

Treadwell closed with a clever patriotic appeal, even got away with citing places like North Korea, Africa, and Bosnia as a call to vigilance, a summons to encourage those who "labor day and night to design the means of ensuring our security and the security of our children's children."

It was corny, but Seth noticed that Stanton, Ms. Stengler, Mrs. Nance, and even Ronald Kimbrough seemed to eat it up. Well, trial work was a swinging pendulum, and after the morning recess, he'd call Crispie as his first witness and hopefully get it swaying back in his direction.

Judge Singer declared the morning recess, and when the jury had left the courtroom, Seth took a heavy hit from the Maalox bottle he kept in his briefcase.

"Stomachache?" said Elena.

"Just a little indigestion, thanks."

"You were wonderful, darling. My knight, my hero. Do you still love me, now that I'm a frump?"

"You're a gorgeous frump."

Elena took his hand in hers. "I love you, Seth. Let's get this behind us. I'm already tired of our 'arrangement.' "

"Soon, Elena," said Seth, and was surprised to spot Simon Stephens in the back of the courtroom, impossible to miss in his tailored Brooks Brothers three-piece suit and restrained Talbot tie. Seth took a step toward him, but Stephens gave him a thumbs-up and lost himself in the crowd surging for the exit.

"Who's that?"

"A friend, sort of. A guy my age pulling down a half million a year with Caldwell and Shaw. Probably has a hearing next door at the law and motion department."

"Here comes your secretary."

"Hey, Ramon. What brings you here?"

"The Queen Mother of Jurisprudence said I should get this to you pronto."

Ramon handed Seth a message from Lev that read simply: *Hold 'em off, Cowboy. The cavalry's coming.*

"Tell us, if you will, Major Christopher, about Sam Barton's capability as a pilot."

After the recess, Seth had quickly carried Crispie through the preliminaries: the stealth program's operational goals, the background of the X-215A and its competitive forerunner, the Northrup B-2 stealth bomber, and the rigid selection process that had led top guns from various bases around the country to Symington Air Force Base in New Mexico to test the Con-Space aircraft.

"Objection," said Treadwell. "Assumes facts not in evidence—that he *had* capability. The evidence seems quite to the contrary. The question also calls for hearsay and the witness's opinion."

"Of course it does, Your Honor. I'm asking Major Christopher to give his opinion as a qualified expert concerning Captain Barton's known reputation as a skilled test pilot. Sam Barton's capability is obvious from the assignment he was given—an assignment that ultimately cost him his life."

"Further objection," countered Treadwell. "If it's so 'known' and 'obvious,' then 'expert' testimony is not permitted under the rules of evidence. Moreover, there is no foundation for this witness's expertise. And finally, Your Honor, Mr. Cameron is now arguing to the jury."

"As, obviously, is Mr. Treadwell, Your Honor. I'll happily stop if he will."

"You both will," said Judge Singer. "Objections overruled, and the jury is admonished to disregard the comments of counsel."

And so it went with almost every question Seth asked. Treadwell had obviously decided to play hardball, a puzzling strategy in Seth's mind, given the fact that juries distrust constant objectors—wonder what they are trying to hide—plus Judge Singer had quickly made his feelings known about technical objections. Midway through the direct examination, not one had been sustained, though Crispie did seem unnerved by them and testified without the conviction Seth had hoped for.

"Was he a careful pilot?"

"Objection. Vague and leading."

"Overruled."

"Yes, he was."

"Was he known to be cool under pressure?"

"Yes."

"Technically skilled?"

"Of course he is. Was. We all were. Are."

"You had simulated air battles as top guns, did you not? Dog-fights, electronically scored?"

"Yes, sir."

"Who had the highest kill rate and best scores in the unit?"

"Objection. Compound question."

"Overruled."

"Captain Barton was the unit leader at the time he was . . . at the time of his death."

"Did Captain Barton teach part-time in the Air Force aviation cadet program?"

"Objection. The captain died trying to fly an airplane, not in a classroom."

"Overruled."

"Yes. Most of us taught one or two ground-school subjects."

"Would you tell the jury what subjects Sam Barton taught?"

"He taught flight safety and emergency procedures."

"Was that because he was known to be the best pilot at dealing with emergencies?"

"Objection! Leading."

"Sustained."

"I'll reframe the question," said Seth. "Why was Sam elected to teach those subjects?"

"Objection. Assumes facts not in evidence—that there was a selection process and that decedent was in fact 'selected.' Also compound—there was apparently more than one subject."

Judge Singer looked at the ceiling and blew air out of puffed cheeks. He was either bored or angry, Seth couldn't tell which, but he could tell it was time to pull in his horns.

"Counsel's objection is technical," he said to the judge, "but well taken. With the court's permission, I'll reframe the question."

"Thank you, Counsel," said Judge Singer, settling back in his chair.

"Major, would you please tell the ladies and gentlemen of the jury what procedure, if any, was used in determining which pilot would teach which course?"

By the time Seth finished with the subject, there could be no doubt that Capt. Sam Barton was one of the most courageous, cool, and competent test pilots to strap himself into a jet since Chuck Yeager broke the sound barrier. Time to roll the dice.

"By the way, Major, what time did Sam Barton take off that night?"

Treadwell leapt to his feet, spewing a compendium of every objection know to the common law system of jurisprudence. The ones that hit home were hearsay and lack of foundation regarding the witness's knowledge concerning the subject matter.

"I haven't a clue," said Crispie, even before the judge had a chance to sustain the objection.

"Your Honor," said Seth, "if I could have a bit of leeway here—"

But Judge Singer had heard Christopher's answer and told Seth to move on.

When Seth tried to move on to questions about the X-215A, however, two Defense Department lawyers behind the rail rose to their feet, triggering a request by Treadwell for a conference in chambers. Judge Singer nodded his assent. When Seth, Treadwell, Bingham, two government lawyers, and Gen. Clement Farnsworth emerged twenty minutes later, Seth was allowed to read but one carefully drawn question to the witness.

"Major Christopher, do you have an opinion as to any defect in the X-215A which more probably than not contributed to the crash in which Captain Barton was killed?"

Crispie glanced at General Farnsworth and snapped out a "No, sir."

"Why are you looking at your commanding officer, Major? Are you afraid you'll be reprimanded if you tell the truth here?"

"Objection!"

Or killed? thought Seth.

"Sustained!" said Judge Singer, glaring at Seth. "The jury is instructed to disregard counsel's remark and counsel is admonished to refrain from making such comments."

"Thank you, Your Honor," said Seth in the time-honored response of an advocate who has just been disemboweled. "Tell me, Major, what you know about the supplier of the canopy system—"

"*Objection, Your Honor!*"

"Counsel!" said Judge Singer. "Were you not in chambers with the rest of us?"

"Let's leave the question of aircraft mechanics, Major," said

Seth. "The standard test-flight route is called Triangle 42-W, is that correct?"

General Farnsworth elbowed a Defense Department lawyer, Crispie looked up at the judge, and Treadwell rose to object—all at once. The judge and counsel again retired to chambers, but Judge Singer was showing irritation at being told how to run his court by Washington bureaucrats, and this time Seth was given permission to proceed.

"The question is relevant," Judge Singer told them before returning to open court, "perhaps even determinative on the statute-of-limitations issue. Moreover, I fail to see how national security can be endangered by discussion of a route of flight. If secrecy is so damned important," he added, glaring at the Defense Department lawyers, "they can change it tomorrow. Proceed, Counsel!"

Back in open court, Seth had the question read back to the witness.

"That's correct," said Crispie.

"This route goes from New Mexico to a point in the state of Washington, then south to Castle Field in California, then generally east back to Symington. Correct?"

"Correct."

"And would that route have taken the captain over the approximate point of the crash in Arizona?"

"Yes."

"And that would normally be on the final leg of the triangular route?"

"Yes."

"So if Sam Barton took off—hypothetically—around eleven-thirty P.M. and flew the standard Triangle 42-W pattern at the speed normally flown in the X-215A, would he not have crashed in Arizona after midnight, on the sixteenth?"

Treadwell objected, but to no avail, and when the arguments were over, Christopher answered that it would indeed have been after midnight.

"Into the morning of the sixteenth?"

"Yes."

Seth thanked him and turned him over for cross-examination.

Treadwell took his time, scribbling some final notes off Bingham's computer monitor. He then took Christopher through a cross-examination that, to Seth's surprise and dismay, appeared to have been rehearsed. Crispie affably cited competitions that Sam had *not* won, several he himself had won, a ground-loop accident Sam had suffered as a cadet, and the fact that Sam could have taken off as late as 10:30 P.M.—"the official reported takeoff time"—and still easily have made it to the crash site well before midnight.

Mice, not troubling nonetheless.

But now Treadwell changed moods, turned serious, took a wide-legged stance between Seth and the witness.

"With whom did you dine the night of October fifteenth, Major?"

"I had dinner commencing around eighteen-thirty hours with Captain Sam Barton, sir."

"That would be around six-thirty in the evening?"

"That's correct. I was OD on the fifteenth."

"That's officer of the day?"

"Yes. Sam joined me for dinner in the dining room of the club."

"Do you have a clear recollection of the event? What you ate? What he ate? How long you dined? What you drank? What he drank?"

How could the son of a bitch not have told us about this? thought Seth, seeing what was coming next.

Indeed, what came next was a clear and credible recitation of Sam Barton's last supper: Caesar salad, rack of lamb, and ... nearly a bottle of red wine! Before that, two vodkas, maybe three!

"He didn't tell me he was flying that night, of course, or I would have intervened before I returned to duty. Sam was my best friend."

I'd hate to be your enemy, thought Seth, then remembered he had become just that. Seth could hear the jurors' gasps of incredulity.

Treadwell finished with a flourish, forcing the ostensibly reluctant witness to support the public information officer's takeoff time of 10:30 P.M., then to cite regulations against drinking before flying and the impact of alcohol on supersonic reaction time. Treadwell even risked an aside to the jury that perhaps ConSpace should be the plaintiff here, not the defendant. To Seth's objection, Treadwell angrily retorted that Barton was obviously "FWI —flying while intoxicated—risking not only a three-hundred-million-dollar aircraft and his own life, but the reputation of a fine defense contractor!"

On redirect, Seth did his best to soften the blow without showing how badly he had been hurt: yes, it could have been just two vodkas; no, Sam didn't appear drunk or impaired; yes, it was an opaque bottle—a Gabbiano Chianti—so he couldn't be certain the bottle was more than half-gone; and so on. But all the pretext of confidence Seth managed could not obscure the fact that he had been wounded badly, perhaps mortally.

He was afraid to look at the jury; he felt their collective disdain. Also Treadwell's eyes, burning into him from behind, laughing at him.

Seth didn't like calling Harold Bostwick next, particularly considering what had happened with his first witness, but the judge had ordered him to put on his statute-of-limitations witnesses first. As Treadwell had argued, why burden the taxpayers and the court's calendar with a drawn-out trial if the plaintiffs' case isn't going anywhere?

Seth's spirits rose somewhat, however, as Bostwick entered the courtroom. The tech officer responded to the bailiff's summons as if he were heading for the gas chamber. Gone was the arrogant strut, the imperious manner; he approached the witness stand as if he were dragging a heavy-duty tractor tire. *This is a man packing a load of anxiety*, thought Seth, noting how the thick fingers of the tech rep's right hand trembled as the clerk administered the oath. Bostwick's obvious discomfiture lead Seth to a snap judgment: he'd skip the preliminaries and go for the jugular before Bostwick could get comfortable.

"Do you recall our visit at Symington early last summer?"

"Yes, sir."

"Do you remember telling me on that occasion, in the presence of Mr. Leviticus Heywood—a licensed, independent investigator—that Captain Barton's flight probably took off after eleven in the evening, so that the crash probably took place early the next morning?"

"Objection!" shouted Treadwell. "Lack of foundation that this witness knows anything about the time of takeoff one way or the other, thus the question is either calling for his opinion, or for hearsay. Also compound and complex."

"I hear you, Mr. Treadwell," said Judge Singer, "but Mr. Bostwick is an officer of the defendant company and has been called as a hostile witness. I'm going to allow some latitude here."

"Thank you, Your Honor," said Seth. "Do you remember the question, Mr. Bostwick?"

"Yes, but I don't know anything about the time of takeoff one way or the other."

Seth moved a step closer, concealing his disappointment. "I think there must be an echo in here. Those were Mr. Treadwell's words. I want yours. Did you or did you not say words to that effect to me."

Bostwick shot a glance at Treadwell. Seth jumped on it.

"You don't need to look at your lawyer. You just need to tell the truth, Mr. Bostwick."

The senior tech rep took a deep breath, then loudly exhaled and said, "Well, you're trying to confuse me. I never told you any such thing."

Seth saw he was beaten on the statute and shifted gears in hope of salvaging something out of this wreck of a day.

"As senior technical adviser on the X-215A project, Mr. Bostwick, what do *you* think caused the crash."

"I think the captain just lost it. Nothing wrong with the bird."

Seth picked up the Justice Department's incriminating Con-Space document Allyn had found—and which Judge Singer had rejected for want of authentication—and leaned in close enough to ensure that Bostwick could see it.

"Isn't it a fact that you investigated the canopy system, thinking it might be creating friction on the insulation harness that protects the X-215A's electrical wiring?"

To Seth's surprise, there was no objection from Treadwell.

"There has never been the slightest hint of a problem with the canopy system," said Bostwick without hesitation, suddenly articulate. "In fact, my routine investigation has established the absence of any friction to the wiring harness that could have caused sparking."

Seth started to head for his seat, then stopped in his tracks, the answer sinking in. "Who said anything about *sparking*, Mr. Bostwick?"

"Well . . . I just assumed, I guess . . . you know, that you meant that it could be . . ."

Bostwick's voice dropped off, smothered in a blanket of confusion.

"The cause of the crash? *Is that what you thought, sir? Is that what you* think?"

"Oh, hell no! It was pilot error caused the crash, like I said. My birds are perfect or they don't fly!"

"*Your* birds, Mr. Bostwick?"

"You know what I mean," said the witness sullenly.

Seth let it go. He could have made Bostwick look even more arrogant and defensive than he was, but he needed to bag more than a nest of mice; he needed to bag an elephant.

He went off into neutral territory for twenty minutes—eliciting information about the importance of electronics in "fly-by-wire" aircraft systems—during which he glanced at the gallery and was somewhat cheered by the sight of Leviticus Heywood taking a seat in back.

After another fifteen minutes of Bostwick's self-serving assurances about the airworthiness of the X-215A, Seth decided it was time to test a long-shot possibility that might get him his elephant.

"Isn't it a fact, Mr. Bostwick, that the X-215A's canopy system is basically a combination of off-the-shelf components?"

Bostwick paused for a moment. "That's true, Mr. Cameron, but there has never been the slightest hint of a problem with the canopy system. In fact," Bostwick continued with the precision of a recording, "my routine investigation has established the absence of any friction to the wiring harness that could have caused sparking."

Seth allowed himself to glance toward the jury. At least half of them were giving him a puzzled look. He cocked his head to one side. "There's that 'sparking' thing again, Mr. Bostwick, and I don't remember saying anything about the wiring harness. I asked you about the canopy system."

Bostwick reddened, looked over at Treadwell, then back at Seth. Panic had seized him again. "I thought . . . well, hell, I know what you were driving at! We've made no major alterations that bear on the airworthiness of the X-215A!"

Slowly now, Seth moved toward him. Then, in a soft voice, almost a whisper, he said, "Tell us about the *minor* alterations you've made, Mr. Bostwick." As he spoke, Seth again held the memo tantalizingly close to Bostwick's bulging eyes.

Treadwell started to rise, but the judge gave his head a quick shake that told the senior partner to save his breath. His witness had inadvertently opened an otherwise closed door.

"Well, we do a lotta things, strictly out of precaution, you understand."

"You got rid of the TDA canopy system, didn't you." It was a statement, not a question. It was also pure bluff.

"Well, most of it."

"And did you change the size of the protective harness around the electrical wiring as well?"

"We may have beefed it up a little."

"You made it thicker?"

"Yeah, but just by an eighth of an inch."

"To protect against friction?"

"Yes."

"To provide protection against electrical failure?"

"As a precaution, not that we—"

"Protection against electrical failure is particularly important in a fly-by-wire aircraft, because the pilot changes the control surfaces electronically, rather than by cables connected between, say, the stick and the rudder. Right?"

"Yes."

"And you made these 'minor changes' *after* the Barton crash, the third X-215A to crash?"

"No, I think we did it after the fourth one."

"Lieutenant Lee Andrews?"

Bostwick nodded. "As a precaution."

"And since that time, there have been no more crashes?"

Bostwick jerked his head down and to the side.

"Is that a yes, Mr. Bostwick?"

"*Yes!*" shouted the witness. "But that doesn't mean a damn thing!"

"We'll let the jury decide that, sir."

Seth had achieved the trial lawyer's goal of gaining control of the witness and, temporarily at least, silencing his adversary. *Let's go for the home run.*

"You'll agree, won't you, sir, that if you had a short circuit in the wiring adjacent to the canopy activation components, the pilot could lose control of the aircraft?"

"That's confidential information, and I won't answer it."

Seth bore in, seeing that Bostwick was close to blowing.

"There's no objection, Mr. Bostwick. *Answer the question!*"

The tech rep cast a pleading look at Treadwell, but saw no rescue there, only anger. Bostwick then looked up at Judge Singer, but found no solace there either.

"Mr. Bostwick," said the judge, "you'll have to answer the question."

"Answer the question, Mr. Bostwick!" said Seth, moving as close to the witness as he could get.

Bostwick recoiled, closed his eyes, and in a barely audible voice—and to Treadwell's manifest horror—began to repeat his canned litany. "There has never been the slightest hint of a problem with the canopy system. In fact, my routine investigation has . . . established . . ."

Seth turned toward the jury. Most had caught on. Maurine Stengler was shaking her head in disgust. Mrs. Nance was frowning. Mr. Velasquez looked angry.

"*The absence,*" said Seth, joining Bostwick in a unison recitation of the last few words of his carefully memorized response, "*of any friction to the wiring harness . . .*"

Bostwick realized what Seth was doing, but the final few words came out anyway, from both the witness and the examiner: "*. . . that could have caused sparking.*"

Seth turned toward the jury. "One last question, sir, then I'll let you go. How much money would it have added to the three-hundred-million-dollar cost per copy of the X-215A to have included that extra one-eighth inch of harness protection for pilots like Sam Barton and Lee Andrews *before* the crash?"

After a long silence, Bostwick mumbled an inaudible response.

"We can't hear you, Mr. Bostwick."

"I said it would have cost around sixty bucks more."

Mrs. Nance gasped out loud. Two other jurors shook their heads in disbelief.

"Did you say . . . *sixty*, Mr. Bostwick?"

"Sixty dollars is what I said. Am I finished?"

"That's one way to put it, sir," said Seth, scanning the jurors' faces, then glancing up at the clock. "Your Honor, I have nothing further. I see the hour is late. Might we argue that motion we discussed tomorrow morning?"

"Yes, Counsel, I think we've had enough for one day. The jury is excused until nine-thirty tomorrow morning. You are admonished not to discuss this case among yourselves or with anyone else. Thank you, ladies and gentlemen, and good day."

Seth shoved his notes into his briefcase, eager to talk to Lev, but saw Senator Traeger and General Farnsworth crab-stepping along the bench seats toward his end of counsel table. Mutt and Jeff.

"Hello, Elena," said the senator. "Hello, Cameron. I'd like you both to meet General Clement Farnsworth."

"I've had the pleasure," said Seth. "What can we do for you, gentlemen? We're a little busy here."

"I'll just take a moment," said Traeger. "May we sit for a moment?"

"I'll see you back at the office, Seth," said Elena, and started to leave.

"I'd like you to listen to this, too, Elena," said Traeger. "After all, it is your case. Such as it is.

"I've been watching from the back, as has the general here. Please consider us to be neutral, albeit interested, observers. I'll come right to the point. Your case is full of holes, Cameron, as you well know. You have a fatal statute-of-limitations problem and a drunken pilot. But you do have a certain leverage, let's face it. You have the ability to embarrass your government's defense effort and to play into the hands of the liberal press and other idiots who would like to see it dismantled."

"I may be one of those idiots, Senator, so you might want to alter your approach here."

"So be it. I'll appeal to you lawyer to lawyer then. The look on the jurors' faces says it all. You lied to them, Cameron, and not even a woman scorned is as vengeful as a jury misled. In your opening statement, you played upon their sympathy and extolled the virtues of Sam Barton. My God, he sounded like a saint. But suddenly they find that the deceased was drunk on duty, trying to fly a supersonic, three-hundred-million-dollar aircraft, and they are angry, Cameron. Very angry. You can see it on their faces."

"I believe you said that, sir."

"All right. I pitched in to help you after your trip to Washington, perhaps even to the point of compromising my public trust, but it's time to resolve this mess.

"I want to help all of us out of a difficult situation and broker a settlement between you and ConSpace that will be fair to everyone. Particularly to my daughter."

Elena blurted out something between a disdainful grunt and a laugh. "When," she said, "have you ever shown a glimmer of fairness? *Particularly* to your daughter!"

"You're hardly in a position to talk, young lady!" shot back the senator. "You claim you wanted to clear your husband's name, but all you've accomplished is to reveal him to have been a common drunk."

"You know nothing about Sam!"

"All right, I take it back. He was an *un*common drunk, whose exploits deserve condemnation, not exoneration. I'd suggest you let your lawyer do the talking, Elena, though he's also done nothing but botch things since the very beginning."

"You've got a nice touch, Senator," said Seth. "I'm surprised you haven't been tapped for diplomatic duty."

"I haven't time for diplomacy, young man. Here it is. I've persuaded ConSpace to treble their earlier indication. Elena, I can get you one hundred and fifty thousand dollars! Today only, take it or leave it."

Elena's eyes betrayed her amazed interest, even before her words did. "Did you say one hundred and fifty thousand dollars?"

Seth silenced her with a motion of his hand and urged her in a forceful tone not to take up poker as a profession. Elena, looking pale, fell back into her chair, and Seth turned back to the senator.

"Does that include clearing Captain Barton's name?" asked Seth. "Plus repair and lost rents to the Tucker estate?"

Traeger glanced at Farnsworth. "I think we can take care of Tucker."

Farnsworth jumped in. "But we can't alter the Air Force ruling, particularly now that the fact of his intoxication is on the record."

"Let's slow down a minute, gentlemen," said Seth. "You, too, Elena. This is only the first day of trial. We took a hit, but we hurt Bostwick. As you know, Senator, anything can happen in a courtroom with a jury around."

Traeger moved a step closer to Seth and glowered at him with cold, bulging eyes. "That's true, Cameron, and anything can happen *outside* a courtroom as well."

Seth turned to Elena. "Just when you think they've run out of new ways to threaten us . . ."

"Don't be absurd," said Traeger. "I was only referring to what you yourself told me at Dulles that day."

Seth shrugged and turned to Elena. "Let me translate for you," he told her. "What it all means is that if they're this scared, we must be on the right track. I can't give you any objective grounds for optimism, but unless they come around, I say we've started it, let's finish it."

Traeger turned to Elena. "Take it, Elena. For God's sake, you're my *daughter!* I've done this for *you!*"

The senator then shocked them all by grabbing the arms of Elena's chair in both hands and lowering himself into a crouch in front of her. "Take it, darling. It's your last chance! It's *our* last chance."

Elena appeared to be even more embarrassed than the others. She gently moved his left hand from the chair, got up, and walked over to the witness box. Leaning against it, she stared into the grain of the wood as if trying to read an answer from the mahogany swirls and shadings.

Slowly then, she turned, walked back, and faced her father.

"You hated Sam, Daddy. You've hated every boy I've ever dated. And now you'll hate me, because I won't jump through your hoop like everybody else does. I think you're afraid this trial will prove that Sam was not only a better man than you think he was, but a better man than *you*—the thing you feared most since the day I met him."

The sound of Traeger's hand across Elena's face snapped like a rifle shot, but she hardly blinked. Seth moved forward, but Elena held him off with a gesture, then addressed her father in a tone of icy intensity.

"Thank you, Daddy dearest, for the first display of emotion since I was expelled from high school in 1978."

She snatched up her purse, looked each of the three men in the eye, then stormed out of the courtroom.

"I think that was a no, gentlemen," said Seth as he turned to follow her.

LEV WAS IN THE CORRIDOR WAITING FOR HIM. "SAW YOUR CROSS OF Bostwick. Nice duet."

"Thanks," said Seth, "but you'd better have good news, podner, or it was also my swan song. The wheels are coming off my case."

"See that old couple on the bench down the hall?"

"Don't tell me. The Lockhorns?"

"Lukens, Seth—Thomas and Grace Lukens. The cop spelled it L-u-*c*-k-e-n-s on the accident report, which cost me an extra two days and you another two thousand dollars. Finally tracked 'em down in a trailer camp outside Tucson after a few wild-goose chases, including a hundred-mile drive north of Taos for a visit with a juiced-up couple named Luckens—spelled with a *c*—who offered to pierce my nose and trip me out on mushrooms."

"You always wanted to see Taos."

"Okay, make it fifteen hundred dollars. Anyway, I finally found the real Lukenses—the Tucson Lukenses without the *c*— and they saw it, Seth. A 'pillar of flame' that shot ten stories high."

"Sounds good, pard. They spell their name right; can they also tell time?"

"Hold on, Cowboy, that's the best part. They were heading for a church retreat campsite east of Phoenix, got lost, ended up on a back road. Saw the explosion and Tom took it as a sign, a perfect end to a disastrous day: late start, flat tire, wrong turn. 'Now they're bombing us, Grace,' he told her. 'The good Lord must not want us at this retreat.'

"Then old Grace—amazing Grace—pipes up and says something like, 'You might be right, Thomas, but it's not the end of a disastrous day, it's the beginning of a new one.' She's looking at her watch and adds, 'It's one twenty in the morning. Maybe this day will be a better one.' "

"Are you shitting me, Mandrake?"

"I matched their location to the coordinates of the crash site," said Lev, turning and flashing a reassuring smile at the Lukenses. "They were only four miles from the point of impact, and the fire they saw was exactly where the crash was relative to their location. Go talk to them. See for yourself."

A quick visit confirmed Lev's assessment and revealed the Lukenses to be completely credible.

"So is it safe to say," said Lev as they walked back to the office, "that you can now win this case in a hurry so I can get paid? Remember, fast pay makes fast friends."

"Good work, pard. Take them to the motel on Market Street. Have 'em here in the morning. Okay?" With a weary smile, Seth handed over his credit card. He would wait until later to reveal to Lev that while the investigator had been out winning a battle in the field, Seth may have lost the war.

Later that evening, Seth sat with Elena and Lev, filling Allyn in on the events of the day.

"Crispie was simply awful," said Elena. "I can't believe he would say those things—even if they were true."

"He's scared, like everybody else in this case," said Seth.

"And based on what Simmons told me," said Leviticus, "he *was* telling the truth. Your husband was seriously into the juice that night, Mrs. Barton."

"Was anything bothering him that day, Elena?" asked Seth.

"What would be bothering him?" she snapped.

Seth and Allyn exchanged a look.

"I was just asking," he said.

"Well, he seemed perfectly fine to me on the telephone."

Lev mentioned that he recognized Crispie from somewhere, and Seth reminded him that he had glimpsed the pilot in the maintenance hangar at Symington the day they posed as magazine reporters. But Lev gave his head a hard rub with the knuckles of his right hand, then stood and slapped his thighs in frustration.

"No, it was somewhere else," he said, then headed down the stairs for home and an attempted reconciliation with his wife.

Allyn was tired from her own long day, but tried to put a positive spin on what they had told her about the day's events. "You aren't dead, yet. The Lukenses will get you past the statute of limitations. Should be some consolation in that fact alone, Cowboy." She reached over and gave him a rough pat on the shoulder. "Plus, it may be the ultimate irony, but now you know you didn't screw up at M and M after all."

Seth stared out the open window, sniffed at the night air. "The Lukenses are wrong," he said quietly.

"Wrong?" said Allyn and Elena in unison.

"Wrong. Incorrect. Lying. I don't know. I'll put 'em on the stand anyway—I'm the lawyer here not the jury—but those folks didn't see the crash. They saw something else."

Allyn frowned, then shrugged in apparent agreement. "Simmons?" she said.

"Yep. I can't think of a reason why he'd lie about seeing Sam out the door at exactly eleven-thirty that night, and he must have been telling the truth or they wouldn't have had to kill him. So tell me, Elena, how does Sam get all the way to the flight line, change into flight gear, preflight an X-215A—which the book says takes three hours—fly the 42-W pattern over Washington, Oregon, and California, then crash in Arizona by one-twenty?"

Allyn nodded. "Any clue yet on the identity of the other officer who left the club with him?"

"Probably Gerald Murphy, which is another reason they had to kill him. But no matter who it was, the fact remains Sam had to crash much later than the Lukenses have it happening."

"*But that's not for you to say!*" said Elena, suddenly aroused out of her languor.

Allyn looked up, startled at the outburst, then squinted at Seth through one eye. "The girl has a point, Seth. Besides, he's dead on the sixteenth either way and you've beat the statute. Why confuse things?"

"Thank you," said Elena, brushing her hair back as she blew air out of pursed lips and sat down. "At least there is *one* real advocate around here." Allyn rolled her eyes to let Seth know she was still on his side. Seth lit a cigarette.

"Okay," continued Allyn, "so he was drinking. That ain't good. But Bostwick has paved a clear path for your expert testimony on the protective harness chafing, and with the statute defense gone, it'll eventually wind up in the hands of the jury, where we know that anything can happen. Okay so far?"

Seth nodded.

"All right. Now what is it that could have such an emotional impact on the jury that they'd find a way around the drinking problem?"

Elena raised her eyebrows.

Seth smiled. "Are you by chance referring to the heartsick widow Barton?"

Allyn nodded. "When you putting her on?"

Seth looked at Elena and said, "Tomorrow, right after the Lukenses."

Elena paled. "You said it would be next week."

"Allyn's right. We've got to start swinging them back our way. If we wait, it'll be too late. It's the way this business works. Don't worry, you're ready."

Elena looked unconvinced. "I'll do my best."

"Good," said Allyn. "I'll bet one of my finest cigars that a few grief-stricken tears from the bereaved widow will wash away what's left of the stain of Christopher's testimony."

"WHAT IN THE HELL ARE YOU DOING?" SAID ALLYN THE NEXT MORNING as she glanced into Seth's office. He was standing in front of his small window, alternately covering one eye, then the other.

"Oh! Hi, Allyn," said Seth, putting his hands behind his back like a kid caught stealing. "Nothing, really."

Allyn shook her head. "You're having that blurred vision again, aren't you." It wasn't a question.

"Nothing serious."

"And you're back on speed?"

Seth reddened and shrugged. "I found a few stragglers in my

desk, and damn lucky I did. I had to work with Elena until two-thirty, then finish my jury instructions and responses to Con-Space's latest series of motions. Caught a one-hour snooze on the cot."

Allyn shook her head and grunted.

"It's temporary."

"Sure, kid. I just fail to see what good it will do you to get back on Montgomery Street if you're brain-dead when you get there."

"I just have to get through this."

"Jesus, Cowboy, you're *in* trial, not *on* trial!"

"Can't say I've ever seen much difference," said Seth, and gave his lapels a shake. "How do I look?"

"The women on the jury will know it's the same suit you wore yesterday, but that might not hurt your David image. But wasn't it Goliath who was supposed to get stoned?"

The Lukenses were perfect, and Treadwell was too smart to take them on. He waived cross-examination, making only a casual reference for the jury's benefit to the complete irrelevance of the testimony. Seth decided to put his damage economist on ahead of Elena to allow them time during the lunch hour for a final run-through.

As Seth turned to watch his witness enter the courtroom, he noticed Si Stephens seated in back again. This was no coincidence. Was Stephens monitoring the trial? What interest did Caldwell and Shaw have in his case? One more thing to worry about.

The expert's testimony for loss of consortium and earnings was predictable, if somewhat dull, and went in without complication or damage on cross. After Christopher's damning evidence, Treadwell had obviously elected a strategy of showing disdain for Seth's damage testimony—"I'll not waste the time of these good ladies and gentlemen, Your Honor"—implying that the jury would never have reason to consider it. It was a boring, anticlimactic morning, for which Seth was exceedingly grateful, given the intermittent buzzing and blurring that had reentered his neurological system.

At the noon recess, Allyn—her own trial finished—approached Seth with a hearty smile. "Treadwell is screwing up," she announced.

"Oh?"

"He's not going to rebut your damage case. He obviously doesn't remember what happened to the defendant who tried that tactic in the Texaco-Pennzoil case."

"You don't either," said Seth, ushering Elena through the rail, "or you'd know that Joe Jamail didn't have to fashion his victory around a drunken test pilot."

Allyn backed off, knowing how the pressures of a trial can spread like cancer cells, assailing the spirit and breeding irritability.

"And you have a nice day, too, Seth," she said under her breath as she watched the jurors leave the courtroom.

"Are you all right?" asked Elena, when Seth had closed the door to the small conference room adjacent to the courtroom. "You were rather short with Allyn, don't you think?"

"She understands," said Seth, rubbing eyes that fatigue and uppers had turned into muddy pools. "Yeah, I'm okay," he added, but his words were belied by the ashen hue of his skin, drawn taut across his prominent cheekbones. "Let's get to work."

At twelve-thirty, Ramon brought in a carrot salad and yogurt for Elena, double espresso and a carton of milk for Seth.

"That's it?" she said, looking at Seth's "lunch."

"Lean and mean," he said, but couldn't conceal the tremor in his hands as he sipped his coffee.

Elena's testimony on direct examination exceeded Seth's wildest expectations. Her manner and appearance were those of a woman whose interest in life had died in the Arizona desert with her husband. She wept at appropriate intervals and within minutes had engendered sympathy in not only the jurors, but the judge as well. She credibly denied that Sam would ever take a drink before a flight and testified that Major Christopher must have his nights confused. The jury might think otherwise, but Seth knew that the important thing was that if jurors *wanted* something to be true, it *would* be true.

She reviewed Sam's awards and honors, his safety record, his publicly expressed concerns about the X-215A, then established her damage case by testifying to her loss of consortium, her undying love for her husband, and the saving influence of her grief counseling.

"How did your grief counselor influence you?" asked Seth.

Elena paused, got herself under control, then spoke in a barely audible voice. "I . . . wanted to die. I was considering . . . suicide."

Seth ended Elena's direct examination by asking her to describe the nightmarish predawn visit by the unit commander and the chaplain on December 16. She was unable to finish and accepted Judge Singer's offer of a recess before cross-examination.

While Elena gathered herself, Seth walked out into the corridor, where he spotted Si Stephens bending over a water fountain.

"Okay, Si," he said, "I've seen you in back since the start of this thing. What's Caldwell and Shaw's interest in this case?"

Stephens looked embarrassed. "It's an interesting case, Seth. National coverage and all. I'm just another trial groupie when it comes to something as hot as this thing."

"Bullshit, Si. You're monitoring the case for the firm."

Stephens spread his palms in an appeal for mercy. "You're putting me on the spot, Seth."

"It's a problem I have." Seth offered him a cigarette. "Let's have it."

Stephens hunched his shoulders and took a deep drag. Then another. "We're not monitoring the trial. We're monitoring you."

"Me?"

"I've been talking you up at the firm ever since you dumped me on the U.S. Minerals motion the day Charlie Branch was too drunk to show up. Then, after you fucked me over on the Pacific Sigma Insurance trial, I told them they should grab you before somebody else did. We've had two retirements on the trial side this year and a ton of new business. I've been authorized to offer you a junior partnership at Caldwell and Shaw if you can beat Treadwell in this case."

Seth tried to conceal his astonishment. Caldwell and Shaw! Partnership?

"Do they know about—"

"Sure they do. But I told them it was never clear who was supposed to have calendared the statute in the first place. More importantly, it now appears you didn't blow the date after all."

"Thanks, Si. I owe you one."

Stephens gave his head a quick shake. "Just keep it to yourself, okay? Hell, I wasn't even supposed to have been noticed, much less have you engage me in conversation."

"What conversation?"

Seth floated back into the courtroom, barely able to contain his elation.

"What are you smiling about?" asked Elena.

"Me? I guess at how well you did on direct."

Treadwell surprised Seth—and the rest of the courtroom—by wading into the witness with neither compassion nor civility, violating the cardinal principle that even the harshest cross-examination of a widow should be preceded by a show of solicitous gentility. Seth put a hand to his stomach. *The senior partner must have a smoking gun.*

"So you even considered suicide? Would you tell what your counselor said when you discussed suicide?"

Seth objected on the grounds of privilege, and Treadwell withdrew the question, though his manner left little doubt that he knew she was lying about the suicide.

"Did you ever discuss your compulsion with Major Christopher?"

Seth objected again to the word *compulsion*, and Treadwell again withdrew and rephrased the question. Then, fearing that he was appearing too overtly protective of his client, Seth decided he would have to let her sink or swim.

"And was Major Christopher your husband's best friend?"

"Yes, I would say so."

"Was he also a good friend of yours?"

Elena had appeared pale and vulnerable on direct examination. Now, she was flushed and betraying a growing anger. Seth felt helpless to block Treadwell's momentum. *Where's the son of a bitch going with this?*

"Yes, of course," she said. "I considered all of Sam's friends to be mine as well."

The senior partner took but a single step toward his goddaughter, but his presence now seemed to engulf her as if he had thrown a plastic bag over her suddenly ashen face. "That's quite commendable," said Treadwell, then turned to watch the jury as he fired his next question.

"But Major Christopher was the only one of Sam's friends you were having sexual intercourse with, wasn't he? Or was he?"

Seth shot to his feet and shouted—with inappropriate and uncontrolled emotion—"*I OBJECT TO THIS!*"

As if in some kind of communal shock, the courtroom froze into still-frame. Went dreadfully silent as Seth's agonized protest hung in the air like a wounded bird.

"Please state your grounds, Mr. Cameron," said Judge Singer at last. "I assume Mr. Treadwell is exploring the credibility of the damage issue here."

Seth searched Elena's face, now pale again, for some sign of denial, but she could not meet his eyes.

"Mr. Cameron? Your grounds, please?"

Seth's brain felt as if it were exploding inside his head. He placed his hands on the table for support, kept staring at Elena. When she finally met his gaze, he saw the truth there. The naked, oozing, filthy truth.

"It appears I have . . . no grounds for objecting, Your Honor. None whatsoever."

Seth collapsed in his chair in dazed and impotent silence and barely followed the exchange after that: heard her stammering, unpersuasive denials, offered in a thin, metallic voice; knew nobody believed her; heard Treadwell savoring the titillating details—How often, *Mrs.* Barton? How recently, *Mrs.* Barton? How about last month in New Mexico, *Mrs.* Barton? The Palomar Hotel?

Seth's bloodshot eyes flickered to the jurors, saw their voyeuristic fascination with Treadwell's relentless attack. He listened as his witness—his client, his lover, his future—denied the charges, time after time, until finally the judge stepped in like a referee protecting a helpless boxer and told Treadwell he had made his point. At last, it was over.

"Any redirect, Mr. Cameron?" said Judge Singer.

Seth knew he should provide a more relaxed opportunity for Elena to rebut the egregious charges made against her, but he could not bring himself to enter into the collusion.

"No redirect, Your Honor," he said in the most casual voice he could muster under the circumstances—the circumstances being the spontaneous, open-court heart surgery he had just endured, coupled with the shattering of his dreams of securing

revenge by defeating the great Treadwell and returning in tri-
umph to Montgomery Street with Caldwell and Shaw and trying
the important cases he felt capable of trying, thereby winning the
respect of his peers and harvesting the fruits of years of hard
work and sacrifice, thus showing his father that he was capable
of playing in the majors after all, damn it, then marrying the
woman he had loved, getting out of debt and off the bennies,
buying a decent car and a new suit and being able to sleep at
night and . . .

SETH SAT IN HIS OFFICE AN HOUR LATER, HALF-DRUNK AND ENTIRELY
alone. Ramon had finished for the day and Allyn had left early,
saying something about self-immolations giving her sinus problems. There was an I-told-you-so in there somewhere, subtly disguised as sympathy, but who could deny her that?

She had been right, of course, about almost everything: certainly about both Elena and the case being certified losers. She
had stopped short of including him in that category, probably
concluding he had suffered enough abuse for one day.

Elena had come by, not to apologize, would you believe, but
to berate *him* for not protecting her better on cross-examination!
Seth poured himself another shot of Cuervo and mused at his
infinite capacity to be fooled by women he thought he loved. She
had never given a rat's ass about him or about clearing her husband's name; it was her debts she had been trying to clear. In
her self-righteous rage she had admitted everything, her disinher-
itance, her pittance of a military insurance policy, her debts, and
her desire to cash in with a big verdict, and her nonexclusive
passion for Crispie. (A hygienic concern tried to nudge its way
into Seth's full dance-card of disasters—how many sexual partners had he taken on every time he slept with Elena?—but dis-

ease and eventual death ranked low on his list of calamities and were summarily dismissed.)

She had persisted in the virtuous heroine myth at first. "I came to you to clear my husband's good name," she had insisted, "and all you accomplished was the destruction of my own."

Bravo. That's when his record for never having hit a woman fell into serious jeopardy. The record was still intact—if you don't count grabbing Elena by the shoulders and slamming her up against the wall (a few inches off the ground, in the interest of accuracy) and telling her she had literally fucked herself out of a verdict and himself out of partnership in the best firm on the West Coast. Which is when she spit in his face, and he lowered her back to the floor (suddenly, in the interest of accuracy), and the ugly truth had poured out of her like green vomit in a horror movie. More truth than he had bargained for, actually; wide-ranging, seemingly unrelated revelations screamed at high volume about having been fucked (literally) by Papa Traeger between the ages of ten and fourteen, then admitting that Sam had found out about her recent promiscuity with an unnamed lover in a midafternoon anonymous phone call the day of his last flight. Little wonder Sam was into some serious drinking that night. She had last spoken with him at eight forty-five from his on-base quarters, and he had already been to the club.

Oh, sure, clearing her husband's name had been part of it, but out of guilt, not love. Crispie had told her a week later about the boozing, and naturally they both felt responsible after he crashed.

"Crispie cared about Sam and he loved me," she had told Seth, which made Seth wonder just how much Crispie had loved Elena and how far he might have been willing to go to have her for his own. Had the major actually encouraged his friend's drinking, knowing he would soon be behind the controls of a machine flying at a speed somewhere between sound and light? Christopher probably envied Sam as much as he loved Elena. Seth would be the last man in town to underestimate another man's capacity for loving Elena Barton.

And the craziest part of all?

She still expected him to see the case through to a verdict! The woman had balls, all right. After slashing up his heart with a razor blade, she stood there with hands on perfect hips, demanding that he continue to prosecute her guaranteed loser of a contingent-fee case, representing the whore wife of a cuckolded drunk who had violated every regulation in the book and smashed up a $300-million airplane in the process!

And he had agreed to do it.

JUST WHEN A TRIAL LAWYER ON A REVERSE ROLL HEADING BACKWARD down a slippery slope to nowhere knows it can't get worse . . . it does. Treadwell started the day by getting permission to call a witness out of order. Seth was sure it would be some paid whore to say he saw twenty or thirty pillars of flame at exactly five minutes before twelve midnight, but it—she—turned out to be an Arizona pathologist who had examined Sam Barton's body at a clinic near the site of the crash.

This was no paid whore. Katherine Margolin's credentials were so solid, in fact, that Seth waived his right to voir dire her to avoid giving her the chance to repeat them. Besides, how much could she hurt? Dead is dead.

But Dr. Margolin had come not just to testify that Sam was dead, but dead drunk. Legally drunk—an estimated .18 at the time of death, and clearly "under the influence."

Bad enough, but it was Dr. Margolin's second revelation that nearly jump-started Seth's heart through his rib cage.

"My opinion as a board-certified pathologist is that the victim had been dead for a minimum of four hours at the time of my examination."

"And that was at what time, Doctor?" asked the smarmy Treadwell.

"My records show that I examined the corpse at three forty-five A.M. on the morning of October sixteenth."

She gave Seth a little slack on cross—*Yes, his body was burned beyond recognition; Yes, that complicated my autopsy; Yes, that increases the margin for error*—but held firm to a four-hour minimum and death "in all medical probability, well before midnight." Thank God for the Lukenses, thought Seth, but Treadwell's statute defense was breathing again.

Seth called Henry Daimler as his next witness. While the professor was entering the courtroom and being sworn, Seth's mind wandered back in time to the night of the fifteenth. Trying to rationalize Simmons's statement and Dr. Margolin's persuasive testimony, he pictured Sam stumbling from the Officers' Club at eleven-thirty, bluffing his way into the X-215A—everyone knew him—somehow skipping preflight, and then, in his inebriated confusion, running Triangle 42-W in reverse and crashing before midnight. A possible, but unhelpful, scenario. Someone had to be lying. Simmons? Crispie? Margolin? The Lukenses?

All of the above?

Professor Daimler performed masterfully. Relying in part on Alan Millstein's partially successful experiment, he testified with conviction and authority that the X-215A's problems were caused by improper interfacing between the electrical system pathways and the off-the-shelf TDA canopy system, resulting in friction fatigue to the main electrical harness. Picking up on Seth's cross of Bostwick, he agreed with the ConSpace tech rep that the problem could have been avoided, and many lives saved, with an investment by ConSpace of an additional $60 to thicken the harness.

Mary Nance and juror number four, Ronald Knowlton, usually inscrutable, looked stunned as Daimler recited how the harness might easily and inexpensively have been toughened "had they but thought about it and cared enough to do it."

Edward Stanton remained unreadable, but Seth saw juror number nine, Ruth Jackson, exchange indignant looks with Barbara Bateman, sitting next to her. Number seven, the bleached-out and amiable Sophie Byers, actually gave Seth a wink and smile. Seth knew how unreliable these expressions could be, but the reactions in this instance were too strong and widespread to be ignored. Maybe he was still in the game after all.

Treadwell's cross-examination of the professor fell flat. *I've seen a lot of forensic experts get eaten alive on cross, Son. That's when you*

*separate the wheat from the chaff. The good ones are like politicians:
no matter what you ask them, they tell you what they want you to
know.* Seth had never forgotten Pop's admonition and had grilled
the professor—a gentle soul with no instinct for the jugular—to
use every question on cross as an excuse to regurgitate something
he had said on direct. It worked to perfection.

"You've never even been inside an X-215A, have you, Mr.
Daimler?"

"No."

"Or even close to one?"

"No, sir, your client refused to permit it."

"Because of security, correct?"

"I doubt it. The details of the X-215A are now an open secret.
I brought a copy of *Jane's* to court with me if you would like me
to read from it, sir."

"That's all right, Prof—"

"The only reason Mr. Bostwick gave me for refusing to discuss
the X-215A was that it might prejudice your defense."

"But wouldn't your testimony be more accurate if you, like
Mr. Bostwick, had seen and studied an actual X-215A?"

"No."

"*No?*"

"The latest version of the X-215A has been altered, according
to Mr. Bostwick, to correct the precise defects that killed Captain
Barton. Inspection of Captain Barton's aircraft was impossible, of
course, given the fact that both Sam Barton and his X-215A were
severely marred by flames."

And so on.

Treadwell realized he was beginning to track blood on the
carpet and quit before it got worse. Seth thanked Professor
Daimler, then caught a thumbs-up from Si Stephens as the C&S
observer headed outside for a cigarette. Seth was relieved. He
had not expected to see Si Stephens in court again after what
had happened the day before. He was also glad to see both Allyn
and Leviticus in the gallery, for he feared he was losing perspective and would value their reactions. Despite all the disasters that
had befallen him, it seemed obvious that the jury didn't like the
defense side of the case either. Maybe this thing could be sal-
vaged. So far today, he had needed only a half bottle of Maalox.

Flushed with his minor victory, Seth decided to try to normalize relations with his client. "Well, it's a new day a-dawning, Elena. One small step for the good guys, huh?"

She said nothing; indeed, she had refused to say a word to him since the night before.

"Look, Elena," he said, swiveling around to face her. "We're finished, you and I. You don't like me, and I don't care a whole lot for you either. But we're stuck with each other, chained together like a couple a cons trying to make a jailbreak. It'll go a lot smoother if we work together."

Elena's response was to rise to her feet and leave the courtroom, brushing off Lev's greeting as he advanced toward the rail.

"That girl ain't a happy camper, Seth," said Lev, watching her stride through the door.

"It's going to be a long, hard trail."

"Who's the guy in back underneath all them medals? He looks real familiar."

"That's the now-notorious Don Juan Christopher. I told you, you got a glimpse of him the day we conned our way into Symington."

"That's not it. I told you before, I know him from somewhere else." Lev stole another look at the major and gave his head an exasperated shake. "Screw it. Who's next?"

"There is no 'next.' What they've seen is what they get."

"You're resting your case?"

"That's customary when you've got no more witnesses."

Lev shook his head again. "You're fucked, man. It ain't gonna fly."

"I might get a break on one of Treadwell's witnesses. It's happened before. He might overtry his case, give me an opening."

Lev exhaled and lifted himself off the rail. "Look, man, I've got a little time on my hands. If you'll spot me another ticket, I'll make a last sweep around Albuquerque."

"For what? Pottery? Turquoise? You've worn out your welcome at Symington. That's for sure."

"I might join up. I'd look good back in uniform."

"I'm afraid it's a little late, Lev."

"For re-upping?"

"For everything."

"Okay, but what's to lose? I've got a hunch or two. Hang out in bars around the base. Employ some shamus secrets I'm not at liberty to share with rank outsiders."

"You're some piece of work, Mr. Heywood."

"You're going down if you got no rebuttal. That's for sure, too."

"I can't ask you to do that, Lev. I already owe you more than—"

"Hey, Cowboy, I still owe them federal motherfuckers something, too."

Seth scribbled out a note to Ramon. "Okay, pard, and thanks. The ticket will be ready right after lunch."

Lev headed out, but stopped midway to the exit and hurried back.

"Hold on to your Stetson, Cowboy. I just found the guy who closed the bar at eleven-thirty with Sam Barton. Now I know why he looked so familiar. He's the spittin' image of the description Simmons gave me that day at Symington. Check the guy under all them medals."

Five minutes later, Elena, Christopher, and Seth sat in a conference room. Bluffing Crispie into the truth had been easy. Deciding what to do with the new information was harder.

"*Why didn't you tell us?*" demanded Elena, her pale eyes verdigrised with anger and glowering at Christopher. "If it hadn't been for the Lukenses, we could have been thrown out of court!"

"I'm trying to tell—"

"You bastard! You were just going to sit there and watch it happen!"

"No way, Elena, just—"

"*Weren't you?*"

Crispie looked at Seth for help.

"Let's hear what he has to say, Elena. Okay?"

Christopher gathered his thoughts and addressed himself to Seth.

"I knew that if they found out I was the officer with Sam that night, I'd have to tell the whole truth."

"Which is?"

"Which is that Sam had three more drinks after dinner at the bar between ten-thirty and eleven. He was shit-faced, Seth. He had found out about . . . Elena and me—except he didn't know

I was the other man—and he was shit-faced drunk. I couldn't stop him from drinking *or* flying, though I slowed him down some."

"So he did leave around eleven-thirty?"

"That's affirmative. I figured going with the official takeoff time was better for Elena; you know, getting him high in the air instead of high at the club."

Christopher turned to Elena. "I almost came forward when it looked like you would lose on the statute, but when Seth came up with the Lukenses' story, I saw I could keep quiet."

Elena appeared mollified, even spoke to Seth for the first time that day. "So what do we do?"

"Nothing," said Seth. "If we put Crispie back on to help on the statute, it will hurt us a hell of a lot more on the drinking. Sam's got too much booze in him as it is. Plus we'd be giving Treadwell another bite at the cheating-wife apple. It's a bad trade-off."

Seth rubbed his face with both hands. "Do you think Treadwell is going to put you back on the stand anyway? To impeach Elena on the adultery issue?"

"I don't think so. I don't know how they found out about Elena and me. But I've drawn the line at going back on the stand. It would ruin me. I'm career."

"Then there's hope, Elena. It's your word against Treadwell's unsupported allegations."

"Seth," said Crispie, "it's none of my business, but nobody on that jury doubts that we were lovers."

"Thanks to the protection of my brilliant lawyer!" said Elena, her lips drawn tightly over her teeth.

"You're right, Major," said Seth, seemingly ignoring the remark. "They see her now as a tramp and a liar. Juries tend to be intuitive that way."

"Now hold on, Cameron," said Christopher, starting to rise.

Seth came up faster, leaned across the small table, and pinned Christopher back into his chair with just a look. "No, *you* hold on, pard, 'cause by the end of this, the jury will see you're two of a kind, neither one of you worth a minute of Sam Barton's time, let alone his life."

Elena leapt to her feet, fists clenched at the end of arms stiff against her sides. "Listen, you smart-ass bastard. You're a loser just like Uncle Tony said. But I'm stuck with you. Now here's what you do. You get that one hundred and fifty thousand dollars back on the table and then you grab it. I need that money."

But Seth was already leaving the room. He turned at the door and flashed a mirthless smile. "That offer's gone the way of your virtue, Elena, which is to say it's irretrievable. Besides, this isn't your case anymore. This is Sam's case—what's left of it anyway— and mine. And of course there's the Tucker estate. You're just extra baggage we're all stuck with."

ON THE THIRD DAY OF TRIAL, TREADWELL MADE HIS ONLY ERROR.

With victory within his grasp had he simply put on one solid expert witness and rested, he committed the unpardonable crime of overtrying his case. Witness followed witness, all articulate forensic technicians and scientists, but most of them parroting the same themes: the X-215A was the closest thing to the perfect flying machine ever developed; the electronics seemed to be operative on every crashed aircraft studied; the TDA canopy system was up to specifications and replaced solely because ConSpace sought a more cost-effective unit; and so on.

Seth, more pallid each day from lack of sleep and a new, persistent cough, laboriously cross-examined each one, first to foster the boredom he observed among the jurors, but most importantly, to stall for time; time for what, he wasn't sure.

"Let it go, Cowboy," said Allyn, succumbing to pessimism at the end of the sixth day. "If you were a boxer, I'd throw in the towel. You should be in a hospital, not a courtroom. You're a burnout, kid. Look at yourself!"

"I'm okay," he said, coughing from deep in his chest, "and thanks for the inspiring vote of confidence. I happen to think the jury is beginning to suspect a cover-up here."

"You mean the two jurors who still bother to wake up at lunchtime?"

"You're exaggerating. Besides, they're getting mad at Treadwell for dragging the thing out, not me."

"Why is Treadwell doing it?"

"It's his style. Take no chances. Wear a belt *and* suspenders. Most important of all, keep the meter running at three thousand dollars a day as long as possible. Lawyers like Treadwell will end no case before its time."

Seth started coughing again, and Ramon held crossed index fingers up as if warding off a vampire. "Could you please spray your viruses another way?" he pleaded.

"Seth," said Allyn, "you're also wearing out the carpet. Sit down."

Seth took a chair.

"You know I'm a fan, Cowboy. But I've seen some of your cross-examinations the last few days."

"And?"

"They are thorough, journeyman stuff, but not the Seth Cameron jugular thrusts we've come to know and fear. Give it a rest. Give yourself a rest. And while you're at the hospital, check into the psychiatric ward and have your head examined."

"You're instincts are off this time, Allyn," said Seth, up again and pacing around Ramon's desk. "The jury is getting suspicious. Why else would ConSpace be trotting out every fucking technician and corporate officer they've got? Not one of them has said he actually inspected the harness at the point we claim it ruptured."

"Someone will."

"Well, I'm ready. Besides, have you forgotten that people have been murdered over this thing?"

"You don't know that. Birds do fly into air scoops."

"They ravage the turbine fans," offered Ramon without looking up from his keyboard, "rip them like tissue. I read it in *USA Today*."

"And Simmons actually might have fallen," Allyn added. "Or jumped."

"And the guys that chased me in North Beach were fraternity hazers, right? Or bill collectors from hell? And Lev's beating was a case of mistaken identity. They thought he was one of the Menendez brothers."

"No," said Ramon, "Lev's taller than either one."

Seth entered the courtroom for the seventh day of trial and saw Treadwell already at counsel table, reviewing notes for his next witness, an outside avionics expert.

Elena drifted in, refusing as usual to acknowledge Seth.

The gallery, including some members of the press, had diminished in number, turned off by the parade of technical experts and Seth's protracted attention to each one. Traeger and Farnsworth remained faithful spectators, as did Treadwell's shadow jury and the two Defense Department lawyers, popping up from time to time "in the interests of national security." Seth was depressed to note that Si Stephens had stopped coming to court.

Another lonely morning passed as he stubbornly struggled against the odds, fighting a losing cause with no rational possibility of a fee, in behalf of a client who refused even to speak to him. During the afternoon recess, he suffered another bout of dizziness and blurred vision. He brushed it off as the normal consequences of averaging three hours' sleep since a week before the trial had begun. He popped a cough drop and two more caffeine pills—he had run out of heavier stimulants—and strolled over to ask the bailiff if it didn't seem unusually cold in the courtroom. The bailiff politely assured him it was seventy degrees, knowing Seth would soon be complaining about its being too hot.

"I think you got a fever, Seth," said the bailiff. "You should see a doc."

"So I've been told."

"*All rise! Department 16 is now in session, Judge Jerome Singer presiding!*"

True to Allyn's prediction, Treadwell's next expert—a forensic aeronautical engineer—said that he had been permitted to examine two of the four crashed X-215A's and had found "no clear evidence of harness deterioration proximately resulting from friction imposed by any component of the TDA canopy system." Seth had objected on the grounds of surprise, but Dr. Harrison testified in chambers that he had only been given access to the

X-215A the day before trial, and Treadwell persuaded the judge that ConSpace should not be penalized because of the military's vacillation and delay in granting their request.

"That's bullshit, Judge," Seth said. "Everybody knows that ConSpace's and the military's interests are identical in this case!"

He then pointed a finger at the Defense Department lawyers, adding, "What the fuck do you think these monkeys are doing here, Judge? Aiding in the pursuit of truth, justice, and beauty?"

"Counsel?" said Judge Singer, an edge in his voice.

"It's not only obvious collusion, Your Honor," said Seth across the judge's desk. *"It's trial by ambush!"*

"Calm yourself, Counsel," said Judge Singer. "You'll have free rein on cross."

"And just what the fuck am I to ask him, Judge? They won't let *my* expert within a hundred miles of an X-215A!"

"That's quite enough out of you, Mr. Cameron!"

As they left chambers, Treadwell put a consoling hand on Seth's shoulder. "Trial by ambush? Cute, Cameron. And quite correct, for once."

"Just another insignificant battle," said Seth through clenched teeth, "and get your hand off me, or you won't be around to see me win the war."

"Now there's where you are wrong, Cameron. This was the battle that *won* the war. Waterloo, Gettysburg, Normandy, and Hiroshima, all in one."

He turned out to be right. Harrison was soft-spoken, brilliant, and persuasive. Seth tried to shake him—*You only saw two of the four X-215A's? In a storage area? Isn't it a fact that the harnesses were fire-damaged beyond analysis one way or the other? You're really saying you were unable to distinguish between precrash and postcrash damage, aren't you? You haven't run any independent tests to corroborate your claimed observations, have you?*—but got nowhere, and at the end of the day, Seth's only consolation was that Judge Singer had arguably committed error by allowing Treadwell to bushwhack him with the previously undisclosed testimony, maybe even reversible error. Small consolation, for not even Seth would be fool enough to appeal, then retry, a turkey like this.

He put his notes away, hardly aware that Elena was still sitting behind him.

"You look tired," she said.

Startled, Seth jumped. "What?"

"You'd better get some sleep tonight. That's a bad cough, and your skin is the same color as your shirt." Seth always wore a white shirt when he was in trial.

"I'll try. Thanks for noticing."

"You mean, thanks for not being a bitch for five minutes?"

"Thanks for that, too."

"I'm sorry, Seth. About all of it. It's gotten pretty crazy, hasn't it?"

"Pretty crazy says it."

"I can't sort it out."

"Join the club."

"It's getting to me, Seth. I need you to tell me the truth."

Seth just gave her a look that had her staring at her hands for the ten count.

"Okay, I know I've lied to you, but even though we're no longer lovers, you're still my lawyer, Seth. And I don't give a damn what you tell the jury, but I've got to know how Sam died in Arizona at the same time he must have been taking off in New Mexico."

"You want the truth, Elena? Okay, here's the truth. I haven't the slightest fucking idea."

"Oh."

"So that's your lawyer's analysis. I tried to avoid getting too technical so you could follow it. Anything else?"

Elena surprised him. No clever, biting retort. Not even a hard look. She seemed beaten, like someone had let the air out of her. "Yes, there is," she said, pushing her hair—what was left of it—over the left side of her head with her right hand—one of the moves that used to kill him. "If you want to dump this thing and walk away, it's all right with me."

"Well, I've already told you—"

"I know. It's your case now. And Sam's. But I just wanted to say it."

"Okay, Elena, you've said it. But the genie's out of the bottle and there's no putting it back in."

"Are you talking about the case or us?"

"Yes," said Seth, and left the courtroom.

*   *   *

As bad as Seth looked as he dragged himself up the last few steps to his office, Allyn looked even worse.

"What's the matter, boss lady? You look like you've just gone three rounds with an oral surgeon."

She sat down behind her desk and beckoned Seth toward a client chair.

"Can't sit," he said, reaching for a cigarette, "gotta get on the phone. What's up?"

"There's bad news," she said without a trace of humor, "and then there's worse news."

Her bleak expression sent a flash of heat through his stomach. "What's the bad news?"

"Elena Barton left a message with Ramon five minutes ago. She's thought it over and decided that it would be best for all concerned if you were replaced by new counsel for the plaintiff."

"Shit!"

She handed him the message. Seth stared at it, willing the words to rearrange themselves into a joke.

"And she said not to bother calling, she's already making new arrangements. Said to tell you 'the genie's out of the bottle.' "

"That's great," said Seth, "and I'm left representing a two-bit case for Ben Tucker's penniless estate. Guess I pissed her off pretty bad."

Allyn nodded. "You've got the knack for it, Cowboy."

Seth stood there for a minute, the unlit cigarette dangling from his lips, then slowly turned and started back down the stairs.

"There's something else, kid. You really better sit down."

Seth took a seat and struck a match.

"No easy way to tell you this so I'll just tell you. Harry Cooper is dead."

"What?"

"It's true. Harry's dead. Last night."

The match died against Seth's flesh. "Thursday night? How?" he asked, his voice thin and flat.

"It wasn't painful. He's over at Ferguson's Mortuary."

"How?"

Allyn looked away, paused, took a deep breath. "He hung himself, Seth."

They sat in silence for a while. A car alarm went off in the alley. An apartment dog answered.

"Leave a note?"

Allyn gave an almost imperceptible nod.

"What did it say?"

"I don't know. I honestly don't."

"You know something."

"I don't know what the note said."

"Well, what in the hell *do* you know?"

Allyn relit the stub of a cigar. "The bastards threw him out."

"What bastards? Threw him out where?"

"Miller and McGrath. They voted him out of the partnership yesterday afternoon."

"Oh, Jesus," said Seth, rising to his feet. He stared out onto the bustling street for a few minutes, hands against the window casing, seeing nothing.

"Oh, Jesus," he said again, then walked out of Allyn's office and down the stairs. She stood watching through the window as he reached the crowded, commute-hour sidewalk and stopped for a minute on the cold, cola-and-blood-splattered pavement, hands gesturing as if he were talking to himself. Looked like just another street crazy. Finally disappeared into the sea of shoppers, clockers, boppers, and other sad-eyed strangers.

Seth was surprised to find himself alone in the small, dimly lighted room at Ferguson's Mortuary, a welcome relief from the mob of self-conscious weirdos storming the bar at Aunt Pearl's Jam House where he had consumed three quick shooters. Harry looked amazingly at peace amidst the flickering candles and linen; better looking than when he was alive.

You're saying some people are better off dead?

No, just that you're prettier now, Harry. Like when we were in law school.

You mean before all the nose candy, then the pipe, then trying to fake my way through M and M like I did law school. Trying to keep smoke in a broken bottle. Hell, Seth, the messed-up memo was just the last straw.

I didn't come here to feel more guilty, man.

Sure you did, asshole. That's your game. One of them. Anyway, the vote was unanimous. They were just waiting. Knew about the drugs, knew everything.

I didn't tell anybody.

Hey, Cowboy, relax. I'm dead, remember? Fucking Treadwell knows everything and everybody, and the rest of them are wannabe clones. I'm well out of the whole messy business.

You don't have to tell me anything about that particular support group.

Seth could swear Harry smiled at that one.

Yeah, I'm well out of it. Trish is damn sure better off, too. I'm insured like fucking King Farouk, but look in on her anyway. She'd have been better off sticking with you, Cowboy. Jesus! Nine years ago.

I guess I'll be heading back.

Thanks for stopping by. Better watch yourself; it's hot down here.

Seth laughed. Shit, Harry, I was sure you'd have the presence of mind to renounce Satan before you kicked the stool.

Hell, no. Like Machiavelli, I figured it was a bad time to be making enemies.

"Excuse me, young man," came a woman's frail voice from behind Seth. "We're Harry's parents. You look very familiar."

Startled, Seth extended his hand, the one not clutching his stomach. "Seth Cameron. I met you at Harry's wedding."

"Why, yes," she said. "You were an usher."

"Yes, ma'am."

"You remember Seth, Harold. He was one of Harry's best friends in law school, then at Miller and McGrath. He was an usher at Harry's wedding."

Harold remembered. "The one with the boots. You don't look so good yourself, son."

"Yeah, well, I'll be going, Mr. and Mrs. Cooper."

"Thank you for coming, Seth," said Mrs. Cooper, and then started to cry.

"Did you spend much time with our son, Seth?" asked Mr. Cooper. "Recently?"

"No, sir. I've been out of Miller and McGrath for quite a while."

Mrs. Cooper was sobbing, losing control, holding on to her husband's arm for support. "We ... we know about the note, Seth. We know ... what they did to him. We just ... don't know *why*."

"They're a tough group, ma'am," said Seth, choosing not to get into his own history.

"I don't mean why *they* did it," she said. "I mean why *Harry* did it!"

Mrs. Cooper had momentarily mobilized her anger and was glaring at Harry's corpse as if he were a child and she had caught him stealing cookies.

"Harry was one of the brightest young men in his class, wasn't he?"

"Yes, ma'am, probably the brightest."

"And well-liked?" asked Mr. Cooper.

Seth suddenly felt a passionate need to get out of Ferguson's.

"Everybody liked Harry," he said with conviction. "And envied his mind, his gifts. Everything seemed easy for him."

"Then *why?*" demanded Mrs. Cooper, grabbing Seth by the arm, her reddened eyes boring into his. "Why would our . . . handsome, popular boy . . . kill himself over partnership in a . . . *law firm.*"

She spat out the last words out as if she were referring to the KKK or the Nazi party.

"That's a complicated question—"

Sarah Cooper strengthened her hold on Seth's arm. Sweat erupted on his forehead and his eyes cast about, looking for a place to sit for a minute. Mrs. Cooper seemed close to hysteria now, and Seth looked at Mr. Cooper for help, or at least some guidance. But Mr. Cooper appeared to be a man whose patience had been tempered by years of reflecting on answers to questions posed by Mrs. Cooper.

The old lady suddenly gave Seth's arm a rude shake, then pulled him closer to the casket with surprising strength, given the fact she looked considerably worse off than Harry as she bent close to his face. Without relinquishing her hold on Seth's arm, she repeated the question in a tone that reached deep into his guts, then lay smoldering there.

"*What could be so important to be killing yourself over it?*" she demanded. "*Give me one good reason!*"

Seth followed her eyes into the casket, into the waxen flesh of the Most Likely to Succeed. Seth smelled something like wet straw and couldn't tell whether it was coming from Harry or Mrs. Cooper's coat. Her words had taken root in his brain, and his brain was racing wildly inside itself, like the search feature of a computer program on auto-replay, looking for something that wasn't there. As her eyes burned into him, the silence in the small room swelled like a tumescent blister. A sudden breeze nearly blew out one of the candles at Harry's feet. Someone must have come in the main door.

Seth slowly turned to face the small woman. "I can't give you a reason, ma'am. Not one. I'm sorry."

He took a last look at Harry, extricated his arm from Mrs. Cooper's grasp, then bolted outside, into the rain.

ALTHOUGH HE EXPECTED HER, SETH WAS STILL JOLTED BY HER APPEAR-ance when she walked in the next day. Even more beautiful than he remembered her, Rosie stood in the doorway to his office, stunning in a navy blazer and pleated, bone-colored skirt.

"Is the lawyer in?" she said, her dark eyes shining. Rosie had lost the few pounds she had put on while living in Mill Valley—too much pot, too many Oreos, too much daytime TV—and her legs were well-toned again, too. A thinner face made her pene-trating eyes seem even larger than before.

But Seth could see there was something else, even in the fad-ing, early-evening light: a new confidence her temporary shyness couldn't conceal.

"The lawyer's always in for you, Rosie. What brings you to the big city?"

"Bank's closed on Saturday. Thought I'd do some shopping."

"You're lookin' swell."

She entered the office and took him in for a minute, then gave him a hug—a sympathy hug—whether for the way he looked or for Harry, Seth couldn't say, but he was grateful either way.

She had called ahead, saying she was "in the area," and Seth had let the pretext slide. He knew she'd be worrying about him once she had heard about Harry and was just masking her need to "be there" whenever and wherever disaster struck. Rosie, the one-woman Red Cross, spreading random acts of generosity and senseless kindness.

"I'm terrible sorry about Harry," she said.

"I wanted to call you. How did you hear about it?"

"Well, they say bad news travels fast," she said, looking away.

"Rosie?"

"Yeah," she said with a shy smile, "I'm dreaming again. Ever since my trip to Canada. Then I called M and M Friday morning to be sure and the receptionist . . . well, you know. Anyway, I'm sorry I couldn't make the funeral this morning. Was it nice?"

"I missed it, too."

"You *missed* it?"

"I've been a little under the weather lately."

She'd been there less than a minute and already he was defending himself and, by the looks of her, not very effectively.

"The good Lord said leave the dead to bury the dead," he added, remembering the mileage he used to get out of his modest collection of New Testament pearls. He winced from a sudden jabbing pain in his stomach and shook a cigarette out of a bent package. "Or something like that."

"He didn't necessarily rule out a little show of respect," she said, eyeballing the cigarette. "What's bothering you? The stomach again?"

Seth put the smoke back in the package and buried the crumpled mess in his pocket. "Yeah. Same as before. It's controllable."

"I'm sorry," said Rosie, looking embarrassed. "Shootin' my mouth off like always."

"No, you're right. I should have tried to make the funeral, but things have been pretty crazy around here."

"I understand."

"It's okay. . . . How's Bakersfield?" he said, offering a chair.

"Same old Bakersfield."

They fell into small talk about Aunt Claire, some mutual friends, Rosie's job, Seth's trial. Then Rosie said she should let Seth get back to work, but Seth talked her into a cup of coffee.

"You're changing, Rosie. The banking world agrees with you."

Rosie laughed. "The bank's just a living, Seth. It's the spirit world that agrees with me."

"You winging out on me, Rosie? Goin' mystic?"

She looked at him for several seconds before answering. Measuring him. "I'm happy, Seth. Happier than I've ever been."

Seth massaged the back of his neck with both hands, then smiled at her, told her he was glad.

"You seem different, too," she said, taking him in again with those laser eyes.

"How so? You've seen me in my trial delirium before."

"Yeah, you've got that coiled-spring look, all right. But you're different."

"I'm afraid I haven't changed all that much."

"Well, I guess you haven't, if you don't think you have."

"What's that supposed to mean?"

Rosie just gave her head a little shake, as if it weren't that important, then switched back to the subject of the trial.

Safe ground.

"How's your jury look?"

Seth had decided not to tell her he'd been fired. Besides, he still had the Tucker estate case, so he was stuck till the end anyway.

"Couldn't have asked for a better shake. All but one or two are affective personality types; you know, come at things emotionally."

"Like me."

"Yes."

"And the others?"

"Cognitive."

"Like you?"

"I get your point," he said with a little sideways smile. "You think that was our main problem?"

"You're the brain here. You tell me."

Seth grunted, then lit up. "It was M and M. You can say it. I put the firm first and everything and everybody else fifth or ninth."

Rosie nodded her head. "You felt you were failin' in your job. Well, I *knew* I was failin' in mine, which was to care for you. You were my whole life, Seth. I couldn't do enough for you—I felt I owed you so much. But there was nothin' for me to do in your life, except the thing I knew deep down you really wanted from me, which was just to leave you alone."

Rosie sighed, picked up the coffee mug, and leaned back in her seat. "I'm a regular motor mouth this evenin'."

"No. I want to know."

"Well, I guess that's when I knew I had to leave if I was going to survive. Get a life, as they say."

She gave a little self-deprecating shoulder shrug and smiled at him with glistening eyes. Seth had almost forgotten how much he liked this person.

"You've got it more or less right, Rosie. I guess I persuaded myself that I'd have time to make it up to you after I made partnership at M and M. I gambled one thing against the other and lost all the way around."

They sat silently for a moment, listening to street sounds.

"I'm sorry I left so quicklike," said Rosie with a tone of genuine contrition. "It's the only way I could do it. But I've felt pretty guilty about it. You know, just up and walkin' out of your life."

"I should be used to it by now," he said without rancor or self-pity, and Rosie nodded.

"That's why I felt so guilty."

Seth laughed. "I hadn't thought about my mother in years. But lately, she's been on my mind. Anyway, you shouldn't have felt guilty. Truth is, there was a certain relief, being alone. After I stopped drinking three meals a day, I was able to focus on the work without the pressure of daily failure."

"Failure?"

"Hell, Rosie, I knew I wasn't making you happy. Wasn't making *anybody* happy, including myself."

Rosie held her coffee mug in both hands as she sipped from it, watching him over the upper edge. "You weren't exactly a barrel of chuckles."

"Still ain't, Rosie." He rubbed his eyes, which felt like a pair of festering blisters. "But at least I don't have to worry about making somebody else miserable."

Rosie put her cup down and slowly raised her eyes to his. "Are you trying to make me feel better about leaving or worse about not leaving sooner?"

Seth flushed. He knew she'd pick up on the implication as soon as the words had escaped his mouth. Worse, her soft presence and sympathetic effort at understanding him was greasing a slow slide into self-pity, a trait he despised, particularly in himself. He put out his cigarette and forced a smile.

"You did exactly the right thing, darlin'. Now tell me about the bank."

"Time out?"

Seth laughed and reached for another cigarette.

"*Cop*-out," he said, and Rosie laughed, too. The tension relieved, they talked about her promotion to supervisor, about night courses at the community college, about a study group she had joined at the Unitarian Church. Seth half listened, mainly watched, stirred anew by her strength and resourcefulness. His thoughts drifted to closed places, doors he had barred because of the pain behind them, windows nailed shut against the good times they had shared. How had she summoned the courage to up and leave him? No job, no money. How bad must it have been here, to make her overcome so much uncertainty and just drive away?

Had it been that bad for his mother? No. Same result, but cases clearly distinguishable, Your Honor. Besides, that door stays shut.

"I'm sorry, Rosie."

"You're sorry I got promoted?"

He laughed, got up, and poured her another cup of coffee. He would have to work all night to catch up on his office backlog, but he didn't want her to go quite yet. There was something else he had to know.

"No, I meant I'm sorry I made it so miserable for you here."

"Don't be. You took care of me. It's just that every time I took something from you, I felt like I was giving away a part of myself. I needed to learn I could survive on my own. It was real hard at first, because I kept thinking I'd backslide and show up on your doorstep like some lost orphan. That's why I've been so cold to you, Seth."

"Is that the only reason?"

"The main reason," she said too quickly. "Oh, sure, I knew something was going on with the Barton woman, if that's what you mean."

The anger was still there. *Change comes slowly,* thought Seth. *Even in the spirit world.*

"Not much was going on, Rosie."

"Not much was going on with you and me, either, Seth. When I saw her, I almost didn't blame you. Almost."

"But you did."

"I don't know who I was blaming. I was going crazy, scared it was my fault that you didn't want me anymore, yet something

inside told me that it had nothin' to do with me, that I was just
the first stage of some rocket you had to shed to go on higher."

Seth poured himself another unneeded cup of coffee. "And
Elena Barton was the second-stage booster rocket that could get
me into the next galaxy?"

"Somethin' like that. Oh, I felt real needed at first, but I guess
I wasn't enough to keep you going, once you commenced to set
your sights on bigger game."

"You think I needed more approval than I could get from you?"

"We all need approval, Seth. That's what was drivin' me buggy
in Marin. It was obvious you didn't want me."

"It wasn't—"

"I know, it was the work, like you kept saying, but alls I could
remember then was how it had been down in Bakersfield where
if I so much as stopped to pick up a sock, you'd be all over me."

Seth looked into his coffee. Rosie stared at the top of his head
as if willing him to look up and meet her eyes.

"That's also why I got so upset when you got mad about me
bein' pawed by that greaser at the restaurant."

"I don't get the connection," said Seth, feeling too tired now, yet
powerless to reverse the direction their conversation was taking.

"*Because a part of me wanted him to!*" she said, then quickly put
her hand to her mouth as she saw Seth's head snap up. "I mean
I was feelin' so unwanted and unattractive and undesirable—"

"So I guess your rolling over and fucking Tom Huckins was
my fault, too," said Seth through tight lips.

"I was wonderin' when we'd get around to that."

"Good, then you're not surprised."

"Only that it took you so long." Then, to Seth's amazement,
she started to cry. Softly, like the rain outside.

"I'm not cryin' over you or over my shame at one lousy fuck,"
she said, opening her purse and removing a wad of Kleenex.
"I'm cryin' because with you it's always the tail waggin' the
darned dog."

"And what's that supposed to mean?" said Seth, grabbing another cigarette.

"It means," she said, the tremulous words and tears coming fast
now, "that I'm sittin' here months later tellin' you that when I was
here, I was dyin' because I loved you so much and felt so useless,
and how when I left, my whole world was crashin' around me,

and alls you can think about is that I spent one stupid night . . . with Tom Huckins tryin' to . . . feel better about myself—"

Rosie tried to control her tears, and Seth reached across and touched her cold hand. "I'm sorry. I had no right—"

"It's not a matter of right, Seth," she said, sitting straighter. "I just wish you weren't so . . . muddled in your head. You always used to say you wanted men on your jury when you were on the defense side of a case because women always deal from 'emotion'—like emotion was some disease just this side of the black plague. I'd just sit there like I didn't know you were puttin' women down—*me* down—for never knowin' what we're doin'. And I guess I *didn't* know what I was doin', but at least I *knew* I didn't know, and *you didn't.* Guys can't admit they don't know what they're doin' about *anything:* love, sex, color of the refrigerator, how a toaster works, inflation, menstruation—"

"Whoa there, Rosie. I get it."

"Sorry." She wiped her cheek and put her Kleenex away. "I guess I got a little off the point somewhere."

"That's okay."

"My point was not that I stopped lovin' you, but that I had forgotten what love was supposed to be. You didn't have time for a companion. I couldn't give you sex 'cause you were always tired. I couldn't even cook for you because you were never home. Alls I could do was clean and wash and wait like some neglected pet for you to come home.

"I finally figured out you can't just put love on hold, waitin' for something like partnership in M and M to turn it all back on like a faucet. I realized by the time you made partnership, we might not be able to find the handle anymore."

"Then I got fired."

"And I felt guilty for shoutin' hallelujah!—to myself, of course. I thought maybe we'd get back to bein' like normal people. Maybe you wouldn't have to go on killin' yourself. Maybe you'd see that I loved *you,* not some big-time lawyer in some big-time law firm."

"It didn't take you long to hit the lifeboats."

Rosie stood abruptly and closed her purse. Seth jumped up, too, reached for her hand. "I'm sorry, Rosie, that was below the belt."

"Yes," she said, suddenly angry again, "but it was also true.

As soon as you got on here with Allyn Friedlander, it was clear nothin' had changed. Nothin' mattered to you but gettin' back on Montgomery Street, the only place where you could win so much respect and approval that even *you* would have to believe you were worthy of being loved and not just some little snot-nosed shit who not even his own mother loved enough to stick around and—"

Rosie again slapped her hand over her mouth, but too late, and her words hung in the air like a cloud of radioactive dust. A muffled, forlorn sound came from deep in her throat as she watched Seth through wide-opened eyes. Seth was holding his stomach as if he had been shot there, and his eyes flickered around the room like birds looking for a place to light.

"Talk about below the belt," he said finally, managing an unconvincing smile.

"Oh, Seth, I'm so sorry—"

"It's okay."

"Just too much stuff comin' up all at once," she said. "I see I've got some heavy work to do on this."

"We've got to stop apologizing to each other, kid. Let's just say I was in the slow reading group and leave it at that."

"Believe me, Seth, I didn't mean to come up here and say these things when I called you today."

"Well, some things need sayin', I guess, and they say themselves when they're ready. It's okay. Really."

Rosie headed for the door. "I've talked way too much, Seth, but I stand by what I said when I first came in here: you're different. I can't put my finger on it, but I feel it. Something's changed."

Seth smiled. "Well, if half the things you said about the way I used to be are true, I guess that's a compliment."

"Take it that way. Good-bye, Seth. Good luck with your trial, and I hope you get what you want."

"Rosie, don't go like this. Have one more cup of coffee."

"I've got to go, Seth. I'm going to end up blaming myself for all this, so the sooner I leave, the less I'll regret tomorrow."

Seth followed her downstairs and saw her into the El Camino, then watched as the trail of exhaust from the retreating vehicle painted white swirls in the cold night air.

It took thirty-six hours over the weekend—fourteen phone calls and seven meetings—for Elena Barton to convince herself she would be unable to find a trial lawyer willing to substitute into the case for Seth, even assuming she could get a mistrial and a continuance, both unlikely possibilities. She did, however, receive five invitations to dinner (two from women lawyers), two flat-out propositions (one from a woman lawyer), and a word of advice in the form of a parable from Terrence X. Kelly, a blotchy-faced old warhorse who confessed he could use the work, but had "read about some of the problems with the case." He was too tactful to mention her publicized adultery, choosing instead, as had most of the other lawyers, to rest his pessimistic appraisal on her husband's drinking the night of the crash. Here was Kelly's parable.

"When Yogi Berra was trying to break into the major leagues as a catcher, he wasn't getting any playing time. One day he begged the manager to let him substitute for the regular right fielder—who I'll call Flannery—at the top of the eighth inning so he'd have a chance to bat in the ninth. The manager finally gave in, and Berra proceeded to either drop or misjudge every ball hit to right field. The manager glared at him as he trotted back to the dugout at the end of the long inning, but Yogi looked him squarely in the eye and said, 'That Flannery's got right field so fucked up, nobody can play it.' "

Elena got the point, and deep down she knew that Seth, like poor Flannery, could hardly be blamed for what had happened to her star-crossed case. She was beginning to regret her impetuous firing, not that she didn't have sufficient grounds. The guy was obviously a burn-out—holding his stomach a lot and peering out of one eye at a time—not to mention turning down $150,000, a third of it in his own pocket, when she knew he could barely afford bus fare. But all that aside, and apart from who was to blame for the mess the trial had become, one thing was clear: her case would not be touched by any lawyer in his right mind.

Which left Seth Cameron.

She had paced the floor of her Pacific Heights condo for nearly an hour late Sunday afternoon, trying to come up with a way to gracefully unfire her lawyer, when, to her amazement, her lawyer obligingly called and did it for her. Seth told her he was calling to apologize for not paying more attention to her desires in regard to her father's offer to broker a settlement. Called it "unprofessional," which gave Elena a chuckle, considering the rest of his conduct. He also hadn't meant to hurt her feelings after court on Friday when she had tried to be nice. Blamed it on end-of-the-week fatigue.

Elena had counted off five full seconds of silence, then magnanimously forgave him and rescinded her "precipitous action"—though not without mentioning that nearly every lawyer she had spoken with had told her she had a clear case of malpractice against him for not advising her to accept the $150,000 offer, given all the circumstances.

"Haven't you heard of double jeopardy?" Seth had said, obviously relieved and trying to lighten things up. "You can only charge me with malpractice once per case."

She had laughed her throaty laugh and suggested a round of peace talks. "I'll meet you halfway," she said. "Literally. How about the Alta Mira in Sausalito? The sun's out this afternoon. You can pick the drinks and the shape of the table."

An hour later, they sipped Irish coffees at a round table on the restaurant deck overlooking San Francisco Bay, host to several multicolored sailboats that had been coaxed out of their moorings by an unseasonably warm January day. San Francisco in the distance looked like a fairy-tale kingdom, with its undulating hills topped by structures of every imaginable configuration, including Coit Tower, claimed by locals to be one of the world's largest phallic symbols.

"I've got to ask you something," she said, after silently watching the sails dancing like water bugs on the relatively calm surface of the bay. "Why *didn't* you want to take the money? I assume you could have put your firm's fifty thousand dollars to good use."

Seth lit a cigarette, then gazed at the tip for a few seconds before answering. "As I told you at the time, the offer didn't include clearing Sam's name, and they damn sure weren't going to admit they had built a bad bird. So Sam's death and the deaths of the other three pilots would be swept under a red, white, and blue rug." He took another deep drag, then made a face and snuffed the cigarette out. "I've got personal reasons, too."

"I thought there might be more to it."

"Yep. There's always more to it. If I get a verdict, I'm a partner back on Montgomery Street. I also have the satisfaction of whipping your uncle Tony's ass and heroically handing the *Chronicle* the goods to make an example of ConSpace, so maybe other contractors will think twice before they lower safety standards to raise their bottom line. You know, quit putting decent people in supersonic tinderboxes?"

"That's a heavy agenda."

"Yeah, and part of it puts me in a potential conflict of interest with you. So if you still want to take the money and run, you'll have to get one of the people you talked with this weekend to handle settlement negotiations. I won't stand in the way."

"You're full of noble thoughts today."

"Don't use Kelly. He's not taken seriously. I'd use Deborah Shaffield or Vic Anderson."

Elena blinked. "How did you—?"

"I've had six calls so far. I'd guess you talked to a dozen lawyers before you realized no one would come in."

Elena smiled in amused resignation. "One other question. What makes you think you've got a chance of winning, given Sam's drinking and my own . . . behavior?"

Seth returned her smile, then killed his Irish. "There's something else you don't know, Elena. Lev found a girl at the phone company in New Mexico who says someone placed a call to Farnsworth from the Caicos Islands—"

"From where?"

"A small tax haven in the Caribbean. Anyway, Farnsworth got this call around eleven, about a half hour before Simmons says the general placed a call to the Officers' Club where Sam and Crispie were hanging out. It's possible Sam was not scheduled to fly that night, which would explain why he was drinking. It's also possible that Farnsworth might have ordered him up, and no one bothered to tell him that Sam was drunk as a billy goat."

"But Crispie would have known. *He* would have told the general!"

Seth grinned. "Yeah, you'd think so, wouldn't you?"

They sat in silence for a minute, Seth watching her, allowing the implication to sink in.

"Anyway," he said, "Lev's in the Caicos working the angle right now."

"That's *wonderful* news," said Elena, and Seth saw a light returning to those pale green eyes, a radiance that had once caused a short-circuit between his brain and his genitals. "When will we know?"

Seth signaled the waitress for another round. "Soon."

Elena extended her half-empty glass in a toast. "Well, then, here's to going the distance, Rocky."

Seth looked at her and smiled. "You're sure?"

"What the hell."

"Okay, then. To the distance."

They sat in silence for a few minutes more, watching the boats heading back to their harbors as the first hint of fog began to blow in from the west. Fresh drinks arrived.

"You must really hate him," she said.

"Who? Treadwell? I don't know what I feel anymore about anything. I've got to do some thinking when this is over."

"Seems like you took the death of your friend pretty hard."

Seth nodded, lit a cigarette. "Left me with some questions I couldn't answer."

"Such as?"

He gave his head a quick shake that told Elena he didn't know or wasn't saying. Took a deep drink from his glass. Looked out at the Bay. A speckled gull swept in and plucked a bread crust from the table next to them.

Elena remembered something else. "Speaking of Crispie, I've got some more good news."

"I'm sure."

"I've been working on him. He'll go back on the stand and say that Sam left the club at eleven-ten P.M., not eleven-thirty."

Seth just stared at her. "Working *on* him? Or *under* him? Forget it. I want nothing more to do with the son of a bitch."

"Be nice, Seth. Don't you see? He's willing to make the Lukenses' sighting at one-twenty more possible."

"I said forget it. First place, there's still not enough time. Second place, it looks to me like your great and good friend Christopher developed a case of lockjaw at a point when he could have saved your husband's life with a word or two. So I don't trust him and the jury won't either. Third place, the *jury* would know what you bartered for the revised testimony, if you take my meaning. Fourth place, Treadwell would hit him with the adultery issues. Fifth place, but not in order of importance, it doesn't happen to be true. Simmons had no motive to lie when he said both of them left at eleven-thirty."

Elena looked to the sky and placed both palms on the table. "Fine, Moses, stay up there on your ethical mountaintop, but write this on your tablet: You're an advocate—or so you told me—not a judge and certainly not a priest!"

Seth laughed sardonically. "Ethics never entered my mind, Elena. It just won't sell. Hell, there's not a shred of ethics or morality in this whole damn case on either side. Or maybe anywhere else in the world either. It's gone, vanished into thick air, like clean water, mom-and-pop grocery stores, and the great auk."

"So?"

"So I won't do it. I was always partial to clean water and mom-and-pop stores."

"Okay, great auk, but I'll get Crispie to volunteer himself somehow. You'll have nothing to do with it."

"You're right about that, Elena, I'll have nothing to do with it. Or the case either, if it happens. You can't separate the dancer from the dance, and I'm the dancer here. I won't be involved in perjury suborned by a piece of ass, even a good one like you."

Elena's expression reflected the battle being waged within her. Seth knew she was dying to fire him again, but knew he was her last and only hope. It bothered him to think that she was his, too. It bothered him even more to be sitting there hating her guts, yet suddenly wanting to take her into one of the rooms behind the restaurant and fuck her brains out.

*   *   *

Seth checked for messages when he arrived at the office early Monday morning. He returned a call from Lev in the Caicos Islands.

"Dead end, Seth. Whoever called Farnsworth from the hotel used an obviously fake name and address on the registration. I'm staying here at the hotel. Nobody remembers him. Claimed to be a Dr. John Phillips. Paid cash for the room."

"Shit."

"Yeah. Shit."

Seth marveled at the clear telephone connection, wondered how much the silence was costing. Wondered what Allyn would say when she saw the bill.

The bill!

"Here's what you do, Lev. Get back to Albuquerque. Talk to your telephonic deep throat again. Have her trace any *other* outgoing calls from the occupant's room to see if our mystery guest was billed for a call to his home or office number while he was down there. It's a long shot, but she could then use her reverse index, maybe find a number that could be his residence or his real office."

"It's a long shot, Cowboy, but it's your money."

"Do it, okay?"

At ten on Tuesday, Seth made his pitch to Judge Singer for a forty-eight-hour continuance within which to develop some new evidence that could dramatically impact the case. When Treadwell strenuously opposed the motion—characterizing it as "yet another example of Mr. Cameron's passion for frolic and detour"—the judge decided to hold a good-cause hearing in chambers. Seth, the court attachés, the defense team, together with the governmental entourage, crowded their way into chambers.

"All right, Mr. Cameron, we're waiting. What possible reason can you give me for recessing this interminable trial, just as it finally seems to be winding down to its less-than-gripping climax."

"It's clear to everyone in the courtroom, Your Honor, that Captain Barton was drinking the night of the crash, probably drunk."

"If that is an offer for a stipulation," interrupted Treadwell, winking at the Defense Department lawyers, "you've got a deal, Cameron."

Seth ignored the remark. "With the court's indulgence, I believe I can prove that the reason Sam Barton was drinking that night was because he wasn't scheduled to fly. I believe he was *ordered* into the air by the base commander late the night of the fifteenth."

"Your Honor," interrupted Treadwell, "this is absurd, and hardly a showing of good cause. Even if it were true—and I can assure the court from talking with General Farnsworth that it is not—it would be irrelevant as to my client, who merely manufactured the plane."

Judge Singer flashed a rare bemused smile. "Come now, Mr. Treadwell. You forget that I was once a trial lawyer myself. This jury will make its determination based largely on whether they believe that Captain Barton was an irresponsible lush—a currently inescapable conclusion given the proof *you* introduced—or, on the other hand, whether he possessed good-faith reasons for believing he had the night off. From what I have learned in this case about the life of a test plot, I would not begrudge one of them a few drinks on a night off."

But Treadwell was tenacious. "Even so, Your Honor, Mr. Cameron has provided no clue as to how he is going to pull this fantasy rabbit out of a nonexistent hat."

"I was coming to that, Counsel. I'd like to hear an offer of proof from you, Mr. Cameron."

This was what Seth had feared, but ultimately, Judge Singer settled for Seth's summary of what he had learned so far and at least did not require the identity of the Albuquerque telephone operator.

"All right. I'll grant the motion. We'll be in recess until Thursday, but don't come back for more, Mr. Cameron. Understood?"

Seth thanked the court, returned to the office, and began to catch up on a backlog of correspondence and pleadings he had been ignoring for two weeks. Allyn was in Santa Clara County on a breach of warranty case, so he had complete access to Ramon and his magic fingers.

"Get ready for some heavy work, Ramon."

"I'm with you, Number Two."

"Good. I have reason to believe there's a desk beneath all this crap, and we're not leaving until I can see it."

"May I suggest a good clean fire?"

Seth dictated for two hours, interrupted only by the occasional sound of the telephone, which, though muted, rattled his heart every time it went off. At twelve-fifteen, he sent a note into the alley, ordering a sub sandwich for Ramon and a cup of soup for himself.

By the time Ramon left at five, Seth had made a satisfactory dent in his paperwork and was dying for a drink.

Still, nothing from Lev. Seth eyed the drawer in Allyn's office, the one containing the pint of Jack Daniel's. He picked up a writing pad instead and tried another approach to his closing argument to the jury. He began writing an outline, which, after a tortured hour, made as little sense as the case itself. He ripped the sheets off his pad, crumpled them into a ball, and hook-shot the wad into the corner basket for two points.

He started over.

Ladies and gentlemen, you've all read about government contractors and their $75 hammers and $400 toilet seats. But this is not just about waste or fraud or taxpayers getting ripped off. This is a case about a man killed in the prime of his life because one of the richest aircraft manufacturers in the world wouldn't put sixty lousy dollars into a harness to protect life-saving electronics in a $300-million airplane.

He tore off the sheet, formed it into a glider, and sent it toward the corner wastebasket. Another deuce.

The phone rang, triggering Seth's heartbeat, but it was only some guy looking for Ramon. Seth took a message, grabbed his coat, and headed home.

It was strange, he thought, commuting across the bridge in four lanes of metal-to-metal traffic at a normal time with normal people on their way home to children and three-bedroom homes with two-car garages and six-figure mortgages. What would it be like?

A barge lumbered its way eastward toward the channel that would take it up the San Joaquin River to the port of Stockton. A half dozen sailboats were still scattered around the bay, looking like toys as they braved the January winds and raced the dying sun back to their safe harbors. He glanced to the west, toward the Farallon Islands and beyond, where a quilt of bruised cumulus clouds touched the horizon, starting to show red as the sun settled beneath them.

Nothing on his answering machine at home. *Fucking Lev.*

He considered, then rejected, the idea of just one shot of tequila, fearful of where it might lead. Instead, he took Fat Dog for a Frisbee session in the park. They romped for an hour under the full moon, then took a turn around the Mill Valley square. Stopping for a minute at D'Angelino's Restaurant, Seth looked through the window like a kid at a candy store. Well-dressed people laughing. Normal people.

Fat Dog made friends with a golden retriever curled by the door, and Seth debated going in for a quick look around. Everyone seemed paired up, no singles. No, wait! Down at the end of the bar, a pair of eights. One maybe a nine. He caught his reflection in the window, unconsciously brushed his hair back. One of the girls glanced in his direction. He smiled, gave her a casual wave. Miraculously, *she* waved, and Seth began to tie Fat Dog to a drainpipe, until he saw a tall young hunk rise from his seat near the window, wave back, and head toward her welcoming face.

"Come on, Fats, let's go home and eat."

At midnight, Seth fell asleep on his couch. At 1:30 A.M., Lev called.

"Looks like the usual good-news-bad-news scenario back here in Albuquerque, Cowboy."

"Yeah?"

"My angel at the phone company found another outgoing call from the room in the Caicos, this one to a Washington, D.C., area code residence. She wanted her five hundred dollars up front like before, delivered personally."

"Personally?"

"She liked me."

"*Liked?*"

"Yeah, liked. My angel has done flown off to heaven. By the time I got to her apartment the place was crawling with cops and emergency wheels. She's dead, Seth. Multiple stab wounds. A crazed slasher from what I could gather."

"Or made to look like one." Seth put a half-cup of coffee into the microwave and hit the switch. "Like a bird in an air scoop or a drunk kid falling off a hotel balcony?"

"Yeah, like that."

"How about another operator?"

"They're not going to want to talk to me after this. Besides, only two others have access to the international computer data codes."

"Did you get into her apartment? See any notes?"

"Are you kidding? I couldn't even get into her building. Security like one of those Elizabeth Taylor weddings. But I'll try to get next to the cops later this morning."

Seth stared at the receiver in his hand, tried to force his beleaguered mind to process this new information, heard Lev's distant voice saying, "Seth, you there? You there? Operator?"

"Yeah, podner, I'm *here* and I want you to get out of *there*. If they knew about her, they know about you."

"How'd they find out?"

"From me. In court. Fucking Farnsworth, or maybe Treadwell himself. Look, I want you to go straight to the airport and get out of Dodge."

Lev said he'd consider it and hung up.

Seth drifted back to sleep around four, and Lev called again at six. "I took your advice for once, Cowboy. I'm at the airport and just picked up the morning edition. The press somehow either got hold of a police photo or took one of their own. The photo shows angel-baby spread out on what looks like a gray linoleum floor. Get this. She tried to leave me a message after the killer left. In blood. Six numbers. It's messy, but I'll fax the front page to your office."

"What are the numbers?"

"Looks like 338310. She couldn't finish."

"I'm heading to the office. Oh, and Lev?"

"Yeah?"

"You're still not out of town. Don't step in nothin', okay?"

"I'll be careful."

Within five minutes, Seth had William Torville on the phone at his office in New Orleans.

"Allyn Friedlander's associate? Remember me?"

"Oh, yes, Mr. Cameron. I remember you quite vividly."

"Look, pard, I know we didn't hit it off all that well, and I have it on good authority that I acted like a first-class asshole. Worst of it is, I wasn't acting. Anyway, I need a hand here. It's for a good cause that could come back around to you, maybe help you with your own investigation into Aubrey Olmstead and TDA."

Torville eventually agreed to use his resources to trace all telephone numbers in the Washington 202 area starting with 338–310 and ending with the numbers one through nine.

Seth hung up. "Hear that, Fats? We may salvage this thing yet." Seth fed Fat Dog, showered, grabbed a piece of toast, and headed across the bridge to his office.

He went straight to the fax machine, and there waiting for him was the blaring headline:

Slasher's Victim Attempts Dying Clue in Own Blood!

To the right of the article lay a young woman named Rochelle Rodriguez, facedown, fully clothed, surrounded by a halo of chalk, her right arm extended toward the six blood-smeared numbers.

$$338\text{-}310$$

The caption read: "Police baffled—can you help?"

Seth fired up the coffee machine, walked into his office, and collapsed into his chair, clutching the page in his hand. The whole thing was crazy. People getting killed—how many now?— Lev out there in jeopardy, himself maybe next, all over a case that couldn't be won. What were these bastards afraid of? What could be so damn important to them? And who the hell were they?

Now, more waiting. Settling back at his desk, his mind wandered back to the $150,000 offer. A verdict of anything less than that—plus Tucker's $25,000 and lost rents—would be a humiliating defeat, even set him up for another malpractice charge. Had his pride run away with him? He leafed through his checkbook and wondered how he would pay his rent this month. He had already taken two advances on his salary. He owed Lev another

$1,000 for finding the Lukenses, and Allyn more than that for financing Lev's Caicos trip. A $50,000 fee out of the settlement would look damn good right now.

Suddenly he was dialing Rosie's number. He couldn't stop himself, or maybe he just didn't try. He had to talk to her, hear her voice. For some reason, the thought of her lately was like a paper cut—fleeting, but painful whenever his memory rubbed against it. He knew it was a mistake, so he just let his mind go blank—maybe like people do when they step off a building or a bridge—and observed his shameless fingers as they pushed buttons on the telephone.

No answer, and—no surprise—no answering machine. As he sat there, eyes closed, listening to the tenth or eleventh ring, a call rang in on another line. It was Torville.

"One of the numbers is listed to an eighty-five-year-old pensioner who lives in a retirement home? Two have been out of service for nearly three years?" Seth had forgotten Torville's irritating habit of ending each declarative phrase with a soaring intonation.

"All the rest are located at a large Catholic convent in Arlington?"

"That's it?"

"That's what we found."

"Any possibility of error?"

"None."

"Shit!"

"Well, you're *welcome*, Cameron!"

"Sorry, Torville, it's just that I was so sure. So damn sure. And now I'm dead."

"Come now, Cameron. I know it's a big case, but there will always be others?"

Seth grunted a sardonic chuckle. "Not for me, Torville, not for me. Thanks anyway." He hung up, stared at the telephone, then whispered into the emptiness that surrounded him.

"Not for me."

Minutes, though it seemed like hours or even days later, Seth was stirred from his melancholy lethargy by the sound of footsteps on the stairs. Heavy, familiar footsteps, then a voice.

"Yo, Cowboy. I'm home, dear."

"Come on up, Lev. Join the wake."

Lev was soaked, Seth's first realization that it was pouring rain outside.

"The numbers didn't pan out?" said Lev, already standing in a pool of water.

"Good try, no cigar."

"Now what?" Lev took off his coat, shook his head like a wet dog.

"I'm out of ideas, old son. No miracles this time, no potato bugs to swallow, no more recesses, nothing. Guess I'll try to act like I came up with something; maybe bluff my way into getting some of that settlement money back on the table."

"Are you're forgetting that the guys you're trying to bluff in this particular game have already seen your hole card?"

"Good point."

"Which leaves us but one thing to do."

Seth grabbed his coat. "I'm with you, podner."

The Brazen Head—the last bar on their tour—cut them both off at twelve minutes before closing time. Lev started drinking straight coffee, having lost the coin toss that had declared him the designated driver thirty minutes earlier at Moose's. That was just before they had been ejected for playing shuffleboard on the bar, using their empty shot glasses.

"So it's back to divorce court for me, Lev. Maybe you'll see me on TV."

"Oh, yeah. Slugging it out with Judge Wapner."

"That's a different venue. Anyway, don't sell uncontested divorces short. They can be verrry tricky sometimes. Things can happen. The judge might not show up, for example. The courtroom might burn down the night before. Just as you think everything's in order, the bubonic plague makes a comeback."

"Bullshit, Cowboy. You'll get another chance."

"No. Not in this league. After this debacle, I'll have clinched the title of 'Career Minor-Leaguer'; winner of the 'Lifetime Valley Journeyman-Lawyer' award. Pop was right."

"Could be worse things than goin' back to the Valley. Rosie's there. You're known there."

Seth swallowed the last of his coffee. "Too easy, pard," he said bitterly. "Too hard."

*　　*　　*

Seth awoke the next morning to a tequila sunrise, a crashing headache, but a full awareness of his situation. He had forgotten to set the alarm, and it was eight. Usually Fat Dog would have awakened him by now. He tried to think whether he had fed Fats when he got home, but couldn't remember getting home. He looked outside. No car. Mouth tasting like a toxic dump, a superfund site. Must have been poured into a taxi by some well-meaning Good Samaritan who should have minded his own business. No—Lev had driven him home.

He dressed in a hurry, trying to think of something to say to Judge Singer, then to the jury.

No sign of Fat Dog. The doors were all closed, so he couldn't have wandered out. Seth gave his head a shake, forced down some buffered aspirin and water, tried to clear his mind. Fats must not have been in the house when he got home.

Seth found his friend a few minutes later, propped against the curb in front, his neck twisted grotesquely and already rigid, his eyes mercifully closed. Seth picked him up and took him inside, cleaned the matted blood from the gray fur around his mouth, then wrapped him in a clean white sheet and buried him in the backyard under a scraggly oak tree with branches as bare as fingernails.

He did everything mechanically, without emotion. *Fetch the shovel. Dig into the dirt. Get through the day. Fetch the dog, sweet, loving dog. My friend. Put the Frisbee in there with him; won't need that anymore. Get through the day, then get even. Smooth the sheet, shovel in the dirt. Dust to dust.*

He tried to shut his mind off, to block thoughts of what it would be like coming home without Fats there. He wondered what General Farnsworth would say about this situation. He'd say accidents like this happen all the time. Dogs get run over.

Don't think. Just do it. That's it, make a mound, so when Fats decomposes the ground will be level. Plant something tomorrow. Cover the little fella with spring flowers. Don't think; especially don't think about the fact that you're alone again.

56

SETH WASHED HIS HANDS AND SAT DOWN TO DRINK A CUP OF COFFEE. His bloodshot eyes fell on the copy of the Albuquerque front page and the ghoulish picture of the courageous victim. Her face was covered by her hair. All he could see of the rest of her head was an ear, as small as a child's. *Five hundred dollars. A couple a dresses, a blouse or two. Jesus.* He shoved it aside, tired of thinking about death and tired of trying not to think about death.

He raised the coffee to his lips, but then slammed the mug on the table and grabbed the page.

He stared at the numbers he had stared at a hundred times, but this time he saw something different.

"Oh, shit!" he shouted to the empty room and raced to the telephone.

"Torville? I think I have it!"

"That's very comforting," came Torville's typically bland reply, "but who is this?"

"Cameron, Seth Cameron from San Francisco. One more favor, Torville, and I'm your fucking slave forever, okay? I gave you area 202 and the numbers 338–310, remember? I was wrong. Run the same check for me, but on numbers 338–31*8!* The woman makes her eights with two circles. She wasn't telling us it was a zero; she was trying to make another eight! Will you do it?"

"Sure, why not?"

"I'm heading for the office. I'll check in the minute I get there."

Seth called a cab and arrived at the office at nine-thirty, only to find that Torville's D.C. contact was at lunch, "due back in a half hour."

Seth poured another cup of coffee, then absently stared at the newspapers Ramon had collected for him months earlier. News of the imminent presidential election dominated the first few pages. Then, on the next-to-last page of the first section of the *Chronicle*, he found a small article about Sam's crash. Ten lines, parroting the Air Force's version, and making no mention of previous crashes. Similar low-key articles appeared in the back sections of the other papers, all attributing the cause to pilot error.

Seth called another cab—he had no idea where his car was—then unaccountably dialed the number of the bank where Rosie worked. He was relieved that she seemed happy to hear from him.

"I hoped you'd call," she said.

"You did?"

"I'm just glad to hear you're okay. I . . . had a dream last night, Seth. Something terrible, but, well, sometimes I'm grateful to be wrong."

"They killed Fats."

"Oh, Seth."

Seth couldn't think of anything to say.

"You won't go and do something stupid, will you, Seth? You know how you can get."

"You know what they say, Rosie. Don't get mad, get even."

"That's what I'm afraid of."

"Listen, Rosie. I'm racing to court. The case is basically dead, except for one last gasp. I'm arguing the case to the jury tomorrow and . . . I was wondering, well, if you had any vacation time coming or anything. I could, uh . . . use . . . some . . ."

Seth swallowed, then listened to the heavy silence, a quiet density broken only by the sound of his own labored breathing. He moved the mouthpiece away from his lips, but the totality of the resulting silence made him feel queasy, and he had to shake his head to stave off an attack of vertigo. He thought he heard his name come through the receiver, but the sound turned into a noxious, glowing mass that transformed the seconds into hours into years, winding through time, back through thirty years of time, slowly forming itself into a fist that . . .

Seth dropped the receiver into the cradle, grabbed his briefcase, and raced down the stairs to the waiting taxi.

He arrived at City Hall at 9:45 A.M. and hurried through the metal detector to the nearest telephone. Torville still had not reached his D.C. contact.

Seth entered the courtroom and took his seat. Treadwell and his entourage were already in place. The bailiff brought the jury in, causing Seth's heart to hammer in his rib cage as he wondered what he would say when the judge told him to call his mystery witness. The clerk entered the courtroom and announced that the judge was on a conference call and would be a few minutes late. Seth considered running for a telephone, but could not take the risk with the jury already in place and the judge about to enter. He tried to relax, took some deep breaths, and removed from his briefcase one of the newspapers—*The New York Times*—the paralegal had produced from the week of Sam's crash.

It was interesting—at least distracting—to read the retrospective account of the political jousting at that time between doves in quest of the so-called peace dividend versus advocates of the Stealth Program, Star Wars, and the Houston supercollider. Senate Bill SB-1857 was up for a vote, a vote to end "continued waste and mismanagement," cried its eighteen sponsors. Also at the top of the news was a lagging economy, unemployment, the death of a movie actress, and the appointment of an independent counsel to investigate the B-2 bomber, now acknowledged to be a multibillion-dollar dinosaur. A piece about one more airplane crash didn't stand a chance against such weighty matters. Against charges and countercharges between the major parties of incompetence, intemperance, inexperience, incontinence, intransigence, and so on. American politics at its best.

So no surprise that there, buried on the back pages, was Sam Barton's fiery death in the Arizona desert.

"All rise!" shouted the bailiff, and Judge Singer shot from his chambers onto the bench.

"Well, Mr. Cameron," he said, "we await your next witness."

Crunch time. Seth had considered putting Elena on as a stall, but was afraid to expose her to further damage. Crispie was willing to lie about Sam's departure from the club—to tie in better with the Lukenses' 1:20 A.M. "pillar of fire" sighting—but putting him on would be not only risky, but illegal.

"Mr. Cameron?"

"Yes, Your Honor." But Seth continued to sit, staring down at his hands, his brow furrowed in thought. A low murmur rose from the spectators, and jurors began to exchange puzzled glances.

"Are you going to call a witness or not, Mr. Cameron?"

Seth glanced over at Treadwell, staring innocently at a jagged crack in the ceiling, a relic of the '89 earthquake. Seth thought he detected one of those infrequent smiles that occasionally slid onto the senior partner's disciplined countenance.

Seth turned his head a little farther and saw Christopher, glowering, challenging. He knew the jury was watching him, waiting. *What the hell.*

"Call Major Jack Christopher as a rebuttal witness, Your Honor."

He heard Elena whisper a *"Yes"* behind him, apparently pleased that her lawyer was following instructions for once, doing something right. The pleasure quickly faded from her face, however, as Seth not only failed to give Crispie the opportunity to perjure himself, but locked him solidly into the eleven-thirty, logically impossible, departure time from the club.

But that was just the beginning.

"Where did Captain Barton go after you left the club, Major?"

"I don't know. I assume to the flight line."

"Where did you go?"

"Objection! Irrelevant."

"Sustained."

"Your Honor, I need a little slack here."

"Mr. Cameron, you have had more than your share of 'slack' in this trial. Objection sustained."

"Remember a phone call you received, Major, just before you left with Captain Barton? To refresh your memory, it was at eleven twenty-five P.M."

"No, I don't recall that."

"Then let me help you. It was from General Farnsworth, the man seated right over there."

"Objection, Your Honor. We're far afield here."

"I'll tie it up, Your Honor."

Judge Singer looked skeptical, but finally said he would allow an aria by José Carreras if it would speed things up.

"Well, Major?"

"It's possible."

"And if he did, it would be quite unusual, wouldn't it? I mean, the base commander doesn't call you at the club every night, does he?"

"No, but you must remember, I was officer of the day."

"Do you remember what he said to you?"

"Haven't a clue."

Out of the corner of his eye, Seth saw General Farnsworth rise as unobtrusively as possible for a man his height and walk toward the door.

"Thank you, Major, that's all for now. But don't you rush off, General Farnsworth. Let's visit."

"What?" said Farnsworth, stopped in his tracks, pointing to his chest. "Me?"

"Your Honor, I call the general as my next witness."

While studying Farnsworth's uncharacteristic disarray, Seth spotted Simon Stephens in the back of the courtroom and didn't know whether to celebrate or lament his return.

Farnsworth scowled, then looked at the Defense Department lawyers, but the senior counsel, the one named Harold Baldwin, simply shrugged. Treadwell offered no consolation either, so the general gave Seth a withering look and marched to the bench, ramrod erect, and addressed the court.

"Your Honor, is this really necessary? I have absolutely nothing new to say about this matter."

"That," replied the judge with a sigh of resignation, "does not seem to disqualify anyone from being called as a witness by Mr. Cameron. Please step over to the box and be sworn, sir."

With another hard look at the Defense Department lawyers, Gen. Clement Farnsworth was sworn and took his seat.

"Well, sir, you did call then-captain Jack Christopher around eleven-thirty P.M., did you not?"

"I might well have done so, sir. For precisely the reason he has already explained. He was officer of the day." Farnsworth's eyes then locked onto Seth's, and a faint smile appeared at the edges of his mouth as he added, "Remember, Counselor, the crash had probably already occurred by then."

Seth met Farnsworth's crooked smile with one of his own, then started nodding his head and dropped a bombshell. "You may be right about that, General."

This remark created a tumultuous reaction at the defense table, with Treadwell the first to leap to his feet.

"Your Honor, the defense renews its motion for dismissal under the one-year statute of limitations. Counsel has just admitted that the crash occurred on the night of the fifteenth, one year and one day preceding the filing of his complaint!"

Judge Singer looked as surprised as anyone. "Counsel?"

Seth appeared unperturbed. "I remind Mr. Treadwell that the remarks of counsel are not evidence, and I have not stipulated to anything. Moreover, I merely said that the general *could* be right, not that he is."

"Motion denied," said Judge Singer, spreading his palms toward Treadwell, seemingly disappointed that Seth was technically correct. "We'll take the morning recess now. The jury is excused with the usual admonition not to discuss the case among yourselves or with anyone else."

Seth raced for the door, then down the hall to the telephones, dogged by his client. "Hold on, you lunatic! Talk to me! What in the hell are you trying to do in there?"

Seth ignored her until she cornered him in the phone booth as he was dialing Torville's number.

"You're supposed to be my lawyer!" she shouted. "Even the judge thinks you've flipped out. This isn't a game, Seth, you're in *trial*, for God's sake!"

"Wrong, as usual, Elena. Haven't you heard? I'm not *in* trial. I'm *on* trial."

Seth pulled the door shut as Torville reported, "I've eliminated all but three names. Got a pencil?"

Seth began scribbling, at least until he got to the third resident, a name that sent a thousand electric needles up his spine and into the back of his head. "Are you sure, Torville?"

"I'm sure. But I need to know what you intend to do with this information."

"Trust me, Torville, I haven't a clue, but they can draw and quarter me before I reveal my source. Not to worry."

Seth thanked him, hung up, and took the long way back to Department 16, clockwise around the perimeter of the fourth floor, trying to think.

TDA, "Father," a major vote on the future of the stealth program with the peace-dividend doves closing for what they thought would be an easy kill, and a stealth crash less than three weeks before the vote. A vote that could have killed the program and Sen. Stanford Traeger's political career along with it.

It was time for these events to be connected, which meant that for Seth Cameron, everything else could soon be coming apart.

"GENERAL, LET'S GET RIGHT TO IT. JUST BEFORE YOU CALLED MAJOR
Christopher at the Officers' Club, you received a call from the
Caicos Islands, isn't that right?"

"Your Honor," said Treadwell, his voice oozing contempt.
"Mr. Cameron's ability to wander afield is bordered neither by
the rules of evidence nor geography, and exceeded only by his
disdain for reality."

"Just state your objection, Mr. Treadwell," said Judge Singer,
his patience obviously frayed, "so that I may sustain it!"

"Irrelevant, argumentative, and patently ludicrous!"

"Sustained on the first two grounds, although the court con-
curs with the third as well."

"Your Honor," said Seth, "permit me to argue the matter at
sidebar."

Judge Singer reluctantly allowed the lawyers to come forward
and, after hearing argument, even more reluctantly reversed himself on the basis of Seth's representation that he was "now prepared to prove that Sam Barton was not scheduled to fly on the
night of the fifteenth."

"You may answer the question, sir."

The general didn't blink. "I did not receive such a call."

Seth walked closer to the witness and held up a phone bill so
that Farnsworth could see him reading off it. "Let me be more
precise. *Isn't it a fact that you received a call from the Beach Cliff
Hotel on Kew in the Caicos Islands at precisely 11:03 P.M., central
time, on the evening of October fifteenth, 1992?*"

The general blinked. His eyes flickered to Traeger, then to
Treadwell. "It's possible," he said, his jaw and neck muscles
jumping as if he had swallowed a live fish, "but I don't recall."

Seth waved the bill in his direction. "You *may* have, is that your testimony?"

Farnsworth glanced at Treadwell again. Seeing no relief forthcoming, he looked Seth squarely in the eye. "I may have."

"And if you did—which I assure you is the case—who would have been calling from the other end?"

Treadwell started to object, but let it go.

"*If* I received such a call, I don't remember who it might have come from."

"Or *why* a person—who *might* have been calling you—*might* have called you from an obscure island over three thousand miles away?"

"I don't remember."

The words were pouring from Seth's mouth like bullets from an Uzi. "Or *why* a person—who *might* have called you and *might* have called from an obscure island more than three thousand miles away—*might* have called you just fifty-seven minutes before midnight?"

"*Objection!* Counsel is berating the witness with his sarcastic manner. He's also assuming facts not in evidence."

"Without conceding either point, Your Honor, I'll withdraw the last question." Seth stole a glance at the jury. They were alert, but obviously couldn't tell where he was going with all this; not surprising, since Seth wasn't sure either.

"Let's see, General, 23:03 hours—three minutes past eleven—would make it predawn back there in the Caicos Islands, would it not?"

"I suppose so."

"Is this something that happens to you a lot, General? Getting mysterious calls late at night from mysterious places?"

"Objection," said Treadwell, affecting a bored, condescending tone. "Argumentative."

"Sustained," said the judge.

Seth walked back to counsel table and slipped the document, his current Marin County Pacific Bell telephone bill, under a notepad.

"Isn't it a fact that you received a call from the Caicos Islands at 23:03 hours, night of the fifteenth, *that resulted in Sam Barton, an unscheduled pilot, being ordered into the air?*"

Seth knew he was pulling the pin from a hand grenade, but

he had underestimated its explosive force. Treadwell leapt to his feet screaming, the Defense Department lawyers barged right through the rail and charged the bench, demanding a conference in chambers, Senator Traeger made a move toward the door, and General Farnsworth looked as if he were going to take a swing at Seth. The front end of the courtroom looked like a prison riot. Chinese New Year's. *Marat/Sade.*

Judge Singer hammered his gavel in an attempt to restore order while the jury and the press shouted at each other, trying to figure out what it all meant.

When things began to settle, Judge Singer sent the Defense Department lawyers back to their seats under threat of a contempt citation and ordered the bailiff to exclude anyone who failed to maintain complete silence. But when Seth said he intended to call Senator Traeger as his next witness, another melee ensued.

Judge Singer gave his gavel another workout and, when things had quieted down again, ordered the witness to answer.

This brought the junior Defense Department lawyer to his feet, strenuously objecting to this line of questioning from his seat in the first row of the gallery. At a glance from the judge, the bailiff escorted him out of the courtroom.

"Of course not," said Farnsworth, finally answering the question.

"Let me get this clear, General. You're not sure about taking the call, but you're sure about what you didn't say?"

"Your Honor!" Treadwell was almost whining.

"I would have remembered that," said Farnsworth.

"Would you also remember threatening me at Nellis Air Force Base in Las Vegas when I came to talk to Gerald Murphy?"

"I remember speaking to you. There were no threats."

"Didn't you tell me you'd shoot me as a spy if I returned to Symington?"

"That's absurd."

"Didn't you tell me I was getting into something way over my head?"

"No, but you are, Counselor. Your case makes no sense whatsoever."

Seth exchanged a long look with the general, then scratched

the back of his head and broke into a broad smile. The courtroom was as silent as a church. "So that's what you think, General?"

"Yes, Mr. Cameron, that's what I think."

Seth broke into a smile and began to bob his head up and down, looking slightly deranged as he stared into the general's fierce eyes. Abruptly then, he slapped both hands against his chest, looked up at the ceiling, and emitted a quiet chuckle. "You know something, General?" he said at last. "You are a lying son of a bitch, but on that point I have to agree with you."

"*Your Honor!*" shouted Treadwell in a reflex action, but then refrained from moving to strike the remark from the record.

"I withdraw the comment, Your Honor, with apologies to the court, and call my next witness. Call Senator Stanford Traeger."

"Your Honor," repeated Treadwell, again taking on a petulant tone.

"*Counsel approach the bench!*"

Seth hated these sidebar conversations, jostling arm against arm with Treadwell. "Sorry, Judge, but the guy *is* a liar and—"

"Listen to me, Mr. Cameron! I've sat on this bench for more than twenty years, and I've neither seen nor heard of anything like this. You seem determined to turn my courtroom into a theater of the absurd, and I won't have it. In a single morning you've admitted the statute of limitations has run against your client and just now that your case makes no sense whatsoever. You have conceded everything except that you are not really even a lawyer, and if that's coming next, I want you to know I'll not be in the least surprised. Now step back, both of you!"

The gavel came down hard as the judge declared the court in recess until two. Seth turned to see Allyn and Lev filing out with the crowd just ahead of Si Stephens, who gave him a troubled look as he disappeared out the door.

Back at the office, Elena, Allyn, Lev, and Seth ate sandwiches in silence until Elena couldn't stand it anymore and demanded to know what Seth was up to.

"Sometimes you got to shake the tree to get the fruit," he said.

"Meaning?"

"Meaning, sometimes you got to shake the tree to—"

Elena slammed her clenched hands down on the desk so hard that some of Lev's Dr Pepper spilled into his lap.

"*Stop it, you nut case!* Save your backwoods homilies for your friends in Modesto!"

"Bakersfield," whispered Allyn as she lit up a cigar.

"Bastards. All of you! Now I've not only got Uncle Tony's army against me but my own lawyers as well!"

Seth and Allyn exchanged a look. "Not necessarily," said Allyn. "Seth, I must admit I'm a little curious myself, concerning your, uh . . . strategy."

"I'm open to suggestions, Allyn," said Seth, lighting a cigarette and dropping the match next to his unfinished sandwich. "Quite frankly, I haven't figured one out yet." He took a deep drag, then blew smoke out the open window. "I'm working on it."

"*Working on it?*"

"Well, Elena, if you're sure you want to know, I don't think we've got a case here."

"Isn't it a bit late for that?" said Elena.

Allyn nodded reluctant concurrence. "Confidence like that might turn you into a prophet, but it won't win a hell of a lot of cases."

"I'm rarely short on confidence, Allyn, but there's the little matter of us all knowing deep in our hearts that there's no fucking way Sam leaves the club at eleven-thirty and gets to Arizona by one-twenty."

Elena's face bloomed red as she railed against Seth, Treadwell, her father, and "that wimpy jerk sitting on the bench!"

Seth took a sip of Maalox.

"What the hell happened," she demanded, "to the art of advocacy?"

Then he lit a new cigarette. "It's alive and well," he said, "but not equipped to alter reality." Lev reached for Seth's sandwich, and Allyn put her feet up on her cluttered desk. Elena paced around the small office, her arms clasped tightly together.

"And just what is the 'reality' in this case, may I ask?"

"I'm not sure yet," said Seth, "but I aim to find out."

"And just how do you propose to do that?"

Seth flashed her a crooked smile. "The art of advocacy."

"Oh, *shit*," she said. "There must be a half million lawyers in the U.S., and I have to draw a certifiable lunatic."

"Madonna here's got a point, Seth," said Allyn. "Not about you being a lunatic, though the jury's still out on that one. I was in the courtroom this morning, and I can tell you those twelve folks smell a government rat big as ol' Lev over there. They don't like Farnsworth, and he's become identified with ConSpace. Plus you got the good senator, who's unlikable on sight—it should be a fucking misdemeanor just to walk around looking like he does. I mean, *Jesus!* No offense, Mrs. Barton, but that ugly fucking insect couldn't be your biological father."

"Don't look at me," said Lev, letting out a cackle.

"Anyway, Seth," continued Allyn, "if they believe Sam didn't expect to fly the night he was sent up, I think they'll clobber ConSpace—despite your client's ... nocturnal intemperance."

Seth felt everyone watching him. Elena apparently knew better than to wreck the moment by saying anything and settled for walking over and resting her hand on his shoulder. Seth was surprised to find her touch mildly offensive. All feeling for her was gone at last, his once-consuming passion now just a corpse stuffed into a trunk. He got up and walked over to Allyn's window, stared across Market and up at the high-rise buildings of the Montgomery Street financial district.

"You can still win, Seth," said Allyn, reaching for Elena's unfinished tuna melt. "Put Traeger on and nail the little bastard."

Everybody piled into Lev's car, but Seth asked to be dropped off a block from City Hall. He needed time alone, time to think. It was one of those miraculous San Francisco days, clear and low seventies, the air coming in fresh and clean off the bay. People eating outside and milling about in shirtsleeves and short skirts. People enjoying the good life.

Ten minutes later, as the elevator doors opened to the darkened fourth-floor lobby, he found himself looking at Stanford Traeger and the senior Defense Department lawyer, Harold Baldwin.

"A word, Counselor?" said Baldwin, a lanky, completely bald lawyer in his fifties.

"Can't hardly stop you," said Seth, walking toward Department 16, pushing through the lunchtime crowd.

"I have reserved a small conference room right here in the law library. I just need five minutes, and it might be the most important five minutes in your life, certainly in your client's life."

Seth stopped for a wheelchair being pushed by a young woman whose face was twisted with suffering. The man had no legs. A woman lawyer walked beside them carrying a trial bag in one hand and blown-up pictures of an intersection in the other.

"Five minutes," Seth said.

Inside the small room the lawyer was all business. His voice sounded like a computer, no words wasted. Traeger looked out the window, saying nothing. He tried to maintain his imperious presence, but could not conceal an anxiety that filled the room like the smell of a dead animal.

"I'll come to the point, Counselor," said Baldwin. "You've got us by the balls and you probably don't even know why. Moreover, you don't need to. All you need to know is that you have somehow obtained a piece of evidence that could trigger great damage to our nation's defense effort and to the integrity of our government as well."

"You mean the integrity of a pair of defense contractors, a certain senator, and a certain air force, don't you?"

"Have it your way, sir, if you really believe any functioning government can be separated from the essential agencies of which it is necessarily comprised."

"Come again?" said Seth, raising his eyebrows. "Look, Mr. Baldwin, I've never been one for splittin' hairs and fancy semantic distinctions. We're both talking about the same thing: something that would make Watergate look like a cotillion intermission."

"Yes, well, let me get to the point. I obviously do not represent the defendant here, and though the senator and I have tried to broker a settlement of your case, I have been unable to do so. ConSpace and its counsel have every reason to believe that the judge will grant their statute motion now or throw out any verdict you might get—in the unlikely event you should get a verdict at all. Given the public attention to this trial, ConSpace now demands full, public vindication."

Seth looked at his watch. "You said something about getting to the point."

"We—the government—make the following offers, in return for your agreement to revoke your decision to call Senator Traeger as a witness, or to otherwise exhume various . . . delicate matters, wholly unnecessary to your case." Baldwin handed Seth a notarized document. Traeger stared at steepled fingers.

"First, this is a notarized statement by the senator here, detailing his role in TDA, admitting his violations of state and federal securities law as well as U.S. Senate ethics codes, et cetera, et cetera. The statement—confession, if you will—fully implicates his confederate Aubrey Olmstead, a resident of Kew, corporate headquarters of TDA, whom the Justice Department has unsuccessfully pursued for years. This may be of more than passing interest to your employer, whom we know has brought a stockholders' class action.

"I also hand you a copy of Senator Traeger's letter of resignation from the Senate, effective immediately.

"Next, as informal amicus to the court, I will inform Judge Singer in the strongest possible terms that the government sees no merit whatsoever to the statute-of-limitations defense in light of the persuasive testimony by Christopher and the Lukenses on the point. I think I can say with reasonable assurance that he will rule accordingly.

"Finally, in the event you agree to rest your case without calling Senator Traeger to the stand, I am authorized to lodge with the court a certified flight schedule showing that Captain Barton was not—I repeat was *not*—scheduled to fly on the night of October fifteenth, 1992."

"Is that it?" said Seth, glancing at the red-faced, shrinking senator.

"My God, man," said Baldwin, "what else could you want? Isn't it obvious that with the statute defense dead and Captain Barton's drinking excused, you can have your victory in this case and, at the same time, minimize what could be irreparable damage to the nation's security and the integrity of the—"

"I think you've covered that. I assume the 'damage' you're referring to is the fact that federal officers with badges have been running around the country murdering innocent citizens."

"That's an unwarranted assumption."

"Maybe, but it doesn't inspire much confidence in my own future longevity."

"We've thought of that. You can make any provision for your future safe conduct you deem appropriate. I believe a registered if-something-should-happen-to-me package to *The New York Times* or *Washington Post* is the most popular modus operandi. You will not be in jeopardy, although once you accept our offer, there would obviously be consequences should you later choose to reveal what you know."

"You mean you'd kill me."

"Of course not. But you would be charged with criminal conspiracy, accessory after the fact—"

Seth stood up, adding, "Et cetera, et cetera."

Small grunts of suppressed rage kept coming out of Traeger, who looked as if he were going to explode.

"Won't Mr. Et Cetera here let you say anything, Stan? Never known a politician to be so quiet."

Traeger bared his teeth and began to spit out words in a manner that reminded Seth of a professional-wrestling commercial. "I'll spend a good part of the rest of my life in a federal prison for what I'm admitting in this document, Cameron. I hope you appreciate what we're giving you."

"You'd be getting something back, Traeger, though nothing of value."

"Like what?"

"Your miserable fucking life. The penalty for conspiracy to commit murder is death, Senator."

Traeger grunted disdainfully. "Trying to prove homicide will accomplish nothing other than wrecking your own chances for what could be a major verdict."

"Might get you fried," said Seth, giving the senator a wide grin. "And speaking of dying, what about Farnsworth? A whole bunch of people got killed over this thing."

"He will cop to complicity in the TDA fraud," said Baldwin, "though of course he had nothing to do with it. He has agreed to accept postdated stock in the company for his 'part' in it. And his invented involvement in TDA is mentioned in the senator's confession."

"So he'll admit to what he didn't do and deny what he did."

"You could say that."

"I believe I just did," said Seth, then turned back to the senator. "How did you get Farnsworth to kill those people."

"I didn't tell anyone to kill *anyone!* Christ, I just told that idiot Farnsworth to control the situation, not to *kill* people."

"That's what's always amazed me about you guys," said Seth, grabbing his briefcase and walking to the door. "You recruit tough guys, train them to kill people, then seemed surprised when they do."

Ten minutes before two and there she was, standing at the door to Department 16, looking lost.

"Rosie. Thanks for coming."

She smiled, though she had to work at it.

"You okay?" he said.

"Just feeling a little guilty, I guess." Her voice was thin as oxygen.

Seth put a hand on her arm. "Forget it. I'm glad you got all that stuff off your chest. You did the right thing."

"No, I mean about phoning in sick. I've never done that."

Seth smiled for the first time in weeks, touched as always by her innocence and candor.

"So how's it going?" she asked. "You look jumpy and awful tired."

"Last time you told me I looked different."

She smiled at that and Seth walked her down the hall, then a few steps down the next corridor to avoid observation by jurors or other lawyers returning from lunch. He told her everything in quick, jerky sentences as he bounced from one foot to another, as jittery as a subway cop. His neurons were firing in an electric frenzy, making it hard to synchronize his mouth with his brain.

Rosie, her eyes wide with concern and wonder, threw in a question now and then, but mainly just listened. When he was finished, they stared at each other as if they were getting ready to jump into a volcano.

"I don't know what to say, Seth. I know how important this case could be to you."

Seth said yeah, it sure could be, then turned and bent over an ashtray mounted on the wall.

"Seth! That's not a water fountain!"

"Oh. Right. Thanks."

"How long since you had a decent night's rest?"

"Tomorrow I rest."

"So what are you going to do today? Now?"

Seth glanced down the hall. "You're good with dreams, Rosie. I'm climbing the face of a cliff, chasing this bird or something that stays just out of reach. I'm scared, but I keep climbing until

I reach the next plateau, where there's always the dead body of someone who died on the way up. Sometimes I go through three levels with a different body at each one. Wake up sweating like a pig."

"I'm still a little weak at the interpretation end, Seth."

Seth saw Treadwell putting a cigarette out down at the end of the hall. Rosie followed his gaze.

"How much does Treadwell know about all this?"

"I don't know," said Seth, rubbing the corners of his eyes with his thumb and forefinger, then jiggling his head to ease the pain in his neck. "Maybe everything, maybe nothing. Oh, oh."

"What?"

"This guy coming up the hall. Name's Si Stephens. He's been in and out of the trial, checking me out."

"Checking you out?"

"Hi, there, Seth," said Stephens, extending his hand and giving Rosie the once-over. "All work and no play, right?"

Seth managed a sickly smile. "Hello, Si. This is my friend from Bakersfield, Rosie Wheeler."

"I'm pleased to meet you, Mr. Stephens."

"My pleasure, Rosie. Our friend here has a tough one on his hands and can use a little moral support. Right, Seth?"

Seth shrugged. "It's a tough one."

"Never seen anything like this. Got everybody talking. The word's out about the hundred-and-fifty-thousand-dollar offer! You must be planning to ring the bell big time, Seth. Good luck, buddy."

Seth nodded and forced another smile.

"Don't forget," added Stephens as he turned to leave, "you win, you're in."

"In?" said Rosie. "In what?"

"Caldwell and Shaw, as a partner. He's a partner there."

"*Caldwell and Shaw?* He looks too young and happy."

Seth shrugged.

Rosie searched Seth's eyes, ducking and darting around his face like an ophthalmologist. "So what *are* you going to do?"

Seth looked at his watch, picked up his briefcase, and gave her hand a hard squeeze.

"Thanks for coming," he said, and followed the defense entourage back into the jammed courtroom.

* * *

"Call your next witness, Mr. Cameron, and I think I speak for this exhausted jury when I express my fervent hope that it's your *last* witness."

Several heads in the jury box nodded in agreement. Even the inscrutable and taciturn Mr. Stanton smiled ruefully at the judge.

"Yes, Your Honor," said Seth without looking up. He was slouched down in his seat, his legs crossed, doodling on a legal pad, his left arm dangled carelessly over the back of his chair.

"Well?"

Seth slowly shook his head. All eyes were on him now, and he knew it. His stomach burned as if a soldering iron had been jammed through his navel.

"We're not going through this again, Mr. Cameron, are we?" asked the judge in a flint-edged voice. "You have thirty seconds in which to call another witness or rest your case."

Seth sucked in an audible deep breath and exhaled himself to his feet.

"Your Honor has not ruled on the statute defense on the Barton case."

"I was going to give you my ruling after you finished presenting your case, Counsel, but I will do so now, since you appear to have been seized by another attack of Hamletian indecisiveness."

Suppressed laughter leaked from the defense side of counsel table.

"I conclude that the facts, interpreted in the light most favorably to the plaintiff—as I must do—require that I deny the defendant's motion for dismissal."

That killed the laughter. Seth shot a look at Treadwell, but could read nothing into his expression. He felt Harold Baldwin's eyes on him though, as palpable as a touch on the shoulder.

"Now, Mr. Cameron, might we move along?"

"Yes, Your Honor." Then, in a thin, barely audible voice, Seth added, "The plaintiff rests."

The judge shot a withering glance in the direction of Baldwin and Traeger, who had succumbed to a minor demonstration, whispering and shaking hands. They stopped in midsmile, however, and Judge Singer quietly put his gavel down. He then instructed Seth to commence his argument to the jury, but Harold

Baldwin leaned over the rail from his front-row seat and whispered something into Treadwell's' ear. The senior partner's jaw twitched and his eyes narrowed, but he shrugged and rose to his feet.

"May all counsel approach the bench, Your Honor?" he said. When they arrived at sidebar, Harold Baldwin handed Judge Singer some documents, then gave copies to Treadwell and Seth.

"The government, appearing as amicus curiáe herein, first offers this certified flight schedule, showing that Captain Barton had flown an X-215A test mission on the night of October thirteenth and was not scheduled to fly again for at least a week. It also shows that Lieutenant David Ames was originally scheduled for the night of October fifteenth. We also offer Lieutenant Ames's personnel records showing him to have been declared absent without leave as of twenty hundred hours—8:00 P.M.—that same night. Finally, with the permission and consent of Senator Stanford Traeger, we offer his notarized statement containing other significant information relevant to these proceedings."

"With all due respect to the government," said Treadwell, "I most strenuously object—"

But Judge Singer cut him off. "The only lawyer with standing to complain about this offer is Mr. Cameron. His earlier document request clearly embraced exactly this kind of evidence, and it should have been produced at that time."

"I can explain that, Your Honor," said Baldwin. "Note the security classification status. Not even Mr. Treadwell was aware of this information. I have just now obtained clearance from the Pentagon and am bringing the matter to the court's attention despite my personal misgivings—in the interest of justice."

"So we were *not* stonewalling," urged Treadwell, raising his voice, his eyebrows, and his shoulders all at once, "and damn it we *object!*"

Seth elbowed his way in front of Treadwell. "I'd like to remind the court who it was that introduced this whole issue of—"

"Captain Barton's drinking," said Judge Singer. "I need no reminding, Mr. Cameron. I've suffered through the evidence like everybody else. I assume you have no objection?"

"Better late than never, Your Honor," said Seth.

"All right, the documents will be admitted into evidence. To minimize its last-minute impact, Mr. Treadwell, I will simply instruct the jury that they are to assume that Barton was not scheduled to fly that night. You may frame your closing arguments accordingly."

Treadwell gave Baldwin a withering glance, but the government lawyer didn't notice. His eyes were fixed on Seth. But Seth didn't notice, because his eyes were fixed on Treadwell, still wondering where he fit into all this. If he was acting, thought Seth, he was good at that, too.

"Step back, Counsel," said the judge. "Let's wrap this damnable case."

Judge Singer apologized to the jury and instructed Seth to proceed with his argument.

As Seth walked back toward counsel table, he glanced at the expectant face of Si Stephens, sitting two rows in front of Rosie, who looked as if she were about to take flight. He gave her a little smile, but Stephens intercepted it and smiled back at him. He turned his gaze to Elena and noticed for the first time that her hair was growing back out—*my God, how long have we been in this nightmare?*—and that she had resumed the use of full makeup. She had become the glamorous Elena again without his noticing. Glamorous Elena now offered him a nod of encouragement, her cool green eyes full of renewed promise as she awaited the justice that was her due. What madness, he wondered, could drive a man to risk everything for such a woman? To believe for a minute that he knew a damn thing about her? Or about himself, for that matter.

The judge cleared his throat.

Judge Singer. There's another piece of work. The system would always survive as long as men like the judge could be induced to serve it. Firm, but fair; earnest, but not lacking in humor; intelligent, but humble and even-handed.

He glanced back the other way. Three rows back on the right side sat Allyn and Lev. What smart, brave souls they were! How could he ever repay them? Allyn winked, and Lev gave him a subtle thumbs-up in his lap that unwittingly came off as an obscene gesture. Seth broke out laughing.

"I'm sorry, folks. Your Honor. Sorry. But really . . ."

He started laughing again. All he could think about was Lev's giant thumb rising up out of his lap. His fatigue was giving way to hysteria, and he started laughing again, so hard this time his body convulsed, and he fell against counsel table—Treadwell's end—tears streaming from lunatic eyes.

"*Mr. Cameron!*" said Judge Singer. "I'm calling a recess of five minutes in which you will either gain control of yourself or be deemed to have waived your right to argument."

Seth reacted to the admonition by pulling himself into a reasonably erect posture and forcing his face into an expression much like that of a drunk driver confronting an arresting officer: eyebrows tilted innocently, lips in a tight smile, radiating penitence.

"No, Your Honor, please. I'm . . . all right. It's just that, well, it's just that I'm tired and . . . Oh, Jesus, am I tired."

He walked toward the jury box, trying to suppress small outbursts of laughter that kept escaping in the form of something sounding like hiccups. Sophie Byers wasn't fooled and started giggling, but some of the jurors recoiled from him as if they were being accosted by a panhandling crackhead. Others leaned forward in amused curiosity, but all had their eyes riveted on the clownish figure before them.

"I'm tired of all the confusion, just like you are, folks. I'm tired of dealing with Mr. Treadwell over there and all his roadies and groupies. Oh, hell, I'm sick and tired of this whole damn lawsuit—if that's what it is."

Seth was vaguely aware of murmurings from the gallery, of Elena loudly clearing her throat, of strange looks flying toward him out of the jury box, but he couldn't stop the outpouring of words his brain was involuntarily generating.

"Well, hold on, folks, I didn't mean that. This is a lawsuit, all right." Seth spread his arms wide and swung them one hundred and eighty degrees in both directions. "We're in a courtroom, aren't we? There are pleadings on file, right? We've got a judge, and we've got a plaintiff sitting here glaring at me. There's a defendant—Mr. Leffingwell—sitting right over there."

Seth paused for a moment, then glanced to his right at Elena. He shook his head and opened his palms toward her in apology. "There's only one problem, folks. Mrs. Barton here isn't the *right* plaintiff . . . *because it wasn't her husband in the X-215A the night it crashed!*"

The courtroom erupted, and Treadwell rose to object—until he realized he had just won his case and dropped back into his seat.

Elena gasped, and a newspaper reporter raced out the door. The jurors looked at the judge, who pounded his gavel and started to speak, but Seth had never stopped and now raised his voice over the din.

"Which means the real plaintiff should have been the widow of poor old David Ames, *because* he's *the pilot this document shows was the scheduled pilot that night, and* he's *the man who crashed in the desert on the night of October fifteenth, 1992!"*

Judge Singer again pounded his gavel, but the courtroom was in chaos. Finally, the judge achieved silence and Seth continued.

"You see, I now know when the flight of the X-215A began, and when it ended. I know *where* it ended and I've known for a long what *caused* it to end. The only thing I hadn't figured out until a few minutes ago was who was at the controls when it crashed."

Seth glanced at General Farnsworth, then back at the jury. *"It wasn't Sam Barton."*

A single gasp went up from the gallery, and if Seth had looked to his right, he would have seen Elena's wide-open eyes imploring Judge Singer to do something. She was wasting her effort, for if Seth had looked to his left, he would have seen that Judge Singer's own wide-open eyes were viewing him with clinical fascination. And if Seth had turned around at that same moment, he would have seen Treadwell and Leffingwell in whispered consultation, and Traeger and Farnsworth exchanging concerned looks. But Seth looked in none of these directions. He was having a conversation with his jury.

"So, it's like this, folks. Sam wasn't in the X-215A that night, but he's dead all the same. What this means to you is that in the case against ConSpace, I've got the wrong plaintiff, and in the case against the people responsible for the death of Sam Barton, I've got the wrong defendant—a sorry comment, you might say, on my pleading skills."

Seth started to laugh again at the irony, but there was something about the twelve completely blank faces staring at him that was more sobering than if he had bitten his tongue. Embarrassed, he took a sip of water, then shrugged his shoulders and added, "Some days, folks, it just doesn't pay to get out of bed."

Susan Wanger, number eleven, smiled at this and ruefully

shook her head in agreement. Sophie Byers giggled. Edward Stanton looked astonished.

"You see, Sam Barton died that night, but it wasn't the X-215A that killed him. Sam Barton was murdered in cold blood by his best friend—"

"Your Honor!"

"By his best friend, Major Jack Christopher, under orders of General Clement Farnsworth—"

"YOUR HONOR!"

"—who had been instructed to 'keep things under control' by United States Senator Stanford Traeger—"

This time there was no controlling the explosion in the courtroom. The gallery was on its feet, most reporters racing for the door, some backtracking, fearful they might miss something. The ever-present gavel was splattering molecules but getting no respect. The spectators finally quieted themselves when they realized Seth was still talking, reading from something that seemed to be an admission of various crimes and misdemeanors by Senator Traeger.

Treadwell, looking as surprised as anyone by the bizarre turn of events, dutifully objected again, but his heart didn't seem to be in it. In fact, if someone had looked closely at the senior partner during Seth's recitation, they might have detected the shadow of a smile on his worn face as he assessed the situation and, as was his nature, already began to count his profit and loss. Later, he would celebrate the preponderance of the former over the latter with his wife, Charlotte, over a bottle of fine Bordeaux. With her, and with her alone, he would share his secret pleasure as he realized that the maverick kid had, in one reckless, ironic stroke, not only exculpated ConSpace from any possible damages in the Barton case, but had *inculpated* Stanford Traeger of numerous felonies—the man who had unjustly delayed his ascension to the helm at M&M for those five bitter and humiliating years.

Seth continued to chronicle the history of TDA, annotating Traeger's confession with editorial comments—tracing the senator's alter ego as Olmstead's "Father" figure, and the Faustian bargain struck between Herbert Leffingwell and Traeger leading to the incorporation of the flawed TDA canopy system.

Judge Singer was pounding his gavel again.

"Your Honor," said Treadwell, "there is not a shred of evidence that—"

"Let him finish, Mr. Treadwell," said Judge Singer. "You've won your case, and damn it, we're entitled to an explanation of all this, even if it's his. You'll have your turn. But let's do stay with *this* case, Mr. Cameron, not some future criminal prosecution."

"Yes, Your Honor. Here's how I think it all happened, ladies and gentlemen. You must have suspected that Sam Barton couldn't have left the club at eleven-thirty, completed preflight, and crashed in Arizona by one-twenty. They don't make 'em quite that fast yet. I believe it to be a fair inference from the evidence," said Seth, glancing at Treadwell, "that by eleven-thirty, the body of David Ames was already stiffening in the cockpit of the crashed X-215A. Yes, the statute had run, even if it had been Barton in the cockpit."

"Excuse me, Counselor," said Judge Singer, resting his forehead in the palm of one hand. "It may seem but a grain of sand on the beach of your theory, but aren't you forgetting the testimony of the Lukenses, *your* key witnesses, on whose sworn testimony I largely based my ruling on the statute?"

"I believe what they saw was a secondary fire, Your Honor, probably set by Farnsworth and Christopher to make the body switch believ—"

"The *what?*" said Treadwell and Judge Singer in unison.

"Look, I'm guessing at some of this, but weird as it sounds, it's the only plausible explanation. A third X-215A crash meant big trouble for some very big people. You all heard Elena Barton and Major Christopher testify that Sam Barton had become a lightning rod at Symington and had openly threatened to go public with his case that the X-215A was a flying coffin, a disclosure that would probably have killed Farnsworth's and Traeger's Stealth Program, and, more importantly, their careers."

The gallery roared its excitement again, and the last of the newspaper reporters with deadlines raced for telephones. Judge Singer picked up his impotent gavel. But the crowd saw that Seth was still speaking and turned silent again.

"Let's play homicide cop for a minute, ladies and gentlemen.

"*Motive?* Plenty. Senator Traeger was not only a major stockholder in TDA, but chairman of the Armed Forces subcommittee responsible for the success of the Stealth Program. Farnsworth there, then a mere full colonel, ran the X-215A testing program and managed to come out of it a general. After the third crash, they both knew that Sam Barton had to be silenced in a way that would not create suspicion. As for Christopher, ask yourselves who stood between him and Elena Barton? Her husband, of course. Christopher also mysteriously won his major's leaves ahead of everyone else in his class. Was that because he was that good or because he was that *bad?* Most officers would have refused Farnsworth's order to kill Barton—have seen it as bizarre and outrageous; I believe Christopher saw it as an opportunity.

"*Means?* Between Traeger and Farnsworth, they literally had an army of trained killers at their disposal. And used them.

"*Opportunity?* We know that Christopher was the last person to see Sam alive, so it's logical to assume he was also the first to see him dead. Following orders, of course, like those guys claimed at Nuremberg." Seth turned and fixed his eyes on Christopher. "It took me too long to figure it out, Crispie, but I finally remembered that only Elena and I knew that Gerald Murphy was ready to blow the whistle on whatever he knew at my scheduled meeting with him in Las Vegas. I didn't tell anybody and Murphy damn sure didn't. That left Elena and pillow talk with you."

The jury looked puzzled, never having heard of Gerald Murphy, as Seth now turned his gaze on his client. "Remember, Elena? You told me that you had reported to Christopher about Murphy's willingness to talk to me. You told me he seemed 'enthusiastic.' You had no way of knowing, of course, but that slip cost Murphy his life.

"So that's it, folks. I know this is no laughing matter, but the irony got to me. Broke me down. Here I got a crooked senator, a murderous general, a felonious canopy supplier, a negligent aircraft builder, a roving pack of cold-blooded killers with federal-marshal badges, acting under orders for Traeger and Farnsworth . . . and none of it adds up to any significant damages against the negligent defendant here because poor old Sam Barton just wasn't in that airplane when it crashed on the night of October fifteenth, 1992."

Elena gasped, causing Seth to turn in her direction. Her eyes had gone dead, bleached out above sagging cheeks and lips thinned into a straight line. Her fingers and knuckles were white from being squeezed together, and still they shook as if connected to a jackhammer. Abruptly, she rose to her feet and, without so much as a glance at Seth, made for the exit, eyes down and streaming with tears, but chin up and head erect, as if she were a model walking down a runway. Seth knew she was learning all this for the first time and didn't blame her for leaving. Even Elena had her limits.

Traeger got to his feet and started to follow his daughter out the door, but Judge Singer ordered the bailiff to return him to his seat. As a precaution, the judge instructed Farnsworth and Christopher to remain seated as well.

Seth saw that Si Stephens had also risen and was standing with hands on his hips, looking at him through incredulous eyes, his features twisted into a pretzel of exasperation. Rosie Wheeler followed Seth's gaze in time to see Stephens turn and disdainfully push his way through the door.

Seth knew that Stephens would not be returning this time.

Anthony Treadwell took advantage of the lull to make a motion for dismissal, but the judge silenced him, saying, "I've suffered through this thing just like the rest of you, and I want to hear how this travesty ends. Your motion will be taken up in due course, Mr. Treadwell."

But Seth stood transfixed, staring at the courtroom door, still swinging from Stephens's departure. "Will there be anything else, Mr. Cameron?" said Judge Singer, his voice now taking on the quietly respectful tone of a headwaiter at the end of a meal. Seth's gaze shifted back toward Rosie, who looked so pale Seth thought she might be ill. But when their eyes met, she managed a proud smile. He nodded, acknowledging the feeling passing between them, then turned back to address Judge Singer.

"That's about it, Your Honor, except for this. For me, ladies and gentlemen, this case started out as a quest to clear a good man's name—at least that's what I told myself. But what I really wanted was a chance to establish myself as a hotshot trial lawyer. Someone who could take on that elegant three-piece mouth sitting over there and beat the hell out of him."

Seth turned and glanced at Rosie again. She had raised a hand to her mouth, and he could see diamond tears glistening on her cheeks in the cold light of the courtroom.

"Okay, so I didn't pull it off, but that doesn't mean your work is finished. Not yet. See, folks, we could sit around here and wring our hands about having the wrong guy in the White House, a U.S. senator off to the 'big house,' and a three-hundred-million-dollar airplane that flies like an outhouse—but there's one thing that still works around here, and believe it or not, it's the judicial system.

"Meaning you.

"Yes, you folks can still clear Sam Barton's name and the names of four other fine pilots who *did* go down in the X-215A, including Lieutenant Lee Andrews, the last pilot to die before they got rid of the TDA system. These were brave, good men, who died in the service of their country as honorably as wartime military heroes; top pilots who were at war and didn't even know it—at war with greed and deceit. When ConSpace entered into an unholy alliance with TDA at the behest of a United States senator, it bartered away the lives of four good men.

"How can you restore honor to their names? Well, here comes another irony. You see, Elena Barton is alive, but her case is dead as yesterday's beer. Ben Tucker, on the other hand, is dead, but his case is very much alive. And his estate is entitled to your finding that the reason Grant Wilburn crashed was the negligence of the defendant, not pilot error.

"Your verdict—though for relatively small change—will send a loud and clear message to our government, and to all its contractors, that the brave people who serve this country are entitled to that extra sixty bucks' worth of safety.

"Finally, you need not concern yourselves with Senator Traeger, General Farnsworth, and Major Jack Christopher. Rest assured, folks: other courts—criminal courts—will deal with them.

"Thank you."

Seth abruptly took his seat. Nobody moved. Nobody. Judge Singer and the jury kept watching him, as if wanting even more. The courtroom had never known such silence.

"Mr. Treadwell," said the judge finally, "your summation?"

Treadwell rose to his feet, but stayed in place behind his table and made a brief, perfunctory closing, "given the admission by counsel that you can award no damages to Elena Barton in this case—not one dime." He glanced at Seth, who nodded his agreement without looking up. Treadwell closed with a denial of negligence and the assertion that the plaintiff's proof on defective manufacture was based solely on circumstantial evidence.

Seth's final argument was equally brief. He didn't even stand up.

"The amount of Tucker's damages—$25,000, plus $4,500 in lost rents—has been stipulated, ladies and gentlemen. The cause—a crashed X-215A—stipulated as well. As for our proof on defective manufacture, of *course* it's largely circumstantial. Did any of you expect that parade of trained seals from ConSpace to come in here and admit they screwed up?

"But there's this to be said for circumstantial evidence: it comes into the courtroom without motive or bias. It doesn't have a reason to lie. It doesn't pontificate. It just *is*. And what it told you is what you already knew: apply enough friction to any material, it wears out. Throw in Traeger's admissions, and that's Tucker's case."

When he had finished, Seth turned around and saw that four men in gray suits, one wearing dark glasses, had entered the courtroom and taken up positions on either side of the door. Treadwell resumed his seat at counsel table and the court excused the jury for the afternoon recess, but ordered counsel to remain to resolve any final motions and the jury instructions Judge Singer would soon be giving. Everyone else was ordered from the courtroom, and Traeger, Farnsworth, and Christopher were taken into custody by the FBI agents summoned by Judge Singer.

Traeger gave way to his frustration, refusing to be handled by the agent, and finally had to be forcibly cuffed. "I'm a United States senator, you morons!" he shouted, then directed his rage against Seth. "Cameron!" he shouted as an agent guided him past Seth and up the aisle. "You double-dealing bastard! I'll deny everything! I'll beat this thing and get you for this!"

Seth didn't look up as the senator was escorted past him.

Next came Farnsworth, more resigned, his discipline seemingly unimpaired by things now clearly beyond his control. But as he was led past counsel table, he, too, glared at Seth. "*Why?*" he demanded, halting his forward progress for an instant. He seemed genuinely offended. "What happened? Didn't we keep our end of it?"

"Cameron!" shouted Christopher from behind Farnsworth, his anger unrestrained as he grappled with the steel cuffs behind his back. "What the hell's the matter with you, you crazy bastard? You blew it for everybody, even yourself. *Why?*"

Seth seemed not to hear them at first. Then he stopped piling papers into his briefcase and looked over his shoulder at his tormentors, answering in a voice so low they had to strain to hear.

"For one thing, you shouldn't have killed my dog."

TREADWELL MOVED FOR A DISMISSAL OF THE BARTON CASE BASED ON Seth's admissions and the motion was granted. The jury then received its instructions from the court on the Tucker estate's property-damage claim. As the jurors filed out of the courtroom behind the bailiff to begin their deliberations, Judge Singer asked to see lead counsel in chambers. Rosie followed Allyn and Lev into the hallway.

Seth and Treadwell stood at their respective tables, packing their trial bags. Another eerie silence descended on the courtroom, broken finally by Treadwell's hushed baritone voice.

"Cameron?"

"Yes?"

"I knew nothing of this. Any of it."

"Okay."

"I hope that you can believe this. My advocacy blinded me to what was going on."

Seth gave his head a little nod to acknowledge the closest thing to an apology the senior partner would ever offer.

"Gentlemen," said the clerk, "the judge will see you now."

Judge Singer smiled broadly at both of them and beckoned them to a chair.

"We don't see many of these," he said, "for which , at my age, I am most grateful." The judge came around from behind his desk, gave Treadwell a perfunctory handshake, saying, "Good job, Anthony, but aren't we both getting a little old for this?"

He then took Seth's hand. "You've been to hell and back, young man, and I fear you'll have precious little to show for it. So let me give you this for what it's worth: I have never seen a more creative demonstration of grit and tenacity in my thirty-eight years as a member of the bar; old-time advocacy that never rested and would not be constrained by the walls of this courtroom. You've been trained well—I understand nearly a year of it under your current adversary."

Seth smiled. "My father was a career court clerk, Judge. He was my teacher. The only thing Joe Cameron and my 'current adversary' have in common is that they both motivated me. Neither one of them thought I had the right stuff."

"And they were both wrong, son," said the judge, unembarrassed tears in his eyes. "I'll be watching your career with great interest."

Seth felt his own eyes moistening, and his legs starting to buckle. Fatigue was buffeting him like ten-foot waves.

A door opened and the bailiff leaned in. "They have a verdict, Judge. They didn't even pick a foreperson."

"Well, then, bring 'em back," said Judge Singer, donning his robe. "I've got my next case waiting for me down at Department One. I hope it's a simple six-month, multiple-defendant antitrust or securities case."

Even Treadwell laughed at the judge's attempt at humor, and as he and Seth reached the door at the same time, the senior partner held it open. "After you, Mr. Cameron."

After a brief, tense wait, the jury returned and Edward Stanton handed the clerk the verdict. It gave Elena nothing, of course, but declared InterContinental Aerospace guilty of negligent design and manufacture and provided the estate of Mr. Tucker sufficient money to repair the motel, together with modest lost rents. The verdict form was supplemented to include a recommendation that, if possible, the court order the U.S. Air Force to purge its files of "pilot error" determinations on all four pilots who had died in X-215A's.

A cheer went up from the gallery.

Judge Singer thanked the jurors for their service and excused them. Mr. Stanton paused at the rail, then turned back to Seth and shook his hand. He told Seth of his regret that their hands had been tied on damages.

"But I'll tell you this, son," he added, giving Seth's hand a final squeeze, "if a verdict could be rendered for heart, you would be a millionaire now."

As the last of the jurors filed out, most of them smiling at Judge Singer or Seth, Anthony Treadwell quickly packed his trial bag, then offered his hand to his adversary. "My client is content to have been spared significant damages, Cameron, but you and I know who won this case."

Seth shook Treadwell's hand and gave him a tired smile. "People who were no longer here to speak for themselves," Seth said. "They were the winners here."

A strange look crossed the senior partner's face as he looked into Seth's eyes, and he seemed about to say something, but Herbert Leffingwell walked up and the moment passed. "You're all over the lot, young man," said Leffingwell, "but you gain high marks for persistence. Better luck next time."

"Next time will be sooner than you think, Mr. Leffingwell," said Allyn, who had joined them unnoticed through the rail. "And next time, better luck is guaranteed."

"Pardon me?" said the amused executive. "Do I know you?"

"No, but you soon will. Name's Allyn Friedlander. Here's my card. I represent Mrs. Lee Andrews, widow of the last pilot killed before you replaced the TDA system."

"What?" said Leffingwell, no longer amused.

"*What?*" said Seth, equally surprised.

"I suggest, Mr. Leffingwell, that you put Mr. Treadwell here back on the job," Allyn continued. "He'll have some bad news for you. It's called collateral estoppel, which means that this jury's verdict of negligence in the Tucker case will be binding on ConSpace in the Andrews trial. All the plaintiff will have to do now is get out the calculator and tote up damages—we're talking mid-seven-figures here, Mr. Leffingwell."

Everyone stared at Allyn, including Seth, an astonished smile on his face.

Treadwell shook his head. "Cowboy, you bastard."

"Can't take credit for this one, Mr. Treadwell. I didn't even know she had filed the damn thing. Why didn't you say something, Allyn?"

"Hell, I don't tell the hired help all my business."

Lev, standing several rows back from the rail, broke into laughter. "She worked you, boy. The Dragon Lady worked you real good!"

Seth joined the laughter, then saw Rosie, shyly approaching behind Lev. Their eyes connected across the rail, across the years, melting into one another.

Allyn continued to spar with Treadwell and Leffingwell as Judge Singer left the bench.

"Here, Allyn," said Seth, handing her his copy of Traeger's confession. "This is yours. These admissions will make your stockholders' suit against Olmstead a slam dunk. In fact, now you've got two big-time cases not even you could lose."

Allyn scanned the document, her eyes popping with each page. "Holy shit, Seth! I feel like I'm holding a winning lottery ticket worth millions. Just pass Go and collect the cash!"

"That's the way I see it," said Seth.

Allyn scanned the last page, then ran a hand through her mop of curls. "But it's your ticket," she said, handing the document back. "So are the cases, Seth, both of them. I've just been holding them in trust for you. Go get 'em."

Treadwell pushed through the rail toward the door, muttering, "God help the poor bastards!"

"You earned it, kid," she added wistfully, "a first-class ticket to ride back to Montgomery Street."

But Seth shook his head. "Keep it, Allyn. What good is a ticket if you don't want to go where it takes you. Besides, none of this would have happened without your help. And Lev's. Call it a down payment."

Rosie looked stunned and exchanged a quick look with Seth, their eyes speaking again without words.

Allyn grabbed Seth and gave him a quick hug, then shouted to the senior partner as he reached the door. "You'll be hearing from us, Mr. Treadwell—from my new partner at Friedlander and Cameron."

Seth turned to look at Allyn, saw that she was serious. "If that was an offer, Allyn, I accept."

"Good boy," said Allyn, heading for the door. "Oh, by the way, there's a contested divorce starting in Marin tomorrow. Stop by later and pick up the file."

Then it was Lev's turn. He offered his hand to Seth, but Seth extended his arms and they embraced warmly. "What can I ever do to repay you, Lev?"

"For starters, Cowboy, you can pay my bill. Check's fine. Money order. Any legal tender will do."

The four of them laughed together once more, then Allyn and Lev left, and Rosie and Seth were alone, holding hands across the rail. Late-afternoon shadows played around the silent room.

"Come back to me, Rosie."

Rosie looked into his eyes, fighting back tears. "I don't think so, Seth."

He moved closer to her. "After Harry died, you said you saw something different in me, Rosie. Give me a chance to prove it."

"You just did, Seth, but I—"

"I know I was stubborn and stupid about your dreams, spending all that energy convincing myself you didn't have some special . . . ability."

"Everybody has it, Seth. I just inherited a little more than most people."

"Whatever, I made you hide it. Maybe deep down I was afraid because you had something to hang your hat on and I only had myself."

Rosie brushed away a tear, then touched his lips with a finger. Seth took her hand, kissed the finger.

"Look, Rosie, I know I've got a ways to go, but even a blind hog comes up with an acorn once in a while. I'm catching on."

"I can see that."

"Then come back to Mill Valley. I love you, Rosie. It's not too late for us."

"Maybe not, Seth darlin'," she said, managing a sad smile, "but I think it may be too soon."

Seth swallowed, started to speak, but saw the truth there swimming in Rosie's dark eyes—and the truth was that she was heading back to Bakersfield. He saw something else there, too, something hopeful, or maybe it was a reflection from his own eyes.

Either way, he knew things would be different now.